Thomas Holt was born in London in 1961. As a child he was fascinated by ancient Greek history and mythology, and went on to read ancient history at Oxford. In addition to his acclaimed historical fiction, under the name of 'Tom Holt' he is the bestselling author of more than twenty comic fantasy novels.

Thomas Holt is married and lives in Chard, Somerset.

MEADOWLAND

A NOVEL

THOMAS HOLT

An *Abacus* Book

Published simultaneously in hardback and paperback
in Great Britain by Abacus 2005

A CIP catalogue record for this book
is available from the British Library.

Hardback ISBN 0 316 72649 4
Paperback ISBN 0 349 11741 1

Typeset in Bembo by M Rules
Printed and bound in Great Britain
by Clays Ltd, St Ives plc

Abacus
An imprint of
Time Warner Book Group UK
Brettenham House
Lancaster Place
London WC2E 7EN

www.twbg.co.uk

For Kitty, Fang and Truffle the Improving Dog;
essential monsters

O my America, my new-found land . . .

JOHN DONNE

CHAPTER
ONE

Many years ago I was at some kind of diplomatic function – I'd been dragged along because I have a knack for languages, and nobody else of my rank could understand a word of what these people were saying. It was very dull and rather embarrassing, because I couldn't think of anything to talk to them about; they were upset because they'd come all that way to discuss trade quotas, and there they were surrounded by silent people who were staring at them, and the only one of us present who could talk to them wouldn't know a trade quota if it built its nest in his ear. Eventually, for want of any other common ground, the ambassador started on about Greek philosophy; he was an Arab, and apparently they think very highly of Aristotle and all those people. Philosophy bores me (I'm an accountant), so I limited myself to making little grunting noises and trying to stay awake. At some point I lost the thread completely, because the ambassador asked me a question and I didn't know what we were meant to be talking about.

'I'm sorry,' I said. 'What was that again?'

The ambassador smiled, rather vaguely. 'I was asking,' he

said, 'what you thought about Plato's decision to exile all poets from his ideal republic.'

By the time I'd remembered who Plato was – actually, family tradition asserts that fifty generations ago, one of my ancestors knew Plato very well, though they weren't friends – he'd figured out that I wasn't paying attention. 'Something we remember in my country,' he said, 'though you seem to have forgotten it, is that Plato was a great wizard. He could do magic.'

'Is that right?' I said.

'Oh yes.' He nodded three times, very quickly. 'There was one time when he was standing in the bazaar and a man asked him to demonstrate his very strongest magic. Plato thought for a moment, then took from his sleeve a bundle wrapped in cloth. In this bundle, he said, I have a very powerful magical object. The other man was most impressed; what does it do, he asked. Ah, Plato replied, if you know how to use it, it will take you anywhere you wish to go in the twinkling of an eye; it will carry you from Spain to India in a heartbeat, or show you the heart of Asia or the deserts of Africa. It can even take you to where you can see the dead and listen to them talking to you.'

'Really,' I said.

'Absolutely,' the ambassador replied. 'Plato knew all about this magic, and of course we have studied him and learned all his secrets. As it happens,' he went on, 'I have with me just such an object. Look.' And he dived about inside the sleeve of his robe and pulled out a bronze tube about the size of a cucumber.

'That's remarkable,' I said, wondering what he was looking to achieve. Obviously whatever the thing in the tube was, it couldn't do all those things he'd said; he'd offer to give me a demonstration, it wouldn't work, and we'd have a major loss of face and a serious diplomatic incident on our hands. Why me, I thought? But the ambassador just smiled and said, 'Would you like to see it?'

Well, I couldn't say no; so he pulled off the lid and started fishing about inside the tube with his fingers. 'It's very easy to use,' he went on. 'All you need is a flat surface to unroll it on, and you're ready to go.'

When he said that, I must confess I felt a trifle uneasy. After all, we've all heard those Arab stories about wizards who put spells on old carpets and rugs to make them fly, and maybe just possibly there was a grain of truth in them. What if the tube really did contain a flying carpet? Was I expected to climb on to it and be whisked away to the ends of the Earth? The fact is, I hate heights and I'm seasick crossing the Bosphorus on a calm day. I was beginning to wish I'd stayed in my chambers and done some work.

'Here we are,' the ambassador said, and he pulled out the contents of the tube; and of course you're way ahead of me, and you guessed quite some time ago that what he'd got in there wasn't some scrap of magical cloth but a plain, ordinary book.

The point being:

My name is John Stethatus. I was born in the year of Our Lord 990. I live in the great city of Constantinople and serve his Imperial majesty Constantine X, Emperor of the Romans, in the capacity of clerk to the exchequer; which means, in practice, that my world consists of a few streets, a small office, a chair and a table. I was born in the City, have been outside it only four times, and never wish to leave it again. It's hard, therefore, to imagine someone less likely or worse suited to announce to the world the discovery of a new island, further north and west than any land hitherto known to us, a place that can only be reached by crossing a sea so cold that in winter it freezes into ice, yet so pleasant and hospitable that both grain and grapes grow there wild, as they did in Eden before Adam's fall. Unfortunately, because I have a knack for languages and a fatal tendency to listen to people, the job has fallen to me, and I shall endeavour to do my best.

It was the spring of the year of Our Lord 1036. I forget who we were at war with that year, or who was plotting with and against whom – stupid of me, because of course that sort of thing is the essence of history, and here I am pretending to be a historian. But I know my limitations, so I'll stick to what I do remember. If you're interested in the big stories, there are plenty of books.

What I remember most clearly was the panic in our office when the rumour filtered down that someone was going to have to accompany the payroll to our forces in Sicily. Our department consisted of me and half a dozen other portly, settled middle-aged eunuchs whose own mothers couldn't have told them apart from me in bright sunlight. None of us wanted to go. I remember the embarrassed silence when the man from the military finally sent for us all and asked for a volunteer. We stood there like guilty schoolchildren – *if nobody owns up, the whole class will be kept in at playtime* – while the soldier waited and scowled, his patience draining away like wine from a cracked jar. Finally he glanced down at the notes he'd brought with him, and observed in a deliberately matter-of-fact voice that John Stethatus was supposed to have a knack for languages.

'Not really,' I muttered, after another long silence. 'I mean, I know a smattering of Arabic and a few words—'

'Arabic,' the soldier interrupted joyfully. 'Excellent.'

Sicily is, of course, crawling with Saracens. I'd forgotten that.

So there I was, a few days later, sitting in a coach that was more of a farm cart, with my back to twelve huge iron chests crammed with fat gold coins, all fresh and sharp-edged from the Mint. I was wrapped up in three woollen cloaks (it was baking hot, but it might turn cold later) and feeling more wretched than you could possibly imagine. It wasn't fear – well, of course it *was* fear up to a point, because there'd be boats and mountain roads and bandit-haunted passes and a bullion train, even an imperial one, is basically an invitation to the entire world to help itself; but it wasn't death or serious injury that I was mostly afraid of. To be honest with you, it was awkwardness, embarrassment. Like I told you, I'd spent my whole life in the City, exclusively in the company of my own kind or my betters, which was precisely how I liked it. Now I was setting out on a two-month journey into the wild unknown – ship to Illyria, down through Greece, ship to Sicily – with no company except the bullion guards, who weren't my sort of people at all. In fact, they weren't even Greeks. They were, of course, Varangians.

Quick explanation. We use the term Varangians to cover the people from the North-West who drift down to the Empire to serve as mercenaries in the emperor's elite per-sonal guard. They're ideally suited for this purpose; partly because they're all huge tall men, trained from birth to be ruthlessly vicious fighters; mostly because they're loyal to whoever pays their wages, and in the Empire, loyalty is an exclusively imported commodity, like beaver pelts and amber. We only have a very vague idea of where the Varangians come from, and we care less. Since it's extremely relevant to the story, however, you should know that they mostly derive from the cold, inhospitable places north of Germany: Norway, Sweden, Russia, Denmark, England and Iceland. Believe it or not, the ones who end up in the Empire tend to be drawn from the upper echelons of their society, what passes for the nobility up there; they want to see the world, or they get into trouble with their neighbours and have to clear out, and so they come south and join the Guard. They're all the sons of wealthy families, so they'll have you believe, and lots of them are noblemen and princes in their own country. You'd find this hard to believe if you'd ever watched them eating.

Or, come to that, listened to them talking, as I did, hour after hour, as we bumped and rattled day after day in those loathsome unsprung carts. I had nothing else to do; you can't read when you're being bounced up and down all the time, sleep's out of the question, so for want of any other amusement whatsoever I found myself eavesdropping on the three men who were sharing my cart. Two of them I'd come across before; they were old-timers who'd been hanging round the treasury complex for years, too past it for active duty, by the same token far too aged to risk going home to their own countries, even if they'd wanted to. But the Guards look after their own and find nice quiet, restful jobs for the elderly and infirm; so I'd got used to seeing these two sitting out in the courtyard behind our office, shields propped against the wall, gobbling bread and playing some complicated-looking board game for hours on end. I was surprised to find that they'd been sent on what seemed to me to be a highly responsible and dangerous mission, but presumably as far as they were concerned it was a nice trip out. The third one was younger: a big, long-haired bear of a man who didn't say much but glowered a lot. I assumed that in the event of any trouble requiring actual fighting, he'd be the one to deal with it. He looked more than capable. In fact, he scared the living daylights out of me; but the two old men seemed to treat him as a sort of combination idiot nephew and pet. They were always saying things, nodding towards him and laughing, which made him scowl even more ferociously, which just made them burst out laughing all over again. As I gradually picked up their language (which didn't take long, it's pretty straightforward compared to some) it turned out that they spent most of their time on the journey teasing this poor man, mostly speculating rather unfavourably about his martial and sexual prowess. Odd, you'd think; more so, in fact, because from what they said it appeared that he was some kind of heir apparent in exile, while neither of them were anything special at all. Now everyone will tell you that the Varangians have a highly volatile attitude to personal honour, and you need to watch your step around them if you want to stay healthy. Clearly, I decided, it wasn't as straightforward as that, and I must admit I was intrigued by the way the balance of power, or pecking order or whatever you care to call it, went inside this group; and so, one evening when we were sitting by the fire – we'd messed up on our itinerary, hadn't reached the town we were meant to stay the night in and ended up having to camp out – I decided to throw caution to the wind and actually talk to them.

I don't know what they'd made of me up till then. Mostly they treated me as if I wasn't there, and I think they were quite surprised when I suddenly opened my face and started talking to them in their own language. Quite probably I hadn't mastered it quite as well as I thought, because after a moment of stunned silence, one of the old men and the prince-in-exile sniggered, and the other old man stuck a finger in his mouth.

'I'm sorry,' I said, with all the dignity I could muster. 'I didn't know I'd said something funny.'

One of the old men grinned, revealing a sad absence of teeth. 'Sorry,' he said, in pure and perfect Greek. 'But *threyja* doesn't mean what you think it does. At least, I hope not, because otherwise you're going to be sadly disappointed.'

That set the other two off again, and I sat there wishing very hard indeed that I'd kept my face shut and not said a word all the way to Sicily. But a curious change came over the three of them; suddenly, it appeared, I existed after all. Instead of facing away from me they shifted round, until without any effort or action of mine I was part of a circle with them, with the fire as its centre.

I wasn't sure I was happy about that. If I came over all aloof and detached at that point, it'd obviously be a deliberate affront, which at the very least would make things awkward on the rest of the journey, and which might ignite this legendary Varangian quick temper I'd heard so much about. So; I didn't really have any choice, I had to be their friend. But I wasn't really sure I wanted to. After all, I was a respectable Greek accountant, deputy head of our department, a career civil servant, one of *us*; and they were, of course, barbarians, savages, not the sort of people anybody would ever dream of talking to back in the City, where the normal rules apply. True, they might all be counts and princes in their own country, but that really didn't enter into it. In the City, in the government buildings, we treat them as a cross between livestock and furniture, it's the only way you can make things work in a place that's always full of foreigners, and anything else would be downright unnatural.

Still, I'd taken the step too far, and there wasn't anything I could do to put it right, so the logical thing seemed to be to make the best of the situation and accept the change in the rules. It's a bit like being in a ship that gets blown off course: you ride out the storm, and if you fetch up in some strange and exotic place, you might as well go ashore and explore a bit while you're there.

'Fine,' I said, in Greek. 'So, what does *threyja* mean?'

The other old man assured me that I really didn't want to know. 'But we're impressed,' he added. 'You're the first one of your lot we've come across who can talk our language. To be honest, you don't look the type.'

I did my modest shrug; I think it was wasted on them. 'It's just something I can do,' I said, in Varangian; showing off, you see. Then, in Greek: 'Did I get that right, or did I say something else funny?'

'No,' replied the first old man gravely, 'that was pretty good. In time, a bit of practice, you could probably make yourself understood. Actually, languages are something our people never seem to have any bother with. We just pick them up as we go along, wherever we happen to be.'

'Really?' I said. 'That's a useful talent.'

The other old man shrugged. 'Nothing special,' he said, 'Easy, really. Specially since we don't mess our heads up with writing things down, like your lot do. I've noticed this while I've been down this way. You get so used to writing, you forget how to talk.'

That made absolutely no sense as far as I was concerned, but I really didn't want to get into a discussion about linguistics. 'Well,' I said, making an effort; in fact, I may even have smiled. 'Since we're talking to each other now, let me introduce myself. My name is John.'

The two old men looked at each other, as though I'd just done something weird or rude. I suppose they decided to make allowances; anyway, the first old man looked a bit sheepish for a moment; then he nodded, and said: 'My name is Eyvind Thorhallson; my friend here is Kari Sighvatson, and the miserable-looking bugger over there is Harald Sigurdson. If he deigns to talk to you he'll probably tell you he's the rightful King of all Norway, but the truth is, his lot slung him out when he was just a kid because they couldn't face the thought of having him around where they'd have to see him every day. So he came here, because he knew you lot aren't particular.'

I guessed that was supposed to be a joke, but probably not the laugh-out-loud kind; so I did a sort of mute-acknow-ledgement sideways nod of the head, and hoped it wasn't a mortal insult or anything. 'You certainly speak Greek well,' I said.

'He doesn't,' said the man called Kari, jerking his head at the purported King of all Norway. 'Mind you, he can barely speak Norse. Eyvind and I, on the other hand, are good at that sort of thing. You need to be, in our line of work. Anyway, what used to be our line of work, before we took up this soldiering business. You never know from one day to the next where you're likely to end up, so it helps if you know how to keep your ears open.'

'Soldiering's better,' the other old man put in. 'Wish I'd known about it years ago.' He shrugged. 'Too late now, though.'

'Funny sort of a language, Greek,' Kari went on. 'When I first started picking it up, seemed to me you could say a whole load of stuff in it that you just couldn't find words for in Norse; and the other way round, too. Now I'm not so sure, though. Truth is, I've been using it so long I have to stop and think before I know which language I'm talking. Same with the rest of the lads, the ones that've been here a while, anyhow. You're talking, like you do, and I'll say something in Greek and you'll answer in Norse, and neither of us'll know we're doing it, after a while it all goes straight into your head, like drinking bad wine fast so you don't taste it. Wine,' he repeated, and shook his head. 'That's another bad sign. Used to hate the stuff, but now I'm getting a taste for it. No choice in the matter, of course.'

That was supposed to be significant, I guessed. 'You don't have wine where you come from?' I said.

Kari laughed. 'Grapes don't grow that far north,' he said. 'We drink beer instead. Though actually, where me and Eyvind are from, Iceland, barley and wheat don't grow either, we have to ship it in from Norway or wherever. Though I was in a place once, I'm talking about years ago now, where grapes and wheat grew wild, everywhere you looked, like weeds. And that was a long way north.' He shrugged. 'One time I was there we had a German with us, he went crazy soon as he saw the grapes; reckoned it had to be the earthly paradise, the one where Adam got thrown out of. He was all for making wine, but we never got round to it, and nobody else fancied the idea anyway. But we took half a shipload of the grapes home with us, only they went bad on the way and we had to ditch them. Pity, we could've done a bloody good trade for them.'

I nodded. 'You used to be a merchant, then.'

Kari grinned. 'Sort of,' he said. 'More like a *karl*; no word for it in Greek, you're all either free men or slaves, and anyhow it's such a different system, I couldn't make you understand. Doesn't matter. Best way to put it is, me and Eyvind used to work for merchants, or with them; we used to help work the ship, and it was the boss who decided where we were headed for. It's—' He rolled his eyes. 'It's much simpler than the way you people do things, and much more complicated at the same time. If you see what I'm getting at.'

'Different,' I said.

'Different, and leave it at that.' Kari yawned. 'Funny,' he said, 'I've been over here I don't know how long, and that's probably the longest conversation I've had with a Greek. I always figured your lot for different, but maybe you aren't as different as all that.'

Was that a compliment? Looking back, I suppose it was, though of course he knew perfectly well when he said it that I'd have to think about it before I could make up my mind; and presumably that's why he phrased it that way. It's one of the things Varangians like to do: they say things in such a way that they sound like insults but turn out to be compliments, or the other way round. I think that's a strange way to behave, since in their culture it's not only acceptable but expected of you to cut a man's head off on the spot if he insults you a certain way; other insults, on the other hand, are just the conventional way of being friendly and good-humoured. I don't think I could live like that. You'd forever be having to think about what you're saying before you actually say it, and that'd be no good for a Greek. Most of what we say is thinking aloud, and most of the rest is the same but without any thinking at all. If we saw things the way the Varangians do, we'd all be dead inside a week.

Before we could take matters any further, the other old man, Eyvind, let off the biggest yawn you could ever imagine, and said he was dead beat and needed to sleep. It was, he pointed out, his watch first; but what the hell was the point of carting around a useless great lump like Harald Sigurdson if you couldn't slide off your duty assignments on him? Harald – the young, silent man – pulled an even sadder face than the one he'd been wearing and pulled his cloak a bit tighter round his shoulders; the other two lay down on their backs without another word, shut their eyes and were both fast asleep a heartbeat later. That's another thing Varangians can do, by the way. Some of them, anyhow.

I suppose friendship is a bit like a disease. Once you've caught it, you're stuck with it, and it spreads. You can't just back out of it once it's begun. Either you stay with it or you bring it to an end, turn it into something else – hatred, contempt – like turning grape must into wine. What I mean is, once I'd taken the step and started talking to the Varangians, I couldn't very well stop, not unless I was prepared to offend them and turn them into enemies. Not that I minded terribly much. It made a pleasant change to have someone to talk to on the long drag through Illyria and down through Greece. I just have this thing about irrevocable steps, that's all. If I can, I stay clear of them, even if I'm pretty sure they'd be no bother, or even to my advantage. It's just the way I am. Sometimes I get the feeling that I've lived my whole life like a man on a beach who's taken off all his clothes but can't actually bring himself to get into the water; so he just stands there naked, can't go back into town with no clothes on, can't go forward into the sea. Not that that's anybody's business but my own.

We talked a lot, the Varangians and I. It was a curious system. Before I opened my mouth that night, they were always nattering away among themselves, and I didn't exist. Then I changed all that; and from then on, they – well, the two old men – they never talked to each other, they always said everything to me, even if they were having a discussion about something. It was like finance committee meetings where, if you want to say something, you've got to address your remarks to the chairman, even when you want to tell the man sitting next to you that he's being a bloody fool. On the other hand, Kari and Eyvind never seemed even the slightest bit interested in anything about my life, or what I did, my family or my home or anything. They wanted to tell me things, things that both of them already knew but usually didn't agree about. It was like I'd suddenly become the official arbitrator for everything. I suppose you could see that as a compliment, but it wasn't really. It puzzled me, until I gathered from things they said that they'd known each other all their lives – born within a week of each other on the same farm, went to sea together, sailed on all the same journeys, left the North and came to the City together – so it sort of stands to reason that they'd long since either reached agreement on everything or else come to a rock-solid impasse, so there simply wasn't any point going over the issues again. Introduce me into the equation, and you've got a whole new set of rules. No wonder they never seemed to shut up, all the way from Heraclea to bloody Corinth.

Which reminds me: it was not far from Corinth that we ran into a spot of trouble. I shouldn't say this, being a loyal servant of the Empire, but once you're south of Thebes, the roads are terrible. Bone dry all the year round, of course, and so much traffic up and down; no wonder the tracks are rutted axle-deep in places, which can be pretty terrifying on those mountain passes, where the highway's just this little scratch on the side of the cliff-face, and most of what there is looks like it's all set to crumble away right under your wheels. All things considered, it's a miracle, and a tribute to good solid Galatian craftsmanship, that our cart axles lasted as long as they did – all that heavy gold coinage bumping up and down, plus four grown men, over ruts and potholes and rocks as big as your head.

The wheel eventually came off on the stretch between Corinth and Sparta. Don't suppose you know it; very dry, very stony, grey and brown dirt with a sort of steel-green blur in the distance as you look out over the olive groves. Now our family's supposed to be from Greece proper, way back – Athens, in case you're interested, and I'm supposed to be a remote descendant of Eupolis the comic poet, who was around at the time of the Great Peloponnesian War between Athens and Sparta; but that's fifteen hundred years ago, so I don't suppose it's true – but as far as I'm concerned, it's a rotten country and you can have it. It's got this all-used-up feeling about it everywhere you go; you can't travel a few miles without seeing bits of ruined building sticking up out of the dirt, like stones in a ploughed field. I find it rather depressing, as if nobody could be bothered to tidy the place up.

But about the wheel. The consensus of opinion was, the axle sheared when we bounced off a rut into the trough, and all the weight of the cart landed on it. Anyhow, even I could see we didn't have a hope in hell of mending the wretched thing ourselves; and the drivers of the other carts in the train were no help at all. The most they'd agree to do for us was find a blacksmith in Sparta and send him out to fix it. I pointed out that there we were, best part of two days from Sparta, further from Corinth, with several million gold tre - misses and just the four of us to keep them safe for the Emperor until help came. My idea was to shift the money over onto the other carts, but that didn't go down at all well. The extra weight, they insisted, would bugger up their axles as well, and then all four carts would be stranded out in the wilderness. I suppose they had a point, of sorts, but their attitude didn't impress me very much. Nor was I materially reassured when they pointed out that I had three soldiers of the Varangian guard at my command to keep the money safe.

Kari and Eyvind, on the other hand, didn't seem bothered at all, even when I told them that the mountains of the Peloponnese were notorious for bandits, free-company men, Saracen pirates and Catalan privateers. Good, they said; let 'em come, and if Harald Sigurdson wouldn't mind leaving a few for us, we can have a bit of sport. I pointed out that neither of them were exactly in the first flush, but they pretended they hadn't heard me, so presumably it was insulting to bring the matter up. It didn't matter to them either way, they insisted; a bloody good scrap, and either victory or Valhalla, what more could anybody ask? I have no idea what Valhalla means, but from the way they said it, I don't suppose it's something I'd like, and I couldn't be bothered to ask them to explain.

So the rest of the train creaked off and left us. I was all for sitting in the shade of the cart and sulking like mad till we were rescued or died of thirst, but Eyvind decided to come over all brisk and useful. He pottered around for a bit until he found a spring of water, and then he pottered around a bit more, came back and told us he'd found a handy abandoned building where we could sleep and get shade from the sun.

Turned out, of course, it was a tomb. Wonderful. At least, that's what I think it must have been, though you never saw the like. Imagine the dome of Saint Sophia, but made of slates, carefully fitted together without fixings or mortar; and the only entrance is a little hole you have to crawl through on your hands and knees—

'This is useless,' I pointed out. 'It'll mean we've got to leave the cart outside.'

Kari made a so-what gesture with his shoulders and hands. 'We can get the money boxes in through the hole, no bother; and the cart's not going anywhere, is it? That's the whole point.'

Actually, unloading the money hadn't even occurred to me; I can be slow sometimes. But I wasn't going to admit that. 'Sure,' I replied. 'But a cart, even a mended cart, isn't going to be much use to us with no horses; and I don't know how things are where you come from, but around here, you don't leave valuable horses unguarded all night next to the public road. Not if you want to see them again.'

'Actually,' Kari replied, 'we don't have horse-thieves in Iceland, the country's just too small, and everybody knows everybody else. But I take your point. I was going to say, we'll have to post a watch anyway, so whoever's on guard can keep an eye on the horses too. Will that be all right by you?'

'Fine,' I said, trying to make it sound like I was giving in for the sake of a quiet life, rather than because he was right. 'You're the guards, I suppose you know your job.' An unpleasant thought occurred to me. 'Post a guard, you said.'

Kari laughed. 'It's all right,' he said, 'Eyvind and me and the boy wonder there'll do it, you can stay in here in the warm and get some sleep.' He looked at me for a moment, then added: 'No offence, but you'd make a lousy guard; and, like you said, we need the horses.'

Another of those double-sided insult-compliments, I suppose. Anyhow, that suited me, and as it turned out, I was let off helping lug the money boxes in through the door, too. All I had to carry was my blanket and my pillow – I'm sadly fussy, so I'd brought my own special pillow with me from the City. They'd probably have fetched them for me if I'd sat there long enough looking helpless, but I reckoned I'd lost enough face already for one day.

The tomb, and I'm pretty sure that's what it had been once, was completely empty inside, though at first there was no way of knowing, because it was as dark as a bag in there. But Harald lit a fire; and when we found out the hard way that there wasn't a chimney or anything like that, he scrambled up on one of the boxes and bashed a hole in the roof with his axe. It was still uncomfortably smoky in there, but not too bad, thanks to the through-draught from the door-hole.

We'd only just settled in when I heard the most appalling roll of thunder, and then the sound of raindrops pecking on the slates, like King Xerxes' two-million-strong army all drumming their fingers at the same time. It doesn't often rain in Greece, but when it does, it gives it the full treatment. Water coming in through Harald's improvised smoke-hole drowned our fire in no time flat, so we had to shift it over a bit and start again. Just as well, in fact, that Eyvind had insisted on us taking shelter for the night, or we'd all have been soaked to the skin.

For a while we just sat there, feeling sorry for ourselves. Then Kari told Harald to go outside and take first watch; and Harald, rather to my surprise, refused. Come to think of it, those were the first words I heard him speak – in Norse, needless to say, not Greek; I'd been expecting a deep, bear-like rumble from a man of his size and disposition, but it turned out that he had a high, quiet, squeaky little voice, and he stuttered. He could be firm when he wanted to, though. No way was he going out in that, he told them, not with his weak chest (I'd just watched him dragging a money box through the door-hole all by himself); and if that meant the bandits stole the horses, he couldn't care less, but in his considered opinion any bandit with enough brains to know how to breathe would be passing the night in a nice dry cave, so if we wanted to get drenched that was fine, but he was staying right where he was, and anybody who had problems with that could discuss the matter with his axe.

He finished his speech – no other word for it; he gabbled

his way through it like an amateur actor in front of a restless audience – and immediately went back to being still and silent. Thinking back, he reminded me of one of those strange mechanical toys they used to make in Alexandria, a thousand years or so back. You know the ones I mean: you boil up a big pot of water, the steam goes up a narrow pipe and pushes against a little gadget like a waterwheel with wings, and that drives a whole lot of cogs and gears, and a little bronze statue of a flute-player spins round and round and makes a whistling noise. Then, when the steam runs out, it stops dead in its tracks. Constantine the Great or someone like that brought a whole lot of them back from Egypt, and when I was a kid they had them set up in the Forum of Arcadius, and they used to set them going sometimes on saints' days.

Anyway: I was expecting Kari and Eyvind to kick up a fuss about that, but instead they just nodded, as if to say fair enough, and after a brief silence Eyvind said he'd better take the first watch, then, and stomped out.

I don't remember exactly how the subject came up. The idea had been that we'd all get some sleep, but for some reason – the noise of the rain on the roof, is my guess – none of us could get off, and there's something inherently silly about three grown men lying on the ground, wide awake, not talking. Eventually, Kari sat up, yawned and fished about in an old goatskin bag that he carried with him everywhere he went.

'Chestnuts,' he explained, when he noticed me watching him. 'Back home, when we can get them, we like to roast them in front of the fire.'

That reminded me of something. 'Food,' I said. 'Have we got any?'

Kari sighed. 'Wondered when anybody'd mention that.

And the answer is no, apart from these chestnuts and the burnt end of yesterday's loaf. Thought we'd be in Sparta by now, see. Not to worry, though. Soon as it's light, we'll send out young Harald to kill something – he's good at that. And meanwhile,' he added cheerfully, 'there's these chestnuts. It's all right, I've got plenty to go round.'

Actually, they weren't bad, considered in the light of there being nothing else, and once I'd got some food inside me I cheered up a bit. Kari and Harald were munching steadily away, and I thought it'd be nice to start up a bit of a conversation. That's me all over, I'm afraid.

'You were saying earlier,' I said, 'about some place you'd been where vines and wheat grew wild. Where was that?'

I think Harald may have made a slight groaning noise, but I didn't think anything of it at the time. 'Ah,' Kari said with his mouth full, 'now there's a story. Wineland we used to call it; it's a big island way out in the north-western sea. Furthest island out there is, as a matter of fact.'

'Wineland,' I repeated. 'After the grapes, I suppose.'

Kari nodded. 'That's right,' he said. 'Of course, that's not what it was supposed to be called. But Leif Eirikson – that's Lucky Leif, the son of the man who founded the Greenland colony – either he misheard it when Bjarni mentioned it, or he thought Wineland sounded better. Anyway, the name sort of stuck, and there you go.'

'Greenland,' I repeated. 'Where's that?'

This time, Harald groaned quite loudly and distinctly. Kari looked all wise, like Minerva's owl on an old statue. 'Tell you what,' he said. 'For a clever man, there's a lot of stuff you don't know.'

I shrugged. 'I was never any good at geography,' I replied. Then, when Kari looked at me: 'The names of places,' I explained, 'countries and cities and rivers and mountains, and where they all are in relation to each other.'

'Right.' Kari nodded slowly. 'Never knew there was a word for it. Which is a bit arse-about-face, because of course I probably know more about that sort of thing than most people, even you clever Greeks in the City. Still,' he went on, 'I'd have expected you to know about Greenland, because it's quite a big settlement these days, practically its own little country.'

'Sorry, no,' I said. 'So,' I went on, because I knew I'd walked straight into a story, like a fox putting its foot in a wire, 'where is it, then?'

Kari swallowed his mouthful of chestnut before answering. 'North,' he said. 'In fact, as far north as you can go, pretty well, before it gets so cold and snowy you can't get any further.'

'Must be an all-right sort of place,' I said, 'with a name like that.'

Kari laughed. 'Don't you believe it,' he said. 'It's a dump. Just a little frilly edge of farmland between the sea and the mountains; sheep and cattle just about survive there, and most years you can scrape together enough hay to see them through the winter, more or less. But the name was just a gag, a trick, to kid people into moving out there. Eirik – that's Red Eirik, who started the settlement – he was the one who decided to call it that.' Kari shifted a little to get comfortable, and scooped some charcoal out of the jar onto the fire. 'But that's all a very long story, and I don't suppose you're interested.'

Chapter
Two

Actually, he wasn't far wrong. But I had the feeling that he wanted to tell me about it, and he'd be sure to get his way somehow or other, sooner or later, so I thought it'd probably be easier all round if I gave in straight away.

'Go on,' I said. 'It's always interesting to learn things you don't know very much about.'

Kari shrugged. 'Suit yourself,' he said. 'Actually, it sort of ties up with what you were asking about earlier – Wineland and all that.'

Well, why not? I thought. Maybe it'll help me get to sleep. 'Tell me about that too,' I said.

There was this man (Kari said) by the name of Red Eirik.

Now, no offence intended, but I reckon you Greeks aren't a patch on us Northerners when it comes to neat, punchy proverbs and sayings. But a few years ago, I heard a Greek talking about someone, and he said trouble followed this man around like crows following the plough; and straight away, it put me in mind of Red Eirik. You see, it's not the plough's fault that the crows follow, it doesn't encourage them or anything; and Eirik never went looking for trouble, because deep down he was a peaceful sort of man who only wanted to live quietly with his neighbours and get on with a bit of work. But it never seemed to come out of the mould that way. First Eirik and his father got thrown out of Norway because of some bother there. I don't know the details, but everybody who knew him said it wasn't Eirik's fault, and he was quite upset that he had to kill those people. Anyhow, Eirik settled in Iceland, like so many Norwegians were doing at that time, and for a while he got on quite nicely in Hauksdal, which is good country, and good people live there. But a couple of bad men, real troublemakers, tried to push Eirik around, and after he'd killed them their relatives kicked up a hell of a fuss – that's next of kin for you, pathetically narrow-minded – so he had to clear out of Hauksdal and move to Breidafjord. By this time he was sick to death of trouble, and he figured it'd be a good idea to stay clear of other people as far as possible – if there weren't any people about for him to kill, he'd be far less likely to kill anybody, and that'd be just fine. So he built a farm on Oxen Island, which is a pretty remote place. Also, he went out of his way to be sociable and pleasant to the few neighbours he had. He even lent one of them his bench-boards—

Sorry, I forgot. Bench-boards are pretty carved panels that you dowel onto the fronts of your benches. You must have benches, even in Constantinople. For sitting on. All right; back home we build our houses long and low, with one big room where everybody sits around in the evenings and in winter when it's too cold and dark to go out. I'm forgetting, you don't have cold in these parts, not *cold* cold, but you'll just have to use your imagination. Anyhow, there's one big long room, and usually one or two smaller rooms leading off it, for the head of the family to sleep in, and storerooms and so on. In the main hall there's usually long benches running the length of the room, and if you're reasonably well-set and a bit of a show-off, you stick on these carved panels— You get the idea, I'm sure.

Anyway, Red Eirik had a fine set of bench-boards which he'd brought with him from Norway, and, trying to be sociable, he lent them to a neighbour for some special occasion, and the neighbour was a miserable bugger and wouldn't give them back. This led to words, words led to other stuff, and pretty soon, Eirik had the deceased's family snapping round his heels yet again and found himself in need of somewhere else to live.

By now, he was more or less at the end of his rope. All the bad stuff in his life, he decided, was because of other people – because, left to himself, he was just a peaceful, harmless farmer who wouldn't hurt a mouse – and the only course left open for him was to up sticks and go where there weren't any other people at all.

A tall order, that; but as luck would have it, he remembered a story he'd heard about some man called Gunnbjorn Ulfson who'd been blown off course trying to reach Iceland, a hundred years or so earlier, and ended up on some island nobody had ever been to before. Now Gunnbjorn just wanted to get to Iceland, he wasn't interested in exploring, so he turned round and sailed back the way he'd come – his luck was in and he made it home. He told people about his adventure, naturally, but even the people who believed him weren't particularly interested. As time went on, what Gunnbjorn had said about where these islands were and how you got there started to rust away a bit, so to speak, and by the time the story reached Eirik it was all thin and flaky. Never mind: if Gunnbjorn was telling the truth, this island of his was completely empty, and that was just the sort of

place Eirik was after. He packed up as much stuff as he could
fit on board a *knoerr* – there I go again: that's our word for
the deep, chubby ships we use for going to places and carrying stuff about, as opposed to your slim, thoroughbred
warship, which is your quintessential rich man's toy and not
really much good for anything useful. Anyhow, he took
along all his farm workers and some neighbours who'd got
into trouble for being on his side, pointed his ship in the
general direction of where he thought Gunnbjorn's islands
might possibly be, and set off. Everybody reckoned that was
the last anyone'd ever see of Red Eirik, and the general view
was that that'd be no bad thing.

Imagine people's surprise, then, when the following
summer Eirik sails back to Breidafjord (where, strictly speaking, he wasn't supposed to set foot ever again, on pain of
death), and announces that he's found Gunnbjorn's island.
Furthermore, he says, it's huge, and it's the most wonderful
country. The sea's crawling with fish and seals, sky full of
gulls, and the pasture's so good that you ought to be able to
keep your cattle out nine months of the year; in fact, Eirik
says, it's so rich and green, the only possible name for the
place is Greenland.

Of course, you've never been to Iceland, so you probably
don't appreciate how something like that would've sounded.
Basically, Iceland is a few blades of grass between the volca-
noes. I'm overstating it, of course, but a lot of it's pretty
rough, nothing but black shingle and rock, when it's not
buried deep in snow. Part of the story, obviously, was that
Eirik wanted to rub his enemies' noses in it. They'd made
him pack up and run for his life, and he'd gone and found
this amazing paradise of green grass where a man'd hardly
have to work at all if he didn't want to. The other thing was,
Eirik was recruiting. Sure, he didn't want to live in a

crowded place again, where you can't stand on top of your own mountain without seeing at least one or two roofs in the distance; but he was realistic enough to know that if he wanted to make a go of settling in Greenland, he needed manpower. The difference would be, he figured, that if he founded a settlement and he was the boss and everybody accepted that and did as they were told, there wouldn't be any reason for upsets and fallings-out and all the rubbish he'd had to put up with all his life.

Give him his due, Eirik was a persuasive man. Someone told me once that when he sailed back to Greenland the next summer, twenty-five ships went with him. Call that forty men to a ship, that's close on a thousand people, and it's news to me that there ever were more than a couple of thousand living out there on the middle-west coast, so they must've come from all over Iceland to join him. Not all of them made it, of course. Some of them came to harm – they ran into an earthquake under the sea, would you believe, which did for two or three ships and scared the shit out of the rest of them, and after that some of them thought better of it and turned back. But there were still close on six hundred people with him when he made landfall right down at the pointy end of Greenland.

The strange thing about it is, Eirik was right. Not about the green grass and the fish and the gulls, of course; he was lying through his teeth about that. But it was true that once he'd settled in and the colony or settlement or whatever you want to call it had found its feet and sorted itself out, that was pretty well the end of Eirik's troubles, at least as far as falling out with people was concerned. Eirik built himself a house and started farming, and pretty soon he had three big barns just to keep the hay in, so you can see he was doing all right. Better still, everybody who went with him seemed to have left their more boisterous habits behind in Iceland, because people managed to get on fairly well without quarrelling or killing each other, and I get the impression it was a good place to live, if you like quiet. Eirik's wife had converted to the Faith – this was fifteen years or so before Iceland went over, so you can see she was ahead of her time and quite daring, even – and he didn't seem to mind in the least; he even built her a little church so she could go and pray and say the holy Mass without disturbing anybody. Shows you how thoughtful and considerate he could be, once he'd shaken off those bad-luck crows.

Now, one of the people who went out with Eirik was a miserable old bastard called Herjolf Bardason—

'Thanks,' I said. 'That's an interesting story. Goes to show, too, how people can change their ways, if they set their mind to it.' I yawned, rather pointedly. 'Well, it's been a long day and I'm bushed, so I think I'll get my head down for a bit.'

Kari looked at me. 'I thought you wanted to hear the story.'

'I did,' I replied, 'and you very kindly told it to me. I enjoyed it. Now—'

'That's only the beginning,' Kari said. 'Actually, it's more like the bit before the beginning, because the story really starts with Herjolf Bardason, the man I was just going to tell you about.'

'Oh,' I said.

'Or rather, his son,' Kari added. 'Bjarni Herjolfson. I knew him very well, of course. You'll enjoy hearing about him, he was an interesting man.'

'I'd like that,' I said, trying to sound like I meant it. 'Maybe tomorrow—'

★

Herjolf Bardason (Kari continued) was a wilful sort of a man, always had to get his own way. People like that can cause a lot of trouble, though sometimes more good than harm comes of it and then we call them determined and resolute and stuff like that, and everybody thinks well of them. Anyhow, Herjolf could be as resolute as a billy goat when he wanted to; and as soon as he heard Red Eirik sounding off about how great Greenland was, he made up his mind right away, he was going to go out there and start a new life.

Bloody stupid idea, because Herjolf was fifty-five if he was a day, and that's an old man where I come from. Not like he had any need to up sticks and start over, either. He was better than well off, good farm, plenty of stock; his son Bjarni was a grown man, he'd never settled to farming so his dad bought him a ship and he'd taken to the merchant life, done very well for himself; so Herjolf never wanted for flour or timber or any of the stuff Icelanders have to bring in from overseas. Absolutely no call to throw it all over and go plunging off into the unknown. But he'd made up his mind to go, and he went.

Now, then—

(Here Kari took a deep breath, like a man about to dive into deep water.)

Now, then: this is where Eyvind and me come into the story. Eyvind and me, we were born and raised at Drepstokk, which was where old Herjolf farmed. Our families were nothing much; they came over on the first ships to Iceland, but they were hired men, and that's what they stayed. My dad was Herjolf's stockman, and Eyvind's dad helped with the horses, watched the charcoal, did pretty well anything he was told. Him and me, we were born three days apart – I'm the eldest, never let him forget it these sixty years – and I don't suppose we've been out of each other's company more than a few days all that time. Well, we both knew Herjolf's son Bjarni since we were kids. He was a good man, Bjarni, though he had more than a bit of his old man's stubborn streak. They were alike in more ways than they were different, so it was bound to happen that they were always falling out, bickering over how things should be done round the farm. Herjolf's ways were tried and tested and he was set in them tighter than a gatepost, Bjarni was always thinking up clever new ideas to do the job better in half the time. Both of them were right, of course, so neither'd ever give way. So, soon as Bjarni was old enough, he decided to get away from the farm and take up trading. Wheat and barley don't grow in Iceland, there's precious little timber for building or firing, no iron for tools, no flax for linen, no tar, no honey; so we trade for what we need with what we've got.

So, that first year, Bjarni filled up the hold of his ship with a load of stuff his dad gave him – wool, broadcloth, sheepskins, tanned and raw hides, tallow, sulphur, six dozen cartwheel cheeses and even a cage of falcons (guess who had the job of snaring the bloody things; and they can give you a nasty nip when they're angry, too) – and started asking round the neighbourhood to see who fancied coming with him.

Important thing you need to remember about Iceland, and it's something I fancy you might have trouble getting hold of. No cities; no towns, no villages. Everybody lives on a farm, whether he's the farmer himself (and that makes him a big man), or one of his brothers or sons or nephews, or just one of the hired men; we all live in the same house, and sleep in the long hall on the benches – except for the farmer and his wife, they have a room to themselves, but all the rest of us just crowd in together like puppies in the straw. Stands to reason, you can't live that way unless you learn pretty quick how to fit in. If you don't, it's best for all concerned if you clear out as soon as you can. Fact was, Eyvind and me didn't fit. All the time we were growing up, it's like there was a little voice in the back of our heads saying, *you boys were never born to be hired hands, doing the same work every day, every year for the rest of your lives, just so you can have food to eat and two yards of a bench to sleep on.* That didn't sit well with living so snug and cosy with sixty-odd other people, and all of them figuring that there wasn't any other way things could possibly be, and anyone who thought different must be touched in the head. So, when Bjarni asked us if we wanted to go off with him trading in Norway, we didn't think about it longer than a heartbeat. We grabbed our coats and shoes and axes and we were halfway out to the boatshed before he called us back and said he wasn't leaving till the spring.

Now, my old mother always said I was born stupid and went steadily downhill from there, and I'm not saying she was altogether wrong. We wanted to leave Drepstokk because we couldn't stick being cooped up close with the same people day after day. And what did we do? We joined a ship's crew. She knew a thing or two about people, my mother.

You see, on the farm it was tight, but at least you spent the day outside, in the open. On a ship, twenty men and a full cargo in a fifty-foot boat, you can't stand up or walk two steps without treading on somebody. If you sneeze the whole crew gets wet; and for five days, seven days, ten, there's absolutely no place to go. You can't just step outside when it all gets too much; and either it's a heavy sea and everybody's working like crazy, elbows in each other's faces, or it's flat and calm and there's absolutely fucking nothing to do, just sit still and quiet, because after a bit on a ship everybody's said everything they've got to say, three or four times over, so if you want to keep from getting your head stove in, you keep your face shut and don't say a word.

Well, that's the seafaring life for you, and I've got to say I never took to it much. But short of jumping off in the middle of the Norway Sea and swimming home there wasn't a lot I could do once we'd started; and once we got there, of course, I forgot all about how shitty the journey was. Once we reached Norway, there were all kinds of amazing things. There were towns, a hundred houses all next to each other, and people making things and selling things I'd never even heard of; and there were strangers. Living on the farm, you knew everybody, you'd see a face you'd never seen before maybe once every five years. I saw more strangers in Norway in an hour than I'd ever set eyes on in my whole life.

So Eyvind and me, we stuck at the trading, in spite of having to be on ships; and Bjarni was a good merchant, he sold fast and bought slow, pretty soon we'd got into a pattern and that was how our lives were going to be. We left Iceland in spring, soon as it was fit to sail; we'd trade up and down the Norwegian coast till winter closed in, then we'd stay over the dark season with one of Bjarni's friends, spend next spring and summer buying, go back to Iceland to trade for new stock over winter till spring came round again.

Like I said, Bjarni was just like his dad except for the differences. Old Herjolf was a man of habit, and so was Bjarni. Didn't take long for Bjarni to get set in this way of doing things, and all the time we were in Norway, he was looking forward to getting home to the farm and spending winter with the old man. He'd even got him a present, a set of fancy carved struts for the tapestry canopy behind his chair – apparently, the old boy had always fancied some, reckoned they'd add a touch of class, and Bjarni was able to pick up a set cheap in Norway. It was just about ideal, he reckoned:

one winter in two away, one at home, which meant that he and his dad got as much of each other's company as they could take without fighting, no more and no less.

And then Herjolf took it into his head to go to Greenland with Red Eirik.

We were in Norway, of course, when he made that decision; so the first Bjarni knew of it was when he walked up from the ship, leaving us to unload, and pushed in through the door of the house and found himself faced with a hall full of strangers.

First off, he couldn't say a word, just stood there like a maiden oak in a meadow. The man who'd bought Herjolf's place was a southerner – he'd had to clear out of his own district because of some trouble or other – and he didn't know Bjarni from a bunch of goose feathers. You can imagine how he felt when a big stranger in fancy foreign clothes bursts into his house and stands there with his face open, staring. Soon as he'd got over the first shock of it, he jumped up, snatched his axe off the wall behind him, and hollers out, 'Who the fuck are you?'

Well, that's just plain bad manners, asking a man his name straight out like that, but I guess he reckoned Bjarni wasn't the sort good manners are due to. Anyhow, Bjarni stares at him a bit more, then laughs down just one side of his face, and says, 'You're asking me?'

'I'm asking you,' the farmer repeats. 'And what the hell are you doing in my house?'

'*Your* house?' Bjarni says; and things could've got a bit fraught there, except the farmer took another look at him and saw the foreign clothes and probably remembered what he'd been told by the neighbours.

'Hold on,' he says. 'Are you Herjolf's boy Bjarni?'

'I know perfectly well who *I* am,' Bjarni says; but by now

the farmer's got a hold on what's happening and he explains. He says his name and tells Bjarni his dad's sold up and moved away.

Takes Bjarni a while to get his head round that. Then he asks: 'Where'd he go?'

'Greenland,' the farmer says.

'Oh,' says Bjarni. 'Where in fuck's name is that?'

Luckily the farmer knows the answer, because he'd asked Herjolf the same question, being curious. 'Well,' he says, 'you sail up north to Snaefellsness. You know where that is?'

'Heard of it,' Bjarni says.

'From Snaefellsness,' says the farmer, 'you keep on going west until you see the Blueshirt glacier, and there you are.'

'Right,' Bjarni says. 'And how many days would that be?'

Farmer shrugs. 'No idea,' he says. 'But what your dad told me Red Eirik told him, it's all pretty straightforward and simple. Due west from Snaefellsness until you see the Blueshirt, you can't miss it.'

Bjarni thinks about things for a while, then he nods his head. 'Thanks,' he says. 'Sorry to have bothered you.'

'No bother at all,' says the farmer.

So Bjarni sets off back down the hill, and we're all on the beach unloading the stuff off the ship, the barrels of flour and malt and the cords of timber and other stuff besides.

'You can skip all that,' Bjarni calls out, 'and get it all loaded up again. We're not stopping.'

We all look at each other. We're thinking Bjarni's had a fight with his dad about something, because we'd all seen him in that sort of a mood before, so we know better than to answer back or ask questions if we know what's good for us. We figure, if Bjarni and Herjolf have fallen out, Bjarni'll head off down the coast in a huff and put in for the winter with a friend. Fine by us. So we do as we're told, and it's only once the anchor's up and we're running out sail that somebody asks, 'Where to, boss?'

And Bjarni says, 'Greenland.'

Bear in mind, we've been away two years, we missed Red Eirik coming back from his first trip and spreading the good word about the earthly paradise and the cattle staying out nine months of the year. None of us had ever heard of the place. So Eyvind asks, 'Where's Greenland, boss?' And Bjarni scowls at him and says, 'Shut up and raise the sail.'

That was Bjarni for you. Every other winter he spent at home with his dad; and if his dad's seen fit to sell up and set out into the northern sea for some place that quite possibly doesn't even exist, why should that change anything? None of us were going to argue with him, not when he was in that frame of mind; besides, we hadn't got a clue where we were headed, but we all assumed Bjarni knew – otherwise, he wouldn't be crazy enough to try and get there.

You think you know people.

Well, we sailed up the coast to Snaefellsness, and that was all right. We were all figuring Greenland must be one of the islands west of the Breidafjord; maybe Bjarni thought so too. We thought we'd maybe put in at Borg, and once we were there Bjarni would cool down a bit after his spat with the old man, we'd spend a few days drinking at Borg with the Egilsons and go home. But we go on clear past Borg and on into the Straumfjord, and as soon as we see the Snaefells volcano, Bjarni sings out, 'West,' and we head out into the open sea.

Not a good moment, that. You hear all kinds of tales, of course, but nobody you'd believe if he told you your own name had ever said anything about there being any land out west of Snaefellsness. As far as we knew, we were going to sail out into open sea until we came to the edge, or got eaten

by the Great Sea-Serpent, or God knows what. Gives you
some idea what sort of a temper Bjarni had when something
got him all riled up, because we all reckoned we were probably going to die, but nobody said a word about turning
back.

Now, I don't know how much experience you've had
with ships—

'Very little,' I said. 'Very little and still far too much, if you
follow me.'

Kari grinned. 'Tell you a secret,' he said, in Greek.
'Eyvind doesn't know this, or the lad, so don't go telling
either of them; but the first time I ever went out to sea, I was
as sick as a dog eating grass. It was my uncle Kotkel who
took me out, just a little fishing boat, him, me and his three
lads, and I guess I was about twelve at the time. To start off
with I felt right as rain; I sat next to Uncle up by the rudder,
wind in my hair and all that, and I thought, nothing to it,
don't know why everybody makes such a fuss. Then the
boat started wriggling about, and next thing I knew I was
flat on my stomach across the rail, puking like a volcano, and
I didn't stop till we got back home, two days later. Where all
that puke came from I couldn't tell you, because there never
was what you'd call a glut of spare food round the house
when I was a kid. But every time I thought I'd fetched up
the last few little scraps, the boat would start rocking or
heaving, and suddenly I'd find just a little bit more, right
down deep inside me, like I was chucking up from the roots
of my toes. The only good part about it was, I was too busy
barfing my guts up to be scared shitless by the high winds
and the heavy seas, and I'm pretty sure I'd have been put off
seafaring for life if the seasickness hadn't taken my mind off
how scary it was.'

Just thinking about it was bringing a nasty sour, sharp taste into my mouth. 'Not like that with me,' I said. 'It didn't matter how sick I was feeling, the thought of how vicious the sea was and how fragile the boat seemed kept coming back at me like a friendly stray dog and wouldn't go away. And that was just a ferry across the Bosphorus.'

Well (Kari said), I'm pretty bad, but not as bad as that. You couldn't be, where I grew up. Fish don't just walk onto the beach, and you can get a lot more in a boat than you can in a cart. But some people take to it and others don't, and I've always been one of the others. Pretty funny, really, when you think I've been a sailor more often than a farmer, or a soldier.

The thing about being on a ship is— Now I'm talking here about proper sailing, not just taking a boat out to the skerries to bring back the grazing stock; real sailing is where the sun comes up and there's nothing but horrible grey sea everywhere you look. That's when you've got to know how to sit still and suffer quietly. You see, it's cramped on a ship. Now I can't talk about warships, they're different. It's the oars rather than the sails that make them go along, some of the time anyway, so at least you've got your oar-bench. It's not much, just a few feet of board with splinters sticking up your bum, but it's yours. If you were raised on a farm, like we all are, that's what you're used to anyhow. On a farm, like I think I told you, everybody except the farmer and his wife dosses down in the big hall, on the benches round the wall. You've got your little bit of board, not very much but between lights-out and dawn it's yours and you make sure it stays that way. Anybody tries to wriggle you out of a thumb's breadth of your bit of space, you see to it they get an elbow in the mouth, or a knee where it really hurts. Same on a warship, I guess. On a normal ship, it doesn't work like that. Your standard deep-sea *knoerr*'s got a quarter-deck fore and aft, and in the middle's the hold, stuffed full of barrels and sacks and buckets, probably livestock as well jammed in tight so they can't get spooked and move about. If you're lucky, it might be fifty, sixty feet long, and because of the hold you can't get from one end to the other without clambering about over stuff, probably stepping on the back of the cattle, so you tend to stay up your end, days on end, sat on your arse or squatting on your heels, trying not to get flung about as the ship pitches; soon as you start off you're soaked through, and you stay that way right up till landfall. No point changing your clothes, because the next wave or squall of rain and you'll be drenched again. You make an effort to get a fire going in a little brazier, but what's the point: you're flicking sparks off your flint onto damp moss, damp kindling, damp charcoal and wood. Food tastes of nothing but water; wet bread and cheese if the captain's got the journey time right, and if he's a day or three out or you're blown off course, it's fish and seagull, half-raw and dripping wet. Either there's a panic on and everybody's standing on each other's heads grabbing for ropes, ducking under the boom, trying not to get a foot caught up in the lines – bloody stupid way to die, that – or else, what mostly happens, there's absolutely nothing to do and absolutely no space to do it in, so you sit still and quiet. Try and talk? You can't pass the time chatting and telling tales when you've got to yell like a Valkyrie to make yourself heard over the wind and the water and the creaking ropes and timbers. Anyway, like I said before, when you're on a ship it's best to keep your mouth shut. Can't play chess or tables, any second the board's liable to go slithering across the deck and over the side. You need a piss; you put it off as long as you possibly can, because it means getting up off your bit of deck, which you've been keeping dry the way cows cover a patch of grass when rain's coming, and you fight your way to the side, and the wind changes and everybody behind you on the deck is yelling curses at you. And then there's always a puker, at least one in every crew, so that's something else you try and keep out the way of, but that's easier said than done. You squash thirty, forty people on a *knoerr* and keep them out to sea seven days and nights, you'll find out who's easygoing and who's brittle like an icicle. And that's a good voyage. When you're a bit lost and the water ran out two days ago, it gets worse. Half the deck's taken up with waxed hides hung flatwise between the rails to catch the rain; there's blokes leaning over you to spear gulls or drag in lines, and when they hook one it comes flying up out of the water and lands in your lap, thrashing and twisting and smacking you in the face with its tail. Two days out and already you hate everybody on the ship. Everything they do bugs you; there's a man who snores like somebody rasping horn, there's the bastard who trod on your hand yesterday morning and still hasn't said he's sorry, the clown who tried to get the fire going and tipped the brazier over on you, hot embers tumbling down in the folds of your cloak. Captain yells at you to do something, you don't hear or you think he's talking to somebody else; so now he thinks you're idle or stupid, and he tells someone else to do your job, and then he hates you all the rest of the way. You get some old-timers, men who've spent more of their lives sitting on decks than standing on grass, and they can handle it, placid and quiet as an old bellwether or a thin old cow being milked by a clumsy kid. The rest of us, though, we never really get used to it. Sure, we know somewhere down inside that it's all just little nuisances and pains in the bum, and the rest of the crew's not really treating you like shit, it's just the way things are on a ship. We know it, but still we get all fraught when someone treads on our legs as he gets up to go on watch, or his piss flies backwards in a gust of wind and ends up in our eyes. It's two thousand little stupid things a day, salt in your eyes all the bloody time and no way you can make any of it stop; that's sailing. Does that remind you of your boat trip across the bay?

'No,' I confessed. 'It's even worse. Do you people enjoy being miserable, or what?'

'Mostly it's a question of getting used to it,' Kari replied solemnly. 'And the way we live on land, all jumbled up together, makes it a bit easier to cope when we're on a journey. Even so, I can't say as I can think of many folks who'd be able to stand it. Like I said, it's the keeping still and quiet that gets to you. Then again, anybody who's lived through a few Norwegian winters, trapped in the house while it's dark outside for weeks on end, knows a thing or two about that. Let's face it, though. Why do men go to sea? Simple, there's only one reason: to make money, to get rich so they can be farmers instead of hired men, or gentlemen instead of farmers. That's the one thing every man on board ship's got in common, and you never mention it but it keeps you together, keeps you going, stops you from fighting and killing each other whenever someone does something that really pisses you off. Strength of will is what it is, determination; because in his mind's eye, every one of you's got this picture of himself the way he wants to be, or rather the way he knows he should be, if only the world worked how it should. All I ever had to do, when I was on a ship and feeling like I really, really didn't want to be there, was shut my eyes and imagine being on my own farm, sleeping in the back room rather than on the benches, having all the space

I wanted all to myself. I thought, in order to have that, it's got to be worth putting up with a lifetime of the exact opposite.' He sighed, then grinned. 'And now look at me,' he said. 'Didn't get there, did I?'

'No,' I had to admit. 'Well,' I qualified, 'I don't know. You ended up in Constantinople, in the imperial palace. I don't imagine you sleep on a bench when we're back home.'

His grin widened. ''Course I do,' he said. 'Oh, we've got a nice big barracks-hall, bigger than any building in the whole of Iceland; stone walls, would you believe it, and a tiled roof, instead of timber and turf. But we all choose to doss down in the drill hall, piled up like fish landed in a net, because it reminds us of home. Anyway—'

Anyway (Kari went on) we sailed three days, out of sight of land, hoping we were going the right way. Then things started to go wrong. The westerly wind dropped, it started blowing hard northerly, and then the fog set in and we knew we were screwed.

High winds scare you, because you're worried the mast or the yards'll snap. Storms frighten the shit out of you, because all it takes is the one vicious bastard of a wave to swamp you, smash you or tip you over. But fog: I'm not saying it's the worst thing that can happen to you, but it's the nastiest, if you see what I'm getting at. You can't see the sun or the stars, so you don't know where you are. If it's a real bugger of a fog, you can hardly tell day from night, so you lose track of time. When the fog closes in, nobody feels like talking; I don't know if you've ever seen a rabbit when you're almost on top of it, bloody thing knows it daren't run so it crouches flat to the ground, ears back, eyes wide open, hoping you won't notice it but knowing you probably have already: that's how I feel in a thick fog, I just want to crouch low,

keep still and hardly even breathe. I give up, in fog. That's all
there is to it.

You're looking at me strangely, like I've just confessed
that I'm scared of the dark. Well, of course, a Greek like you
doesn't know about fog, any more than you know about
cold. You get low cloud on the mountains, a bit of mist
sometimes, but it's no big deal. Where I come from, you get
fog where you can't see the man sat next to you, even
though you can feel his shoulder pressed up against you. It's
lonely in fog, enough to break your heart, and you know
there's nothing you can do, absolutely nothing. Not if you
were King Hrolf Kraki, or Sigurd the Dragon-Killer; being
big and strong and good with a sword won't help you, or
being clever, or brave. I remember seeing an uncle of mine,
huge man the size of a bear, but he was really ill, dying. He
lay on his bed with his eyes wide open, sweating like dew on
summer grass – I think he was trying to say something but
his lips just moved a bit and no sound came out. I thought,
this is stupid, a big strong man with shoulders like rocks,
nobody on the farm could wrestle him or beat him in a
weightlifting match, but here's something I can't see or hear
or smell or touch and it's killing him, bit by bit while I'm
watching. Helplessness, that's what I'm trying to make you
understand. In a fog you're helpless, I feel like I'm a tree
standing in the forest and I'm gradually rotting away from
inside. When I'm fogbound on a ship, I can't put it out of
my mind. It's like the worries that settle on you in the small
hours, just before first light: the more you try and flush
them out of your head, the worse they get, you more you
dwell on them. If I really want to make myself feel bad, I
imagine that death is a fog, and it's never going to clear, ever.

How long were we there? Were we moving or stood still?
Truth is, I can't tell you. Later, Bjarni said he reckoned we

were being carried along on a stiff northerly wind. Could be right, but I'd like to hear how he knew. My impression was, we just sat there and cowered, but maybe my memory isn't what it was. I remember someone, not next to me but close, muttering prayers, but I couldn't make out what he was saying. I thought about joining in, but I've never been what you might call a religious person. I thought, if Thor's still God, and Odin and all that lot, then from what I know of them they couldn't care less, and even if they could, what could they do to help a few poor buggers lost in the fog? But if what they were saying when we left Iceland summer before last is true, and Christ has driven out Thor and killed him and Christ's father's now God, then I'd really be better off staying quiet here where He can't see me, because they reckon He takes a dim view of sinners, and by all accounts I'm one. So, praying didn't seem like a clever thing to do, so I didn't.

Just when I was sure I was going off my head, I fell asleep. When I woke up, everything was different, thank God. It was broad daylight, we were running before a sharp north wind, and my first thought was, well, I was all wrong about prayer after all, obviously it worked a charm for whoever it was doing it. So I sang out, 'Who was that praying just now?'

Nobody answered; I said it again.

'I was praying, if it's any of your business,' said Thorgils Ulfsson, the forecastle man. 'But that was two days ago.'

'Must've been you I heard, then. Anyway, who were you praying to?'

'Christ,' he replied. 'Want to make something of it?'

I didn't say anything, because people can be funny about religion and stuff. But from that day to this, I've been a really strong Christian, because of getting out of that fog;

and if Thor was to come in here right now and offer me a drink with his own hands, I wouldn't even talk to him. I'd like to say it was the turning point of my life and it's been the making of me, but I'll be straight with you, I can't say it's made a whole lot of difference. Loads of other times I've prayed and bugger all's happened, or things have gone the opposite way to how I asked, so clearly what counts is who's doing the praying, and He can't be bothered listening to a sinner like me. Also, though I didn't find this out till much later when it happened to come up in conversation, Thorgils had said a prayer to Thor before he called on our Heavenly Father, so maybe that was what I'd heard after all; or maybe it was Thor who answered, but he took a while getting round to it. Anyhow, that's enough about that.

We ran with this new wind a whole day and night; and when it got light again, Bjarni jumped up and started yelling, 'Land, land,' and we were all craning our necks and trying to see round each other, and pretty soon there were quite a few of us joining in the shouting. I was one of the last to see it, because there was a stack of malt barrels blocking my view, but eventually I caught sight of a grey blur, dead ahead, smack in the middle between the sky and the sea.

'Greenland,' somebody said. But Bjarni was frowning. He had far and away the best eyesight, and he'd gone quiet.

'Don't think so,' he said.

We weren't happy about that, I can tell you. Someone said, 'Well, if it's not Greenland, where the fuck is it? There's nothing else out this far, and for sure we didn't turn round on ourselves.'

'That's not Greenland,' Bjarni repeated. 'I was told, look for the Blueshirt glacier; soon as you see it, you know you're there. There's no glacier on whatever that is – it's as flat as a board.'

'Maybe it's a different bit of Greenland,' someone else said.

'Then it's no good to me, is it?' Bjarni snapped back at him. 'I want to find my dad, not go exploring.'

It took us a while, but at last we persuaded him to take the ship in closer so we could see if there was a glacier. But there wasn't. There were hills, but they were low and rounded off and covered in woods that came right down to the beach. Now we looked at all those trees, and I don't suppose I was the only one who thought what a good price a full load of long, straight timber'd fetch in Iceland, where they cut down all the trees back in grandad's time to build their houses, if we could only get it back so far. If we dumped Bjarni's cargo from Norway and filled up the hold with lumber, we could double our takings, and since we were there on the spot and none of us knew where we were or how to find it again, I thought it'd make good sense to take the opportunity while it was there. But when someone suggested it, Bjarni got quite uptight about it, and told us to come about and keep going till we saw the blue glacier. Until then, he said, we could forget all about going ashore.

That didn't go down too well. I remember there was a man called Einar Teeth – called him that because he didn't have any, and that's Northern humour for you – and he'd been sat quite close to me all the way from Iceland. He hadn't said hardly a word, only got up from his place when something needed doing or someone needed to get past; just stayed quite still, like a good horse being shod. But when Bjarni said that, Einar jumped up and started yelling and creating, about how he'd joined up to trade sheepskins in Norway, not drift around the edge of the world looking for Bjarni's old man, who was dead anyway because there wasn't any such place as Greenland, so his ship must be at the bottom of the sea right now, and served the old fool right.

'Shut up, Teeth,' Bjarni said quietly. 'You aren't helping.'

But Teeth carried on ranting, and it was a laugh because you could only make out one word in five he said, and one or two of us started sniggering, and that just made him madder still. 'I'm telling you,' said Teeth, 'this whole thing's a bloody disaster, trying to find a place that nobody's ever been to before, nobody's ever heard of, except it's out west of Snaefellsness and there's a glacier. What kind of a damn fool does that? It's only a miracle and the mercy of our Heavenly Father we aren't drowned already, and since He's seen fit to bring us to this place, which looks a damn good place to me and a hell of a lot better than home into the bargain; then isn't it just sinfully ungrateful to say no, we're not stopping here, we aren't even going ashore to take on wood and water, because I want to get to Greenland and see my old man? That's spitting in the face of His mercy, and there's no end of evil going to come of that. Only I don't reckon on drowning out there in the fog, which is no way for a grown man to die, so you just give me an axe and a bag of flour, and I'll swim ashore and let you go to hell your own sweet way.'

Bjarni sighed, like Teeth was the dog you never could teach not to shit under the benches; then he jumped off the foredeck, skipped over the hold on the tops of three beer barrels, lighted on the rear deck and punched old Teeth in the gut so hard we could all hear a rib go. Of course, Teeth sat down in a hurry and sort of cuddled there, hugging himself with his mouth open and no sound coming out, and Bjarni looked round, all slow and careful, and said, 'Anyone else?'

Well, there were one or two of us could've given Bjarni a hard time, particularly all ganged up on him, but somehow nobody seemed to be in the mood. It was like Bjarni had won the argument, and so it'd be pointless just going over the same ground again. Also, we didn't need to go ashore for anything, except a walk and a stretch; we had fourteen barrels of flour in the hold, and beer, and charcoal, and even if the food and the beer ran out, you don't die starving or parching on a ship, when the sea's full of fish and the sky's full of rain. Bjarni was right on that score. He was thinking, he had a good wind behind him and for the moment he was clear of the fog, but we were right at the end of the sailing season, God only knew what the weather was going to do. Bloody fools we'd look if we loafed around on this island two or three days and then got caught in blizzards or ice. Of course, Bjarni could've said all that instead of scatting Einar's ribs in, but it'd have taken longer and the outcome would've been the same, so never mind.

So we set off again, leaving this island with all the trees on the port quarter, and pretty soon we were out in the open again, nothing to see except a blurry line where the sky smudged into the sea. Two days we sailed, with that good wind behind us. Some of us were getting a little edgy, because the nights were cloudy and we couldn't see squat. But at dawn on the third day, just when I was waking up and shaking the water out of the folds of my cloak, someone up front starts yelling, 'Land!' and this time everybody hops up to look, hoping they'll see that old blue glacier.

No such thing. We went in close to take a look, just in case we could make out the Blueshirt, but it was as flat as a blanket. Trees, now: you never saw woods like it, crowding right down to the beach like they were looking at us, the way the young bullocks do when you climb the hurdles into the fold. Very pretty it looked too, and such a difference from home, where there's one little scraggly tree per farm if you're lucky. I remember old Eyvind saying he was sure there'd be deer in those woods, and maybe bear and pigs too, and if that wasn't a good beach for fishing, he didn't know one when he saw it. Now usually you wouldn't take Eyvind's word about hunting any more than you'd take mine, but over the last two days a lot of us'd been thinking that maybe old Einar had had a point, even if he'd had his rib busted for him by the captain, and at the very least it'd do no harm to lay up there just for a day or two; give the ship a looking-over for one thing, check the caulking and the ropes. So we all started looking meaningfully at Bjarni. But soon as he'd made sure there wasn't a big blue glacier anywhere to be seen, he kind of shook himself like a wet dog, and there wasn't any need for him to say a word: we knew we weren't going to land.

And maybe that'd have been a good thing, only our Heavenly Father took a hand, or maybe it was old Thor meaning to play games with us; because before we could up sail the wind died away, the sails hung there empty as an old woman's tits, and obviously we weren't going anywhere in a hurry.

'No offence,' someone said, 'but we might as well launch the boat.'

Bjarni looked round to see who'd spoken, then said, 'No.'

'Just to fetch in some water and some kindling,' the man said. Don't ask me who, I couldn't see from where I was.

'No,' Bjarni said again. 'We don't need it. Stay put, and soon as the wind gets up, we're leaving.'

Well, nobody was in a hurry to get his ribs caved in, so that was that. We all sat there like kids when their parents are fighting, because Bjarni was being plain stubborn and con-trary, but we knew we couldn't change his mind when he was in that kind of mood. But when it got dark, I found I'd got the fidgets.

Now that's a terrible ailment for a man on board a ship, when you're becalmed, no place to go, nothing to do. I tried sitting still, shutting my eyes, trying to think of nothing at all, but it wasn't any good. It was like when you get the toothache, and try as you might you can't get it out of your mind. I knew I just had to get up off the deck and go somewhere or do something, or else I was going to burst.

So I stood up, nice and slow, making sure that nobody was watching me; then I tiptoed best I could past where people were asleep on the deck. Not easy in the dark, and just when I thought I'd made it, I felt something soft under my foot and knew I'd just stood on someone's hand.

'Here,' said a very pissed-off voice, and I recognised that it was Eyvind. 'Mind where you're going.'

Now you've met Eyvind, you think you know him; but who you actually know is Eyvind in his old age, with the burrs ground down and the edges knocked off; like a helmet you've worn for five years, so you've had a chance to pad the places where the rivets chafe, and you've got the lining just nice. When Eyvind was a young man, he wasn't quite so comfortable as he is now. In fact, he could be a right pain in the bum when he wanted to, like for example when somebody woke him up in the middle of a deep sleep. I could tell you some tales about that; like the time we were staying over winter in some rich farmer's house in Norway, and the steward's son had just got married. Like I think I told you, everybody but the farmer bunks down in the main hall; which means you get to hear all kinds of noises once the fire's died down, if you get my meaning – well, possibly you don't, you being what you are, but I'm sure they didn't prune off your imagination when they gave you the snip. Anyhow, let's say the steward's son and his new wife were very much in love; and the drill is, the rest of you just lie still and try not to listen. You can hum quietly to yourself, or wrap a fur scarf round your head, but aside from a few words of encouragement at the start of the proceedings, it's very bad manners to pass comments or anything during the actual performance, as you might say.

Now Eyvind put up with it the first night, and the second and the third, though he moaned like hell during the day about not getting any sleep, and some people having no consideration for others. Of course, I put it down to your basic jealousy, because the steward's son was having a good time and Eyvind wasn't, nor likely to for the foreseeable future. Probably I was right about that; anyhow, on the fourth night I could hear him muttering and clicking his tongue – you can tell how loud he was because he was audible over all that racket going on up the other end of the hall – and I was thinking, here we go again, when suddenly he jumps up and starts yelling, all sorts of nasty things, because he's got a way with words, no question about that.

Talk about uproar. The steward's son starts yelling back, the girl's in floods of tears, great heaving sobs like someone tearing up old rags; then everybody else joins in calling Eyvind names, until the farmer comes busting out in a high old temper. That drags Bjarni into it, because of course we're his responsibility, and Bjarni's main concern is that the lot of us aren't slung out on our ears in the middle of winter, snow drifted up seven foot deep outside and no place to go. So Bjarni stomps over – someone's lit a lamp by now – and he grabs up somebody's boot that's lying there on the floor, and he gives Eyvind the most almighty scat round the head. Eyvind stops moaning very quick and just lies there, and everybody's gone dead quiet, even the girl; Bjarni puts the boot back where he got it from, heaves a big sigh, nods to the steward's son and says, 'Right, carry on.' Actually, we left that place as soon as there was a break in the weather and headed off to the next farm down the valley, where I'm delighted to say they took us in without too much of a fuss, in return for a dozen sheepskins and three barrels of powdered sulphur. Even so, it was a two days' trudge through the deep snow to get there, and Eyvind kept the lid on his opinions the rest of that year until well after Yule.

So that's Eyvind; and you can guess from what I've just told you that when I trod on his hand in the middle of the night, he wasn't just going to grunt and roll over and go back to sleep. 'Shut up,' I hissed at him, but he reached out and grabbed my ankle, and said, 'Kari, what the fuck do you think you're playing at?'

Wonderful. Now everybody on the ship's awake, cussing at me and yelling, shut up, lie down, there's people trying to sleep here. I muttered something about going to the side for a shit; but that was my chance of getting off the boat gone for the night. See, I was planning on sneaking nice and quiet to the anchor rope, shinning down, swimming to land, scarfing up an armful of firewood and getting back on board before anybody was awake. Sounds like a stupid idea, and I suppose it was. But remember, I'd been on that bloody ship all the way across from Norway to Iceland, then straight back on without hardly any time ashore, and after that lost at sea, in the fog. I had this painful need to get off that crowded deck and be away from everybody else; and if that meant a midnight swim in the cold water, well, small price to pay.

I lay awake all that night, fretting and brooding. Dawn came, but no wind. Bjarni was just sitting there, chin on hand, staring at the open sea with his back to the land. I guess somebody got up, lit a fire, cooked breakfast, went round with the pan and the plates handing it out. Nobody else stirred, we all just stayed where we were, like cattle in stalls over winter. I tried not to look at the land in the distance, but I just couldn't help it. At times I could feel it, firm under my feet, and all that space around me. I thought about running, or lying down with my arms and legs spread wide without five men yelling at me. It was like my brain had turned into rotten planking and shipworms were burrowing into it.

That was a long day.

At last it got dark and people slowly dropped off to sleep. By now, I could tell if the others were asleep or not just by listening to how they breathed; I recognised each one's own special way of snoring, grunting, whuffling, and I counted. Silly thing was, after all that, I could hardly keep my own eyes open. But there: those that know me will tell you that I've got a stubborn streak. I don't think so, but I do know my own mind. I forced myself to stay awake, and when I was the only one left, I got up, tiptoed ever so carefully round Eyvind and the man next to him, and felt for the side of the ship. Soon as I'd got it, I followed it uphill – the decks slanted a little, see – until I felt the anchor rope under my hand. Then it was overboard and into the horrible icy cold water, and a long hard swim to shore.

Even while I was swimming, I was calling myself every bad name I could remember. Crazy fool, I thought; what if a good wind suddenly gets up while I'm fooling about on shore? Bjarni wouldn't stop to count heads, he'd call up sail and away, and then I'd be stuck here on this island for the rest of my life, not that that'd be a terribly long time. Or suppose I lost my way swimming about in the dark, went straight on past the ship, got frozen through or cramped up in the water and sank? Risks? I'd have been safer hunting bear with a leek-stalk for a spear. And what for? Because I wanted the stupid firewood? I'd burn it all up drying myself out, always assuming I'd dare light it and explain where I got it from. The thrill of being the first man to set foot on the undiscovered island? Who'd risk his life for something like that? No, I told myself, it's your bloody wilfulness, like when you were a kid. Dad said don't climb up on the roof or you'll fall off; so I climbed up and I fell off. Bjarni said no going ashore, and here I am, freezing my nuts off in the sea in the dark. I wish just once someone'd forbid me to do something sensible, and then I'd go and do it.

You can imagine how glad I was when I fetched up on the sand, though of course it was spoiled by knowing how far back again it all was. Still, I'd made it; and the light was coming up, very pale in the east, and I could just make out the trees in the distance, and the faint gleam of the sky reflected in a river snaking lazily away. I turned round to look at where I'd come ashore and I couldn't help but notice what a good convenient harbour the bay made; also, after a few yards of sand I was standing on turf, firm and springy. Hadn't seen it from the ship, of course, because of the angle and the lie of the ground, but there was actually a wide strip of flat grass between the beach and the tree line. As I walked through it I could feel how lush and thick it was, not like the short, coarse, wiry stuff back home. Good pasture, I thought.

Then I walked along a bit, and next thing I knew I was on my face in the mud. I groped round to see what I'd tripped over, and it felt like a branch. Driftwood, I thought, that'll do, and I tried to pick it up, but it was heavy; also, it felt odd. I bent my head down so I could see, and I realised it wasn't just some old bit of tree, it was a proper worked post, all carved up and down with twisted snakes, Norwegian style. That got me going for a moment, and then I figured out what I'd got hold of. It was one of the canopy struts Bjarni had bought as a present for his dad.

That gave me a really funny turn, you can imagine. Well, no, actually you can't, because you don't know what I'm on about. See, there's an old tradition going right back to when Iceland was settled. The original settlers, when they first came in sight of land, used to get their canopy struts and chuck them over the side. Then, when they'd landed, they'd go up and down the beach till they found where the struts had been washed up, and that was where they built their houses. It sounds like a really stupid way of choosing a new home, till you think that even back then there was bugger-all wood in Iceland, apart from driftwood. It made a lot of sense to build at the point where the currents pitched driftwood ashore – and other useful stuff too: you'd be surprised what you can pick up off a beach.

Anyhow, there they were, these canopy struts; and I stood there for a bit like an idiot, wondering how on earth they'd got there. I guess they must've been washed overboard at some point while we were bobbing about in the fog, and what with one thing and another we hadn't noticed they'd gone. It struck me as pretty funny: Bjarni'd been so dead set against landing, but the sea had other ideas and pinched his struts to show him where to build a house; sort of like when the dog really wants to play chasing sticks, and it comes running up with the stick in its mouth so you can't help but get the message. Of course, there was no way I'd be able to tell Bjarni what'd become of his dad's present, since I wasn't meant to be there. Seemed a shame to leave them, but what could I do?

So I left them sticking up out of the sand on the edge of the turf line and went to look for firewood. I had to walk right up to the trees to find even a twig. I'd been counting on scooping up an armful of driftwood off the sand, but I hadn't reckoned on the belt of grass. The trees were all familiar shapes, masur birch (made me feel a little better about not loading up with the stuff; grows quick, burns quick, rots quick, and the best you can say of it is, it's better than nothing), and I grabbed a half-armful of fallen stuff and brash and scuttled back to the beach, hoping it was light enough by now to see the ship, rather than try and remember where it was. Of course, trying to swim one-handed with a load of sticks gripped under my arm was a waste of time. I had to dump the whole lot just to keep from going under. But I got back to the ship, and my fingers weren't quite so frozen that I couldn't climb the rope. Hauled myself over the side, dragged myself back to my place, slopped down all wringing wet and fell straight to sleep; woke up with Eyvind's boot in my side, saw from the light it was no more than an hour or so later.

'Get up, you idle bugger,' Eyvind was saying. 'The wind's up, we're on our way.' Then he stopped and looked at me. 'You're all wet,' he said.

Luckily, I had my answer ready. 'Yeah, well,' I said. 'Got up in the night for a pee, lost my balance and fell in the water. Had to climb back in up the anchor rope.'

Eyvind grunted, which told me that he believed me; and then Bjarni was shouting orders, and I jumped to it along with the rest of them. Nobody else said anything about me being all wet. Fairly soon the whole lot of us were drenched through, all of them as wet as me or wetter, so I guess I was no worse off for my adventure.

It was three days before we saw land again. When eventually it popped its head up out of the water, we could see glaciers plain as anything. The trouble was, there were too many of them. Bjarni was on the lookout for one big blue one, but this place that we'd come to had loads of them, crowning a huge mountain range, and once again Bjarni told us to keep going. We weren't too badly upset by that. It was a fair way from the sea to the foot of the mountains, and a more desolate landscape you never saw, not even the lava coast of southern Iceland. No good to anybody, Bjarni called it, and for once we all agreed with him.

We kept the sail full and followed the coastline for a bit. Turned out that the worthless place was an island, not that that had any bearing on anything. Soon we were sick of the sight of that flat waste of rubble, so we set a course away from it, due east into the open sea. Our luck was in: we picked up a nice brisk wind, which pretty soon thickened up into a regular gale. Shorten the sails, Bjarni said, not that we needed telling; we didn't want the sail in rags and all the ropes busted.

We hung on for four days, like men breaking a wild pony clinging to the training rein. Nothing we could do except hold on. The wind knew where it wanted to go and the best we could hope for was that it'd take us somewhere, not just drag us out into the middle of open sea and then suddenly die away. I'm not sure which was worse, that or the fog. On balance I'd say the fog, but not by much. Cooking was out of the question. Moving about on the ship was just asking to get swept over the side. We were fairly flying along, and I remember Bjarni saying that if we were headed in the right direction, you couldn't ask for a better wind, since each day we went twice as far, maybe three times, as you'd expect to go under normal conditions. Me, I could've put up with taking a bit longer and going a bit more steady. Actually, I was in no hurry at all. See, the difference between Bjarni and me was that Bjarni really wanted to see his old man and the rest of his family again. Not so in my case. We never got on all that well, my dad and me, and of course he'd gone west with the rest of the Drepstokk household, so I was going home too.

Not sure what this has got to do with anything, but let me tell you a bit about my old man. Mum died when I was quite small, I don't hardly remember her. I had a sister but she was ten years older than me; she married out of the house when I was five and moved fifteen miles away, so I only saw her once or twice a year, at County Fair and Government Assembly, assuming I got taken with the rest of the family. So it was just Dad and me most of the time, and the two of us got along like a fox in a henhouse, each of us taking turns to be the fox, if you get my meaning. If he saw something one way, I'd see it the opposite. Like, he was head stockman; it was an important job and he did it well, all credit to him. He valued those cattle more than old Herjolf himself did. Nobody ever had to tell him what to do, because he'd thought of it already; and he always went the extra mile, made the extra effort, did that little bit more than the boss would've asked of him. Me, I could never see the point. Why wear yourself to the bone for another man's herd, was how I saw it; half the time, old Herjolf wasn't aware of the pains the old man was going to, so he got no extra thanks. Different if it's your own stock, that goes without saying, but grinding yourself thin when nobody's even looking – I couldn't see the point. My attitude was, do what's expected of you and no more. That riled Dad no end. What else were you planning on doing with your time, he'd say; you just sit around in the house or in the barn. He couldn't understand anybody wanting to be idle when there was work he could be doing. He was the kind of man who can't sit still and just be, with his hands folded across his belly.

Truth is (and I can see it now I've lived with myself all these years) I'm not so different from him after all, but back then I sort of took pride in making myself the opposite of the old man, just to spite him. He'd call me shiftless and no good, and I'd make like I thought he was stupid, working so hard and getting nothing in return. I was wrong, of course. Maybe Herjolf didn't notice every single time that Dad put in extra work, but he was no fool, he could see that his cattle were the best in the district and he knew they weren't that way by chance. In return, he treated Dad as a cut above the rest of the hired men, because he knew he could depend on him; didn't treat him as a servant, more like a member of the family. That way, Dad was really working for himself as much as for Herjolf, and he had the wit to see it. I was just young, though, and never saw it that way. As far as I was concerned, there was this line drawn right across the world, farmers on one side, hired men on the other, and never a day but I knew which side I'd been born on; and whose fault was that? Dad's, of course, for bringing me into the world on the wrong side.

So anyhow, you can understand why he and I never got on when I was a kid, and why I was so keen to get away from the farm when Bjarni came looking for a crew. Fool to myself, because it meant I turned into a sailor when the sailing life doesn't suit me at all. The comedy of it is, deep down I must've learned Dad's lesson without even knowing it, because when we were on a trip I was just like him. Nobody ever had to give me an order, I'd already seen what needed doing and done it. Partly, I guess, that was because I got so bored sitting still that anything was a welcome change, but really I think it was me being like the old man in my chosen path, as you might say. No bad thing in some ways, because a man gets a reputation for being a good worker, and then he'll never be out of a place when they're hiring for a voyage. On the other hand, there's this thin line between knowing what to do without needing to be asked, which is good, and thinking you always know what needs to be done better than anybody else, which leads to wilfulness, specially when other folk think otherwise. Like for instance, I thought somebody should go ashore and get firewood when we were sat there becalmed off the sandy beach, so I went and did it, in spite of what I'd been told; and you'll hear about what came of that.

So there we were, skimming along ahead of the gale and going God only knew where; and on the fifth day the wind drops, the sky clears, and suddenly Bjarni's stood up by the prow, leaping about like a salmon and yelling his head off. At first I was sure he must've scat his shin on the rail or dropped the weight on his foot; but then he calls out, 'Land, land,' and we all crane our necks to see, and sure enough, standing up out of the sea is a mountain capped with a glacier as blue as steel. 'Greenland,' Bjarni shouts. 'We made it.'

I guess you can say we were pleased.

Well, so we were. We were thrilled to buggery, because it meant we'd be getting off the ship and going ashore after all that time. Even so, I remember thinking if that's Greenland, I can't see the point. Fair enough, there are worse places. It's not that different from the rougher bits of back home; there's an apron of green grass between the mountains and the fjord, enough to keep the stock alive, provided you can get in enough hay in the season. No trees, mind, and precious little between you and the weather, and you knew as soon as you looked at it that winter'd be a long haul each year, but no worse than many places in Iceland. No better, either. Which raised the question: why bother? Why uproot yourself and go all that way for something that's pretty much the same as what you left behind? Only answer I could think of was, Herjolf and Red Eirik and all those people had made up their minds to go, and now here they were and that's all there was to it.

But I didn't waste much time thinking that kind of stuff, because as soon as we made landfall I was so bloody over-joyed to be off the ship that it passed clean out of my head. Didn't care where the hell I was, so long as I didn't have to sleep another night in wet clothes with the wind freezing my bollocks off.

Now here's a remarkable thing, and I've often wondered about it since. We hadn't just found Greenland. When we drew the ship up we could see a farm away yonder, tucked in under the mountain. Bjarni dashes off to find out where we are, and who's the first man he meets when he walks in the door but Herjolf, his old man.

'Dad?' he says.

'Hello, son,' Herjolf replies. 'What're you doing here?'

'Come to spend winter, same as usual,' Bjarni says, cool as you like. At least, that's what he told us; but Fat Thorhalla who worked in the dairy told us later that she was watching from just inside the door, and the next moment they're both in floods of tears and hugging each other like a pair of wrestlers.

CHAPTER
THREE

'So what did he tell you, then?' Eyvind asked.

It was Kari's turn to go on watch. Eyvind had come back inside the tomb, wringing wet and miserable as a cheap funeral. He'd heard voices, he said; or rather, he'd heard Kari's voice bleating endlessly on and on. He hoped the old fool hadn't bored me to the point where gangrene set in.

'Hang on,' I objected. 'I thought you and he were old friends.'

An extraordinary expression came over Eyvind's face. It was as if God, creating Man, hadn't been able to make up His mind whether His ultimate creation should look amused, outraged, disgusted or depressed; so He'd emptied all four jars into the mix and waited to see what'd happen.

'He told you that?'

I nodded.

'Figures.' Eyvind was quiet for a moment, as though he was trying to digest a medium-sized brick. 'Well, it's true that we've known each other ever since we were kids. We've done everything together, been everywhere together, hardly—' (He took a deep breath.) 'Hardly been out of one another's sight these sixty-whatever years. That doesn't mean we're friends,' he added, quiet and savage. 'Any more than the mule is friends with the treadmill, if you see what I mean. Truth is, I've been chained to that bastard my whole life, and every bloody thing that ever went wrong with me is his damn fault.'

'Oh,' I said.

He nodded vigorously. (That's a Varangian thing that used to bother me a lot until I figured out what it meant. They aren't like us. They don't lower their heads for yes and lift their heads for no like civilised people do; they waggle their heads up and down for yes and side to side for no, and obviously that takes some getting used to. First time I saw one of them do it, I couldn't make it out. I thought he was saying no-yes-no-yes-no, like he was changing his mind several times in the space of a heartbeat. The side-to-side thing was even worse; I assumed he was being buzzed by a wasp.) 'Every damn thing,' Eyvind repeated. 'Like, I only went to sea in the first place to get away from the farm, because I couldn't stick having Kari around all the time. So what happens? Kari joins up too. So, instead of being cooped up with Kari on one of the largest farms in south-west Iceland, I'm cooped up with Kari on a fifty-foot ship. We reach Norway, winter comes round, and I'm cooped up with Kari in some stranger's house for the whole of the snowy season. And so it goes on. Finally, when I can't take any more, I leave the North and come to Micklegarth to join the Guard. Guess what happens.' He sighed down to the nails in his boot-soles. 'Now it looks like I'm stuck with him till the day I die. Which is why,' he added sadly, 'I gave up believing in Christ and our Heavenly Father some time ago. I heard the bishop, see, in the big round church in the City, telling us that when we die we don't just sit in the mound twiddling our thumbs, like the wicked pagans believe. Instead, we're taken to Heaven and we're reunited with all the family and friends we knew when we were alive.' He sat quite still for a moment, staring into the fire. 'In all other respects,' he said, 'Thor and Odin haven't got much going for them. Thor's an idiot and Odin's a bastard, and I wouldn't give you the snot off my sleeve for Frey. But at least with them, when you're dead, you're dead.'

'I see,' I said. 'I hadn't realised it was like that with you two.'

This time Eyvind groaned, quite loudly. 'The worst part about it is,' he said, 'neither does he. Kari thinks he and I are best friends in the whole world. Can't think why he thinks that. I've told him, to his face: Kari, I think you're a total arsehole and I hate you more than anybody I ever met. Bloody fool thinks I'm kidding.' He shook his head sadly, then shrugged like a wet dog. 'So,' he said, 'what was he drivelling on about?'

I pursed my lips. 'He was telling me about how you went to the unknown country with Bjarni Herjolfson,' I said.

'Was he, now.' Eyvind frowned. 'Did he tell you how he snuck ashore, even though Bjarni expressly said we were all to stay on the ship?'

'He mentioned it,' I replied.

'Really? No shame, that man. If it'd been me did that, I'd keep damn quiet about it. You see, everything went wrong because of that. Because of *him*,' he amended viciously. 'The settlement failed, all those people died – I can't prove it, of course, nobody ever listens to me, but I know it was his fault.' He'd twisted his fingers together like a woman making a basket; I was afraid he'd never get them apart again. 'I could tell you,' he said. 'You're an outsider, maybe you could see it, if I told you the true story. But you aren't interested.'

I say some stupid things on the spur of the moment. 'I'm interested,' I said. 'Tell me what happened.'

Well (Eyvind said), it was like this.

I suppose he told you how we eventually found old Herjolf in Greenland. Which is true, actually, and wasn't that the damnedest thing ever? We anchor the first place in Greenland we come to, march up to the first house, and there's Herjolf, standing there grinning, saying, Hello, boys, you took your time getting here. Of course, it's easier to credit if you believe in Odin, like I do. That's another thing I never could stomach about our Heavenly Father. Never the slightest hint of a sense of humour. Odin, though, he's a laugh a minute. Drawback is, the laugh's always at your expense. So, that was exactly the sort of thing you'd expect Odin to arrange, just to fuck our heads up completely.

But we got there in the end, which is the main thing. Also, it had no end of an effect on Bjarni Herjolfson. It made him realise he'd had enough of the sea and ships. He'd tried to put a brave face on it, but being lost like that had really scared him. Then when he found Herjolf, and saw what a good life he'd made for himself there at the Greenland settlement, he made his mind up right away. It was time he packed in sailing and trading, and settled down on the farm to do something useful and make something of his life.

Now, it was all very well for him, but what about the rest of us? Bjarni was quite sure, you couldn't shake him on it. He had the ship drawn up out of the water and he and his father built a boat shed and laid it up there. The ship wasn't going anywhere; so, it stood to reason, neither were we.

It so happened that there was an unpleasant bit of news waiting for me when I landed in Greenland. My mother and father and my elder brother and my kid sister were on one of the ships that went with Red Eirik, but they never got to Greenland. Did Kari tell you about the underwater volcano? He mentioned it; typical. My family were on one of the ships that got smashed up in the terrible storms Red Eirik's party ran into. It happened right out in the open sea so their bodies were never found, but one of Herjolf's men told me that he'd seen the ship go down and there was no way anybody on board her could've survived.

That knocked me about a bit, believe me. I'd always been close to my family, especially my father. Like I told you, I'd only left home to go with Bjarni so as to get away from Kari; I'd have been perfectly happy staying on the farm if it hadn't been for him. Now maybe you're beginning to see why I reckon everything bad that's ever happened to me is Kari's fault—

'You say that,' I interrupted. 'But think about it, will you?'

'Think about it?' Eyvind repeated. 'I've done little else these forty years.'

'All right,' I said, wishing I'd never started on the subject. 'But the way I see it, if you hadn't gone away with Bjarni, you'd have been at home when Herjolf decided to go away with Red Eirik. So isn't it likely that you'd have been on that ship with the rest of your family? You'd have drowned too.'

There are times when I wish it had been my tongue my parents had cut out when I was a baby, rather than the other thing. True, you can get up to a lot of mischief with either of them, but perhaps I'd have been less trouble to the world if I'd never been able to talk.

'I see what you mean,' Eyvind said eventually. 'And yes, I suppose you've got a point there. Whether it makes it any better that I owe my life to that bastard isn't something I can give you an opinion on straight away. Ask me again in another forty years, when I've had time to think it through.'

'I'm sorry,' I said.

He shrugged. 'Not your fault,' he said. 'Anyhow—'

Anyhow (Eyvind went on), that was what was waiting for me in Greenland, and as you can imagine, it knocked me out of true for a while. We Northerners put on a great big show about life and death, like we really aren't bothered one way or another. We'd have you believe that we don't care whether we die today or tomorrow or in fifty years' time, and that we take the deaths of others in the same easy way. We pretend – to you, to ourselves – that a life is like a coat or a shirt; doesn't matter whether it's long or short so long as it's good quality; and quality, of course, means honour, the way other people see you. So, it's better if you die young and respected than old and pitiful, and the longer you live the harder it is to keep your life from getting frayed and tatty, so really you're better off getting killed in the spear-storm, Odin's tempest of axes (that's poetry-language for fighting) rather than ending up weak and blind and having to be helped outside each time you need a shit, and everybody saying behind your back what a bloody nuisance you are since you lost all your teeth. Now like I said just now, I turned my back on the True Faith some time ago and went skulking back to Odin like a stray dog, so what I'm talking about here is Valhalla; that's the place where you go when you die in battle, and just before you get your leg chopped off or your brains crushed, the Choosers come to you – they're these beautiful women that you can only see when it's your turn, and they tell you that Odin has chosen you, and they scoop you up out of your body and carry you up to Odin's wonderful house, where the dead heroes slaughter each other all day and come back to life and drink and feast all night, and so on for ever and ever. But if you die in your bed or drown in the sea or starve in a bad season or a branch drops off a tree on your head, they don't come for you. Then it's not so good, for you or anybody else. They stick you in a hole in the ground and there you stay; unless you're stroppy and a troublemaker, in which case you're liable to get up and start wandering about at night, dancing on rooftops and smashing things up and killing the living. In which case, they'll bury you under a big mound of earth, to stop you getting out; and if that doesn't do the trick and you still get out and make a pain of yourself, they dig you up at noon and burn you and piss on the ashes till they're cold; and that's the end of you for good and all. Even now, when we're all supposed to be good Christians, and our Heavenly Father takes us when we die, they still worry about what happens when someone dies and the farm's snowed in, say, so they can't get the body to consecrated ground. In which case, they bury you in a temporary grave and stick a big wooden stake through your guts to keep you down till the thaw comes and you can be moved.

Valhalla's just a name that we give to memory, of course. If you live a good-quality life, people remember you after you've gone, which is a way of saying you live for ever. If you weren't anybody, you're quickly forgotten and that's that. Personally, I can't make up my mind about any of this stuff. It's probably because I know that our Heavenly Father's lot are winning and Odin and Thor are losing, and you've got to be truly noble or really stupid to stay loyal to the losing side when you know it can only end one way. But I'm pretty sure of this. If there's a life everlasting, I don't want it. This one's been quite enough for me. It's like the big beer-horn in a rich man's house: you've got to drink it all down in one go or people laugh at you. I'm having my work cut out getting through this life. Last thing I want is some bugger filling the horn up again and handing it back to me.

No; the way I see it, life is like a lathe or a potter's wheel. You know that our lives go in circles: day and night, the seasons, the years. I think of myself as a piece of work on a spinning stock or a wheel, and as I turn through each set of cycles the craftsman presses on me with his chisel or his thumb, and that shapes my life. But sometimes he presses too hard and a big chunk of wood splits off, or the clay gets squashed out of shape, and for a while I'm flying round out of true, maybe so hard that I fly out from between the centres or off the wheel, and that's the end, I'm just scrap for ever. That's more or less how I felt when I fetched up in Greenland and they told me everybody was dead. Didn't matter to me, see, whether they'd lived well and gone to Valhalla or whether they were in Heaven or lying on the seabed slowly rotting. One way or another they were clear of the headstock and the wheel and the slip of the chisel, and I couldn't really find it in my heart to feel sorry for them on that score. It was me I felt sorry for, because I was still here, only now I was on my own, with nobody for company except bloody Kari Sighvatson. And what the hell had I ever done to deserve that?

'Is that really what happens in your country?' I asked. 'When a bad man dies, I mean. Do they come back and do all those things you said, dancing on roofs and everything?'

Eyvind shrugged. 'Everybody thinks so,' he replied. 'I don't, but everybody else does, so it's just common sense that they're right and I'm wrong. Mind you,' he added, 'there was this time when I was a kid and we were lying there asleep in the big hall, and suddenly there was this horrible thumping noise coming from directly overhead: stomp, stomp, stomp, like trolls doing ring dances in heavy boots. Everybody lay there dead still, pretending they were still asleep; but you could tell by the sound of them, they all stopped snoring and held their breath. But I didn't believe in that stuff, even then; so I jump up before my dad could catch hold of me and head for the door. Now Dad wasn't afraid of anything, but he wasn't going out after me; because if a dead man catches hold of you and snaps your head off, you'll end up restless too, or so they reckon. So he just groaned and let me go – don't suppose he thought he'd ever see me alive again. Anyway, I take the bar off the door and heave it open – had to shove like crazy, because I was only little – and out I went. It was a bright moonlit night, and I strolled round to where the eaves stuck out.

'In case you don't know, we build our houses out of turf, with short fat walls and big wide roofs, so the eaves are only a foot or so off the ground. It saves on timber, doing it that way, and the best part of it is that after a year or so all the turf's grown in together, so in effect you've got a house that's alive and growing. You Greeks are clever all right and your houses look bloody impressive and grand, but they're all made of stone and brick, they're dead.

'So there I was, snot-nosed kid looking up at the roof, trying to see the dead men trampling up and down. But it wasn't dead men after all. It was just three fat ewes and the old ram, they'd scrambled up onto the roof to get at the wild leeks growing in the ridges. So I stood there grinning for a bit, and then I went up and drove the sheep off, and went back inside. I was all set to tell them my amazing discovery, that it's not dead men who make all that racket at night, it's just sheep. But as I came in, I could feel them all sitting up in the dark and staring at me, wondering if the dead men

had got me and I'd turned into a troll who'd murder them all
where they lay. Silly of me, but I was so pissed off by that,
because they didn't trust me, thought I'd suddenly become a
monster, that I just went back to my place and lay down
without saying a word. And nobody ever mentioned it
again; but from that day on, I knew people thought I was,
well, odd somehow. They'd look at me when my back was
turned, or stop talking when I came along. Probably, you
know, that's why I decided to go with Bjarni, to get away
from all that once and for all.'

I couldn't help it; Greek cleverness, which is never your
friend. 'So in a sense,' I said, 'the dead men *did* get you and
turn you into one of them.'

He looked at me. 'Because everybody believed it, that
must be what happened?'

I nodded down. 'And maybe one of the things they did
was scrape the memory of your mind and make you believe
that all you saw was sheep. But that's not what I was thinking of. What I meant was, they brought about the end of
your old life, even though they were never actually there.' I
smiled. 'We Greeks believe that there are things that are real
that we can see and hear and touch, and other things that are
just as real that we can't. Maybe the dead men were real but
you couldn't see them.'

'Ah,' Eyvind said, with a slight click of the tongue. 'Plato.'

You could've sharpened my head and bashed me into the
ground for a gatepost. 'You know about Plato?' I said.

'I know a lot of stuff,' he replied, with a grin. 'Been out
here fifteen years, you hear all kinds of old nonsense. Wasn't
it Plato said that once upon a time men and women were
joined together, and then God came along and cut them
apart, and that's how Love started?' He sighed. 'And you
Greeks are meant to be smarter than us.'

'Forget about Plato,' I said. 'In fact, forget about all that stuff about dead men and so on. What happened after you'd heard about your family?'

Well (Eyvind said), the simple answer is, not much. Bjarni said he was through with sea-trading; he settled down in Greenland on his dad's place, Herjolfsness, and a day or so later he'd turned into a farmer; like one of those people in stories who can shapeshift, turn themselves into bears or wolves or eagles. There weren't any ships leaving Greenland any time soon, so we had no choice in the matter. We settled down too and worked on the farm. Talk about shapeshifters: Kari and me were gradually turning into our fathers – which is what most people do, I guess, sooner or later.

Now they say time goes by really fast when you're having fun and drags along slow when you're miserable, but that's not how it's always been for me. I've generally found time slips away quickest when I'm really bored. To start off, when you're only a bit bored, like you've got three days of turf-cutting or mucking-out to look forward to, time creaks along like a snail on a wall. But once you've gone past that and you just get used to it, time sort of freezes on you. One day's exactly like another, and you lose count, and next time you wake up and snap out of it, it's ten years later.

Things happened. Like, I got married. Thorgerd, her name was, and I suppose I was lucky to get her, since we were short on women to start off with at the Greenland colony. But she was still available, on account of a really filthy temper among other things, and I wasn't bothered one way or another. Can't say it made much difference, to her life or mine. I was outside all day, she worked in the dairy, or spinning. At night we all slept in the big hall, and come the cold season we were all cooped up inside till spring anyhow. I can't really say I noticed being married very much. There was sex, of course, except that the having-an-audience thing really puts me off, and she took it personally, because women are funny about stuff like that, so really that was all something and nothing. She took to sneaking off at quiet moments with Hallvard the shepherd. People said, why don't you divorce her? And I said, same reason she doesn't divorce me; why bother? Actually, there was another girl I got quite keen on, but after a bit she dumped me and went off with somebody else. Guess who.

The point is, my life was turning fast and smooth; like when you look at a pot on the wheel, and it's going round and round so quick that it looks like it's actually standing still. It all seemed like no time at all had passed, but the fact is that when I first came to Greenland I was seventeen, and I was thirty-two when Bjarni sent Kari and me with a load of logs over to Brattahlid, and we met Leif Eirikson.

(At this point, Eyvind suddenly stood up, as though he needed to go outside or something. He sat down again, closed his eyes, and sat quiet for a bit before going on with his story.)

It would still have been all right (he said) if it hadn't been for the rock. Wasn't a big rock, a bit smaller than a man's head, but it was big enough to knock the wheel off our cart, because bloody Kari wasn't looking where he was going. Well, the Brattahlid smith fixed the axle easily enough, but while he was at it a blizzard came up, and we were stuck there for four days till it was clear to go home. Never had any luck with cartwheels, me.

Even a place like Brattahlid, which was Red Eirik's farm

and the biggest in the Eastern Settlement, they didn't get many strangers; so we were sat down in the middle of the table for dinner, and we did more talking than eating. Mostly just the usual stuff, like how much hay we'd made that autumn and were our hens still laying; but once we'd got all that out of the way, this tall, thin man, about my age or a bit younger, started looking at us and frowning. I asked the woman sitting next to me, nice and quiet, who the skinny man was.

'That's Leif,' she replied. 'Eirik's eldest boy.'

'Right,' I said. 'He's not much like his dad, then.'

She shrugged. 'He is and he isn't,' she said. 'He's quiet and Eirik's noisy, and the old man'd make two of him with enough left over for a shirt; but they're both stubborn as anchors when they want to be.'

I thanked her and turned away before anybody saw me whispering; and Leif was still glowering at Kari and me, which made me feel a bit itchy and uncomfortable. Kari didn't seem bothered; the man next to him was telling him dirty stories, so he was all right. I told myself Leif must just be a bit cautious around strangers, like the way the cows all look at you when you open the gate; or maybe he'd just eaten his food too quick and his guts were playing him up.

But the next day, when the men went out to shovel the snow so they could get to the cattle stalls, Leif stayed in and stood in the doorway, looking at us again. Well, I'd had enough of that, I'd rather dig snow than get stared at, even when it's not my snow. I went to leave the hall, but as I went past he shifted a bit to block me.

'You're one of Bjarni's men, right?' he said.

Well, he knew that already, so I just nodded.

'And your mate there.'

'Kari,' I said. 'I'm Eyvind.'

He didn't nod or anything, just gave me a like-it-matters stare. 'You wouldn't happen to know,' he said, 'if Bjarni'd be interested in selling his ship.'

Well, it's always nice when someone asks you a question you know the answer to. Also, it made sense of the staring, which was kind of a relief. So I said cheerfully, 'Funny you should mention that, because just last spring – no, sorry, the spring before that – we hauled it out of the shed for its yearly pitching and tidying up, and Bjarni was saying he might as well get shot of the bloody thing, he didn't plan on using it again.'

Leif nodded. 'Thanks,' he said.

'But Herjolf, that's Bjarni's dad, he said we might as well keep it as get rid of it, just in case we ever wanted something from the old country or Norway, timber or anything like that. Bjarni said he wasn't bothered, so—'

'He's still got the ship, though,' Leif interrupted.

'Oh yes, still there. And we tar and caulk it every year, so it's pretty much up together. Ropes might need seeing to, but that's about all.'

I was babbling and I didn't know why. But Leif was one of those people: when you're talking to him and he's not saying anything, you can't help chattering away just to fill up the enormous silences.

'So,' I said, 'you thinking of buying it off him?'

He didn't answer that, he only nodded (just enough of a nod to be polite) and went out. But when the thaw came and we were ready to go home, he came out while we were harnessing up and asked if he could come with us. 'Sure,' Kari said (and I can't really blame him for that; we couldn't very well have said, 'No, piss off') and he hopped in the back without a word and sat there quiet as a rock all the way back to Herjolfsness. Talk about a miserable ride. Kari didn't seem to notice, mind; he chatted away to me, and I didn't answer, and he chattered over his shoulder at Leif, and Leif may have grunted once or twice; but it'd take a knife across his throat to shut Kari up, not that that'd be a bad thing at all.

It was a long drive home, I'm telling you. When finally we got there, Leif hopped off the cart without saying a word and strode off on his long thin shanks to the house. We took our time about putting the cart away and seeing to the horses, just in case Leif managed to offend someone with his unfortunate manner and we got blamed for bringing him.

Leif hung round Herjolfsness a day or two, but we didn't see a lot of him. Nights he drank up on the top table, with Bjarni and the old man; during the day he was mostly down at the boat shed, crawling about on his back poking at the strakes to see if they'd sprung, and trying to slide a knife blade in the joints. But he must've been satisfied in the end, because one night he stood up just as the dishes were being cleared away and banged the table with his fist for quiet.

'Maybe you know me,' he said. 'I'm Leif Eirikson. My father's Red Eirik, who was the first man to come here. The point is, I've just bought Bjarni Herjolfson's ship, and I want a crew to sail to the new islands that he found when he was blown off course on his way here, fifteen years ago. Stands to reason his old crew would be right for the job, since they've been to the islands and they know the ship.'

He paused a heartbeat or two, and the hall was dead quiet. Not that Leif was a shouter; in fact, sometimes you had a problem hearing what he said, because he spoke very soft; mumbled sometimes, so the words sort of strained out through his moustache, like draining the wort off the mash when you're brewing.

'I'll be straight with you,' he said. 'Assuming we get there in one piece, we'll be stopping a while. Maybe a year, maybe two – longer than that, even. We'll be building houses, fishing, hunting, maybe planting some grain to find out if it'll grow. So, anybody thinking of coming along but who doesn't want to be away that long, forget it, we'll have to make do without you.'

He stopped again, and this time there was a soft buzz going round the hall as what he'd been saying began sinking in. A lot of the men who'd been with Bjarni weren't likely to go; I knew that, either they'd told me straight out or I'd heard from someone else that they'd had it with sailing after what had happened that time. You could see their point. After all, we'd been blown right off course and fetched up God knew where. It was pure chance that we stumbled across the islands, and an even bigger one that we'd got that fine wind that blew us straight back there. Far more likely that we'd have come to harm, and either died or ended up wandering around through the fog and the ice for months, drinking rainwater and eating seagulls.

To start with, I was one of them. Now I'd enjoyed my time on the Norway run, don't get me wrong. But the sea-road between Iceland and Norway's pretty well known, though even so it only takes one bastard of a storm and you're way out and completely lost. Ships go down every year and men die. I wasn't having the best fun ever carrying hay and mending rails in Greenland, but it was a life, I could put up with it. I didn't really want to go to sea again.

And then – it was all in the few heartbeats after Leif stopped talking – then I remembered Kari telling me he felt exactly the same way. Fuck seafaring, he'd said to me, more than once. Fuck being cramped up and wet through. It's just about all right when you're a kid and you want to go to new places and see new things, but a man in his thirties wants to be settling down and doing some proper work.

There's only been a few times these sixty-odd years that I've agreed with Kari Sighvatson, but that was one of them – which meant, I realised, that Kari wouldn't be going. And if Kari wasn't going, then I was.

Sounds like a really stupid reason, doesn't it? But think about it. You've known him, what, a few weeks? I'd been putting up with him, the endless chattering, always saying the wrong bloody thing, getting to me like a dry boot chafing your heel, for nigh on thirty years. He spoiled my life for me, and that's no exaggeration. Listen: a few years years ago I was at some scraggy little Greek monastery somewhere, and they had a book. Bloody proud of it they were; it had pictures, and every page was written on both sides – psalms, I think it was, or something of the sort. But at some point some fool had spilt wine on it, and there was this dark blue stain. You'd turn the pages, and each one you came to would have the same-shaped blue mark on it, blotting out the words and muddying the pictures and spoiling the whole thing. They'd come to put up with it, because it was their book, and most of the time they hardly noticed, but it was always there, and try as they might, they couldn't ever look at it without hating the clumsy bastard who ruined it. Same with me. Every day of my life was a stained page with Kari all over it. So, I said to myself, if Kari's not going on the trip, Leif Eirikson can count me in.

And then I thought – it was still only a half-dozen heart-beats since he'd finished his little speech – if I stick my hand up right now and say I'm going, what's the betting that Kari'll do exactly the same? Perfectly capable of it; the stupid bastard'd think he was doing me a favour, coming along to keep me company. You know, maybe that's the very worst bit of all. He thinks I like him. I actually believe he likes me.

God only knows how he does it, but I wouldn't put anything past that bugger.

So I made up my mind. I'd wait till the very last moment, make absolutely sure Kari wasn't going, and then I'd join up. Or maybe Kari'd join, and that'd be even better, because that way I could stay home; at any rate, the sensible thing to do was not commit myself either way until Kari'd said what he was going to do. Meanwhile, I thanked our Heavenly Father (Leif was a Christian, so it seemed only polite) for putting it into Leif's mind to buy Bjarni's old ship and go exploring, and maybe just possibly give me my life back.

Anyhow; Leif hadn't quite finished yet. He said he was stopping at Herjolfsness one more night, and he'd be going back to Brattahlid next morning, just after milking. Anybody wanting to join him had till then to let him know, because after that he'd be going on to Stokkaness, and maybe the Western Settlement after that. Then he sat down, and Herjolf waved to the women to fetch round the beer.

Clearly I didn't have much time; I had to find out what Kari was going to do before sunup next day. So I hopped up from my bench, making it look like I was going out for a piss. I actually went out the door and stood outside in the dark and the cold for a bit. Then I came back in, and on my way down along the benches I stopped next to where Kari was sitting.

'Well,' I said, shoving in next to him. 'What d'you reckon?'

He looked at me. 'What, about going on this trip?' he said. 'No bloody chance. We were there, remember, we know what happened. It'd be just plain stupid – we'd have to be touched in the head.'

I nodded. 'That's what I was thinking,' I said.

'Well, of course you were,' he said, and the way he said it

put my teeth on edge. 'I mean, just look at the facts. Last time, we only fetched up there because of a fucking great storm, followed by days and days in the fog. Point being, we haven't got a bloody clue where those islands are. No way in hell we'd ever find them again.'

I looked at him thoughtfully. Twice in one night I'd found myself thinking the same way as Kari. Bad sign. 'Still,' I said, more to myself than him, 'we know the way back, don't we? That strong north-easterly took us straight from the useless rocky place with the glaciers to here; so if we just set a course south-west, then follow the coast straight down once we get there—'

He shook his head, bloody annoying know-it-all. 'It's all right you saying south-west,' he said. 'But I don't remember you or Bjarni or any of us taking the position of the stars or cutting a bearing-dial or anything like that at the time; we were too busy keeping our heads down in that gale, trying to keep the sheets from splitting. The last thing on our minds was making notes of how to get back there, we just wanted to get to Greenland.' He sighed, drank some beer, spilt most of it down his beard. 'South-west you said,' he muttered. 'You only got to be a tickle out either way, you could sail straight past an island, specially in the fog or if a big wind gets up, and then where'd we be? Lost in the middle of the sea counting ice floes. No, you take my tip, don't you have anything to do with it. If this Leif wants to get himself drowned, I say let him get on with it. You and me are staying put.'

Well, that was pretty definite, so I'd got what I wanted. Good. But as I went back to where I'd been sitting, it started preying on my mind. I hate it when Kari's right. I hate it when the truth smells of him, if you get my meaning. But he *was* right, sure enough. A man'd have to be completely crazy to launch off into the open sea with nothing to go on but what we knew. I was so frustrated I could've cried. Here was my chance to get away from that pain in the bum after thirty years, but it'd mean I'd probably be going to my death. Would it be worth it, I asked myself? Just how much did I hate Kari: enough to risk dying for?

Well, yes.

But that wasn't the issue, was it? Where'd be the point of going on this trip in order to get Kari out of my life, if my life only lasted a week or so? I might just as well go back out, there and then, and cut my own throat, save myself getting wet through on a poxy ship. There were all sorts of things to think about. Sure, Leif was the son of the man who'd discovered Greenland; but did that necessarily mean he knew anything about sailing or finding his way at sea? He'd been bloody vague about what his actual plans were if he did manage to find Bjarni's islands. Was he planning on starting a settlement, like his dad, or was he simply after a cargo of lumber? I hadn't wanted to start a new life in Greenland, but I hadn't had much choice in the matter. The Greenland settlement had at least been up and running when we got there. Buggered if I wanted to pioneer a place from scratch: camping out nights in the rain, no way of knowing where your next meal was coming from, and what about the islands themselves? We hadn't gone ashore, so we didn't know if there was anybody living there already who might not want us to take their land away from them. Or there could be huge ferocious wild animals, dragons, God knows what. Suppose we decided to stay and something happened to the ship; Leif hadn't said anything about taking any women along, so we'd be stuck there for the rest of our lives, no kids to look after us when we got too old to work. I could picture it in my mind's eye, the bunch of us all grey and hobbling and feeble, trying to hunt deer and drag logs lest we starve and freeze to death. Problem was, I could also picture this farm. It was set in the crook of a fat green-edged fjord, with a forest on the skyline and a sparkly silver river tumbling down the mountain into the plain; there were sheep on the upper slopes and cows on the flat, a hay meadow as far as the eye could see, and barns and outhouses and beehives and a boat shed, and a smiling old man standing in the porch watching his grandchildren playing happily, and the name of that farm was Eyvindsfjord.

Most of that night I lay in the dark staring up, and when I wasn't watching a ship getting smashed into kindling by storm-waves I was either staggering home empty-handed through the blizzard with my tottery old knees buckling under me, or else counting my six dozen newly shorn sheep as the shepherd brought them down from the shieling in spring.

Probably it was counting the sheep that eventually put me to sleep. I woke up, and I saw light streaming in through the smoke-hole. That was when I realised I'd made up my mind: a pity, really, because I found I'd decided to go with Leif Eirikson, only he'd said he was leaving at sunup.

Don't suppose I've ever moved so quick in my life. I was wearing my shirt; I stuck my feet in the nearest pair of boots, which turned out not to be mine, grabbed my coat and my short-handled axe, and ran.

Running isn't my thing. I can walk all day, or I could back then, but more than twenty yards running and I feel like my heart's about to burst. No sign of Leif in the yard, so I raced off in the direction in which we'd come back from Brattahlid. If he was walking, I might catch up with him, but the chances were he'd have borrowed a horse, or a wagon if he'd got any volunteers from our lot. Anyhow, I ran. Despite what I said about the strain of it, that wasn't a total pain, because running warms you up, and I wasn't wearing any trousers.

A few piles of horseshit, still warm and steaming, told me that I was on Leif's trail, and I forced myself to run faster. Just when I thought I couldn't bring myself to run another step, I saw a wagon in the distance. It was just ambling along, or I'd never have caught up with it. Luckily, someone must've looked back and chanced to see me sprinting along and waving like a lunatic; they stopped when I was about half a mile from them, and waited for me.

It was Leif all right, and half a dozen of the Herjolfsness men. I noticed that only one of them had been in Bjarni's crew. Unfortunately, I only noticed that after I'd panted out to Leif that I was coming with him, if that was all right, and he'd grunted, 'Fine.' That was when I saw Kari sitting there in the wagon.

One of those moments. Had a few of them in my life; like the time I was carrying a big load of logs on my shoulders across the middle of a frozen lake, and the ice broke. Of course, I should've just turned round and gone home again; except that Leif saw me hesitate and he said, 'Well, get in,' and I knew it was too late. I'd joined up, see, and men like Leif don't take kindly to people breaking their word. You can get an axe blade between the eyebrows for that sort of thing, unless you can get out of the way quick enough, as one of Eirik's men had found out the hard way according to Brattahlid gossip. After all that running, I'd never be able to outpace Leif. Best I could hope for was waiting till dark and sneaking off nice and quiet, hoping that Leif wouldn't come after me for fear of getting behind on his schedule.

So I sat down in the wagon next to Kari, because there wasn't anywhere else to sit; and as soon as I'd put bum to board, he scowled at me and said, 'What the hell are you doing here?'

I couldn't have killed him because I didn't have the strength. I could've bust out crying, though, or laughing like a head case. 'Screw that,' I said. 'Why're *you* here, more to the point? After all that stuff you said—'

Kari shrugged. 'Maybe I laid it on a bit thick,' he said. 'Actually, a lot thick. See, it turns out Bjarni carved a bearing-dial on the way home, and he's told Leif precisely where to find the islands, and Leif's a red-hot navigator, like his old man.'

'Bloody hell,' I said. 'So why did you tell me all those lies about—?'

'Not lies,' Kari said, sounding hurt. 'Just the truth with a slant. All right,' he went on, with a deep sigh. 'The fact is, I'd decided to go and I didn't want you coming too.'

Men have died of less. For less, too.

'Is that right?' was all I said, though.

'Well.' He seemed annoyed with me for screwing things up. 'We've been mates a long time, you and me, and when we're on dry land, you're a pleasant enough bloke. But when you're on a ship, I don't know, you do tend to get a bit uptight and difficult. Like the time with Bjarni when we were becalmed off the second island, and you got all snotty with me for sneaking ashore in the night. No offence, old chum, but on a long voyage, that sort of thing's a real drag. But never mind,' he added cheerfully. 'So long as you try and make an effort not to be so inconsiderate, I expect we'll rub along all right.'

It was a long ride to Brattahlid.

At this point, Eyvind stood up and wandered round the tomb for a bit. I decided he wouldn't want to hear anything

I had to say, so I kept my teeth together and my face shut. After a while, he sat down again and asked the young Guardsman, Harald, if he thought that it was time he replaced Kari on watch. Harald shrugged, and said he'd take the next watch.

'No, that's fine,' Eyvind said. 'I could do with a breath of air.' He sighed, then turned back to me. 'One thing,' he said. 'You may've noticed, we Northerners like to give each other nicknames. Mostly it's because we're an unimaginative bunch when it comes to our regular names. We haven't got many to choose from, and most of the ones we've got begin with Thor–. When four of your neighbours are called Thorstein and the fifth is Thorgils and the sixth is Thorbjorn, it's a damn sight easier to say Red or Fats or Flat-nose. Well, that was the occasion on which I got my nickname, and I've been Bare-arse Eyvind ever since. I just thought I'd mention it,' he added, 'in case one of the others uses it, and you're wondering who they're talking about.'

Then he ducked his head under the low doorway and went out.

CHAPTER
FOUR

'We've been mates longer than I can remember,' Kari said, 'but he can be a funny bugger. You don't want to go taking anything he says at face value.'

When Kari'd come in from his stint on watch, he'd made me give him a precis of what Eyvind had told me. I'd left out quite a lot. Even so, Kari seemed concerned that I shouldn't be misled or misinformed. Personally, I was prepared to take anything either of them said with a healthy drop of olive oil, but it seemed to matter to Kari that I believed his story, and that if Eyvind's version contradicted his own, it was because Eyvind was an unreliable witness. Mostly, of course, I wanted to go to sleep. Unfortunately, I couldn't make Kari see that. Maybe he'd promised his mother not to take hints from strange men.

'I could hear him banging on all the time I was out there,' he went on. 'Not the words, just the sound of his voice. He does talk rather a lot, bless him. Always has. The trick is making it look like you're listening. Nodding your head from time to time and grunting helps, but you've got to be careful you don't agree to do something. Like most things, it comes with lots of practice.'

'Mostly he was telling me why he decided to go with Leif Eirikson,' I said.

'Ah, right.' Kari nodded, apparently satisfied. 'I talked him round in the end. Stupid bugger, he'd have missed out if it hadn't been for me, and then he'd have spent the rest of his life kicking himself. Still, he came, and that's what matters. And we were glad of him in the end, no doubt about it.'

'Really,' I said, without thinking. 'What—?'

(Only myself to blame. I'm like a cat with a bit of string; the story twitches, and I lash out for it.)

Of course (said Kari) Leif Eirikson could've used his dad's ship, or bought one off one of the other settlers; but he'd set his heart on having Bjarni's old *knoerr*. Superstition, mostly. He reckoned that if it'd been to Bjarni's islands once it could go there again. Actually, a lot of people think like that: they get the notion that a ship knows the way, if you see what I mean.

Bloody thing was a right old relic, of course. We'd had it out of the shed every year, given it a dab of pitch and wool grease, stuffed a bit of caulking in the cracks. But the ropes were all shot, the strakes were warped, we ended up stripping it down to the frame and putting it back together again; easier to start over from scratch, if you ask me.

But Leif had to know best and get his own way. He wanted Bjarni's ship. He also wanted Bjarni's crew, but all he got was us, Eyvind and me. Never mind; we'd have to do. Besides, what he really wanted most of all was me, because I was the only one who'd set foot on shore. I'd happened to mention it, more bragging about how brave and contrary I'd been defying the captain, and he got it into his head that I'd be able to guide him to the best landfall. All right, I might have exaggerated a bit, because you do, when you've had a drop and somebody's listening. But Leif should've realised that.

By the time we'd got the ship in a fit state, time was getting on. Something you've got to remember about sailing up north: once it gets cold and the ice floes start to form, you stay home, or stay wherever you are, until the thaw comes. That's not a big deal when you're sailing known waters, but if you're planning on zooming off into the unknown, you need to give yourself plenty of time. While we were working on the ship—

'Excuse me,' I said. 'Just one thing.'

'What?'

'You were working on the ship for some time.'

He nodded.

'And Eyvind was happy about that, was he? I mean, he didn't try and sneak off, or quit the expedition?'

Kari laughed. 'God, no. Dead keen, he was. Only thing, he kept banging on about how late we were getting, how if we didn't get a move on, the trip'd have to be put back till the spring.'

I thought about that. 'He was more worried about that than the rest of you?'

Kari smiled. 'He talked about it a lot more than anybody else, but that's Eyvind for you.'

'I see,' I said. 'Sorry, do go on.'

Like I was saying (Kari went on) we were all fretting a bit; and some of us started thinking about what Leif had said, or rather what he didn't say – his plans for the trip, I mean, whether we were going there to cut timber and come back, or stop there and build a settlement. General view was that Leif didn't know himself, and that was reasonable enough:

nobody except me'd set foot on the islands, so he couldn't make the decision until he'd seen what sort of a place it was, whether it was fit for farming or just somewhere to cut lumber. I wasn't so sure, though. It struck me that if we sailed late, we'd end up having to stay the winter, and maybe that was what Leif intended. In other words, he wanted to have a stab at founding a settlement but he reckoned nobody'd be interested in that, so he was planning on stranding us there deliberately. But I kept that to myself, since I wasn't bothered one way or the other. Far as I was concerned, I hadn't wanted to come to Greenland, but there I was, and Greenland wasn't doing me any favours. If Leif settled Bjarni's islands, there'd be land up for grabs, assuming it was any good. I could maybe have a farm of my own, marry, settle down, be somebody for a change. Sure it'd be hard work and suffering and a whole lot of shit, but Greenland was all that, working for somebody else. On the other hand, if we just filled up with lumber and came home, there'd be money in it for me, maybe enough to set me up. Either way, I didn't have anything to lose, so what the hell.

Something was going on, though; because when the ship was finished and we were all getting ready to go, we got word that there'd been a change of plan. Talk about surprises; we all met up at the boat shed, thirty-four of us plus Leif himself, and right out of the blue he told us he was coming along but he wouldn't be leading the expedition. Red Eirik had suddenly decided he was taking charge.

Well, we were in two minds about that. Sure, nobody knew more about building settlements than Red Eirik, because he'd done it already and made a pretty decent job of it, say what you like about the man. On the other hand, Eirik had something of a reputation for not caring how he went about getting his own way. Leif was an unknown quantity on that score, but everybody knew what sort of man Red Eirik was. Also there was the small matter of why, at his age, he felt the need to up sticks and go exploring again, when by rights he'd already got everything he could possibly want: the Greenland settlements, with him as the undisputed leader – oh, he didn't call himself King Eirik or Earl Eirik or any shit like that, but in Greenland, if Red Eirik told you to bugger yourself to death with a pointed stake, about the only thing you'd dare ask was whether you could borrow a billhook to sharpen it with.

Nobody wanted to raise the issue, though, so we all stood there murmuring 'Good' and 'Splendid news' and 'How wonderful', and then Leif said to be ready to set sail at first light next morning.

It gets better. We all showed up as ordered, huddled there in our fur cloaks in the cold glow of sunrise. Leif comes riding up on a big black horse, but no sign of the old man.

'Accident,' Leif tells us. 'Sorry to have to tell you this, but when we were riding over here just now, Dad's horse stumbled and threw him, and he hurt his leg. So he's not coming.'

So that was that. I'm not saying anything about what was or wasn't going on, but it strikes me as funny the way it happened. Particularly the falling-off-his-horse part. See, where I come from it's a real sign of bad luck, falling off your horse on the way to do something. Well, obviously it's bad if you fall off and land the wrong way, you can break your neck like that, let alone your leg. What I mean is, it's like an omen, telling you to stay home. Point is, instead of acting all glum and put out, Leif seemed a lot more cheerful after that, like he never wanted Dad along anyway.

Be that as it may: we set sail from Brattahlid, and the first few days we puddled along the Greenland coast, heading north. Nobody had any idea why we were doing this, except presumably Leif and he wasn't inclined to share. One of the men told me that he'd spent hours talking with Bjarni about stars and winds and currents, but I'd been there when Leif was over at our place, and I didn't remember seeing anything of the sort. I didn't say anything, of course.

Three days out and the bloody fog came down. Did I mention I don't like fog? It made a bit of a nonsense of hugging the coast, since we couldn't see the width of the ship, let alone the land. I was sat aft, and I could just about see into the hold, as far as a big stack of barrels. That set me thinking. I'd done my bit helping to get the stores on board. There were three big water butts, as you'd expect. There were loads of barrels of flour and beer, which was good; also blankets and furs, charcoal for cooking, also good; dried fish and honey and cheese and a tub of apples wrapped in straw. Fine; we had no idea how long we were going to be at sea, or whether we'd find anything to eat once we got to the island. There were spades and mattocks and half a dozen scythes; three big cauldrons, a spit and other bits and pieces of cooking gear. Also we'd loaded three dozen long axes, a good collection of froes and wedges, plenty of rope, all the stuff you'd need if you were planning a logging trip. So far, fine by me. Then we'd had to build a little pen, separated off from the rest of the hold with withy hurdles, for the live-stock – two cows (but no bull), four goats, six sheep and a big wooden cage full of chickens – and the rest of the hold space was taken up with hay and barley and onions and the like, for feeding the stock. Oh, and tucked away in a corner there was an anvil, a set of hammers, stakes and swedges, and two tanned hides for making bellows – but no iron. And that, aside from what we'd each of us brought along to keep by us, was that.

Sitting there in the fog with nothing to occupy my mind,

I tried to figure out what the cargo had to tell me about what Leif was planning to do. Mostly I thought about fetching along two cows but no bull. Eighteen months, that said to me; a cow'll give milk for eighteen months, but then it's got to be put in calf or it'll run dry. On the other hand, we'd brought a ram and a billy goat, so we'd not be without milk if we were planning on staying longer. The logging stuff made sense whether we were planning on staying or not; but I couldn't for the life of me figure out why you'd bring along a forge but no iron. In the end, I decided that Leif was either too smart for me to second-guess, or very stupid.

The northerly wind that'd carried us up the coast for three days changed when the fog came down. We were becalmed for maybe twelve hours. Then a stiff westerly came up. Leif hopped up from where he'd been sitting, staring out at the sea and the fog. We put on as much sail as we dared. Didn't take long for the fog to blow away, but when it had cleared there wasn't any sign of Greenland to be seen.

That night was lovely and clear, and I could see the stars. The wind was down. Everybody else was asleep, dead to the world, except me. Strange feeling. A man with an imagination could make himself believe that he was completely alone out there. I remember thinking, well, this is what you wanted, isn't it, to get away from living right under the armpits of the same old people every day. Maybe our Heavenly Father was listening, and He thought, if that's what old Kari wants, he can have it. And you know how one thought leads to another when you're awake in the middle of the night; I got to thinking, what if He'd been thinking about me the night I swam ashore to Bjarni's second island? What if He'd got up a sudden squall of wind and blown the ship far out to sea and left me there on shore all alone? I could almost imagine Him grinning to Himself, and saying, well, Kari, you wanted a big rap of land all your very own, yours as far as the eye can see; don't say I never give you anything.

Now you ask any bishop, he'll tell you that's not the way our Heavenly Father does things. There's times, though, when I wonder.

Next morning, not long after dawn, the wind got up again. It had changed a bit, so we had to tack a little to keep holding due west. Leif was worried about the mast. He was sure he could hear a nasty groaning noise, and he clambered out over the barrels and sat directly under it, looking up to see if he could spot a crack opening anywhere. Of course, that made the whole lot of us nervous as hell; if your mast goes, out in the middle of the sea, you're screwed. So we all sat dead quiet trying to hear this funny noise Leif was on about, and you know how it is. If you listen for something hard enough, sooner or later you'll hear it, whether it's there or not. Somebody piped up that he could hear it too, a sort of long, high creaking; somebody else said no, that was just the ropes straining; what he could hear was a sort of low rumbling growly noise; someone else said, 'Don't be stupid, that's just the boards flexing against each other, what the captain means is that sharp clicking sound.' Leif didn't join in, except every now and then he'd tell the lot of us to shut up. By the time it got dark we'd got ourselves in a right old state, even though deep down we all knew we were fussing over nothing and really there wasn't a funny noise at all.

That was when the rudder snapped.

God knows why. True, it was old and we hadn't replaced it when we were giving the ship its refit. I suppose there must've been a big wave or a gust of wind twisting us in the water. Anyhow, there was a sudden loud crack, just like a man's arm breaking. We all jumped in the air, looked up at the mast and saw it was still there in one piece, then started staring all round trying to see what'd gone.

Soon as we realised what'd happened, Leif snapped out of his mood and started giving orders. We dropped anchor, got the rudder up out of the water and had a good look at the damage. It could've been worse. The break was just above where the handle meets the blade and it wasn't all the way through. There was still a hinge of sound wood holding it together; so we took a coil of good tarred rope and pulled the plies apart till we had a strand about the thickness of your little finger, and served the break up good and tight – two men straining on the cord, three men slowly turning the rudder to wind the strand on. We melted up a block of pine pitch we'd fetched along just in case, and sealed the splice up to keep it tight. Proud of ourselves we were, when we'd finished. It was as though we'd all known we were due a disaster of some sort, and now that it'd come and we'd coped with it and nobody was drowned or killed we could all relax. We hauled the anchor up and got in a good four hours before the wind dropped again.

Nothing happened the next day, except that we got a light wind that kept us pottering along, nothing like so fast as we'd been going, but we didn't mind too much taking it a bit steady because we were a bit concerned about the strain on the mended rudder. About mid-afternoon we saw a whale, but it was too far out to risk launching the boat, and besides, we were well set as far as food was concerned. What got me going wasn't the whale but a handful of gulls, the first we'd seen since the fog. I heard them first of all, nearly did my neck in trying to catch a glimpse of them. Anyhow, what with one thing and another we were all suddenly feeling bright and cheerful; we started talking to each other again rather than just huddling down against the spray.

People kept asking Eyvind and me what the islands were like. Of course, we'd told them over and over again everything we could remember, which wasn't much, but they were all in the mood to hear it one more time, and naturally we spiced it up a bit, like you do with the salt beef in midwinter. Something seemed to be telling us that we'd sight land the next day. It was a sort of everything's-going-right feeling, and it made a pleasant change.

The rain started around midnight. Now, when you've been wet through for days and your feet squelch every time you put your weight on them, and your hair's flat to your head and caked in salt, you may find yourself thinking that you can't really get any wetter, not if you were to jump off the ship into the sea. A really good rainstorm sets you right on that score. If you ask me, heavy rain with the wind behind it is wetter than being in the water. It's like the difference between wearing a mail shirt and carrying it: you don't really notice the weight when it's on, but it's a bloody lumpy thing to carry in a sack over your shoulder all day. Same with water. When you're swimming it sort of shrugs off you. Rain stays with you, works its way down from your head and on down inside your clothes into your boots, where it's trapped.

That rain was something else. When it hit you in the face it was like being slapped. I'm not sure which was worse, trying to move about in it and get some work done, or sitting all still and huddled and taking the pounding. Not that we got much of a chance to sit, because along with the rain there was one hell of a wind. Leif was still fretting about the mast, so we shortened the sails. The waves were up so high it was like being in a valley, so we were tossed around plenty. The stores broke loose. Barrels and bales and sacks and kegs got bounced right up in the air, came down and split – we lost one of our three water vats, and we weren't at all happy about that. Two big sacks of flour went straight over the side and the water got into another three where they tore against the sharp edges of smashed barrels. Then the sheep got loose and jumped up on the forward quarterdeck, and we had real fun and games catching them and hobbling them so they'd stay put. Soon as we'd done that, the apple barrel landed on the chicken crate and stove it in. Chickens everywhere under our feet when we were trying to haul on the lines, and every now and then when you stopped to catch your breath a bloody great wave'd sweep in out of nowhere and smack you in the face. It seemed to go on for ever, and as soon as we'd coped with one disaster another one started off. The rudder held, thank God, and so did the mast, but a couple of boards sprang and we shipped an awful lot of water in the hold before we could stop up the leak with the dry clothes we'd been carefully saving for when we finally made land. It was a bloody miracle nobody went over the side. I was sure we were going to capsize at least twice, when big waves got under the keel and lifted us right out of the water, like a salmon jumping a waterfall. It was bloody cold and we were all soaked, but a lot of the time I was sweating.

Rain stopped about midday; wind fell, and we all dropped right where we happened to be standing, completely shattered. On the farm you work hard all day every day, and you get to thinking what a soft life it must be to sit in a boat letting the wind carry you along. But real work is when you're on board ship in a filthy bloody storm like that one. It may not happen all that often, but when it does you find out what it means to be weary right down to your bones. Half a dozen of the men just fell asleep where they'd slumped. I guess the rest of us were too tired to sleep. We sat or sprawled and breathed – it was all we could manage to do.

And then someone called out, 'Land.'

Fuck me. We'd been sitting there becalmed, don't know how long but quite some time, and nobody had thought to look where we'd ended up. It was a man called Thorgrim Sigurdson, Thorgrim Feet to us, who just chanced to look over his shoulder and suddenly there it was, like it'd snuck up on us while our backs were turned. I was looking the other way and thinking about a whole load of other stuff when he started to holler. I remember thinking, Land? as though I didn't know what the word meant. Then it dawned on me. Land. *Land*, for fuck's sake, we made it, we're here.

We were too whacked to dance around and yell or anything of that sort. We didn't even cheer, it was more a general sigh of relief, like the feeling after you've just mown five acres and you cut the last clump of grass. Even Leif seemed like he didn't really care. He turned his head and stared at it, then went back to looking down at his feet; he'd lost a boot scrambling about in the hold, and he didn't have the energy to go and fetch it. All this way, I thought to myself, and now we're here he spares it a passing glance, like your dad used to do when you were a kid, riding in the hay cart with him and you suddenly pointed and yelled out, 'Look, Dad, a cow.'

Well, I thought, if he can't be arsed to look happy, neither can I; so I lay down on my back and looked up at the sky for a long time.

It was Leif's voice that woke me up. 'Right,' he said. 'Swimmer and Bare-arse' – that meant me and Eyvind – 'on your feet and tell me where the hell we are.'

I wanted to tell him to go away and do something or other, but I hauled myself up on the nearest rope and dragged myself over to the rail. Eyvind joined me; he's got better eyesight than me, and I hear better. He says that's because I talk so much I haven't worn my ears out with listening.

'Well?' Leif said, and I didn't answer. My eyes were all red and bleary with salt, for one thing. But Eyvind was peering about, and after a bit he said, 'That's the third island Bjarni found. The one with the flat stone beach and the glaciers.' He paused a moment, then added, 'The useless one.'

I have a feeling that Eyvind promised his mum when he was young that he wouldn't tell lies, and somehow he stuck like it. Yes, Bjarni had said it was useless, but that really wasn't the time to mention it. Straight off the blokes started to mutter, like it was Eyvind's fault, and probably mine too for being his best mate. Leif sagged just a little bit, round the shoulders; then he seemed to snap out of it, and barked out orders like a small dog yapping. We raised sails and crept in as close to the shore as we dared. Then Leif had them launch the rowboat, and told Eyvind and me to get in it. Wasn't thrilled about that. I figure the smaller the boat, the more there is to be scared of. Wouldn't want to be in that thing if the rain and the big wind came back. I sort of wished I hadn't been so cocky when I was on Bjarni's crew; if I hadn't swum ashore when Bjarni'd told me not to, Leif wouldn't have been so determined to have me with him, and I'd have been back in Greenland mucking out cows instead of clambering into a little boat on the very edge of the world.

Still, it had to be done. I muttered a prayer to our Heavenly Father and asked him please not to blow up a big wind and take the ship away while I was on the island; and then we were rowing like hell towards the shore. Me, Eyvind, a German called Tyrkir and Leif Eirikson.

It was a miserable rotten place, right enough. The closer we got, the less I liked the look of it. Imagine a flat plain, black and grey shingle with hardly a smudge of green, pitted with big, sharp rocks. Far away, where the ground met the sky, a line of triangular white mountains like the teeth of a saw.

'Wonderful,' Leif said — it was the first thing anybody'd said since we left the ship. 'Just one great big useless slab of nothing.'

'That's what Bjarni said,' I reminded him. 'This is where we came last of all. It's good, it means we know where we are. All we got to do is follow the coastline down and we'll reach the good bit.'

Leif made a short grunting noise, like a pig.

Don't know why we bothered, but we beached the boat, got out and walked about a bit. Just so we could say we'd done it, I suppose. Nobody said anything (and that was unusual, because generally the trick was getting Tyrkir the German to shut up: he couldn't speak Norse worth shit, but not for want of practice) and after a bit Leif picked up a couple of small rocks and walked back to the boat. I was glad to leave that place. It gave me the creeps. There's places every bit as bad, in Greenland and Iceland too, that seem to go on for ever and ever. But at least you know that if you keep going far enough you'll eventually see some green grass and a roof or two in the distance. There it was so flat you could see for miles, and it was all the same.

'Right,' Leif said, as the German pushed the boat off and scrambled in, and we picked up our oars. 'Next time, I suppose we'd better build a cairn or something as a seamark, so we'll know where we are when we come this way.'

Eyvind and I made vague what-a-good-idea noises to keep him happy, and we headed back to the ship. I tell you, it was like coming home after a long and horrible journey. Never thought Bjarni's old *knoerr* could feel so cosy and safe. Getting back on board was like sunrise.

'So that's Slabland,' Leif announced. 'Anyway, we've done better than Bjarni Herjolfson; at least we had the balls to land.' He turned his head and scowled at the distant mountains, like they were a dog that wouldn't come when he whistled. 'Screw it. Let's go south.'

So we did. Actually, we didn't have much choice in the matter. We picked up a strong southbound current, combined with a stiff wind that tried to crowd us up against the shore. We didn't fancy getting dragged along the beaches like a knife being ground on a wheel, so we held out into the open sea rather more than we'd have normally done. We could still see the land as a grey smudge, but that was about it. I was trying to remember how long it'd taken us the last time to get from the third island to the second, but we'd had a gale up our arses then, if you remember, and now we were chugging along rather more sedately, so I wasn't going to be much help. Eyvind, on the other hand, was pretty sure of himself. At the rate we were going, he said, we needed to hold this course eight days and seven nights, and that ought to bring us out just where we'd been becalmed, and where I'd swum ashore.

Well, either he'd been back there since and hadn't told me, or he was very observant and a bloody good navigator, or he was making it up so as to be important; but Leif took him at his word and we kept going. Made me wish I hadn't been so honest. Eight days at sea, when we could've gone ashore and at least stretched our legs, even if the scenery turned out to be as miserable as Slabland. Thanks to all that rain we were all right for water, even with one of the casks trashed, and food wasn't a worry, though about half the hens went off lay for the moult, so Leif told us to eat them instead. We were able to get a fire going some of the time, too. But it was four days before our clothes began to dry out;

if we'd gone ashore, we could've had a proper fire and been warm and comfortable, at least for a bit. Couldn't suggest anything like that to Leif, though. He seemed to go a bit funny once he'd set foot on shore that first time; he was impatient, always in a hurry, like a man getting the chores done before setting off for the fair. I don't suppose he was any less cold and damp and miserable than the rest of us, but he took it a different way. It was like all the discomfort was an itch, and only getting to my landing site would scratch it. Strange attitude: we were going past all that coastline without even getting close enough to take a look. For all we knew, the land that we were hurrying past might've been just what he was looking for, but he couldn't be bothered to stop and find out. He'd set his heart on the place I'd described, and he wasn't interested in anywhere else, even if it was better.

They were eight long days and seven even longer nights. Middle of the eighth afternoon, though, Leif stood up by the prow, highest point on the ship, and peered at the grey smudge for a very long time. Then he called Eyvind and me over.

'Well?' he said.

Well the fuck what, I thought, but Eyvind said, 'It'll be here or hereabouts,' so Leif had us bring the ship in tight to shore. Closer in we got, the more I could see; and I couldn't help thinking it wasn't much of an improvement on the Slab place. True, there were trees. You never saw the like. I mean, they think they've got forests in Norway, but I never saw anything over there to compare with what we saw as we skimmed along, and anybody thinking of felling a load to take back to Greenland would've gone mad with delight. One thing I could see, though, was that it wasn't much like Bjarni's second place. You had a long, very pale beach, the sand almost white, and the trees crowding down onto it like a whole bunch of families come to see you off on a journey. But no grass, except for a few sad tufts here and there. It'd been the broad strip of grassland that'd lodged in my mind, and for sure it wasn't there. Either we hadn't reached that place yet, or we'd gone straight past it. Either way I was pretty sure that Leif wasn't going to be happy, and I was glad I'd kept quiet and told the truth after all.

Even when it was quite clear that we'd come to the wrong place, Leif told us to keep going and make landfall. We put the boat out and the same party of four – me, Eyvind, Leif and the gabby German – rowed across and had a look.

Wasn't any better close up. The beach sloped gently up to the forest edge and then it was just trees. Eyvind went all quiet, I hung back out of the way, but Tyrkir the German went bounding off like a dog into the forest, leaving the three of us behind.

'Well,' Leif said after a while. 'This isn't it, is it?'

'Cracking good place for lumber,' I said.

'That's not what I asked,' Leif replied.

'Bet you anything you like those woods are bloody crawling with deer,' I said. 'And it doesn't look like anybody lives here, so they won't be used to people – you could probably walk right up to them. And bears, too. Never tried it myself, but they reckon bear's as good as the best beef.'

Leif looked down his nose at me, and I gave up. 'This isn't where I came ashore,' I said.

'Thought not,' said Leif. 'Where's that bloody Tyrkir got to?'

'While we're here, though,' I said, 'we could beach the ship, see to those sprung boards, maybe build a fire, dry out a bit. Really, we could do with making a new rudder, with all this timber. Silly to take risks with something like that.'

He didn't answer, and I decided to shut my face before I

got on his nerves. So we walked up and down the beach for a bit, and I wondered if we were the first men who'd ever come there, and if so what were my chances of getting a loan of a ship back in Greenland and coming back here for a cargo of lumber, since nobody else seemed to want the place – waste not, want not, as my old mum used to say. But then I thought of all the trouble we'd had, and how I've never really liked sailing much anyway, and if I were to kid someone into lending me a ship, I'd have to go halves on the profits with him, so fuck that. It was very quiet there. I don't mind a bit of quiet, but too much of it makes me nervous.

Then Tyrkir came loping back out of the trees. He hadn't brought anything back with him and he didn't say where he'd been or what he'd been looking for, so for all I know he'd just been searching for somewhere he could have a shit without thirty-four men watching. Soon as he'd joined us we went back to the boat, and that was that.

It was pretty quiet on the ship, too, when we got back on board. There wasn't the babble of questions you'd have expected – well, what's it like, then? Are we going ashore or what? Is this where you were looking for? What about fresh water and all that? Instead, they all waited for Leif to say something, but he wasn't in any hurry.

'Suppose we'd better call it something,' he said at last. 'Forestland all right with you lot?'

Nobody answered him, so presumably it was. Then we raised anchor and left.

By now I guess everybody was thinking the same thing: had we not reached the place I'd come ashore at yet, or had we gone past it? Not something you wanted to dwell on, particularly since we still didn't really know what we were supposed to be doing out here. Well, probably not felling lumber, for obvious reasons. Wouldn't have taken us more than a few days to fell enough to fill our ship, and then we could have gone home. (Except we'd have trouble breaking out of that current enough to strike out east; nobody was forgetting that we didn't actually know the way home from here, bar turning round and going back the way we'd come, which wasn't possible because of the current and the winds.) All in all, it was hardly surprising that nobody spoke much as we left Forestland behind us, because there wasn't anything cheerful to be said, and we were wound up enough without making it worse by arguing.

The next two days were pretty grim. We didn't have much control over where we were going, or how fast. The wind made all the decisions for us. It wanted us to go south, fortunately, so we hung on and tried not to dwell on all the things that could've gone wrong so far. There comes a point where either you go with it and hope everything'll end up fitting into place, like a tenon in a mortice, or else you jump over the side and spare yourself the pain. Nobody jumped over the side, so I guess we all found our own ways of coping. By now, though, as a crew we were pretty much all pulled apart, like the boards of an old abandoned ship laid up on a beach. We'd long since run out of things to say to one another, and we'd reached the stage where talking to someone wasn't much less of an assault than smacking him in the face. We did our work because we knew we had to, because otherwise the ship was going to drift or sink. Nobody was interested in Bjarni's second island any more; except possibly Leif, and he might as well have been on a different ship. We'd given up hope of anything good happening; by the same token, we were far less worried than maybe we should have been about not knowing where we were, stuff like that. Mostly we weren't living in the here and now. We were thinking about home, about things that had happened years ago, things we could've said or done but didn't, things we did or said and wished we hadn't. We all thought about the past, because it seemed like the present was just turning endlessly and slipping, like a cartwheel in the mud. As for the future, I think a lot of us had more or less made up our minds that there wasn't going to be one. Maybe you're wondering what'd got into us all, why we'd suddenly turned so miserable in two days. Not sure. After all, we knew we weren't all that far from dry land, and the weather wasn't kicking our teeth in. I think we'd just been on the ship rather too long, without a reliable end to look forward to. Let's say it was the difference between climbing down a ladder and jumping with your eyes shut.

Morning of the third day out of Forestland, I was asleep with my back to the rails. I woke up, and the first thing that hit me was that I'd got drenched with water during the night. Maybe rain, or a big wave; made no odds. I just felt tired, a bit angry that I'd gone to sleep almost dry and now I was soaked to the skin again. Sun was coming up; half a glowing orange egg yolk in the seaward sky. Cold; but it wouldn't have been too bad if only I hadn't been sopping wet. Another day on the ship.

Well, I like to start the day with a piss if I possibly can; so I stood up, staggered to the rail and started to pull my trousers down. And then I saw it.

You always assume that other people will do the important stuff, like keep an eye out. But sometimes they're assuming the same thing, and it doesn't get done. At that moment, nobody was keeping a lookout. They were waking up, cussing and muttering, stretching and whining about cricked necks and ricked backs. So it was me, with my trousers down round my knees, who saw it first.

I thought: can't be, or someone would've mentioned it. So I looked again, and there it still was. I had this crazy flash in my mind of us sailing right on past it because I'd felt all shy about yelling and disturbing people. So I yelled. 'Land,' I shouted.

Leif was squatting right up front, coat and cloaks snuggled round him. You'd have bet he was fast asleep, but as soon as I opened my mouth he jumped up like he'd got a bit of string nailed to the top of his head and someone had just given it a sharp tug.

'Land,' I repeated. 'Over there, for crying out loud. Look.' I pointed. People were blinking, rubbing their eyes – it took a quarter of a heartbeat or something like that before they could start looking. But Leif was staring at it, the woods with hills behind, the flat white beach. He turned his head and looked at me – I'm not making this up – looked at me the way a cow does just before you cut its throat.

'Is this it?' he asked me.

'Think so,' I replied.

I'd said something wrong, because he went off at me like pouring water into a crucible of melted lead. 'You *think* so,' he said. 'Fuck you, is that it or isn't it?'

Suddenly everybody was waiting for me to say something. 'I think so,' I repeated, and he flared up again, like the famous hot-water spout at Geisir back home. 'I can't bloody well see from here, can I?' I yelled. 'Soon as we're close enough, I'll tell you if we're there or not.'

While I was saying this, I was thinking. I was asking myself, You clown, it doesn't matter, nobody's seen the place where you went ashore except you, and that was in the dark; so if you lie, nobody'll ever know and you'll get all these angry people off your back. And supposing this isn't the place: are you going to tell them that, and have them throw you overboard out of frustration? And the really weird, crazy thing was, my answer to that was, Well, yes. I couldn't have told a lie about it if I'd tried. If it hadn't been Bjarni's second island, and the place where I'd landed, I'd have told them so, because – I have absolutely no idea why – *it mattered*.

Just as well, really, that I didn't have to.

It was Eyvind who spoke up before I did, bless him. He said, 'Yes, this is it, we're here,' in a quite calm voice, almost cold, bored. 'And a bit further on, there's a sort of rounded point that leads into the straits.'

What straits? I was asking myself; but the good bit was, I'd stopped being the centre of attention. Now why they were all so quick to take Eyvind's word for it when he'd been completely wrong the last time, I couldn't begin to tell you. My guess is, because he was telling them what they wanted to hear. Makes you popular for a while, but bad policy in the long run.

'Are you sure?' Leif was saying, and Eyvind was nodding and wagging his beard, all wet and caked with salt into little rats' tails. 'Quite sure,' he was saying. 'Couldn't mistake it for anywhere else. There's the wooded hills, see, and the beach, and the rounded point in the distance. You can't see the grassy plain from here, of course, but we never noticed it the first time.'

People started looking back at me over their shoulders, since of course it was only me who reckoned there was a grassy plain on Bjarni's second island. It was the first island that'd had the nice flat green meadows; but for some reason Leif had never seemed particularly interested in that.

Stands to reason I couldn't have held my breath all the time we were drawing in to land; it took the best part of half a day, I'd have choked. It must just've felt like it. While we were getting there, I was thinking to myself that maybe there was something about this place that brought out the worst in all these strong-minded leader types. Like, Bjarni Herjolfson had been dead set against us setting foot on any of the three islands, even though we'd had good reason to go ashore. And here was Leif Eirikson dead set on doing the opposite and landing – what's more, landing at the place where I'd landed, and nowhere else, like I was someone clever or important, or I knew some wonderful secret.

It must've been around midday when we got close enough to launch the boat, and the sun was bright and high. We dropped anchor off the rounded point Eyvind had mentioned – it was there right enough, though I had no memory of it – and rowed in up the sound a short way till we came to a little bay.

This time there were six of us in the boat: a couple of Greenlanders called Thorvald Salmon and Lazy Hrafn came along, I'm not sure why. It was a bit of a struggle rowing in, but we got there, ran the boat up on the sand and hurried up the beach.

Now I could be slandering you, but my guess is that you're a City boy—

'That's not slander,' I said. 'That's a compliment.'

He looked at me, smiled wryly and sighed. 'Thought so,' he said. 'You're a City boy all right.'

In which case (Kari went on) you may have trouble understanding why we ran up the beach. In fact, if you'd been there watching, you'd probably have thought we'd been drinking salt water on the journey and had gone off our heads.

You'd have seen us dashing up the beach till we reached the point where the sand stopped and the grass began. You'd have watched us dropping down on our knees, trawling our hands through the grass, licking our fingers and suddenly bursting out in whoops of joy, hugging each other, jumping up and dancing round in circles. Very sad, you'd have said to yourself; to get so far and then break down, brains eaten away with worm by the looks of it—

The point being, you don't understand about grass. You think it's just a weed that grows up between paving stones, or a green colour in the background. You don't know about the difference between sour and sweet grass, or why it's a matter of life and death which sort you've got when, or why a man'd go to all the trouble of ploughing up a meadow just to sow grass seed. All a closed book to you, isn't it?

Well, in that case, you'll just have to take it on trust from me that the grass that grew between the beach and the trees in that place was enough to make us think the whole trip'd been worthwhile. You see, if the grass is right, you can keep your cattle outside in the open right through the autumn and into the winter; and then you can bring them in under cover and feed them hay until the spring. Result: you start off the new year with pretty much the same number as you ended the old year with. But if the grass isn't right, you can't leave them out when the weather starts turning cold. First their milk'll dwindle away till they go dry, and then they'll starve or get sick. So you bring them in early; but now you've got to feed them hay for a third of the year, and there's never enough. You've got no choice but to pick out the best and slaughter all the others, preserve the meat as best you can to see you through the winter in place of milk and butter and cheese, and try and make the numbers up by bringing the calves on next year, which of course means less milk for you. Iceland's a green country, large parts of it, but the grass is pretty grudging, if you follow me. It's all right when it's full and fat in summer, but it wanes with the cold till there's not enough sweetness in it. You can make reasonable hay out of it some years, but other times it'll let you down. Then you get shortages, and the fun starts. Good men'll rob and kill each other for hay, when they've got stalls full of cattle starving down into bags full of bones. Greenland was a little better, the good land there anyhow, but the poor land was rubbish. It's a green country all right, but just ever so slightly the wrong shade of green, which makes all the difference. I guess you could say that water and piss look very much the same, if you don't know what you're looking at; but you can drink one, and not the other.

So what we were doing, when we knelt down in the wet grass there, was scooping up the dew and tasting it; and I'm telling you, the beer the angels serve in golden jugs to our Heavenly Father in Paradise couldn't be sweeter than the dew on the beautiful green grass of that landfall. The others were slurping it off their fingers and crowing like cocks and grinning; and I was kneeling there completely stunned, thinking, What the hell is going on here? Because this was the place where I'd come ashore that night when I swam over from Bjarni's ship, absolutely no doubt about that at all. But I'd come there in the dark, I hadn't even seen the grass, just felt it under my feet, so of course I hadn't known it was so good, so bloody wonderfully good. So if it wasn't me who'd known what a marvellous country this was, it must've been Leif, who'd been so determined to come here, ignoring all other possibilities. But he couldn't have known, because I was the only one who'd been here. I couldn't make it out, and I still can't to this day.

At last, when we were all wet through and tired with making noises and prancing about, Leif looked at me and said, 'This is the place. We're here.' And he smiled. It was a huge smile that said I was right and he'd been right, and he'd believed and I hadn't let him down. All that fog and rain and storms and miserable bare rocks and sitting huddled and not talking on the ship just seemed to thaw and melt away. It'd all been just unimportant stuff that we could forget about, now that we'd found what we came for.

'All that,' I said, 'because of some grass.'

Kari looked at me. 'Knew you wouldn't understand,' he said. 'Because you're a City boy, see.'

I was getting a bit sick of that. 'And proud of it,' I said. 'But I've read books about agric— about farming. I've read Hesiod, and Virgil's *Georgics*, and Theophrastus on plants, and Varro and Cato and Columella, and Apollodorus of Sicyon, and Magnentius on the care and breeding of dairy cattle, and—'

The look on Kari's face would've withered a fresh rose.

'All right,' I said. 'So reading books isn't quite the same. But just because I don't know all about something doesn't mean I can't understand how important it is. But it was still just grass. You make it sound like you'd found gold, or pearls.'

He carried on looking at me for a bit; then he said: 'Another thing about you City boys, you never bloody listen. I mean, you ask a man a question, but you don't pay him any mind because secretly you think you know the answer already, and you don't.' He sighed, like Christ for the sins of the world. 'Which means I can't explain, because you won't listen, so I won't bother. You'll just have to take my word for it.'

Carrying on much longer with this thread would've led to bad tempers, so I shrugged. 'It was nice grass,' I said. 'Really, really nice grass. So then what?'

*

So then (Kari said) we got back in the boat and rowed to the ship; and everybody looked at us as we climbed back on board, and Leif just said quietly, 'We're here.'

After that, they got the anchor up so fast you wouldn't believe it. We steered between the headland and the island into that little bay I told you about. It was pretty shallow water and we ran aground, but nobody could face waiting for the tide to come in and float us off. Instead, they jumped over the side, came down with a splash and a squelch and waded ashore like there were wolves after them. They knew good grass when they saw it too, see.

Suppose I'd better tell you a bit about the place, so you can picture it in your mind's eye, assuming you've still got one after reading all those books.

If you'd been standing on the beach with us that day, you'd have been looking at a small, lazy river, winding in loops like an adder on a sunny day until it came out into a small bay. In the background you'd have seen a wall of birch forest, tall and rather spindly because nobody had ever been in there thinning out the trees. Between the beach and the woods you'd have seen a raised shelf of grass meadow. I think you'd have liked it, because you strike me as the sort – no offence intended – who gets a kick out of pretty flowers and stuff. There was heather beside the brook, blue iris and yellow cloudberry and the like; more to the point, there were blueberries, crowberries, gooseberries, red and black currants and a small thicket of raspberry canes. Up along the river there was a large boggy patch, which had Tyrkir the German pointing like a dog and sniffing; he seemed more interested in it than the fat green grass, which we couldn't understand at the time. Behind us, the bay was sheltered and free of ice, with only a few rocks sticking up above the water here and there; out in the distance you could just have seen the closest of the litter of small islands, where the gulls lived. You could've been in southern Norway, or Denmark even. If you'd have been dressed like us, in a coat down to the knees and thick baggy trousers, you'd have been sweating a little – well, *you* wouldn't, because you were brought up in this godforsaken bloody south-eastern oven, but by any reasonable standards it was pleasantly warm. If you'd looked for them you'd have seen deer-slots in the mud by the river, maybe the silver flash of a salmon struggling upstream. And you'd have thought, even a miserable bugger like you, that by some extraordinary stroke of luck you'd fetched up in a place that was as good as anywhere and better than most.

Tyrkir the German managed to control himself for about as long as it takes to boil a fish kettle, and then he darted off, straight at the bog, like an arrow. He squelched about for a bit, up to his knees in black mud; then he dropped down on all fours and crawled around, clawing chunks of something up out of the ground and stuffing it down his sleeves. Mad as a rat in a churn, I thought, till it struck me that we'd all been carrying on just as strangely not so long ago, when we'd been drinking dew off the grass. We stood there watching him for a bit, until he dragged himself up out of the muck and came scampering back to us, grinning like a skull and waving a handful of slimy black lumps under our noses.

'What've you got there, Tyrkir?' Leif asked.

Tyrkir beamed at him. 'Iron,' he said.

Bugger me if he wasn't right. Black as charcoal till you rub it between your fingers, and it starts to blush brown through the dirt; but as far as we were concerned, it was better than finding gold nuggets. Bog-iron they call it, and of course Tyrkir would've known what to look for, being a German. All they care about there is iron and steel. I've been there, Germany, and if you walk through one of their towns you can't hear yourself think for the chinking of hammers on anvils. No wonder the poor bloody fool was beside himself with joy. A bog full of iron ore and a forest just waiting to be burned for charcoal, and it just so happened that there was an anvil and a full set of smith's gear in the hold of the ship.

So Tyrkir was happy, standing there pawing at his lumps of grubby black rock. The rest of us were staring at the grass, or the trees, or looking out for deer or birds. Apart from me, of course. I wasn't really taking it in, except out of the corners of my eyes, if you follow me. All I could think of was, Well, I found this place: Aren't I the clever one?

You know, there are moments so perfect that you can hardly bear to move for fear of spoiling them.

CHAPTER
FIVE

Anyway (Kari went on), there we were. Soon as we'd got over our excitement, we made a proper survey of the place. Turned out that the river flowed out of a lake, big and deep and alive with ducks; so we brought the ship up the river – we had to haul it with ropes most of the way – and anchored it in the lake, where it'd be safe from storms or a sudden freeze. It was easier to unload the cargo, too.

That night, we slung hammocks between the trees on the edge of the wood, but none of us slept worth a damn. Our minds were too busy with what we were going to do tomorrow.

First on the list would be housebuilding, because we'd all had about as much as we could take of the cold and the wet and, although it was surprisingly mild still, we all knew winter'd be along sooner rather than later. Of course—

'Excuse me,' I said.

'What?'

'No offence,' I said, 'but hadn't someone better go and

relieve Eyvind on watch? He's been out there an awfully long time.'

Kari blinked, like a surprised rabbit. 'Bugger me, so he has,' he said. 'My fault, I got caught up with the story. I'll go and take over.'

I frowned. 'Isn't it the lad's turn?' Just then, I couldn't remember his name. 'He hasn't had a go yet.'

'What, him?' He grinned. 'Didn't we tell you? Harald's the Prince of Norway, or he would've been if they hadn't slung him out on his ear. Princes in exile don't sit out in the cold, freezing their bollocks off, not when there's commoners to do it for them. Also, he's a pathetic sentry. Much more use in here, in case some of the local toe-rags bust their way in after all that money. He may not be the brightest lamp on the wall, our Harald, but he's not bad when it comes to crushing skulls and chopping off legs at the knee.'

Kari scooped up his blanket and pottered out into the night, leaving me alone with the royal exile. I looked at him, trying not to be too obvious about it. He was sitting on one of the money chests, leaning slightly forward, arms rested on knees, and he was scraping out his fingernails with the pointed horn of his axe. I couldn't help thinking that Norway had had a lucky escape.

A clumping noise from the tomb entrance.

'Right.' Eyvind shook a triple handful of charcoal out of the scuttle onto the fire, then sat down where Kari had been sitting. 'So where did he get up to?'

'The story, you mean?' Stupid question. 'Well, I gather he'd more or less reached the end,' I went on, disingenuous as they come. 'You'd all finally got to the place with the really nice grass.'

'That's not the end.'

Somehow, I'd suspected that'd be the case. 'Oh,' I said. 'Is there more?'

Eyvind grinned, but without the underlying sense of fun. 'Oh yes,' he said. 'There's more.'

'How splendid. Perhaps we could start again tomorrow, when they've come and fixed the wheel.'

Kari's probably told you (said Eyvind) what a rotten time we had, crossing over from Greenland. And then, I suppose, he went on a bit about how wonderful the place he discovered was. Right?

Thought so. I've heard him tell the story scores of times since we've been stuck out here in the East. Practically every new recruit in the Guards has had to listen through it. Apparently it's regarded as some kind of initiation ritual: if they can survive Kari telling them about discovering Meadowland, then pitched battle against the Saracens the length and breadth of Sicily will hold no terrors for them. The truth is—

'Meadowland?' I interrupted.

Eyvind nodded. 'That's what Leif decided to call the place. When it came to naming places, I reckon he took after his father.'

'What? Oh, I see. You mean Red Eirik choosing the name for Greenland. But Kari said there were wonderful meadows in the new country. He went on at some length about the grass.'

'That,' said Eyvind, 'I can believe. And yes, there were meadows. And good grass, no doubt about that. Not an awful lot of it, though: just that strip between the beach and the forest.'

'I see,' I replied. 'So really it wasn't anything special.'

'I didn't say that,' Eyvind replied cautiously. 'But it wasn't a country of endless rolling meadows, that's all I'm saying. It'd be like calling this place Figland because from time to time you come across a fig tree.'

I wasn't quite sure I grasped the point he was trying to make. 'You were saying,' I said.

All right (said Eyvind), it was a good place; or it could have been worse. That doesn't change the fact that we were effectively stranded there till spring. Which meant, of course, that we had no choice but to dig in and get ready to spend the winter there. Before we started work, though, Leif insisted on a little ceremony. He got in the boat and had a couple of men row him up and down while he chucked bits of stick he'd gathered earlier over the side; he'd marked the bits of stick with notches, and the idea was to see where he'd need to have the ship anchored so that he could chuck his canopy struts out and be sure they washed up in the place he wanted to set up camp.

Now, you won't have a clue what I'm talking about when I say canopy struts— Oh, right, you know about that. You Greeks know some funny old stuff, don't you?

Anyhow: after he'd slung out all the notched sticks, he waited till the tide turned; and sure enough, one of them pitched up right where we'd first come ashore. Fine. He'd taken bearings off the dial while he was throwing out the notched sticks, so he knew exactly where he'd been when he slung each one. Result: he was able to take the ship to precisely that point, chuck out the canopy struts – and, sure enough, they washed up right where he wanted them to, which proved by the age-old traditional method that that was the place where Providence had chosen for him to build his house.

I'll say this for the lads, they managed not to laugh while they were watching. Anyway, that was Leif Eirikson for you;

when all else fails, trust to the family luck, provided you can cheat.

First thing that needed doing, of course, was putting up some kind of shelter. Before we could make a start on that, though, we needed to get a few things straight. Mostly, how long were we planning on stopping there? All along, you'll remember, Leif had been pretty cagey on that score. Finally, we thought, we're going to get a straight answer.

No chance. We asked the question, but he didn't answer. Instead, he had us all cutting turf for the next two days.

I don't have to ask if you've ever done any turf-cutting. Bloody horrible job. It's a bit easier if you've got the proper tools, which we hadn't. Instead, we had to chop each turf out with a spade. It's not exactly challenging work, but it takes a long time and it's pretty exhausting. The hard bit isn't chopping the turf out of the ground; it's getting down on your hands and knees, rolling the turf up like a bit of old mat and lugging it over to where it's needed. Kari and I got put on that, while Leif swanned about supervising the actual building side of things. Credit where it's due, they made a nice, neat job. Building houses out of turf isn't nearly as easy as it looks. If you don't have decent footings and a good, solid inside framework of timber, you're wasting your time. It's not like building in stone – or whatever those things are that you people seem to like so much: bricks. See, the grass carries on growing; and as it grows, it pushes upwards, just as the grass underneath is pushing up into it. True, once it's established, the roots tie the whole thing together far better than mortar between stones or dowels in wood, assuming you've got a sound frame to keep everything in place. If not, your turf wall will quite literally tear itself apart, given time; the walls start bulging outwards, and eventually, the whole lot slowly and quietly collapses. It's so quiet, in fact, that there's no warning: no creaking or groaning or splitting noises to give you a chance to get out. First thing you know about it, you're buried under a couple of tons of living roof.

But, like I said, Leif made a pretty good job of it. We didn't hang about, either; and a couple of days later, we had walls about five feet high, supported by an adequate timber frame. All the wood was green, of course, since it was fresh-cut. Now, people back home'll tell you green wood's no bad thing for building. It's still soft and bendy, so as the house settles down, the timber sort of moulds itself to the shape, where seasoned wood's more likely to crack than flex under the weight. Me, I'm not so sure. There's such a thing as bending too much, and you run the risk of the frame getting out of true. Then you're screwed, of course.

Anyhow, once we'd done the walls, we were all ready to go back and cut more turf and timber for the roof. But Leif said no. Turned out he wasn't planning on building an actual house; what he had in mind was booths.

Right, you haven't got a clue what I'm talking about. Fine. Back in Iceland, we have this meeting every year. Everybody comes along from all over the country. Mostly it's a big market and hiring fair and a chance to drink beer with people you don't see every day of your life; also there's lawsuits and political stuff and all sorts of other excuses for the well-off farmers to pick fights with each other. Pretty much everything that gets done is done at the meeting, which is why we call it the Everything Meeting. Point is, you've got several thousand people spending a week or so at a place that's deserted the rest of the year. They've got to sleep somewhere. So we invented booths.

Basically, booths are four walls, a door and no roof. They sit there all year quietly growing; and when people crowd in for the meeting, they fetch along tanned hides and faggots of brushwood and all manner of stuff to make temporary roofs out of. When the meeting's over, they strip it all off again and take it home with them. It's nowhere near as warm and cosy as a proper house, but it's better than nothing. Besides, most people are pretty well tanked up by the first night of the meeting, and when you've got a skinful you don't feel the cold so much, or the damp.

So you can maybe understand why we all felt a bit confused when Leif told us to build booths rather than a proper house. After all, we were stuck there over winter at the very least. It'd have taken a couple of days longer to roof over the structures with turf in the usual way, but the fact is there wasn't a lot else to do with our time. We still had a fair bit of flour left in the barrels, it wasn't as though our few cows and goats and sheep took a lot of looking after, the deer in the forest – bloody great big things the size of horses, some of them – were so unused to people you could practically walk up and bash them over the head, and you could tickle the salmon out of the river barehanded. And if that wasn't good enough, Tyrkir the German came back the second evening with a basket full of funny-looking grassy stuff he'd found growing wild, which he reckoned was every bit as good as wheat. He wasn't far wrong, either. You could grind it and make flour, or you could just boil it till it went soft, scoop it up in your fingers and shovel it into your face. Didn't taste of much, but so what, when all you had to do was stroll about picking great handfuls of the stuff?

And there's a funny thing. Naturally, we assumed it was some strange, rare grass that only grows up there and nowhere else. But guess what? I've seen people selling it in the streets in the City. Rice, I think you call it, and it comes from away over east.

I'm wandering off, aren't I? What I was saying was, since

we had so little else to do and all winter to do it in, why did Leif have us building booths instead of proper houses? It was like he still couldn't make up his mind what he was planning to do: was he there just to cut timber, maybe bring in a few bales of furs and the like, and go home as soon as spring came? Or were we going to build a settlement, like his dad had done in Greenland?

'You've asked that question before, I think,' I interrupted. 'I take it you're going to answer it.'

Eyvind looked at me. 'Impatient, aren't you?'

'No, not really,' I said, pulling my cloak up round my chin. Unfortunately, that meant uncovering my ankles, which were also starting to get uncomfortably chilly. Still, I was making a point. 'And everybody tells me you Northerners have a fine tradition of oral storytelling, and presumably this is all part of your narrative technique. But can't we just take it that I'm impressed, and get to the point?'

He sighed. 'Trouble is,' he said, 'you've had to sit there listening to Kari drivelling on about how horrible the fog was and how scared we all were, and your patience is starting to wear thin. Now if I'd been telling the story from the beginning—'

'Please,' I said. 'Do go on.'

You're right, though (Eyvind said). That question was starting to bug all of us, but nobody quite had the balls to walk up to him and ask him straight, what're we doing here and how long are you planning on staying? I suppose we were hoping that we'd figure out what he had in mind without needing to ask, just by what he told us to do. But the booths thing was pretty much the last straw. By the time they were finished and we were able to move in – he kept us hanging about an extra day, mind, because he reckoned one of the corners wasn't dead square, so we had to pull it apart and do it again – by the time the walls were finished to his nit-picky satisfaction, and we'd taken the sail off the ship and spread it over a frame of poles to serve as a roof: well, things were beginning to get a bit fraught. So what does Leif do? Does he gather us all round and explain? Hell as like. While we're lashing in the poles and bashing in tethering pegs, he buggers off into the woods with his bow, hunting deer.

That didn't sit too well with us. Sure, a bit of fresh meat goes down nicely when you've been working; and the best way to hunt deer is with a bow, and we only had one bow with us, and it belonged to Leif, so it was hard to fault the logic. It was the way he went about it that pissed us all off. Even Lazy Hrafn started muttering, and usually he was the sort who never has a word to say against the captain. But he'd been up in the roof cutting mortices for the poles, and he'd got tired, slipped, and cut himself to the bone with his axe, so he wasn't in a good mood. 'Bugger this for a day's work,' he said, while Kari and Thorvald Salmon tried to get him to hold still while they tied up his hand. 'We're building his booths for him and he goes prancing off in the green-wood like a bloody earl.'

Of course, Kari has to be contrary. If Hrafn had been sticking up for Leif, he'd have sung a different tune. Instead, he pulls a face and says, 'Don't talk daft, Hrafn. We need the meat, and he's the best shot. You couldn't hit a barn wall if you were locked inside.'

A couple of the men laughed at that, which just got Hrafn riled up. 'You know what I'm talking about,' he said. 'He brings us out here, never says a word about what he's got in mind. Now we've been here, what, three days, and still we don't know.'

'Well, it's pretty clear that we'll be staying the winter,' said Thorstein Troll-Ears. 'No choice about that.'

'Fine,' said Hrafn. 'So why've we built stay-at-Meeting huts instead of a proper house, with the cold weather on the way?'

'We don't know what winter's going to be like here,' said Kari, all sweet reason. 'You don't need to be told that it's a damn sight milder here than at home. If we were back in Greenland, we'd have had to get the stock indoors by now – we'd have had the first heavy snow. Instead, it's like autumn. Loads of grass left for the animals, hardly need a fire at all during the day. Booths'll do just fine.'

'You don't know that,' said Troll-Ears, who loved being contrary almost as much as Kari. 'For all you know, winter comes down sudden here. We could wake up tomorrow morning and have three feet of snow. Not saying that's what's going to happen, but it might; we don't know any different, and nor does he. But instead of staying here and talking it through with the rest of us, he's away hunting the deer, like he's Good King Hrolf or someone.'

'Fine,' I snapped, because I was getting fed up with all the moaning. 'You don't have to eat your share of the venison, I'll have it.'

'That's not the point and you know it,' said Lazy Hrafn. 'And we can stay here all night arguing with each other, and it won't do anybody any good. Here's what I think. I say that when he gets back, we ask him, to his face, what his plans are. Agreed?'

Well, it's so much easier when you think it's not just you, it's everybody. 'Fine,' I said.

'Good,' Hrafn said. 'So, soon as he gets back, you go and ask him.'

It's like when you're on deck in a squall, and the wind's so loud you don't hear everybody yelling at you to look out, and the boom comes swinging round and a loose rope smacks you in the teeth. I hadn't expected that, and by the time I'd thought of what to say it was too late: I'd been elected.

There was no getting out of it; they'd all have been on at me all the bloody time, and when you're stuck in a closed place with a bunch of people, the last thing you want is everybody nagging at you. Even so, I decided that the smart thing to do would be to bide my time and wait for an opening so the question looked like it was just sort of bubbling up out of the conversation.

Got my chance sooner than I'd expected, or hoped. That night Leif came back looking absolutely livid. Turned out he'd tracked a nice big doe, got a perfect easy shot at no more than fifteen yards. He draws the bow and the stupid thing snaps at the handle. It's a bugger when that happens, because you can bet that when a bow fails at full draw, the top half's going to smack you in the face and the lower half'll give you a kick in the nuts you won't forget in a hurry. Leif didn't say that's what had happened to him; but when he came back he had the makings of a top-flight black eye, and he was limping. 'Bastard,' he was saying. 'Bloody useless bastard.'

First off I assumed he must've been talking about me; then I realised it was the busted bow and the scat round the head. 'That's a nuisance,' I said, all sympathetic. 'Can you fix it?'

He sat down and looked at it for a while. Now some breaks near the handle can be spliced, glued and wrapped in rawhide. Not this one, it was too square. 'I'll have to make a new one,' he said. 'Pity. Dad gave me this bow just before we left. Still, there it is, nothing lasts for ever.'

So next morning we left early, just Leif and me, and we poked about in the woods till we found what he was after: a tall, spindly straight-grown ash no more than eight inches across at the foot. It'd been brought down at least two years earlier. A big fat old oak had got blown down in a storm; one of its branches had smacked into our tree and levered its roots out of the ground, but had left it still just about standing, leant right over but still well clear of the leaf mould so it wouldn't be rotten and stuck full of beetles.

After we'd felled it properly and cut off the branches and the brash, Leif split it open with his axe and we worked our way down it with wedges and froes, splitting it longways down the grain. Bows are a real cow to make. You've got to keep to one growth ring on the back – you know, the rings you see when you chop down a tree – or else it'll crack first time you draw it. It's not all that hard a job to do, but it does take time. That suited me: I could hang around making myself useful while Leif was rough-hewing out the inside curves, and maybe find a good moment to slip in the question.

Coincidence, I guess; because asking a tricky question's just like splitting timber. You tap the nose of your wedge into a little thin shake in the wood, then you tap it some more, gently so as not to knock the wedge out; once you're in, you can whack the wedge as hard as you like with the maul or the back of the axe, and if you've gone about it right, the log splits open and falls in two neat halves. Or you can get it wrong, the wedge jams in the cross-grain, and you end up sawing or burning it out, buggering up your wedge and spoiling the log.

'So,' I asked him, 'what exactly are we doing here?'

He looked up at me. Now there's an odd thing about Leif Eirikson. You ask most people who'd met him once or twice to describe him, and they'd tell you he was a big, strong, impressive man: big shoulders, broad back, strong arms and piercing eyes. Of course, I was with him for a long time, so I know he didn't look like that. He was skinny, with a long neck and a big Adam's apple that stuck out, like he'd tried to swallow a pear without chewing it. He had a big sharp nose like a hatchet, and his eyes were small and a bit squinty. I've seen him struggle to move a hay-bale that a fifteen-year-old kid could've pitched up into the wagon without straining; he had a weak bladder, too. But most people went away thinking they'd just met a big, fierce warrior, the sort of man whose bench in Valhalla's been set aside for him practically since he was weaned. I think he came across that way because, deep down, that's who he believed he was; and if his reflection in a pool or a bowl of water said otherwise, it was the reflection's word against his, and he knew who he trusted. Came of being Red Eirik's son, I guess. Eirik was every inch the big, bad man. He could hold up an ox-cart with one hand while you changed the wheel, carry a six-year-old ram up the mountain on his shoulders; and if he told you something, you believed him, even when you knew he was lying. A difficult man to have for a father, especially if you're long and weedy. They were different in a lot of ways, mind. Eirik was a great talker, so long as you didn't interrupt; Leif was quiet, but everybody shut up as soon as he opened his mouth. And I wouldn't say Eirik was stupid, far from it; and Leif wasn't amazingly clever and wise, he got things wrong sometimes, just like the rest of us. But Eirik thought aloud, and nobody contradicted him even when he was way off the mark. People stood still and quiet while Leif was thinking, and waited to hear what he said. If you saw the two of them together, it wouldn't take you long to say this one's brawn and this one's brains. You wouldn't be entirely right, but close enough. What Leif had going for him was this unshakeable belief that he was as good a man as his father, and in many respects better. It was also his weak spot, because he never actually figured out why.

'That's an odd question,' Leif said.

'Humour me.'

He straightened his back and let his right hand with the drawknife in it hang by his side. 'Well,' he said, 'I first heard about this place from old Herjolf, Bjarni's dad; he was boasting about his son the explorer, trying to make out that Bjarni was smarter and luckier than Dad because he'd found this wonderful country nobody knew about, while Dad had someone else's journey to guide him, and Greenland's nothing special anyhow. That got me going, and I thought, sooner or later someone's going to go looking for the places Bjarni discovered, so why not me?'

I frowned. 'That's not what I asked,' I said. 'I'm sure you didn't drag out all this way just to score points off Bjarni Herjolfson – or off your father. Why did we come here? Just to fill the ship with stuff they'll want back home, or are we stopping here for good?'

He laughed. 'That,' he said, 'is a very good question.'

'Fine,' I said. 'So what's the answer?'

Leif was quiet for rather a long time. 'I'm not sure,' he said. 'You lot don't know because I don't know.' He sighed, and put the drawknife down. 'It was different when we were back in the Greenland colony,' he said. 'I knew then. But somehow——' He was staring past me, like he was talking to someone standing behind me. 'This sounds crazy, but I've forgotten. I know I wanted to come here, that it seemed really important to come here; and it was like someone had told me and I'd believed him, but he hadn't explained the reason, so I had to figure it out for myself. So I thought about what your mate Kari said, about feeling lush grass under his feet; and I thought about what Bjarni and everybody else said, all that timber there for the taking. Seemed to make sense, there was a good reason to come. But what didn't seem to sink in was that there were *two* good reasons, and they were pulling in different directions. One said, go there and come back, the other said, go there and stay. But the voice in the back of my mind was just saying, go.'

He shrugged his bony shoulders and still didn't look at me. 'I never said any of this to Dad, he'd have reckoned the trolls had addled my brains. God only knows why I'm telling *you*. You'll assume I'm crazy, tell the others, and everything'll get very tense.'

'It's that way already,' I told him. 'Better to get it out in the open.'

'Balls.' Leif grinned. 'Last thing people need is to be in a strange place miles from home and then find out their leader's brain's sprung a leak. But—' He closed his eyes, then opened them again. 'I'm not as crazy as I'm making myself sound,' he said. 'I've been negotiating with that little voice in my head ever since it started nagging at me. It kept saying, go; I kept asking why. So I reached a decision. If the little voice wouldn't tell me why I had to come here, I'd come here and find out for myself. Maybe it's just for a shipload of building timber, or maybe I'm going to build a settlement here and wind up as King Leif of Meadowland, the richest and most powerful man in the world. Stands to reason, actually. How could I possibly know what this place has to offer until I've seen it for myself?'

'That's not crazy,' I said. 'In fact, it's downright sensible.'

He smiled. 'It is, isn't it? Only thing is, that's me talking, not the little voice. The voice just keeps saying, this is where you need to go, this is where you need to be. I'm just trying to explain it away, like a woman with a drunken husband. But you don't need to tell the others that, do you?'

'I guess not,' I replied. 'So, what's the verdict? We're here, you've had a look, what do you plan to do?'

'I'm not sure.' Leif shook his head. 'Just imagine that, will you? My father's son, unsure about something. The old bugger'd have a stroke if he knew.' He leaned forward, picked the drawknife up and tested its edge with his thumb. 'We're a load of funny buggers, you know? Right down deep in the heartwood, right down as far as our names. When we say who we are, I mean. Half of my name says, I'm Leif; but the other half tells you I'm Eirik's son, like that's just as important as who I am. I can't even say my name without dragging him into it. Do you see what I'm getting at? Half of me wants to look at this place and make a sensible decision: the grass is good, there's fish and game, it's warm, we've got a river and woods, there's even iron ore. But it's a hell of a long way from home – there's no way we can make it work here unless we can get at least a hundred people, a hundred and fifty's more like it, and who's going to want to come all this way just because I say it's a good idea? So I'm turning that over in my mind, and immediately I'm thinking, well, Dad managed it; he managed to kid all those people into settling Greenland, and Greenland's a dump compared to this. If I'm as good a man as he is— You remember,' he went on, 'how, just before we were about to set off, the old bastard suddenly announced he was coming along too? I tell you, I was so close to sticking my axe between his eyebrows, I don't know how I stopped myself. It took me all my strength not to; and I only managed it because I managed to keep my mind clear and realised that killing Dad would cause so much trouble I'd never be clear of it. So instead,' he went on, 'I lent him a horse.'

That didn't make sense. 'You lent him—?'

Big smile. 'I lent him my chestnut mare, for the ride over from Brattahlid. Forgot to mention what a dirty, filthy temper the bloody thing's got. See, Dad's not what you'd call a gentle rider. He likes to impose his will. But my chestnut mare won't stand for that.'

I stared at Leif; I didn't know what to think.

Sorry, I keep forgetting how ignorant you are. We're not too superstitious up North, but there's some things we reckon are just plain unlucky. Like falling off your horse, for instance, when you're just about to set off on a journey. That's not superstition, that's a bloody great big heavy hint from Them Up There: stay home. Now I'd already figured out for myself that Leif was a strong-willed sort. But setting up your own father like that—

Clever too, of course. I never said he wasn't clever.

'So I thought,' Leif went on, 'I'll start off near the end of the sailing season, which means we'll have no choice but to spend the winter here. Come spring, we ought to have a better idea of whether we're here to cut timber or here to build a settlement. Till then—' He shrugged. 'I can put off choosing till then. Fact is, I think this is a bloody marvellous place. But I also *know*—' He turned his head and stared at me, like he wanted to see the inside of my head. 'I know that if I stay here, I won't live long. But that's the bitch of it, when you know the answer but you don't know how you came by it. Now, does any of that make any sense?'

I looked at him. 'Some of it,' I said.

'That's good, then.' He seemed to relax, or shrink, I wasn't sure which. 'Besides,' he went on, 'it's all your mate Kari's fault, finding this place and all. And since the two of you are closer than staves in a barrel, it's your fault just as much as it's his.'

'You know,' I said quietly. 'I'm not really surprised to hear you say that.'

So (Eyvind went on) I passed the word along, or bits of it, anyway. I told the others I'd asked Leif straight out what his plans were, and he'd told me we were here to spy out the country, make up our mind whether it was a good place for a settlement or only fit for logging. They all thought that was pretty reasonable, though they were still a bit snotty that Leif hadn't told them earlier. In fact, the only person who wasn't reassured and happy was me. There you go, though; you can fool other people, but you can't fool yourself. And believe me, I've tried.

Now we all knew where we stood, we didn't mind putting our backs into the jobs that needed doing. Plenty of those to go round.

I hadn't said anything when I'd talked to Leif, because there's no point falling out with the boss over something that's done and can't be helped, but – well, you're an intelligent man, or you'd never have risen to be chief assistant bean-counter to the King of the Greeks, so I don't need to dwell on it. Simply, Leif had been bloody irresponsible, stranding us in a country that he knew bugger all about, with only the food we'd brought with us. What if it'd all been stone and shingle, like Slabland? True, he'd brought livestock: two cows (but no bull), four goats, six sheep and a dozen hens, to feed thirty-five men. No chance. Well, it's obvious now, with hindsight, why he brought them, just to see if they'd survive here, how well they'd do, in case he decided to settle here after all. I'd have had no quarrel with that, if he'd fetched along something for us to eat as well.

But as luck would have it, food wasn't a problem. Getting enough to eat didn't even take up more than half our time, which is more than you can say of life in the old country. That said, you can get really tired of salmon and venison, and wild goose now and then as a treat. We stretched out the flour we'd brought with us as long as we could, likewise the malting barley. We tried cutting it half and half with flour we ground from the wild corn, but that was a waste of both resources. When the flour ran out we made porridge from the wild stuff – boil a handful with an equal amount of water and any bits of meat or herbs you can find to mask the godawful cloying mushy taste, and when the water's soaked into the grain, you gobble it down with a spoon. Then we had nuts and berries, which would've been fine if we'd been squirrels, and a thin sliver of cheese, just enough to remind us of how much we missed the stuff. There were seals when we arrived, but we ate the ones who were stupid enough to hang around, and the rest buggered off. We rowed out to the islands hoping to find gulls' eggs, but that was a waste of time. Oh, we all got enough to eat, no question about it; and as winter dragged on we smoked and salted more than enough to see us through the journey home. No shortages; but it was either horrible or boring, and by midwinter we'd have traded a week's rations for one meal of salt cod or smoked lamb.

Same with everything else. Our clothes had pretty well rotted off our backs after all that huddling in the wet on the way over. No wool, no linen; instead, we tanned the deer hides into buckskin, and that's a job I wouldn't wish on an enemy. In case you don't know, it means hours and hours of scraping with a dull knife or a flint, and then you scoop the deer's brains out of its skull with a stick, beat them up in water to make a thickish goo, and squidge them into the hide with your fingers. Cures the hide a treat, and five hides make you a shirt and a pair of trousers – except they soak up the water when it rains, and turn as stiff as bark when they dry out. At least we weren't cold, with all that timber, and Tyrkir the mad German was as happy as a lamb with all the charcoal we made for him, so he could smelt the ore out of the bog-iron to make nails for building. At least, he was happy till the malt ran out and there was no more beer. Then he got very sad, and you'd find him sat behind his anvil, all droopy and weeping and not getting any work done. Finally, when the warm spring weather started, he went a bit strange in the head and vanished for two whole weeks. We thought we'd seen the last of him, and we thought that was a pity but something we could learn to live with, given time; but no, he came back, wet and smelly and covered in mud and bits of leaf and stick, dragging a huge sack. He'd been a long way, he said, walking south, always south, because he knew he'd find what he was looking for, he could smell it, a very faint scent but no mistaking it— When we asked what he was yammering on about, he yanked open the sack – three flour-sacks ripped up and sewn together again as one – and bugger me if it wasn't full of grapes.

'They grow wild,' he said. 'Many vines, hanging from the tree, just like in my home. Make the good wine, better than beer.'

Well, that cheered us up, no question. I'd had wine in Norway, as a special treat; can't say I liked it much, too sour for my taste, but give me a choice between wine and no beer and I don't have to lie awake all night before I make my mind up. Same with the rest of us; so we asked him, Tyrkir, are there more where these came from, do you think you could find the place again? And Tyrkir nodded madly; of course, he could find it blindfold, just following his nose, he'd lead us there and we'd fill all the empty sacks and barrels and fill the ship and the boat and make a fortune selling grapes in Greenland. So the very next day off we sent him off again with ten men and a whole lot of sacks; and two weeks later they brought the sacks back, and one very sad-looking German, but no grapes.

'Never mind,' Leif said, 'they'll still be there next year, when we come back, and we've got time to look properly and find them again.' We all nodded, and Tyrkir went on being sad. Meanwhile, we decided against making wine with the grapes he'd brought back the first time, since we'd be leaving soon, once the sea warmed up and thawed the ice. Instead, we loaded them onto the ship. They went bad almost overnight, halfway into the journey, and we had to pitch them overboard because of the smell.

Not that that mattered too much; we had a decent enough cargo without them. I can't remember offhand how much building-lumber was fetching in Greenland in those days, but it was some ridiculous price. Obviously you couldn't get very much in the way of planked timber on board a sixty-foot *knoerr*; but it wouldn't take all that much to turn a handsome profit, enough to mean that our winter in Meadowland had been well worth the effort and the misery. We slaughtered what was left of the livestock and had a bloody good feed, we left behind everything we didn't absolutely need for the journey, and we filled the hold with planked wood, till the ship was riding dangerously low in the water. It was all right after all, we decided, in spite of Leif and his indecision and the little voices in his head. We were going home, and when we got there we were going to have a cargo to sell. Credit where it's due, Leif had said when we set off that it'd be equal shares for all, and he never once tried to go back on that. I'm sure he meant it, too, except— Well, I'll come to that directly.

Came the day, and we had a good wind to see us on our way. By then we were so bright and breezy and full of it that most of us were saying yes, of course we'd be back next year; it hadn't been so bad really, and next time we'd bring more flour and a lot more malting barley, and another ship just to carry the livestock; we'd do this and we'd do that, and now we knew a bit about the place there really wasn't any good reason we couldn't make a go of the business. We were going to build proper houses, and some of us'd stay there all year round, felling and logging and planking up, while the rest of us ferried to and fro to Greenland and Iceland (because the price back in the old country was higher still, and it wasn't that far from Brattahlid to Snaefellsness, was it?) and pretty soon we'd all be farmers and earls and God knows what, and everything had turned out for the best, just as we'd always known it would. Things couldn't have been better, in fact. Leif had made up his mind to do the return trip in one straight dash – he didn't tell us that was what he had in mind, of course, because we'd have tied him to the anchor and thrown him in the sea – and as soon as we set sail, we picked up a brisk north-easterly wind that sent us skimming along like an arrow. The sea was beautifully behaved, so it didn't matter a damn that we were ridiculously over-laden. The ice had already broken up, there was almost no fog. We hardly got wet, even. Before we knew it, there on the skyline were the blue caps of the Greenland glaciers. We were home and safe.

Which was when Leif changed course and started taking us close into the wind.

'What's the bloody fool doing?' Kari shouted to me, and buggered if I knew. We were all muttering, and a man called Thorgrim Otter jumped up on the aft deck and tried to grab the rudder. Leif kicked him back down into the hold, then yelled to us that it was all right, he knew what he was about. We weren't so sure about that – little voices in his head and all that – and we started asking him what the hell he thought he was playing at.

'Look for yourselves,' he said.

Well, none of us had thought to do that, so we looked. At first there wasn't anything to see, but then Thorvald Salmon, who had good eyes, called out that there was something there but he couldn't tell what it was.

'It's a ship on a reef,' Leif said. 'My guess is they're stuck. Anyhow, we're going in closer to have a look.'

We couldn't argue with that, so we shut up and let him get on with it; and sure enough, it was a middling-sized *knoerr*, which some fool had run aground on a sunken reef. We could see the people aboard, jumping up and down and waving at us. We'd shown up just in time, because the reef had made a real mess of their hull. A few hours later and they'd all have drowned.

Leif could steer a ship, no question. Getting in close to the reef without trashing our own ship wasn't a simple matter, particularly since we had all that valuable timber on board. But he held in tight to the wind until we were sure that we were going to run aground ourselves, then at exactly the right moment he swung her broadside on, dropped sail and called for the anchor and the boat. Neatest thing you ever saw.

'Hello,' he called out, leaning over the rail. 'Who the hell are you?'

Someone shouted something back, but we were too far away to hear it. But we were close enough to see that there were fifteen people on the deck of the *knoerr*; fourteen men, and a woman.

'Screw it,' Leif said, after a moment's thought. 'We'll take the boat and pick them up, and if they're raiders you can share my beer ration in Valhalla.'

Guess who pulled boat duty. It hadn't actually occurred to me before Leif raised the possibility that these people were vikings—

'Excuse me?' I said.

'Vikings,' Eyvind repeated. 'Pirates to you. The word actually means, "evil bastards who drop anchor just outside the entrance to a fjord and pounce on cargo ships as they come out". It can also mean "evil bastards who loot farms and settlements on the coast or a mile or so inland". Or it can mean "a landowner's son and a bunch of hired hands and neighbours turning an honest penny when there's nothing much needing doing on the farm, depending on how you look at it, and which ship you're on".'

'I see,' I said. 'What's a fjord?'

Probably the thought hadn't occurred to me (Eyvind went on) because the castaways were on a *knoerr*, and vikings prefer to use warships; also, they don't tend to take women along with them. But there's no hard and fast rules, so I guess Leif was right to be concerned. I took my axe with me on the boat just in case, and I wasn't the only one. Kari was in the boat with me, and Tyrkir the mad German, and Leif himself and three others. When we were in hailing range, Leif prodded Tyrkir in the ribs with his elbow; Tyrkir stood up and called out, 'Who are you?'

A short, frail-looking man leaned out and yelled back that his name was Thorir: he and his crew were from Norway. Leif looked at me and Kari, but we just shrugged: Norway's a big country, and just because we'd been there a few times, we didn't know everybody who lived there. Leif shrugged too and stood up.

'My name is Leif Eirikson,' he said.

The short man looked interested. 'Are you the son of Red Eirik from Brattahlid?' he said. Leif nodded, and the short bloke laughed. 'That's a good one,' he said. 'We were on our way to see you.'

That sounded odd, since they were closer to the Western Settlement; if they'd come from Norway, they'd have sailed right past Brattahlid to get there. But maybe they got carried past by a storm or something.

'Splendid,' Leif said. 'In that case, we'll give you a lift.'

Just as well, I thought, that the rest of our lot hadn't heard that. Think about it. We were still several days from home; if Leif was thinking about taking these people on board, there wouldn't be room. Not unless we dumped the cargo . . .

Thorir must've had the same thought, looking at how low our ship was riding in the water; he'd have guessed we had a full load on board. 'You sure?' he said.

'Of course,' Leif called back. 'We'll ferry you across four at a time in the boat. Bring your stuff along, we'll have plenty of space.'

Fuck, I thought, there goes all that valuable building timber, and my winter's earnings. But Leif was right, of course, we couldn't just leave the poor buggers there to drown. I was surprised to see how little fuss the rest of the crew made when we got back to the ship and told them what we were going to do. Still, it was a blow, no doubt about it.

Thorir reckoned so too once we'd fetched him across to the ship and he'd taken a look at our cargo. 'It must've taken you for ever to put together that lot,' he said. 'Look, maybe some of us could go in the boat and you could tow us in; and the rest could perch up top of your cargo hold. It'd only be for a few hours. Got to be better than jettisoning all that lumber.'

Credit where it's due, Leif wasn't even tempted. He had the wit to realise it wasn't about room so much as weight. If we took on ten men lying on top of the cargo, we'd be down so low in the water that the first little wave would swamp us. 'I've got a better idea,' he said. 'We'll offload our cargo here, on this reef. Then, when we come back to salvage your ship, we can pick it up and bring it on.'

Thorir agreed to that, not that he really had any say in the matter, and we spent the rest of the day hauling planked wood into the boat and sending it across to the reef, bringing back men from the stranded ship. We made the last three trips in the dark, which was no fun at all, but Leif was positive that if we didn't Thorir's ship wouldn't still be there in the morning. At least I got to stay on board our ship, hauling on a block and tackle, rather than going on the reef to unload. All the same, I couldn't have felt more miserable if I'd tried. It was fine for Leif to shoot his mouth off about coming back for the cargo. But the reason we were doing this was because the wrecked ship could wash off at any moment, and naturally the same went for our beautiful lovingly planked timber. Heartbreaking was the only word for it.

'That was a good day's work,' I remember Leif saying, after we'd brought the boat back for the last time.

'For us, anyhow,' Thorir replied. At least he sounded like he appreciated what this was going to mean to us. But Leif only laughed and said that there was plenty more where that'd come from in Meadowland, where we'd been all winter. Naturally, Thorir replied with, 'Meadowland? Where's that?' So Leif told him, and you could practically see the idea putting out roots in Thorir's mind. From his point of view, it must've been hard to resist. He'd just lost his own cargo, in all likelihood his ship as well. To a merchant, that was a crippling blow, his entire livelihood gone. And now here was his heroic rescuer telling him about an amazing opportunity to make up those losses in the lumber trade. I could've strangled Leif with my bare hands.

So why'd he do it? I'll give you three guesses.

That's right. The woman I mentioned earlier had come across in the first boatload of survivors from the ship. Her name was Gudrid, and she was Thorir's wife; and the moment Leif set eyes on her, I knew there was going to be big trouble at some point in the proceedings.

It didn't help, of course, that she was the first woman any of us had seen since we'd left Greenland the previous autumn. But Gudrid would've caused problems under any circumstances. Not on purpose, mind, she wasn't that sort at all. On the contrary. I guess you could say she was the sort that brings out the best in any man, and on balance that's the most dangerous kind of all.

Have I got to explain to you – try and explain, anyway – about women? After all, you can't be expected to know, seeing as how you're— Well, if you say so. I guess even you must've at least met some, from time to time. But – I don't know how to put this without sounding offensive, so I'll say sorry in advance and just crack on, right?

The thing is – well, it stands to reason you can't ever have felt about women the way ordinary men do; the most you can do is try and get some idea from what they tell you, same as you're trying to picture Meadowland in your mind, based on what Kari and me have said about it. But you've never been there. Same, obviously, with how men feel about women. Right?

But of course, it's in a man's nature that he'll never tell you, or anybody, the actual truth about that particular subject. No, he'll tell you what he wants you to believe, because he reckons that it's one of the main ways of keeping score, of figuring out who's better and who's worse than everyone else. Stupid bloody way to carry on, of course, and I'm not kidding you when I tell you there've been times in my life when I'd gladly have traded places with one of your lot, and to hell with all the fun-and-games side of things. Be that as it may: if you believe what men tell you about the way they deal with women, then there's got to be a bit of your brain missing, as well as the other thing.

So you're just going to have to take this on trust. Men just can't help liking certain women, even when they know it's a really bad idea – like he's already married, or she is, or she's a farmer's daughter and he's just a field hand, or her dad killed his uncle in a feud, or whatever. And when they feel the tug – like a hook in a fish's lip, it hurts like fuck but you've got to go with it – it's not a blind bit of use people telling you how bloody stupid you're being. You already know that, thanks very much. But you still carry on, because the hook draws you. Maybe you know she can't stand the sight of you, it still makes no odds. The best you can hope for is, you make sure you try your hardest not to let it lead you into doing something stupid or dangerous.

Like I just told you: if you think you understand the subject just from listening to what I've been saying, you're clearly so stupid it's a toss-up whether we cook you a dinner come suppertime, or just water you. Don't try and understand. You'll only get confused.

So yes, Leif was taken with Gudrid. Smitten. A really bad case. And he'd just saved her life, and he was the captain of the ship, and he was just back from a wonderful adventure (it was a wonderful adventure the way he told it, and she hadn't been there so how would she know otherwise?) and her husband was a waste of good cargo space, it was his fault they'd missed Greenland and ploughed into that reef, he was short and fat and his beard looked like weeds growing up through barley stubble. I wouldn't say she was anything really special to look at. Her face was a bit flat and so was her chest, and she had big hands, like a man's; but she had great big eyes for gazing with, and a way of staying perfectly still when someone was talking to her, like she was almost too enthralled to breathe. Bad news.

Thorir, her husband, wasn't blind, he could see what was going on. But he was on Leif's ship, and if it hadn't been for us he'd have drowned, and we'd dumped a fortune in building lumber just to rescue them, so what could he do? What anybody would've done in that situation: he pretended he hadn't noticed, and hoped we'd make landfall sooner rather than later.

Which we did. Nice helpful wind whisked us down the Greenland coast, round the point and straight up Eiriksfjord to Brattahlid. First thing we saw was half a dozen skinny ponies grazing between the rocks, on the narrow shelf of grass at the foot of the white mountain. Goes to show how quickly you get used to things: after winter in Meadowland, it amazed me that anybody could scratch a living in such a miserable place.

The Brattahlid people saw our sail before we beached, and a bunch of them came down to see us come in. Truth is, I was a bit disappointed by the reception. In my mind, we were mighty heroes of navigation who'd come back from the ends of the Earth, and quite likely from the dead. Far as they were concerned, we might just as well have been a Norway trader come to sell them malt and buttons: they were pleased to see us, but that was about all.

Even the pleased-to-see-us wore off a bit when they found out that we'd ditched a holdful of building lumber in favour of fifteen destitute Norwegians who were going to need board and lodging until someone showed up who'd be prepared to take them home. Certainly that side of it wasn't lost on Red Eirik, who came limping down as we were drawing the ship up to the sheds. His first words to his son, after he'd stopped and given Thorir and his gang a good long glare, were, 'Who the hell are these?' Well, I guess he was entitled, since it'd be up to him to put them up, or at the very least pay the neighbours to billet them. For what it's worth, I think he was genuinely pleased to see Leif home again and safe, but he wasn't at all impressed when he heard about all that good timber stuck out on the reef.

Kari and I stayed just the one night at Brattahlid; the atmosphere was a bit too fraught for my liking, and Kari was itching to get back to Herjolfsness and tell everybody there how wonderful the place *he'd* discovered had turned out to be. We took on a couple of Thorir's men as guests (Eirik insisted), and Leif saw to it that we got the loan of four ponies. We left early in the morning, before the house woke up. After all those months together, it seemed odd to be riding away without Leif or anybody to see us off. You'd have thought we'd come over for the day to return a borrowed plough.

Nothing worth mentioning had changed at Herjolfsness, which was a pity as far as I was concerned. Bjarni Herjolfson was pleased to see us, mostly because he couldn't wait to hear about the new countries he'd seen but never set foot on. He'd changed his tune, you can guess. Quite likely he was jealous, because Leif Eirikson was going to get all the glory when he'd been the one to find those places, albeit entirely by accident. What the hell: we answered all his questions and told him a few of the better stories, some of which were actually true, in parts.

Didn't take long for us to get back into the rhythm of Herjolfsness; and pretty soon Kari and me just had the memory, like when an arrowhead's too dangerously placed to be pulled out, so you have to leave it in the wound, and the skin grows back over it. The general attitude wasn't so much hail-the-conquering-hero as: Well, now you're back you might as well get on with some useful work. Thinking of Leif and Gudrid, I had a few goes at telling our adventures to one or two of the girls, but I might just as well have held my breath. The sad fact is that I told them the truth, straight as an arrow, but most of them didn't believe me. But there – I always do better with women when I tell them lies.

Life drifted on. Within a month of us getting back, our holiday wasn't a big deal any more; in fact, the two Norwegians were in greater demand than we were, come storytelling time at night; they could drivel on about the towns back home and the merchants and the splendid houses and everything, while all we had to tell about was fog and Slabland and why we hadn't brought anything useful back home with us. Winter came on, none of the ships that called wanted to take the Norwegians home so they got settled in, and Kari and I went back to our regular jobs. Then, just as the long nights came round and we were getting ready for the heavy snow, we got word that there was bad sickness at Brattahlid, mostly among Thorir's men. Next thing we heard from the world outside was that Thorir had died of it, but (oddly enough) it hadn't spread to Eirik's people or the farms outside the immediate area, apart from those that had taken in any of the Norwegians. Coincidence.

Since he got back, people had taken to referring to Leif Eirikson as 'Lucky' Leif, since he'd just so happened to turn up when Thorir's ship had been on the verge of sinking. Now I think he deserved the name, though not just because of that. It was luck that found the way for him, luck that got us home; and it was luck he'd rescued Gudrid, and then that her husband was so obliging as to drop dead and leave her free for Leif to marry.

So he asked her. And there, I guess, was where Leif's luck ran out. Because she refused him.

CHAPTER
SIX

'So then what?' I asked.

Eyvind stood up. 'I'm tired out,' he said. 'I don't know about you Greeks, but we need our sleep, and it's past midnight already. Remind me, and I'll tell you the rest of the story in the morning.' He picked up a blanket, wrapped himself in it, sat himself down with his back to the tomb wall, and almost immediately began to snore. Harald, the younger man who didn't talk much, got up, made a soft grunting noise, and went out. A moment later, Kari came back in. He looked at the fire, heaped rather too much charcoal on it from the bucket, and sat down opposite me.

'He snores,' Kari said, rather superfluously. 'I've known the bugger all my life, slept in the same hall with him for most of it, and the bugger snores. And you know what? When he's snoring, I can't sleep. Anybody else's snoring I can sleep through, it puts me straight out, like a lullaby. But his *particular* snoring – I don't know, it's the whatsitsname, the pitch or something. I could recognise his snore out of a thousand others, and it doesn't matter how tired I am, I can't sleep with it going on. So I lie down and I really, really hope I'll drop off before he does; but you know what it's like when you're *trying* to get to sleep — there's no surer way of staying awake.' He sighed. 'Well, I'll say this for him. He's trained me to get by on no more than a catnap, and I've had loads and loads of opportunities for just lying there on my back in the dark, thinking. Probably I've done more thinking than anybody else in the history of the world.'

'That's pretty impressive,' I said cautiously. 'We Greeks have produced more great philosophers than any other race on earth, so I'd always assumed that we were the ones to beat when it came to deep thought, but maybe I was wrong. So, what do you think about?'

Kari considered his reply. 'Mostly,' he said, 'how Eyvind's snoring really pisses me off. But after I've been thinking about that for half the night I get so mad I want to jump up and stick my axe between his eyebrows, so I've practised thinking about other stuff, to take my mind off it.'

'Ah,' I said. 'What other stuff?'

He shrugged. 'Stuff,' he said. 'Like, here's a thing I noticed. Back home, in the winter, it stays dark for months on end. Down here, some days are longer than others — depending on the time of year — but there's always a day and a night, one after the other. And in Meadowland, in winter, on the shortest day, it was light by breakfast-time, and it didn't get dark till mid-afternoon. I've thought a lot about that,' said Kari.

'Interesting,' I said. 'And what conclusions have you reached?'

'Search me,' Kari replied. 'I guess it's just one of those things, really. And here's another one. In your Greek sea, down around Sicily and those places, you don't have proper tides, like we've got at home. Oh, you get a bit of a swell on the beach when there's a squall, but mostly the sea just sits there like an old, lazy dog in the rushes. I've spent whole nights puzzling over that, but I can't make head nor tail of it.'

'Me neither,' I admitted. 'Though I heard once that a Greek philosopher living in France round about the time the Huns came reckoned that it was something to do with the phases of the moon.'

Kari looked at me. 'Balls,' he said. 'Same moon down here as we got at home, so that can't be right. No offence, but you Greeks'll say the first thing that comes into your heads; anything rather than just bide quiet and admit that there's stuff you simply don't know.'

'There's an element of truth in that,' I conceded. 'Anyhow, if it's all right with you, I think I'll just get my head down for a bit.'

He ignored me. 'So,' he said, 'where did the old fool get up to? Had he got as far as where Leif Eirikson murdered his father?'

For some reason, I wasn't quite so sleepy. 'He did that?'

Kari nodded. 'Oh yes,' he said. 'I mean, nobody could ever prove it or anything; and even if they could've, nobody could've done a blind thing about it, what with Leif being Eirik's closest kin and heir. Back home, see, when someone gets himself killed in a fight or whatever, it's the duty of the nearest relative to take revenge or claim compensation. And since Leif was Eirik's eldest son, only he could do it and nobody else. I'm all for our ways most of the time, but I must say I think that's a bit of a loophole in the system, because what it amounts to is that you can murder your next of kin and there's not a lot anybody can do about it. Mind you, it's a pretty useless loophole, because as a general rule sons don't particularly want to kill their fathers, or the other way around.'

I was interested in spite of myself. 'Is that right, though?' I said. 'Only the closest relative can take action over a murder?'

He nodded. 'Well, strictly speaking that's not true: you can hand over the right to somebody else — like, suppose you're a substantial farmer and I'm a nobody, and your worst enemy kills my son. I can't do anything much about it, but you can, so I give you my right of taking revenge, or sell it to you more like, and then you can get your enemy and I get my revenge and a bag of silver-scrap, and everybody's happy. But it's up to me — you can't steal my right from me when I'm asleep or anything like that.'

I thought about that for a moment, then made a decision not to think about it any more. 'But you said Leif murdered Red Eirik,' I said. 'You're sure about that?'

'Oh yes.' He grinned. 'Now what everybody in Greenland'll tell you is that Eirik died of the sickness that did for Thorir the Norwegian. But don't you think it's odd, the two main people who die of this sickness are the husband of the woman Leif's besotted with, and Leif's old man? And what's more, the sickness only started after Leif invited a witch from the old country to stop over a few nights. Think on, as the saying goes.'

'But it still doesn't make any sense,' I objected. 'Why would Leif want his own father dead?'

'Ah,' said Kari, 'I was coming to that. You see, I'm absolutely sure that what Leif wanted was to be the boss, in charge. Now that wasn't going to happen in Greenland while Eirik was still alive, and everybody reckoned he was strong as an ox and likely to live to be eighty. So Leif set his heart on starting up a settlement of his own someplace, just like Eirik did at Brattahlid. But Leif goes to Meadowland minded to found his colony there, but for some reason or other he doesn't take to it there; and then on the way home he meets Gudrid, and that makes him all the more deter-mined to get out from under Eirik's shadow. So he — let's say he forcibly inherits Eirik's household. Now he's got what he wanted, he loses interest in Meadowland completely. Instead, he settles down at Brattahlid and he's perfectly happy. Or else he would've been, if he'd married Gudrid. Only, that didn't happen, though of course there was no way in the world he could've seen that one coming.'

'What one?' I asked.

'Gudrid falling head over heels for Leif's kid brother Thorstein. Which proves another point,' Kari went on. 'Like, we've all got this picture in our minds of our nearest and dearest; but often as not, that picture's out of date, or just plain wrong. My guess is, in his mind's eye Leif had this picture of Thorstein the way he was when he was still a kid. But Thorstein's all grown up now, big and tall and strong and good-looking, with all the girls sighing after him. When Leif looks at him, he doesn't notice how he's changed, he still thinks of Thorstein as a snot-nosed little boy sailing his toy ship in a puddle. So Thorstein cuts in and gets the lovely Gudrid, and Leif's been too slow to do anything about it.'

'I see,' I said.

'Served him right,' Kari went on, 'for not paying attention. Still, he'd got Brattahlid, so I'm guessing he made a decision to make the best of it and not worry unduly about not getting the girl. And at least it wasn't a total dead loss,' he went on, 'because as soon as he was able, he took the ship back to the reef where he'd found Thorir's ship – Eyvind told you about that, did he? – and picks up all that lumber he'd ditched there in order to mount his big noble rescue.'

'Ah,' I said. 'So you got your share of the proceeds in the end, then.'

Kari made a strange noise. 'Did we hell as like. No, when Leif came back home to Brattahlid with the timber, he announced that it'd become salvage, on account of it being abandoned at sea, and he was keeping all of it for himself. Which he wouldn't have done,' Kari admitted, 'if it'd just been straightforward greed. But he wanted that timber so he could build a new barn at Brattahlid now that he'd inherited the place. We didn't argue, of course, because it'd have been pointless, Leif wasn't going to give way on something he really wanted. So we never got our money. But Leif sort of made it up to us, or to me and Eyvind at any rate. He said we didn't have to go back to Herjolfsness if we didn't want to, we could stay on as hired hands at Brattahlid. Which we did, of course, because Brattahlid was a bigger place, and we wanted a change. And then, when Thorvald made up his mind to go to Meadowland—'

I frowned. 'Who's Thorvald?' I asked.

Thorvald (said Kari) was Leif's brother; not to be confused with Thorstein, the other brother who married Gudrid. Thorvald was the odd one out in that family: he was the easygoing, no-worries, good-natured type, the one who everybody liked and got on with. How he managed to get that way and stay like it with Red Eirik for his dad I couldn't tell you, but he did it. I think the strain got to him sometimes, though.

But when Eirik died and Leif took over as the farmer at Brattahlid, my guess is that something gave way, and Thorvald decided that he didn't want to live with the family any more. Mind, I never spent a lot of time over there while Eirik was alive, so this is just me making it up as I go along; but I think the difference between Eirik and his children was that the old man had nothing much left to prove.

It's all different down here in the South. All of you have so many *things*. You walk through the streets of the City any day of the year, and there's shops and stalls smothered and crammed with stuff: clothes and pots and shoes and little ivory pen-and-inkwell sets and mirrors and jewellery and carpets and furniture and tapestries for your walls and lampstands and cushions and gentlemen's personal business seals and firedogs and books and table silver and little pictures of the Blessed Virgin all covered in gold leaf and candlesticks and boxes for keeping things in and padlocks and dog collars and God alone knows what else. You have a city full of people who do nothing but make things and sell things to all the other people who make and sell things, and somewhere at the end of a very long chain there's a bunch of farmers you all buy your food and your wool from. I guess it all seems perfectly natural to you, but I've been here a long time now and I still don't get it. Seems to me that you do everything sideways-and-backwards, like the picture in a mirror. Oh, it's all amazingly rich and wonderful, and a poor bugger like me from the North can hardly keep his bowels closed for the sheer glory of it all, first time he sees it.

It's different back home. Where I come from, even a rich man can shut his eyes and picture in his mind every single thing he owns. You ask him, and he'll describe them all for you, in detail, every last scratch and crack and rust spot and busted handle mended with rawhide, and it won't take him too long, either. Oh, we like our things, no doubt about that. We show them off, and when guests come to stay we take them down from the rafters and pass them round the hall so that everybody can see them; and we've got some nice things, too – gold and silver, walrus ivory and carved wood, embroidered clothes and old pattern-welded swords that've been in the family since Odin was still God. The difference is, though, the way I see it, that where I come from the things only matter because of the people they belong to. Like, there's a street in the City where you can buy old second-hand tools; and very good tools they are too, from all over the place, and dirt cheap for what they are; but they're just things, and all you've got to do in order to own them is pay money. Back home, if someone picks up an axe or a stir-rup on the road in the middle of the mountains, chances are he'll be able to tell you whose it is and who made it just by looking at it. No kidding. What's more, it's a safe bet that the man it belongs to inherited it from his father, who got it from his father, and so on back as far as anyone can remem-ber; and he'll have had to wait until the old man was dead and in his grave before he got his hands on it, because we really hate being parted from our stuff. It's supposed to have been done away with now we're all Christians, but a lot of us, when we die, we want all our very favourite things buried in the ground with us. The idea used to be that we'd take them with us to the next life, but that's all rubbish. Truth is, they're our things and we're buggered if anybody else is going to have them once we're gone. The point being, things matter to us because there are so few of them; and when I look at your city streets jam-packed with strangers, I guess the same goes for you people, too. There's precious few of us, surrounded by a hell of a lot of landscape, which I think is what makes us stand out. What I'm trying to say is, we have so little compared with you, but that means that everything matters; and what matters most of all is people, the sort of men and women we are. What people think about us, what we think about ourselves, that's the only thing we care about. Who we are is all we've got.

In which case, Red Eirik was richer than any of you – he was richer than King Michael of All the Greeks. He'd been a big man in Norway, got so big he had to leave so he went to Iceland until it got too small to hold him, so the only course left open to him was start up a brand new country of his very own. He may only have owned three shirts when he died, but everybody in the North knew his name, and we think that makes you very rich indeed.

Now think what it was like for Leif Eirikson, and you can begin to see why he went to Meadowland; also, why he came back and, I'm absolutely positive, did in his old man. Of course, while Red Eirik was alive, his kids were like holly bushes in a birch forest: they could only grow so high before they ran out of light. When Eirik died, though, and the light came flooding back in, a mild, easygoing lad like Thorvald has two choices. He can buckle down and get used to taking the same kind of shit from his big brother that he always took from his dad; or he can go away on a very long journey. Just lucky, in the circumstances, that there was somewhere worth going to – all in the family, so to speak.

So Thorvald goes to Leif and tells him he quite fancies taking the ship to Meadowland, if that'd be all right. Now you'd have thought that Leif would be only too pleased to see the back of him, since it means there'll only be his other brother Thorstein and his sister Freydis left for him to lock horns with. But Leif's not like that. The way he sees it, he got up off his bum and went out and found something, something big of his very own, not just one of the old man's things. True, now he's the farmer at Brattahlid and his mind's full of milk yields and grazing for the sheep and whether the hay'll see out the winter, so he knows in his heart of hearts he probably won't have any use for a great big green island across the sea, so why not let the kid have it? He won't say that out loud, though. When Thorvald tells him what he's got planned, Leif just nods his head a little bit, doesn't actually say anything; and then Thorvald says, 'So it's all right if I take the ship?' and Leif frowns a bit, because 'take' can mean 'borrow' or it can mean 'have'. 'I guess we could do with some timber for the new barns,' Leif says, and that's entirely true, as far as it goes. Thorvald thinks it's close enough to 'yes' to be going on with; Leif knows exactly what he meant by it, but he's smart enough to know that it's what you don't say that carries most weight. 'And if it's all right by you,' Thorvald goes on, 'can we have the booths you built when you were over there? Makes no sense building new ones when there's perfectly good walls out there already.'

Now Leif goes all quiet, because this time Thorvald's said 'have', and that's crossing the line. So he frowns a bit more; Thorvald waits quiet, Leif makes a show of thinking about it. 'Don't know about that,' he says, 'I'll have to think about it. You can have the *use* of them if that'll do you.'

There's a heartbeat or so when nobody says anything. Thorvald thinks: It's right out on the edge of the world, Leif's never going out there again so he won't know, God knows why I even bothered to ask. Leif thinks: Just so long as he knows they're only lent. Then Thorvald says thank you, nicely, and buggers off quick before Leif can change his mind.

Now comes the merry dance. Leif wants to show how rich and generous he is, because that's what being the farmer of Brattahlid is all about; so when Thorvald asks, can he have ten barrels of flour and five barrels of malt, Eirik says, don't be stupid, you'll want twice that at least, and you'll want bacon and salt fish and smoked lamb and apples, and anything else you can think of; also shirts and blankets and coats, livestock, all the sort of thing that comes from the farm, which means that by this time next year Leif'll have made up the loss and never even felt it. But when Thorvald starts asking for farm tools and axes and hoes and knives, stuff that's got to be sent out for if it's going to get replaced, that's another matter entirely. Take felling-axes, for example.

Obviously, Thorvald wants a good axe for cutting lumber, and there's three long axes at Brattahlid. There's the good Danish axe that Eirik brought from Norway; but that's been in the family since God knows when, so he's not having that. There's the four-pound broad axe with the nick out of the edge; but Leif had to earn that, Eirik made him work all one summer riving logs and putting up fences before he'd give it to him, so obviously that's not available; which only leaves the fancy axe that some great-uncle brought back from Sweden as a gift from the King – it's got silver inlay and something written on the poll that you can't actually read any more, but it was in a fire forty years ago and goes blunt soon as look at it so it's actually not much use for anything. Besides, Thorstein likes the fancy axe, and Thorvald doesn't like using the four-pounder, he's always used the Dane-axe because the helve fits his hands better; and getting a fourth axe made specially for Thorvald's out of the question, because there's not enough hardening steel in the smithy to make a good edge, and the pedlar won't be calling out that way again till April. So in the end, Leif takes a horse and rides over to Ketilsfjord, which is a long way away and a rough old road even in summer, because he knows Ketil's got two spare axes his dad brought home from a viking trip and never uses; and he trades them for three months' hay that he can hardly spare. Result: Leif's pissed right off because of the hay, and because Thorvald doesn't seem properly grateful. Thorvald's all resentful because he wanted the axe he's used to. Brother Thorstein says, if he can have a new axe why can't I have one too? Sister Freydis is mad as hell because Leif's gone and wasted all that valuable hay when there's three perfectly good axes hanging up on the wall already.

And so on, for months on bloody end. And don't imagine it was just the family at each other's throats. When things get fraught round the farm, everybody gets sucked in, taking sides, falling out, not speaking, till you reach the point where it's a miracle blood's not shed. Which is why, when Thorvald came round all quiet and furtive, sounding us out one by one to see who fancied coming with him, I said yes, straight off, without thinking.

I do a lot of that, not thinking. Oh, I thought about it later, when it was too late. Me, go back to Meadowland, again. Why the hell would I want to do a thing like that?

First, of course, because I happened to know that Thorvald had already asked Eyvind, and he'd said yes, so really I didn't have much choice. Second, because I was sick and tired of Brattahlid, especially now everybody was so uptight and snotty over sharing out the things. Third—

Third, because I really *wanted* to go back, and buggered if I know why, looking back on it. Going through all that again, the fog and the getting wet and the sitting still on a boat, with the cows roaring their heads off in the hold and waves bashing your face in. But I wasn't thinking of any of that. I was thinking of that imaginary house of mine, Karisfjord or Karisholt or Karisness. You probably don't know it, but we have an old kids' story about the elves' castle, which you stumble across by accident one time and spend the rest of your life vainly searching for, because it can never be found on purpose. Well, I knew my house, my farm, my country of my very own was out there some-where, out back of the lake the river flowed down from, or round the second headland down from Leif's Booths; in my mind's eye I could picture me standing on top of one of the mountains beyond the forest, and from where I was stood I could just see the green flash of its roof, round the rocks and over the treetops, not terribly far away. You lie in the hall at night, squashed up on your bit of bench with someone's knee in the small of your back, and everybody dreams about their own place, their own valley and lake and mountain and fjord, far as the eye can see. That's dreams, and they're all right in their place but you know it'll never happen. But I'd already been there, for God's sake, I'd seen all that grass and flat land with no bugger at all living on it; and once a man like me's got a picture like that snagged in his mind, it won't go away. You can't snap off the shaft and pull it out with the smithy tongs. It's there inside you, for keeps.

Kari sat still and quiet for a while, until I thought he'd fallen asleep. Wishful thinking on my part; because when I stood up and started tiptoeing outside for a pee (which I'd been wanting to do for some time) he lifted his head and looked at me. His eyes were very wide open and bright, but I couldn't begin to guess what he was thinking.

'Anyway,' he said; so I had no choice but to go back to where I'd been sitting.

Anyway (Kari said), we went back to Meadowland.

I don't seem to remember much about that crossing. Yes, there was fog, and rain, and it wasn't a lot of fun. I think we sprang a leak at some point, and had to plug it with all our dry spare clothes stuffed into hide sacks; and there was a hell of a storm that lasted two days and one night, with the ship trying to stand on its tail like a begging dog; stores falling out of the hold and flour barrels bursting, the decks slimy with salt-water porridge, the sail splitting, all that. It was a bad storm, but it shoved us on the way we wanted to go and shaved the best part of a day off the run, so it wasn't all bad. Leif had given Thorvald the bearing-dial he'd got from Bjarni Herjolfson, so quite a lot of the time we knew more or less where we were. I like it when that happens. But you look like you've heard quite enough sea stories for one night, so I'll skip ahead to where we'd sighted land and followed down the coast a day and a night, and the next morning Eyvind was on watch, and he yelled out that he could see the walls of Leif's Booths.

It's a funny thing. Here in Greece there's fallen-down old buildings everywhere you look: busted walls and bits of cut stone poking up out of the dirt, chunks of that shiny white stuff, marble, stuck in the sides of farmhouses and pigsties and dry-rubble boundary walls. I have no idea what you Greeks have got up to over the years, but you must've been bastards for smashing up buildings. Wars, I suppose. Back home we're not like that. When we have a war, we kill the people and leave the buildings alone. Still, it wouldn't do if everybody was alike.

But in the whole of Meadowland there was just the one lot of buildings in the whole country, and even they didn't have roofs; so they stuck out, you could see them from a long way off, even though they were small and low. Soon as I saw them, I knew we were back, and it was like going home to Greenland had just been a dream. Strange, that, because when we were at Brattahlid after Leif came home I'd lie in the dark at night and try and remember what Meadowland looked like, and I couldn't picture it for the life of me. All I could see was my imaginary farm, Karistead or Karisvatn or whatever we decided it was called; the real thing just sort of slipped through the meshes, like sprats through a cod net.

Anyhow: the booths were just where we'd left them, and the only difference was that the grass had grown up nicely through the stacked turfs, binding them together good and tight, which is what you want, of course. Back home we reckon it takes three years for a house to grow properly weathertight; then you cut out the original inside timbers, if they're birch or pine, and replace them with something that'll last. No point doing that until the walls have grown together because they settle and shift and spring the tenons out of the mortices, and it'd be a waste of good lumber. Before we landed we did the business with the canopy struts. At least, we tried to. We said a little prayer to Our Heavenly Father and chucked them overboard into the water, splosh; but instead of bobbing up and floating they sank like stones and we never saw them again, not for a very long time.

We landed the stores, and that wasn't good. We already knew we'd lost a bit of the flour. What we didn't know was that the damp had got into most of the rest and spoiled it; also the malt, which was a cruel blow and likely to make our lives very sad indeed, unless we could find the place where old Tyrkir's vines grew. The livestock hadn't done too badly – it was funny to see them wobbling about after standing still all that time. They went crazy once they started nibbling the grass. You could see they thought it was a damn sight better than bloody Greenland. Even so, the fact remained that we were going to have to live off the country if we planned on stopping there any length of time.

Not that we had much choice in the matter, with almost no flour. We were stuck there till we could stock up with provisions for the return trip, at the very least, and looked at sensibly that meant spending the winter. And that meant fish.

Shows how picky I've got living here, all my meals brought out to me on a plate instead of having to work for a living; I've gone off fish. Not a problem back in the Guards barracks in the City, we get given white wheat-bread and cheese and sausage and eggs and big jugs of that red wine with the tree-sap in, you've only got to eat fish once a week, and that's only because it says so in the Bible. That winter, in Meadowland, we ate fish. Fish followed by fish, with fish for a change when you got bored. Salmon, mostly. There were so many salmon you could stand on the riverbank and spear them with a pointed stick. Not that there's anything wrong with salmon. Two of you can have a good feed off one fish, and the skin and scales boil down into the best glue you can possibly make. But I tell you what; even now, all these years later, I can shut my eyes and the taste of bloody salmon comes straight back to me, and it makes me want to go outside and throw up.

Now and then we'd get so sick of it we'd haul down the ship and go out a way and catch something else – cod mostly, and flatfish; but most of the cod we stuck out in the wind on racks to dry, provisions for the trip home. We smoked some too, and salmon as well, of course, and from time to time someone'd go off into the woods and shoot a deer, or we'd get lucky and a load of seals would turn up. And there was the wild corn too, though there wasn't nearly as much of that as there had been the previous times, and nuts and berries and stuff like that. It'd have been all right if we'd had the time to spend all day finding things to eat; but we didn't.

I said that Thorvald was the easygoing type. Well, he changed. Being in charge, I suppose, or maybe it was the situation we were in, I don't know. It was a slow thing, not a sudden change; but he was always coming up with ideas, finding things for us all to do. First it was putting roofs on the booths. Just dragging the sails over the tops wasn't good enough for him, we had to go up into the woods and cut beams for rafters, make a proper job. Then we were on turf-cutting for days on end, and that's a job I've never liked, it buggers up your elbows and knees like nothing else. I remember thinking, if Leif could see what Thorvald was up to, putting proper roofs on the booths, he'd be mad as hell about it, since the whole idea was that he'd only lent them to Thorvald, and here he was setting up like he planned on staying there for good.

After we'd done that, next thing was building a proper boat shed for the ship. Well, you can see the sense in that. If anything happened to the ship, we were completely screwed. But I've seen earls' houses in Norway that were less well built than that bloody shed. Just cutting mortices and slotting the timbers together wasn't good enough, oh no. We had to go scrabbling about in the bog for iron nuggets, so Thorvald could cook them up in the smithy forge and draw them down into nails, nails by the bucketful, just to build a boat shed. Then, with winter really starting to come on and big fat chunks of ice starting to form in the bay, he had us outside riving great hundred-foot trees up into posts and rails to build a huge stock-pen. Comical it looked, with our four cows, three goats and half a dozen sheep standing in the middle of all that open space. As if that wasn't enough, he made us cut about a ton of withies and wind them into hurdles, God only knew what for. I never did find out what he had in mind; when we'd finished making them we stacked them neatly round the back of the houses, and there they stayed until the damp got in them and they fell to bits. All in all, we were glad when winter set in and it was too cold to be outside, even though there was only fish to eat and nothing whatsoever to drink, only water.

Spring came, and we all came bounding out of the houses like calves turned out of the stalls. Thorvald had gone very quiet indeed over winter, just sitting there in the corner hardly saying a word, and we all had a nasty feeling he'd spent the time thinking up more bloody silly things for us to do. We weren't far wrong. What needed doing, he told us all one morning, was a proper survey of the island, so we'd know where we were. We'd launch the ship and sail right round the island, keeping an eye out for the best places for farms. We'd start off heading west, because nobody had been that way before; for all we knew, Leif's Booths was the crummiest spot in the whole of Meadowland, and just round the corner we'd find meadows where the grass dripped with butter, streams where the salmon crawled along on each others' backs, and God only knew what else. Maybe, he added when he saw our faces go all sad, we'd even find the place where the vines grew, or a big rap of the wild corn, which (he felt sure) would probably make decent malt if only we could figure out how.

That last bit got our attention, after a winter spent drinking water. It's surprising how well thirty men cooped up in a small space with no women and no booze can cope; I guess it's the unspoken fact that if one of them blows his top and starts getting stroppy, chances are that the other twenty-nine will follow suit, and the only possible outcome after that would be a short but bloody fight, with not enough survivors to get the ship home again. But those thirty men will be hard to motivate, unless you can offer them something they actually want. After the long, fraught winter, nobody gave a damn about exploring a strange new country or looking for greener pastures and crisp, cold rivers teeming with salmon. What twenty-nine of us really wanted to do, of course, was go home; it was because we wanted it so badly, I guess, that nobody actually dared say so. That would've been the hole in the planks that lets the sea in. Now that the thaw had come we needed to do something other than scrape along catching fish and burning charcoal, and it had to be something that'd break the tension. An epic quest for Tyrkir's vines was exactly what we needed.

So we loaded the ship with dried and smoked fish, and set off westwards. It was a good season for exploring, a warm, pleasant spring and early summer, with helpful winds, and we cruised along the coast at a nice easy pace. We didn't find any vines, but we saw great forests sweeping down to white sandy beaches, and it was easy to get lost in daydreams about bringing great cargoes of priceless lumber back to Iceland, without giving much thought to precisely how we'd get them there. All that raw material, just waiting to be cut, logged and planked; just looking at it did something to your brains. I remember spending several days hatching out a cock-eyed scheme of building a great raft of floating logs and towing it home all the way to Brattahlid. Completely impossible, needless to say; but I wasn't the only one who let his mind wander, so to speak. It was like those kids' stories about the hero who gets carried off to the land of the giants, where he sees gold rings the size of cartwheels and cups and plates as big as houses; all that wealth, and not a hope in hell of getting it home. If you stopped to think about it clear-headed, it'd have broken your heart.

I remember, we were cruising through a little group of islands, and we had to put in for fresh water. We saw a lake with a river flowing out of it, so we landed; and there it was, the thing that changed everything.

Strange; but it was so ordinary that we nearly missed it. No big deal at all, you see them all the time at home, so you don't notice them. It was a rick-cover: a bundle of long sticks rigged up on top of a hayrick to support the thatch that keeps out the rain. The only difference was that the thatching was birch-bark rather than reed. When it's time to cart off the hay, you pull out the sticks, bundle them up and put them aside ready for next year, you don't think about them any more. Someone had done just that, only by the looks of it they'd forgotten all about it, because the grass and weeds had grown up through the bundle – it was only when you got up close and saw the woven-grass cords they were tied with that you realised what you were looking at.

I can't remember who noticed it first; but someone called out, 'Here, look at this.' Nobody panicked or went wild with excitement, but we stopped what we were doing and gathered round, staring at those weed-covered poles like we knew we were looking at something but we couldn't figure out what was such a big deal. It dawned on us gradually. Someone had tied those poles together, and it hadn't been us.

'Here, Eyvind,' Thorvald said, in a perfectly calm voice. 'When you came this way with Bjarni Herjolfson – did you stop here?'

Eyvind didn't say anything, just shook his head. I was trying to figure out how long the sticks had been there by the length of the overgrowth: three years, I thought, maybe four. I was thinking, so we aren't the first to come here after all. Obviously, someone else had heard about Bjarni's trip and come exploring, and for some reason they'd built a rick here; or maybe the cover was for cords of wood, which'd make more sense, since why would anybody bring hay out here to an island? It didn't occur to me, or to any of us, I think, that whoever left those poles there might not have been a Greenlander or an Icelander or just possibly a Norwegian. We stared at it for a while, then shrugged and went back to filling our water-barrels. It was a mystery, and maybe we felt a bit put out that someone had beaten us to it, but it wasn't like it mattered, after all.

We spent all summer fooling about like that, but we never found any vines. Instead, we found honey, which was even better.

Stands to reason, really. Where you've got wild flowers and fruit trees and all that, there's got to be bees. The stupid thing was that it took us so long to think of it. But it was only when a man called Sigurd Squint was cutting brushwood, stuck his hook into a wild bees' nest and got horribly stung all over that we realised what we'd been overlooking all that time.

'You've lost me,' I said.

Kari looked at me as though I was simple, and said a word I'd never heard before. It began with M.

'Say again,' I said.

He sighed. 'You Greeks,' he said. 'All right. Basically, it's like beer, only you make it out of honey. You ferment it, and—'

'Oh, right,' I said. 'I know what you're talking about. It's mentioned in Homer, but nobody makes it any more.'

Kari grinned. 'Yes, they bloody well do,' he said, 'though back home it's sort of like showing off, because there's so many other things we need the honey for: preserving meat, that sort of thing. You only make (the M-word) if you're filthy rich and have more honey than you can use. But as far as we were concerned, booze wasn't a luxury any more, it was an essential; so we gave up exploring and turned all our attention to bee-hunting.

It's a bastard thing about bees (Kari said): when you aren't looking for them, the bloody things are everywhere, stinging you. When you want to find them, it's another matter entirely. Each one of us reckoned he knew the sort of places where bees like to nest: hollow trees, for instance, or the forks of old oaks. Turned out we hadn't got a clue, because back home we've been keeping bees for as long as anyone can remember. It was like looking for wild cows. But we couldn't wait for a swarm to show up, like you do at home; we needed to find them as quickly as possible. So we spent weeks poking about on the edges of the woods, prodding rotten trees with long sticks, climbing up in the branches like a load of kids. A man called Big Thorbjorn hit on the idea of following bees back to their nest; he'd wander around in the open till he saw one, then he'd follow it, stalking it like a rabbit while it buzzed around drinking from flowers, then running after it when it started flying – he never found a single nest, but he kept at it for days on end, till at last he tripped over a great big stone while he was chasing a bee and bashed his knee so hard that he couldn't walk for a week.

In the end, though, we found a dozen hives – and didn't we all get stung busting them open. Two of them were empty, no honey at all, but we finished up with enough comb to brew from; and then we waited. Of course, every-body had slightly different ideas about how you brew the stuff, and in particular how long you've got to leave it till it's ready. What's more, it turned out that none of us had ever done any actual brewing; we'd maybe watched our mother or our wife or our aunt do it, but we hadn't actually paid close attention, because it wasn't our job. After all the effort and bother we'd gone to in collecting the honey, the last thing we wanted to do was screw it up by tapping it before it'd finished working; but thirty men who haven't had a drink for best part of a year find it hard to be patient. Thorvald organised a guard rota, to make sure nobody got at it while the rest of us were asleep; we kept watch in pairs, since one man on his own might be tempted. It was all very tense, specially the last few days, and I think we were all wor-ried about what'd happen if we tried it and found it'd gone off or something; there'd have been bloodshed, for certain.

Luckily, it was all right. It was better than all right, actually. It went down a treat, hardly touched the sides, and for a couple of days we were all very happy and pleased with ourselves. Then we woke up, and there wasn't any more left, and our heads hurt.

Things were pretty subdued around Leif's Booths for a while after that. It wasn't just because there wasn't any booze, though of course that didn't help. The whole point of booze is that it helps make you forget how shitty your life is; on the other hand, when the booze runs out, you find yourself remembering all the shitty things the booze helped you forget, and then you get *really* depressed. In particular, we all found ourselves asking what the hell we thought we were supposed to be doing there. I mean, it was a fine country, with the most wonderful grazing and all that valuable lumber, but that didn't alter the fact that we were living off dried fish and there wasn't anything to drink. Just for the sake of being there, it seemed a high price to pay. It didn't help that autumn was closing in, so even if we'd decided to pack it all in and go back to Greenland, we couldn't, not till spring. The only answer was to find more honey – or grapes, or wild grain, or any bloody thing we could squash into a pulp and leave to ferment.

It was all a bit ridiculous by that stage. I mean, back home, in winter, the one thing you take for granted is loads of salt beef and bacon washed down with gallons of beer. We were busy all that autumn, but we ended up rationing ourselves to one mug of disgusting mixed-fruit rotgut per man per day to wash down our dried cod and smoked salmon. Over winter, stuck indoors all bundled in together, we mostly went quiet. We'd been together so long that there was nothing left to talk about, and if we tried to talk it just flared up into arguments and bad temper, so mostly we just sat. Now you Greeks know a lot more about Religion than we do, but there's one important thing you've got wrong. You say that if a man's evil and wicked and he dies and goes to the bad place, what's waiting for him there is a huge bonfire stoked with sulphur and pitch, for ever and ever, along with a whole load of other wicked people. No disrespect, but that can't be right. For one thing, you don't know spit about the cold. Sitting in Leif's Booths in the middle of winter, even with the thick turf walls and the hearth stoked right up, you were cold right down inside your bones. Give me this pitch-and-sulphur furnace of yours any time. Also, if I've got this right, most people are evil and wicked, so most people are going to end up in the bad place, which means there'll be plenty of different people to talk to; what's more, since what you call evil and wicked is pretty much what we call interesting, I can't help but think the company'll be better there. Sounds to me like the good place hasn't got much going for it, because if the bad place is hot, it figures the good place has got to be the opposite, cold. Add in being stuck there for ever with a small number of boring people, and it seems to me I've been there already and I didn't like it much.

We got through the winter, but I couldn't tell you how. Mostly I think we went to sleep with our eyes open. When spring came, there weren't any arguments. We were going to get the ship up together as soon as it was warm enough to be outside, and then we were going home.

Well, we got the ship overhauled and seaworthy in no time flat; you never saw thirty men work so hard. True, we were very low on stores, apart from water, but we didn't care; we'd put lines over the side and lures for seagulls, just so long as we could get under way as soon as the ice broke up. Once we could get out and start working on something, the tension broke up faster than the ice in the bay. I was chatting and laughing with men I hadn't said two words to all winter, mostly because we finally had something to talk about. Different if we'd been women, of course, because it's my experience that what women mostly talk about is nothing at all; but men need to talk about *something*, or else they just sit there staring at the wall.

Came the day when we cast off, and all of us agreed that whatever happened we weren't coming back to Leif's Booths again, not ever; we'd rather drown or get crunched on the rocks. We headed east, then north-east, following the lines scored on old Bjarni's bearing-dial, keeping the coast in sight but making the most of the current.

All went well until we came to a headland. I remembered it vaguely, but last time and the times before we'd kept much further out, so all I'd seen of it was a sort of grey smudge at the bottom of the sky. This time, we took a chance and held closer in, because the current was so good. Seemed like a good idea at the time.

Stuff always happens in the middle of the night. We'd actually had the sense to drop anchor, because we weren't happy about being that close in. But a dirty great squall blew up and sprang the anchors, and then we were off. In the pitch dark and the sea throwing us about we couldn't actually be precise about where we were headed, but it didn't feel good at all. We hopped about trying to get the sails up and tack out of it — just as well we failed, because that'd probably have made things a whole lot worse — and then there was the most almighty bang, loudest noise I've ever heard, and we were all thrown up in the air. I came down badly, landed awkwardly on the rim of a bucket, of all things. I felt at least one rib go, and then something heavy gave me a bloody great scat on the side of the head, and I was excused duty, as we say in the Guards.

When I opened my eyes, the first thing I noticed was how much the daylight hurt. Then I realised I wasn't on the ship any more. I was lying on my back on a rock, looking up at the sky, which was grey and miserable, and I was soaked to the skin. Also my left arm hurt, though not nearly as much as my ribs; and there was Eyvind, with a bit of bloody rag tied round his head, looking down at me all thoughtful.

'You're alive, then,' he said.

''Course I'm bloody alive,' I said, swearing because it hurt like buggery to talk. 'What happened?'

He sighed. 'Actually, could've been a lot worse. The keel's all smashed in, but most of the rest of the damage we can probably patch up, eventually. And nobody got killed,' he added as an afterthought. 'In fact, you're probably the worst hurt.'

That didn't sound good, so I called him a bastard and asked what was wrong with me. 'Two busted ribs,' he told me. 'But your arm's probably all right, apart from a bit of bruising.'

'My head hurts,' I told him.

'Well, it would, wouldn't it?' Eyvind replied, and walked away, even though I yelled at him to come back. As it happened, I went to sleep for a while after that, and it was dark when I woke up again There was a fire going nearby, and it was just spitting with rain. Someone said, 'Kari's awake', and next thing Thorvald himself had come to see me. Which was nice of him, I guess.

'We ran aground,' he said, after he'd asked me how I was and I'd lied to him. 'We'll get her afloat again, no worries on that score, but it's going to be a long job. A bloody long job,' he added, in a tone of voice I didn't like one bit. 'Doesn't help that half our stuff's at the bottom of the sea,' he went on. 'We lost the cross-cut saw and the carpenter's chest, and we've got just the one long axe between us.'

'That's bad,' I said. 'Eyvind said the keel's not too clever.'

'It's a mess,' Thorvald said sadly. 'We're going to have to make a new one from scratch – we can't even salvage the nails.'

That was when I really wanted to cry. If we had to build and fit a new keel, we'd need more than just timber; we'd need the right tools, and most of all (because you can do a lot with a hand-axe if you've really got to) we'd need nails. If we hadn't got any, we'd have to make some; and to make nails, of course, you need a forge and an anvil and bellows and all that, not to mention raw iron.

'We're going back to Leif's Booths, then,' I said, all quiet.

Thorvald nodded; I could see the silhouette of his beard wagging up and down against the firelight. 'Might as well,' he said. 'We used up the last of the charcoal before we came on, so we'll need to burn a stack before we can get the forge going. With only one long axe between us, that means everybody pitching in with hand-axes. It's a real bugger when you've got to make every damn thing for yourself.'

I nodded and pretended that I was feeling sleepy again, because I didn't feel like talking any more. Of course, I hadn't had time to figure it all out in my mind, how long each job'd take before we could move on to the next stage, but I didn't need to know the details. You see, it wasn't just a matter of doing the work. Three-quarters of our time'd be spent just gathering food and fuel. The plain fact was, we were going to be stuck in bloody Meadowland all summer, probably all winter too. It was like the place had got its teeth stuck into us and wasn't going to let us go.

CHAPTER
SEVEN

'What?' I muttered.

'You fell asleep.'

I opened my eyes to the sight of Eyvind's long, bony, beard-fringed face hovering over me. 'Rubbish,' I said. 'I was just resting my eyes.'

I could see light soaking through the shadows at the mouth of the tomb. Furthermore, I had a crick in my neck, pins and needles in my left arm and a sharp pain in the small of my back. It was just possible that Eyvind was right.

'Understandable,' he went on. 'In fact, it's amazing you lasted as long as you did, with that old fool sitting there, spouting his drivel at you. I always said he missed his calling in life. Should've been a surgeon's assistant. Get Kari to talk to a man for an hour, you can cut off both his feet and he'd never notice a thing.'

'Actually,' I said, 'I was paying close attention. He'd just got to the part where Thorvald Eirikson ran the ship aground.'

Eyvind grunted. Behind him, I could see the taciturn Harald mixing porridge in an iron pot over the fire. For choice, I like to start the day with freshly baked wheat-bread dipped in wine with cheese grated over the top; porridge, on the other hand, has the great virtue of being better than nothing. 'You mean,' he said, 'the part where I saved that bastard from drowning.'

I frowned. 'I don't think he mentioned that,' I said.

Eyvind's face clouded over like the prelude to a thunder-storm. 'You're joking.'

Yet another thing I probably shouldn't have mentioned. 'Well,' I added, 'he did say he passed out when he hit his head on something during the storm, and the next thing he knew was being on dry land, so presumably he wasn't actu-ally aware who saved him, through being unconscious at the time—'

'Balls,' said Eyvind succinctly. ''Course he knew. I told him.'

'Ah,' I said. 'In that case, maybe I misheard him or some-thing. I was nearly asleep, wasn't I?'

'You said you were resting your eyes, not your ears.'

'Well, anyhow,' I said, as firmly as I could, 'I know now, don't I? Though that rather raises the question: if you've always hated his guts as much as you claim to, why didn't you just let him drown?'

Eyvind sighed. 'Because that's not how it works, on a ship,' he said. 'Look, it's not anything noble or heroic or any shit like that. It's more that, if you couldn't absolutely rely on knowing that anybody on that ship'd do as much for you, even your worst enemy in the whole world, people simply wouldn't be able to go to sea, there'd be nothing on Earth that'd induce them to set foot on the deck of a ship. All right,' he added, as I pulled a not-convinced face, 'let's take an example you can understand. Your orthodox Christians, right, hate the heretics. They hate them so much that they round them up and kill them like sheep in winter. But if the

Greeks were attacked by the heathen Saracens, they'd forget their differences for the time being and fight together. Right?'

'Actually,' I said, 'no, they wouldn't. But I think I see what you mean. The sea is your common enemy, and you'd rather risk your life to save someone you can't stand than give the sea the satisfaction of getting him.'

Eyvind nodded. 'Something like that,' he said. 'Anyhow, I don't know about you, but I can't see the point of staying inside when it's warm and sunny out. Let's go and sit outside, and I'll tell you what happened next.'

Took us the best part of a week to walk back to Leif's Booths (Eyvind said), carrying all the gear we hadn't lost in the storm. Can't say we were overjoyed to see the place again, even though it was looking very cheerful and fine with all its spring flowers and stuff. But it didn't take us very long to get over being pissed off at being there again, and after that we just slotted back into the routine: catching fish, cutting wood, burning charcoal. Well, it was just ordinary life, except we were doing it a slightly harder way than if we'd been back at Brattahlid or Herjolfsness. Meanwhile, Thorvald was in the forge, with Fat Osvif working the bellows for him, banging out nails day after day. Not that Thorvald was the handiest man with a hammer I ever did see, but that's how we do things. We believe that who you are decides what you can do. Like, in the City there's men who do nothing but weave rugs or make silver jugs, and they do that because they're good at it. You can get away with doing things that way round in a city, where there's thousands of people all living together. On the farms, though, back home, there's three or four dozen of you at most, so we can't afford to have experts, men who only do one thing all year round. Even a big place like Brattahlid, there's only, what, five days' worth of blacksmith work needed in a year; maybe fourteen days of carpentering, about the same amount of time tanning or building. So we say, the more responsible a job is, the more important the man who does it has got to be. Really, it's a case of the farmer saying, I need this done right, I'd better do it myself.

So, since making the nails was an important job, obviously Thorvald had to do it; and he did all right, because bashing out a few nails is hardly skilled work. But it took time, best part of a month, what with gathering lumps of ore in the bog, making the charcoal, drawing the iron out of the ore, beating it into a bloom, cutting it, all that. Then, when he'd done that, we needed tools for making the new keel: chisels, augers, a square. So Thorvald had to start all over, making more iron and then turning it into steel by getting it white hot, dipping it in the charcoal dust and forging it all up together. That was just the start of it, mind. Next, he had to draw down iron rods the same thickness as the steel ones, twist them together and weld them, draw the welded bars down and fold them, then another weld and another fold, and so on till he'd got something that'd hold an edge. I'll say this much for him: it was a lot of work for one man to do on his own, with just Fat Osvif to do the bellows and the striking, but he didn't waste much time standing about and looking out of the doorway.

Once he'd finished the ironwork, back we went to the place where we'd left the ship, and we got to work on making the new keel. Took us two whole days of wandering about in the forest just to find a tree with the right bend in it – and we had to use maple, because we couldn't find any elm; then another two days' chipping away with hand-axes to shape it, because we had to be pretty bloody precise or it wouldn't fit. Of course, nothing like that ever does fit, no matter how careful you are, so we made it a bit big and counted on having to work it down a little.

Next was the tricky bit. You see, you can't just tear the keel off a ship and knock in a new one, because the keel's what holds the front end of the ship together. If you cracked on and took it out, all the frames and strakes and boards'd spring out of place and you'd never ever get them all back in again. So what we had to do was, we had to haul the ship up onto the flat and build a cradle of timbers for it to sit in; then we had to cut a whole lot of poles and jam them in hard against the sides of the ship to hold everything in place once we'd taken out the keel. That was a bastard of a job, because of course the front end of a ship's all curves, it's not like propping something easy and flat, like a wall; and we couldn't afford to get it wrong, or there we'd be with no bloody ship.

We managed it, though, somehow; and after that came a really nasty job. Because the keel had taken such a scat running aground, the keel-bolts were all bent and bowed out of shape and we couldn't just drift them out, they had to be cut through with a chisel, each one. No fun, that: working on your back reaching up, and hardly able to swing your axe – no hammers, of course, so we had to use the polls of our hand-axes, which meant having the sharp edge buzzing back and forward an inch from your nose all day long.

Once we'd done that, though, it got easier. We got the new keel scarfed into the stem-post good and tight, and the new bolts were a good fit, and we didn't have to shave the keel down nearly as much as we'd expected. It just took a long time, a bloody long time. We tried to work faster, we even tried working at night, with big fires to light the job, but that didn't come to anything and we nearly screwed the whole job up, trying to do fine work when we couldn't see. Anyhow, the point came where we knew we weren't going to get finished before winter. At least, we might *just* have done it and got launched before the ice started to form; but if we didn't make it, we'd be in deep trouble, because if we carried on working on the ship we couldn't lay in food and fuel for the winter, which would mean that as soon as it got cold we'd all be dead. So we had to take the decision: we'd be spending another winter in Meadowland.

We split into two groups. Thorvald and nine others stayed working on the ship, the other twenty took the long walk back to Leif's Booths to get ready for the winter. Now I'm a pretty reasonable carpenter, though I do say so myself; and Kari's lucky if he can cut a mortice in a fence-post and still have ten fingers. So that was good. Kari went back to the Booths, I stayed on with Thorvald.

You know, this sounds really sad, but that was possibly the happiest time of my life. Yes, I was working all day in the cold and the wet, lying on my back on frozen mud, sleeping in the open under one threadbare blanket, eating last spring's wind-dried cod, with everybody in a right mood because Thorvald had gone all quiet with guilt and worry; and yes, we stayed on a week too long because Thorvald insisted on getting the scarf-joint finished, which meant we got caught in a blizzard on the way back to the Booths, got lost, and came within an inch of freezing to death. But that didn't bother me as much as it might've done, because it was six weeks without that bastard Kari. Wonderful feeling, like you've had toothache all your life and suddenly it goes away.

Trouble with that is, though, it just makes it ten times worse when it starts up again.

I remember when we staggered out of that blizzard into the Booths, when we saw the shape of the roofs against the skyline. Part of me was thinking, thank God, I'm not going to freeze and die after all; the rest was wishing we could all stay out there just a little bit longer, to put off the moment when I had to see that stupid face grinning at me again. Now if you'd ever been so cold your fingers and toes *stop* hurting, you'd understand.

That was a very long winter. Didn't just seem that way: the snow kept on falling, the thaw was late, we were rationing the food and the firewood, and every extra day we had to spend in the Booths was like torture. It'd have been bad enough if it'd been like the previous winter, where we'd all sat quiet. But it was worse than that. About halfway through, some of the men started picking quarrels, quarrels turned to fights, a man called Thorbjorn Elbow nearly got killed. Any other time, Thorvald would've stopped it before it got that far; but Thorvald seemed like he'd practically given up being in charge. All he wanted to do was huddle in a dark place up against the wall and worry himself sick about what the frost and the wet were doing to his ship, stuck up on a lot of poles with its belly open and its guts only held in with a few sticks. So when the yelling and the bad temper started, he just pretended he couldn't hear it; and that made it all worse, of course. Really, it's a miracle we didn't all chop each other to pieces, like the heroes in Valhalla, except there wouldn't have been any Choosers of the Slain to sort out the bits and put us all back together again.

But spring came, eventually, and still we hadn't killed each other, so that was all right. The snow was still on the ground as we trudged back to where we'd left the ship, and all the way we were wondering if the bloody thing'd still be there, or whether the winds had blown it down or the thaw-waters had washed it out to sea. Last time I'd seen it − seemed like another life − it'd been stranded up in the air, which is a bloody funny place for a ship to be, and all those poles and props holding it together had made it look like a crane-fly caught in a cobweb. What I was expecting to see was a mess of smashed-up boards and timbers, scattered all over the place, like the mad woman's shit.

Instead, there she was, bless her heart, more or less how we'd left her. She did all right by me, that ship. Remember, it was Bjarni Herjolfson's boat to start with, and she wasn't new when he got her. This was the third time she'd been in those parts, and she'd had to put up with heavy winds, pounding waves, a fair old bashing from rocks and floating ice. Now she'd just had her backbone ripped out and a new one stuck in, a rushed job instead of slow and careful, not to mention spending winter with damn great holes in her, with the melted snow trickling in and out. If she'd been a horse, you'd have knocked her on the head out of simple kindness, but we were relying on her to get us home again. That's a lot to ask, really. I reckon if ships were human instead of made out of wood and nails, we'd all drown.

Of course there were a few bits and pieces that needed tidying up, where some of the props had slipped, or timbers had warped. Bear in mind, our new keel was all green wood, so really we had no idea how much or which way it was going to move as it seasoned. We'd just done our best to get the frames up snug to it so that they'd go some way towards holding it in shape, and hoped for the best. As it turned out, it wasn't too bad at all – a few shakes and wobbles here and there, but nothing we couldn't live with. We finished off the work in no time flat, proofed and caulked the hull as best we could, broke up the scaffolding and launched the ship into the sea. It was a nasty moment when our home-made keel went under water, but she just sort of gave a little wiggle, sat up and floated on as though nothing had happened. I think, any other time, we'd have screamed and yelled and cheered and carried on like anything, but we stood there and looked at her and didn't say a word. There's times when you celebrate, and other times when you're just grateful.

One thing: it perked Thorvald up no end, once we'd got the ship launched and given her a couple of days of trials up and down the coast and back. He wasn't right back to his old self, mind. Mostly, if you wanted to know what you were supposed to be doing next, you'd have to ask him, else he'd just stay put and not say anything. It's like after you've been ill with a fever, and then it breaks: you know the worst of it's passed but you're weak as a baby for days. Thorvald was back with us again from wherever it was he'd been in his mind all winter, but he'd lost all his strength. Really it was just as well we were going home, because he wasn't any use at all.

Just as we were getting ready to leave, Thorvald called us all up onto the beach, where the wreck of the old keel was lying where we'd left it. 'Look,' he said, 'I know it's been tough and we're all in a hurry to get under way, but there's something I'd like you to do for me. I want to set up what's left of the old keel here on the headland, as a sea-mark.'

Well, we didn't argue; but I don't reckon I was the only one who thought: right, and who're we putting this mark up *for*? I couldn't imagine for a moment that Thorvald was planning on coming back there ever again; same for all of us, should go without saying. Maybe he meant it more as a symbolic thing, like a thank-you to God or whatever. Anyhow, we did as he said; and then we pushed on east till we came to a place where the mouths of two fjords joined. There was a little tongue sticking out between them, all covered in dense forest. We didn't need to stop for anything, but Thorvald told us to put in and take on some extra firewood. I think it was just an excuse on his part, so he could get off the ship and walk about for a bit. Why he wanted to do that, I have no idea; but he could be like that sometimes, right down one moment and right up the next. Anyway, we went ashore and stood about, not really having any idea what we were supposed to be doing; Thorvald walked up and down a bit, looking around him like a man at a farm sale, and then he stopped and grinned.

'You know what,' he said, 'I like it here. I think this is where I'd like to build a farm.'

Well, we didn't say anything, but you didn't have to be clever to guess he'd finally come loose from his pins, as we say back home. Not difficult to see why: winter at Leif's Booths, the worry about the ship, everything going wrong and the tension in the crew. Obviously he was somewhere else inside his head, because that was no place for a farm: no grass, no meadows, just a rocky finger covered in trees stuck out into the sea. No, my guess is that, just like all of us, he had a picture of his farm which he'd been carrying round inside him for God knew how long, the place he went back to when he shut his eyes. Now we were going home and the whole trip had been a failure, he must've known deep down that he was never going to find his imaginary house, same as the rest of us; so I think he'd got to the stage where, instead of it just being there when he closed his eyes, it was starting to be there all the time. It's sad when somebody goes like that, and it makes things awkward even if he isn't supposed to be in charge of the ship and everything.

Just then, somebody (Big Thorbjorn I think it was, the man who followed the bees) got all excited and started pointing at something a way up the beach. Once we realised he wasn't kidding around we looked where he was pointing, and sure enough there was something.

First off, it looked like three small sand dunes; except there weren't any dunes anywhere else on the beach. We went a bit closer and saw it was three little boats up-ended. Funny things they were, too. Not made of wood, like proper boats; they had frames made of skinny old poles with hides stretched over them. Sigurd Squint reckoned he'd seen something of the kind in Ireland, or rather his grandfather had. Not that we could give a damn.

For a moment, I thought maybe they'd been washed up there; but as we got closer, I knew I could forget about that, because they weren't just thrown up on the beach like driftwood, they'd been hauled up and set carefully straight and side by side.

Question was, of course: who by?

We couldn't see anybody, naturally. So we stood around for a bit, talking in whispers; then Thorvald seemed to remember who he was supposed to be, and started giving orders. He told Big Thorbjorn and Kari and me to come with him, and fetch along our axes just in case.

Must admit I felt a bit of a fool, creeping along the beach in broad daylight like I was stalking birds. A few moments earlier we'd all been strolling up and down talking out loud, so it was a bit late for stealth; also we could see a long way up and down the beach, which was open and flat, no place to take cover, and there wasn't anyone besides us. But what the hell, we crept along on the sides of our feet until we were right up close to the first boat. Thorvald held up three fingers, then folded them down one by one to count us down, and when he'd folded down the third finger we jumped on the boat and turned it over.

Bugger me if there wasn't someone under it, fast asleep. Three men, all snuggled up together like puppies in the barn. Can't say they looked all that different from us; they were dressed in buckskins and furs, with hide boots on their feet and their hoods pulled up over their heads. Their skins were a bit darker than ours and they didn't have beards. Sound sleepers, though, because they didn't wake up.

When he'd done staring at them, Thorvald turned round and beckoned to where the rest of our lot were standing by; so up the beach they came, obviously wondering what the hell was going on. Between us we lifted off the other two boats, and sure enough there were another two lots of three men, also sound asleep.

It's a good many years now, but I still can't really figure out what happened after that. Kari reckons he saw one of the men reach for something inside his coat, and the way he did it made it look like he'd got an axe in there, or a knife. Helgi Thormodson told me afterwards that Thorvald gave the order, but if that was the case I didn't hear him, and nobody else remembered it either. Sigurd Squint said many years later that Thorvald started it and we all pitched in after him, and that's how I prefer to remember it. Doesn't make a great deal of difference. You look for a moment, a point where the balance tips or something gives way and breaks, but generally it doesn't matter, the details. It's the main thing that leads to all the stuff that comes afterwards, and you're just acting like kids if you try and say it was his fault more than mine.

Anyhow, we killed them; any rate, eight out of nine. The ninth one sort of got overlooked. He stayed there quite still while we were laying into his mates with our axes and our boots and what have you, and I guess we all thought some-one else had seen to him; then, quick as you like, he jumped up and started running like a deer, not looking round to see if anybody was chasing him. He just ran, and we charged off after him, of course; he led us up the beach a fair way – he was quick, light on his feet – then suddenly doubled back and slipped through between us, neat as anything. We tried to grab him, but he was too nimble – it was like when you're trying to catch up the chickens, and the last one always nips in between your legs and darts off across the yard before you can lay hold to her – and next thing we knew, the cheeky bugger'd dragged down one of the boats into the water and was paddling away like mad.

Four or five of us went splashing in after him, but they were too late, they just got wet and gave up. Thorvald dashed back to the ship after his bow and arrows, but he was wasting his time. The rest of us stood and watched the little boat getting smaller, and I was saying to myself, What the hell was all that about? We just killed eight men and I haven't got a clue why.

I say *we*. Me, I know I killed one of them for sure. He was right there at my feet, and I bent my knees and scat my axe into the top of his head, like you do when you're cutting coppice and you stick your axe into a stump so you won't lose it in the brash. I'd never done anything like that before, and I remember how it jarred my arm right up to the elbow, and I thought, Fuck me, that hurt – Then it was a bit of a struggle getting the axe out again, and he was twitching even though he was dead; and by then it was all done, and we had the ninth man running away to take our minds off it. I've thought about it a bit since then, and for some reason it seems to matter to me whether I killed that one before or after everybody else pitched in; but to be honest with you, I've got no idea. Don't get me wrong, I haven't been losing sleep all these years, or burning myself up with guilt. I've done worse things in my life, specially since I've been here in the Guards with you Greeks; got the commendations to prove it, too. And back home, of course, people are always a bit free with their axes, which causes no end of trouble; but there always seems to be a reason, just like when you're a soldier and the officer says, 'That lot over there, and don't let any of them get away,' so you don't. No: I think that what's stuck in my mind was the way that bugger ran. It wasn't human, it was like an animal; the way, I don't know, the way they're always expecting to get attacked, so when you startle them they just run, no panic, no fear; and if you don't happen to get the deer or the pig or whatever, you watch it into the distance, and when it's half a mile away and it knows it's safe, it just stops and drops its head and starts feeding again, because that's how life is.

'Well?' I said.

'What?' Eyvind had been squinting up at the sun. In the distance, Kari and Harald were playing some sort of bastard chess with only one king. Their games tended to last a very long time, and always ended in bad temper and sulking. I noticed that both of them, the old man and the young, sat with their sword-scabbards pulled round on their belts and laid across their knees, the right hand resting on the grip. I'd always assumed that it was more comfortable that way.

'So what happened next?' I asked.

Eyvind smiled, though not at me. 'Ah,' he said.

For a while nobody said anything; we just stood, catching our breath. Then someone or other – it may have been Saemund Limp, but who cares? – someone said, 'So who do you reckon they were, then?'

Helgi Thormodson turned one of them over with his boot. 'Leather boats,' he said. 'I think they could be Irish.'

'That's right,' said Sigurd Squint. 'They use leather boats in Ireland, for fishing and hauling peat.'

Thorvald shook his head. 'You're trying to tell me they came all the way from Ireland in those?'

'Not necessarily,' someone else said. 'Maybe these are just, you know, lighters. Like, we've got a small boat of our own, for coming ashore when you can't beach the ship—'

'Thank you,' Thorvald snapped, 'I know what a boat's for.'

'That'd mean there's three Irish ships,' Sigurd said.

'Or a big ship with three boats,' someone else suggested.

Helgi was kneeling down beside the dead man, turning his head back and forth by the chin. 'Doesn't look Irish to me,' he said. 'And no, I haven't been to Ireland, since you ask. But I never heard the Irish don't have hair on their chins.'

'Maybe they're monks,' someone said. 'Monks shave their beards off, someone told me once. And there's loads of monks in Ireland. They live on remote islands, for the peace and quiet.'

Someone said he'd heard that, too. 'I heard tell there were Irish monks living in Iceland when the first settlers came,' he added. 'They go places where nobody lives, so they can pray without being disturbed. Then, when anybody shows up, they move on.'

Thorvald thought about that. 'Might account for why we haven't run into them before,' he said. 'But if they've been living here any time, you'd have thought we'd have seen *something*.'

Helgi reminded him about the rick-cover we'd found last summer. 'That could've been them,' he said. 'Mind you, it's hard to tell from a few sticks and bits of bark.'

'If we'd caught that other bugger, we could've asked him,' Big Thorbjorn said. Nobody pointed out that we could have asked all nine if we hadn't been in such a hurry to split heads.

'Anyhow,' Thorvald said, 'we're going home, so who gives a damn? Whoever they are, I don't suppose they know the way to Brattahlid.'

Nobody had anything to add to that; so we made a fire and burned the leather boats, then got back in the ship and cast off. We were all ready to get started for home, but the wind had dropped away completely, and all we could do was sit and wait.

We'd been there a while, when Helgi, who was down in the stern by the post, called out, 'You know those Irish boats?'

'Well?' Thorvald said.

'There's a whole lot of them,' said Helgi, 'coming down the fjord.'

That wasn't so good, we thought. Helgi counted them; there were thirty at least, he said, and they were cutting along at a great lick, headed straight at us. As they closed in, Helgi added that he could see a lot of the men in them were waving bows and arrows at us.

'We're screwed,' someone moaned and, to be fair, he had a point there. My guess is that they saw the smoke from the fire when we burned the boats, or else the one who'd got away had raised the alarm. If we were dead in the water and they had bows and arrows with them, they could simply buzz round us and sting us to death, if that was what they had in mind – and something told me they weren't rushing up at us just to see if we wanted to buy any local pottery or baskets.

'Right,' Thorvald said, suddenly, like he'd just woken up. 'We'll need to run out the spare sail along the gunwales. If we rig it pretty slack, their arrows'll just get snagged up in it.' And that's true, too: a good tip, if you're ever in that situation. Kari and me jumped up and fetched out the sail, while some of the others set up posts to hang it from. We didn't have any proper shields, of course, or any armour or stuff like that, since the last thing we thought we'd be doing was any fighting. As for weapons, Thorvald was the only man with a bow, and it was a pissy little short-range deer-hunter's job; the rest of us had our hand-axes and knives. Like the man had said, we were screwed, really.

They started shooting at us from about seventy yards, and sure enough, the sail stopped most of the arrows; they got tangled up and fell on the deck, or into the sea. I got the impression they weren't aiming at any of us in particular, just loosing away at the ship generally. Even so, one arrow came a bit too close for my taste. It cut through the sail and buzzed past the end of my nose, so close I could smell the bloody thing. Then it stuck into the deck-boards and the tip of the head snapped off. There wasn't anything sensible I could do, so I picked it up and had a look at it. Very thin in the shaft it was, like some sort of very tough reed. The fletchings were long and tied on with backstrap sinew, and the reason it'd bust off in the deck was that the head was made of grey flint.

I was crouching there with that stupid arrow in my hand when someone started to yell, and I looked up to see that the sail was beginning to fill. That was a welcome sight; the wind just sort of picked up out of nowhere, just at the right time, and almost immediately we were whisking along at a good pace, leaving the leather boats behind. A few more arrows sailed over and flopped down, but there was hardly any force behind them. Pretty close, I said to myself, but we'd got away with it, so that was all right.

'Did anybody else get hit?' Thorvald called out.

We all sang out that no, we were fine; then it struck me what he'd said: did anybody *else* get hit. I stood up, and I wasn't the only one.

Thorvald was leaning against the rail, with his left hand pressed into his right armpit. There was blood running out between his fingers, and it wasn't looking very good. I was thinking, that ought to be seen to, before he loses any more blood. Then he wobbled a bit, like a drunk, and sat down hard on his arse.

The arrow, he told us, was a ricochet; it'd hit the gunwale and flown up, and of course, as soon as Thorvald had seen arrows incoming, instinctively he'd raised his right arm to shield his face. It'd gone in pretty deep, and when he'd tried to pull it out the shaft had busted off in his hand. He was as surprised as any of us when we showed him the flint arrow-heads; you wouldn't have thought a bit of old flaked stone'd cut so well, he said. He was genuinely relieved, I think, that nobody else'd been hurt. The impression I got was that he didn't reckon he mattered very much by that stage; no great loss, he said, with a grin, which was his way of telling us he didn't want us to go back and take it out on the leather-boat people. We were glad to hear him say that, because none of us fancied the idea much, I don't think.

Anyhow, Thorvald died pretty soon after that. We put in at the next headland we came to and buried him there. Then we realised, none of us could remember if he was a Christian or followed the old ways; fair enough, I guess, because it's not the sort of thing you talk about much, since people can be touchy about that stuff. In the end, we decided that our Heavenly Father tended to be a bit fussy about doing things properly, while Thor couldn't give a toss how you get rid of a dead body; so we made up a pair of crosses out of cord-wood and stuck them at Thorvald's head and feet, and someone said a bit of the Mass, and then we left him.

Well (Eyvind went on, after a while), that's about all there is to tell about Thorvald's trip to Meadowland. All of us except Thorvald got home all right; we picked up the wind a few days later and it blew us back to Greenland, about three days up the west coast from Eiriksfjord. We hadn't been looking forward to telling the Eiriksons how we'd come home without their brother; but Leif took it pretty well, said it couldn't be helped and anyhow, it wasn't our fault. Thorstein Eirikson didn't say anything, just stumped off and sat on his own. Freydis, the sister, got in a bit of a state, but she was like that. Anyhow, nobody seemed inclined to get stroppy with us, so that was all right.

Thinking about it − I've done a lot of that over the years, thought about some of the things that happened on that trip, and what keeps coming back to me is that it all started to go bad on us once we'd already decided to go home again: first the keel getting smashed, which meant we were stranded there another winter; then the whole thing with the leather-boat people, and Thorvald getting killed right at the very last moment, if you see what I mean.

Sometimes I think that maybe Meadowland didn't want us to go, like it'd grown fond of us or something stupid like that. When we got there, that first time we landed, with Leif, we found everything we needed to live laid out for us ready and waiting: food you could just go out and help yourself to, wood and turf for building and fuel, right down to the iron ore in the bog. It even tried to give us booze when it found we couldn't get along without it. Then, when we made up our minds to leave, it got nasty with us − or how else do you explain that we'd been there three times, stayed for several years in Thorvald's case, and it was only when we were sailing away that we ran into the locals for the first time? Oh, they weren't Irish after all, the leather-boat people; Sigurd Squint had got that completely wrong. We found that out right enough the next time we went there.

CHAPTER
EIGHT

'Can I ask you a question?' I said.

Kari looked up from his bowl of porridge. 'Sure,' he said. 'Anything you like.'

I took a moment to choose my words. 'Tell me,' I said, 'why Harald Sigurdson cooks our food.'

Kari laughed. 'You mean,' he said, 'why do we make him do the cooking, when he hates doing it and he's so useless at it?'

I nodded. 'I'm just curious,' I added.

'Good for him,' Kari said. 'You see, he's had a hard life, young Harald. When he was just a kid, his brother, King Olaf the Saint, went to war with the Danes and the Swedes and got himself killed. Harald got away, just about; he made his way to Russia – he's an off-relation of King Jaroslav, I think on his mother's side. But they didn't really want him hanging around there, so he came South and joined the Guards, because we'll take anybody so long as they're big and vicious. Of course, being a prince of the blood and half-brother to a genuine martyred saint, he reckons cooking porridge is beneath his dignity; so, naturally, we make him do it. Character-forming, see.'

'Ah,' I said. 'That sort of makes sense, I suppose.'

'He's absolute crap at it, mind,' Kari said with a sigh. 'Which shows that he's not as thick as he looks. It's a basic rule in the Guards. If there's something you really don't want to do, volunteer to do it and do it very, very badly; you won't be asked again, and sooner or later you'll find something you *are* good at, and everyone's happy. But that approach doesn't work with old hands like Eyvind and me. The worse he cooks, the more we make him do it. It's tough being a mentor, but he'll thank us when he comes into his own and gets his throne back.'

'Right,' I said. 'Why?'

'Why what?'

'Why will he thank you for humiliating him?'

Kari clicked his tongue. 'It's an honour thing,' he said. 'You're probably too civilised and effete to understand. Basically, though, it's the same idea as when a boy starts off helping his dad and his uncles with the coppicing, and they send him back to the house to fetch the left-handed billhook.'

'I see,' I said, frowning slightly. 'This teaches him obedience and stamina, presumably.'

Kari looked at me. 'There's no such thing as a left-handed billhook,' he explained. 'The point is, your elders make a fool out of you when you're young, so you can make a fool out of the next generation when you've grown old and wise. It's all part of becoming a man, or something.'

I grinned at him. 'I wouldn't know about that,' I said.

Kari nodded slightly, to acknowledge a point scored. 'Well, quite,' he said. 'But presumably you've got some similar kind of initiation thing in the clerking trade, haven't you?'

'No, actually,' I lied. 'When a young man starts work in the chancellery or the records office, the older clerks go out of their way to teach him the best practice, and help him out with anything he may have difficulties with. That way, he fits in straight away and there's no disruption to the work of the office.'

Kari shrugged. 'It's like I always say,' he replied. 'You Greeks are bloody clever, but you haven't got a clue.'

I was getting just a little tired of these Northerners' attitude towards my people and my City. 'For a start,' I said, 'you can stop calling us Greeks, when we're the great and indivisible Roman Empire, and we've been in business for just on a thousand years – longer, if you don't make a distinction between the Empire and the Republic, which was founded seventeen hundred and eighty years ago—'

'You can't be Romans,' Kari interrupted. 'Rome's in Italy. And it's hundreds of years since Rome was part of the empire. And you don't talk Latin, you talk Greek, and none of you are Italians. In fact, most of you aren't even Greeks any more, you're bits and pieces of all sorts of things, all bundled up together and cross-bred, foreigners in your own City. Which is silly, if you ask me.'

I tried to look all dignified and aloof, but I've never had the knack. 'Being Roman is more a state of mind than a simple accident of birth,' I said. 'It's something you aspire to. We tend to judge a man by where he's arrived at, not where he came from.'

'Whatever,' Kari said, with a grin. 'My lot, we reckon a man's no better and no worse than what his neighbours think of him. It's a pretty hit-and-miss way of putting a value on someone, but it's the same with all your various systems of weights and measures: doesn't matter what the standard is so long as everybody's agreed on using it.'

I had an uncomfortable feeling that I was losing an argument here, though I wasn't quite sure what the argument was about, or which side I was on. 'At any rate,' I said, 'we're a nation, not just a bunch of unruly individuals. We work together, under the direction of the Emperor and our superiors, which is how we manage to get things done. You people—' I shrugged dismissively. 'Look, even this story you two've been telling me proves my point exactly. You people can't do anything, you can't take an opportunity when it presents itself.'

'Right,' Kari said, nodding. 'Like we couldn't settle Iceland, or Greenland.'

I laughed. 'My point exactly. When we Romans came to Britain, we settled it and held it for four hundred years; we built roads and towns and bridges, we brought the natives into the Empire, taught them to speak Latin, made them into Romans, like us. And then—'

'And then,' Kari said, 'a bunch of Swedes and Danes came along and took it away from you, and last time I heard, they're still there. Mind you,' he added, 'I'd never have known about that if I hadn't come here, because in the North nobody's ever heard of your lot being in England. They think all the big stone walls and houses were built by the giants, before Thor wiped them all out. See what I mean? Apart from a few fallen-down old buildings, which'll be grown over with grass some day and forgotten, it's like you people were never there at all. You stayed for a while, did a bit of building work and left. You remember it, but they don't.'

'Right.' I smiled. Never argue with a Greek. 'Just like you and Meadowland.'

'Ah.' Kari shook his head. 'That was different.'

'Was it?'

'Of course,' Kari replied. 'You haven't heard the whole story yet.'

★

Thorstein Eirikson (Kari said) was the youngest son. He was the one who married Gudrid, the girl that Leif rescued from the wrecked ship. He'd been old Eirik's favourite, which probably explains why Leif and he never got on. The way Leif saw it, Thorstein got the best of everything without ever having to earn it; Leif had to prove he was worthy of taking over Brattahlid before Eirik'd give him any responsibility in running the place, which meant Leif had to work twice as hard as anybody else just to be treated equally with the others. Thorstein, on the other hand, could laze around the house half the day and not get yelled at for being bone idle; and when he did do a day's work, he got praised for it, instead of it just being taken for granted.

Thorstein saw it a bit differently. He reckoned that there wasn't any point in him working himself to the bone when he wasn't ever going to inherit, with two elder brothers in the way. True, Eirik tried to make it up to him by favouring him over the other two – I think the old man saw more of himself in Thorstein than in the youngster's brothers, and there was some truth in that – but that just pissed Thorstein off all the more, because he knew that he was just as good as the other two, he could've earned fair and square what Eirik gave him for doing nothing, if only he'd been given the chance, but of course he never was. Unfairness cuts both ways, see: it's even more humiliating to be unfairly favoured than unfairly put upon, if you're someone with a bit of spirit, like Thorstein was.

While they were all kids, of course, there was Thorvald in the middle to keep the peace; and Thorvald was the quiet, easygoing one, had to be or else there'd have been bloodshed. But when Thorvald didn't come back from Meadowland and there was just Leif and Thorstein left, things started to get a bit fraught. Of course, it didn't help that Leif had got the farm and Thorstein had got the girl. Far worse, they had their sister Freydis unmarried and still at home, and she had the knack of making things just that little bit worse that makes all the difference.

It all caught fire one night at dinner. Leif had been out all day with us, turning the hay. We'd cut it during a dry spell in a wet summer, and before we could get it stacked and covered, the rain started again, so it was lying out in the wet, spoiling. Couldn't be helped, but Leif seemed to think it was somehow his fault, for not reading the weather better. Thorstein hadn't said a word, but he didn't really need to; Leif just assumed that Thorstein was looking down his nose at him, thinking he wouldn't have screwed up like that if he'd been the farmer at Brattahlid instead of Leif. Probably Thorstein *was* thinking that way; but he'd stayed home all day while Leif was out in the meadows. Actually, he'd been working hard, shoring up the wall of the long barn where it'd been weakened by the damp; if he hadn't noticed there was something wrong and spent all day fixing it, we'd have had the barn collapse and then we'd have been really screwed. But Thorstein didn't think to tell Leif what he'd done, he expected Leif to notice it himself and thank him. Leif, meanwhile, reckoned Thorstein had stayed home because he was lazy, and because he'd washed his hands of the haymaking because Leif had cut too early.

So you had Leif and Thorstein sitting up on the top table not saying a word all evening; and Freydis yapping away in a loud voice about how bad it'd be if the hay spoiled, because nobody else had any to spare, and what a pity it'd be if they had to slaughter all the young stock for want of fodder. Then Gudrid tried to make things nice between the brothers, but that didn't go right at all: she started telling Leif how hard Thorstein had been working on the barn wall, and Leif took that as a personal criticism, because he hadn't noticed it as well as cutting the hay too early, and Thorstein got angry with Gudrid for telling Leif about the wall, and Leif got angry with Thorstein for shouting at Gudrid; and before long, the rest of us were sitting there looking down at our feet and hoping it wasn't going to come to fighting, because whose side were we meant to be on? It was like that a lot of the time at Brattahlid, mind you, but not usually as out in the open.

Then Thorstein started up a completely new line of attack, and it caught Leif by surprise. It was a bloody shame, Thorstein said, that Leif should've left their poor brother's body to rot in Meadowland, in unconsecrated ground, putting his eternal soul at risk, when anyone with a shred of decent feeling would've gone out there and brought him home. Particularly, Thorstein went on, since Leif knew the place so well, even had houses over there to stay in. Somehow he made it sound like Leif refusing to give Thorvald the houses – you remember, he only lent him Leif's Booths, he wouldn't give him them – had been the real reason why everything had gone wrong at the end and Thorvald had died. Of course, that was complete bullshit; but Thorstein hadn't said it out straight, he'd only implied it, so Leif couldn't very well defend himself, all he could do was let the accusation lie. Anyway, the long and short of it was that Thorstein worked himself up into a real state, while Leif just sat there getting icier and icier, and the end of it was Thorstein declaring that if nobody else was prepared to bring Thorvald home, he'd have to do it. Leif looked at him hard and silent for quite a long time, and then said, fine, you do that; and then he got up and went to bed.

Well, in most places I've been, you'd have expected that next morning the brothers'd have made it up, blamed it all on the booze, and that would've been that. No chance. First thing, when Leif came out of the back room into the hall, Thorstein was waiting for him. All polite and formal, he asked him if he could borrow the ship and some of the men for his trip to Meadowland. Leif never batted an eye; help yourself, he said, when were you planning on leaving? Thorstein said, as soon as possible, and I don't think they spoke to each other again until the ship was ready to launch.

Now I'm only too glad to admit that I'm not the brightest man who ever lived; but as soon as I heard that, I made a pretty sensible decision. Nothing on Earth, I decided, was going to get me on that ship again; not money or duty or threats, nothing. They could tie me up in a sack while I was asleep and carry me on board, but I'd jump over the side before we were clear of Eiriksfjord. You don't need me to tell you why, not if you've been listening to a word I've said. As far as I was concerned, my seafaring career was over, and as for Meadowland, I never wanted to see it ever again. Even when Eyvind suddenly made up his mind he was going (and you could've knocked me down with a cobweb when I heard), I never wavered, not one little bit. And if Thorstein tried to pressure me into going, I'd climb up on the roof, jump off and bust my leg. You never came across such a determined man in all your life.

So, two days before the ship's due to sail, Thorstein comes up to me in the barn, where I'm carrying hay down to the sheds. 'You haven't come to see me yet about joining my crew,' he says.

'That's right,' I tell him. 'Look, no offence, but I'm not going. Nothing personal, but I've had enough of that ship, and Meadowland too. I wish you all the best, of course, but my mind's made up.'

Thorstein rubbed his eye, like he'd got a bit of dust in it.

'That's a pity,' he said. 'You know the ship and the run inside out. You'd be an asset.'

'Very kind of you,' I said firmly, 'but I've made up my mind.'

'I see.' He looked away, but stayed where he was. 'I tell you what,' he said. 'If you come with us this time, I'll give you a farm of your own.'

You know how it is when you get that sinking, oh-shit feeling in your stomach, when you know something really bad's about to happen; like, the tree you're cutting down starts creaking before you expected it to, and there's no time to look round, your only chance is to run for it and hope you can sprint the length of the tree before it comes down and flattens you.

'When you say a farm of my own,' I said quietly, 'what exactly do you—?'

'I mean,' Thorstein said, 'I'll give you a house, over in the Western Settlement, and three hundred acres of good grazing; I'll throw in six cows, a dozen sheep and a bull-calf, and enough flour and hay to see you over winter. In case you're wondering, it's part of my share of what I inherited from Thorvald. I couldn't think of a better use to put it to than helping fetch him home.'

My head was starting to hurt. 'Is there any water with it?' I asked him

He nodded. 'River runs all the way down the southern boundary,' he said. 'And if I remember right, there's a well in the yard and another in your north top field. Water won't be a problem at all.'

I gave him a long, hard look. 'Don't get me wrong,' I said, 'but that's a hell of a price to pay just so I'll tag along. I mean, it's not like there's anything I can actually do, apart from coiling and uncoiling rope.'

'I'll be the judge of that,' he said. 'And remember, we're only going there to pick up my brother's body, nothing more. With a bit of luck, we could be there and back in one season, before the ice starts to form; so no having to spend another winter at Leif's Booths. It won't be a big party, I'm taking twenty instead of thirty-five, so it won't be all hellish cramped on the ship.'

I looked at him again. 'My own farm,' I said.

'That's right,' he said, grinning at me. 'You could call it Karisvatn, after the lake.'

'There's a lake?'

'Didn't I mention the lake?' Bastard knew he'd got me then. 'Oh yes, whopping great big lake, and in the season it's completely covered with ducks and geese. All you'd need to do is sit in your porch and throw a stone, and there's dinner.'

I suppose some bugger must've told him, about me wanting my very own lake. And the Western Settlement wasn't so bad, a bit chilly in winter maybe but good land, not so crowded as the eastern region.

'Thanks,' I said, 'but no. I made my decision, and I'm sticking to it.'

He sighed. 'That's a great shame,' he said. 'Eyvind'll be disappointed, too. See, I'm giving him the land on the other side of the lake, so you'd have been neighbours.'

You can only stand so much. The one thing that'd been bothering me was the thought of leaving my oldest and best mate behind at Brattahlid when I moved out west. But if Eyvind was going to be right next to me, the other side of my lake—

'All right,' I said.

Well, it's different, isn't it, doing things for other people rather than yourself. As I lay in bed that night, listening to everybody else snoring, I found myself thinking, I don't really need the whole lake; maybe Eyvind and I can sort of share it between us; he can have the side nearest his place, and I'll have the other half – assuming, of course, that the ducks and the geese don't all hang around on his side.

Thorstein smiled, thanked me and pushed off, leaving me with the hay and my own long thoughts. I was still thinking those thoughts when it came time to get our few personal bits and pieces on board, then cast off and go. They were still just as long, but now at least I didn't have the option of doing as they told me.

Leif had come down to see Thorstein off; like I told you, they didn't exchange a word all the time Thorstein had been doing up the ship. Now he stood on the beach looking all solemn, and he'd brought along a going-away present for his brother, all parcelled up in a bundle of old wool offcuts. 'I'd like you to have this,' he said. 'It used to belong to Dad.'

Thorstein frowned and pulled off the bits of rags. It was a sword; not just any sword, either, but the one that hung off the wall right next to where Leif sat in the hall. You've got to admire how he went about it; because a sword's a real aristocratic gift, like kings give to their favourite earls. Also, Leif had absolutely no use for it, so his wonderful gesture hadn't actually cost him anything. But the real idea behind it was to play on Thorstein's nerves just a little bit. Give a man a sword, you're telling him he's probably going to get mixed up in fighting sooner or later; and the one thing that'd been preying on Thorstein's mind about the trip was the fear of running into the leather-boat people while he was over there. Like I said, Leif had a flair for that sort of thing.

'Now hang on,' I interrupted. 'I think you're being a bit too cynical about this sword business. Now I don't know very much about your people or the North, but it seems to me that giving your brother your father's sword has got to be a pretty significant gesture of reconciliation. I mean, don't you people make a great fuss about the family sword? You hand them down from generation to generation, or you bury them with your great heroes. This is a big deal, right?'

Kari smirked at me. 'You're right, of course,' he said. 'And completely wrong at the same time, again of course. Yes, there are old swords that've been in families for a very long time, particularly the big, rich families in Norway and Denmark and Sweden, kings and earls and so on. But that's not being sentimental; back in the good old days, they made them the hard way, by twisting and folding and welding. Then, about five generations ago, traders started fetching home cheap German swords by the barrelful, made from solid steel rather than the old way. Nobody could be bothered making folded swords any more, when you could buy one almost as good for a third of the price, so the Northern smiths got out of the sword business. But the German swords aren't really up to the same standard, or at least that's what the rich farmers reckon, and they're the only ones who can afford to own the things. And as for what you said about Leif – well, yes, the sword he gave Thorstein had belonged to Red Eirik, but I don't imagine he ever pulled it out of its scabbard. He was a regular killer, Eirik, but he did his killing with a hand-axe, same as everybody else, and he did it from behind or when the bloke was tying his bootlace or looking the other way, because he may've been a vicious bugger but he wasn't an idiot. No, Eirik got hold of that sword because a Danish trader stayed the winter at Brattahlid, but he buggered off in the middle of the night without paying for his board and lodging; but in the dark, he left one of his bundles of stock behind – twelve ells of foreign coloured cloth, a walrus-ivory chess set and that sword. Naturally, Eirik kept the stuff as part settlement of the trader's bill. He only hung the sword on the wall because he reckoned it gave the place a touch of class.'

Anyhow (Kari went on) we set sail from Eiriksfjord on a bright, warm summer morning. The biggest surprise, as far as I was concerned, was that Thorstein insisted on dragging his wife along – you remember, Gudrid, the woman from the shipwreck that Leif was so keen on. My guess is, he didn't want to leave her behind at Brattahlid, and I think he may have had a point there. She didn't seem particularly happy to be on the trip, but she soon proved she was perfectly at home on a ship. In fact, she coped rather better than most of us, as it turned out.

We had a really smooth, fast run of it, right up to the point where we caught sight of Leif's Booths in the distance. Then the weather changed, just a little bit.

First we got caught in a right bastard of a gale. Ironically, it was the same wind we'd ridden on each of our return journeys from Meadowland, and I've told you already how fast it carried us along . This time, though, made the other times look like a gentle sneeze. How we didn't capsize I don't know. There wasn't anything we could do except ride it out and hope we stayed afloat and in one piece. It carried us two days and one night; on the second evening it stopped dead, and then the fog came down. It was bad. You could shut your eyes and not notice any difference in the light.

Don't ask me how long we sat in that bloody fog, with no wind and not a clue about where we were. It was a long wait until the fog lifted; and when it did, it was still too hazy to get a fix by the sun, let alone by the stars at night. Long and short of it was, we were lost. All we knew was, we were somewhere in the sea between Meadowland and Greenland, which was a fat lot of use. So Thorstein took his best guess, just before the fog closed in again. A bit of a wind came up after we'd been there three or four days. Thorstein reckoned it was north-west, so we followed it as best we could. Seemed, as they say, like a good idea at the time. When next the fog lifted, we were still none the wiser about where we were. Thorstein said, let's press on, we must be nearly there by now. He was wrong, of course. We'd been plodding along for nine days or so when eventually the sun came out enough for Thorstein to hazard a guess about where we'd pitched up. The bad news was, we appeared to have been sailing round in a big circle.

Things were starting to get a bit tense, mostly because the food had run out. Now really there's no excuse for starving to death in the middle of the sea, not so long as you've got a few fish-hooks, and spare rope you can unwind to make lines. But it's a bugger having to eat your fish raw because there's no charcoal. Water wasn't an issue, because it rained most nights, enough to fill half a dozen buckets.

By now, we'd all had about as much as we could take. Tempers were starting to fray, and nobody had anything good to say about Thorstein's navigating. Actually, that was unfair, because nobody could've done much in that fog. Even with a bearing-dial you need to be able to see the sun. Also, we wouldn't have got lost to begin with if we hadn't been hit by that freak wind that blew us away from Leif's Booths. But the crew weren't in a mood to be reasonable. Quite a few of them were all for chucking Thorstein over the side; in fact, we'd probably have done it, except nobody else seemed to fancy the job of finding our way home. So instead we contented ourselves by giving Thorstein a hard time. He tried to bluster us down but that didn't get him very far, probably because we could tell he was scared. If you want to control a ship by making threats, you've got to make the men believe you'll carry them out. Once Thorstein realised he was a hair's breadth away from being knocked on the head and pitched into the sea, he went very quiet and sat huddled up next to the sternpost, which didn't help anything.

Believe it or not, it was Gudrid who made us snap out of it. Someone'd got on her nerves with their constant whining and complaining, and out of the blue she went for him; jumped up from where she'd been sitting, grabbed the nearest thing to hand, which happened to be one of the buckets we'd put out to catch rainwater, and gave the poor bastard such a scat round the head you could hear it right down the other end of the ship: a thick, chunky thumping noise, like driving in a fence post with an oak maul. Made me jump, I can tell you; I thought the ship had run aground or something. Anyhow, the whole ship was dead quiet for two or three heartbeats, and then someone laughed, and everybody else joined in, laughing and cheering. For some reason, that made Gudrid lose it completely; she started yelling and shrieking at us, called us all a load of stupid kids. 'It's all your fault,' she shouted. 'You've been on this route before, you're supposed to know the way.' Actually, that was overstating it, because out of the twenty of us only five, me and Eyvind included, had been on any of the previous Meadowland trips. But there's nothing like being yelled at by a woman to stop you in your tracks. I mean, if a man kicks up a fuss and starts calling you names, you can bash his face in and that somehow proves that you were right and he was wrong. Can't do that with women. You try and argue with them, and that's a bit like trying to swat bees with your hand; mostly they just dance out of the way, and if you do manage to connect, they just sting you anyway. Or you shut your face and try and keep a dignified silence, and of course that doesn't work either. So, she told us our fortunes loud and clear, and we just sat still and quiet, feeling embarrassed, so that when she stopped we were all so relieved we couldn't be bothered snarling at each other any more. I mean, there was a very long silence, and then we started talking to each other nice and friendly, as though nothing had happened.

Finally the fog lifted for good, and we picked up a slow but steady wind, which we held for three days. The fourth morning, Thorstein woke us up, yelling and bawling: land, at last.

Turned out we were back to Greenland, off the northern edge of the Western Settlement.

Well, we had mixed feelings about that. Yes, it was bloody fantastic to draw the ship up on shore and walk away from it; but you couldn't help feeling a bit stupid, all those weeks getting soaked to the skin and floundering about in the fog, and we ended up a couple of days' sail from where we started out from. We were going to get laughed at, we knew, soon as we showed up back in Eiriksfjord with nothing to show for our adventure; so when the farmer at Lysufjord, which was where we were, offered to put us up for a day or two before we went home, we were happy to accept.

Now I can see where a foreigner like you might get confused by Northern names, because there's so few of them. The farmer at Lysufjord was called Thorstein; but I can tell you won't be able to tell him apart from Thorstein Eirikson, unless I help you out a little. That first evening, when we'd had a good feed and a few drinks, he told us people called him Black Thorstein, so I'll do the same.

God only knows why Black Thorstein offered to put us up in the first place, because he was a miserable bugger, not sociable. He was well off, at least by Greenland standards, and he didn't begrudge us his food and beer; but he wasn't interested in hearing about our adventures, outside of a very short summary – 'We were headed somewhere but there was a storm and we got lost' – and he wasn't too keen on talking himself, either. In fact, the only one of us he seemed to have any time for was Gudrid, and he was all over her like a hand-me-down shirt. That didn't go down terribly well with his wife, a big woman by the name of Grimhild. When I say big, by the way, I don't just mean fat, or even tall. She was bloody massive: arms and legs like a troll, great big hands and feet. She wasn't all that fat, actually, just large all over. Black Thorstein was a big man, but stood next to Grimhild he looked like her kid brother. Me, I wouldn't have wanted to get on her wrong side by sniffing round the skirts of another woman, in her house, sitting at her table; but Black Thorstein acted like she wasn't there. That was Gudrid for you, though. I've seen better-looking women, and women who flirt with anything on two legs. She wasn't like that. She was quiet, mostly, except when she flew off the handle. I think what got you going was the way she had of sitting looking at you and listening, like you were the most fascinating man she'd ever come across. She had big round eyes, sort of a cloudy brown colour; and when you were talking to her, you felt like it was terribly important that she thought well of you. At least, that was how men reacted. She didn't talk to women much, and other women tended to skirt round her with their ears back, if you see what I mean. Big Grimhild didn't like her at all, you could see that the moment they set eyes on each other. Understandable, I guess. I mean, Grimhild was just the sort of woman you'd want to marry if you were fixing to move out to the Western Settlement, because she could cut turf and pitch hay all day long, carry a sick calf over her shoulder down from the shieling to the farm, and that counts for a whole lot more than glamour when you're living right out on the edge of the world. Gudrid – well, she could card and spin and cure bacon, but I never knew her stir out of doors unless she had to, particularly if it was cold.

So it wasn't a comfortable atmosphere at Lysufjord, and the best I could say for it was that we weren't going to be stopping there long; at least, that was the idea. Didn't quite work out that way, unfortunately.

The day we'd set for leaving, a hell of a storm came up out of nowhere. Thorstein Eirikson said, it's just a bit of a squall, we'll be fine; but it was obvious he just wanted to get his wife away from Black Thorstein. We wouldn't have gone a mile in that weather. So we stayed another night, and the weather got worse instead of better, and then we looked out one morning and the sea was full of floating ice, and we knew we were stuck there for the winter.

It's hard to say who was least happy about that, Thorstein Eirikson or Big Grimhild. The only one who didn't seem to mind was our host. Of course you're welcome to stay, he said; but he said it to Gudrid, without even looking at anybody else. I could hear Thorstein Eirikson growling down the other end of the table, and Grimhild got up and snatched away the dinner plates so hard that she scattered bones and bits of gristle. Black Thorstein's farmhands were looking down their noses; our lot were sat there cowering, because we knew there was going to be trouble sooner or later. We outnumbered the locals five to one, so if it came to a straight fight we'd probably be all right, but none of us wanted it to come to that if it could be helped.

Well, it all ended badly, but not the way we thought it would. After we'd been there about a month, Grimhild woke up one morning and announced that she was staying in bed. We all assumed it was a temper tantrum, but one of the farm women came out mid-afternoon and said the mistress was sweating buckets and couldn't lie still. That was bad news. The last thing you want in a house shut in for the winter is someone going down with something nasty, because if it spreads, chances are you'll all get it. Sure enough, next morning one of the farmhands was taken bad the same way, and later on that day one of our lot. Thorstein Eirikson was next; he woke up next day and told us he was burning up, so we went out and broke up some ice, and packed it all over him till just his eyes and nose were showing. That stopped it getting any worse, but he lay there moaning and swearing and calling out that he was being murdered. That wasn't the brightest thing to say under the circumstances, but by then he was off his head most of the time. The farm people got a bit uptight about it, but Black Thorstein didn't seem to care. He was more worried about Grimhild, credit where it's due; he spent all his time sitting next to her bed, holding her enormous hand, except when he went out with his axe to bust up more ice. Gudrid seemed to have pulled herself together a bit as well. She stayed close to her husband all day, but she was wasting her time because he didn't recognise her, even though he kept yelling for her and asking us all if we knew where she was.

Six more of our men went down. Curiously, the last to fall ill was the first to die; he just seemed to shrivel up, like a ball of wool on the fire. There was no chance of burying him while the ground was frozen solid, so we put him outside and covered him with three foot of snow, so he'd keep fresh till the thaw came. Next to go was one of the farm women, then three of our men, and the rest of us figured that it wouldn't be long till it was our turn. Talk about a miserable time: stuck in the main hall all day, nothing to do except listen to the rantings of the sick and the dying, unless it was your turn to go out in the freezing cold and break up ice. In the end, Eyvind and a man called Thormod Eyes and me decided we'd move out to the cattle sheds and take our chances there. True, it was bloody cold, but no worse than in the house, because they weren't keeping up much of a fire in there so as not to melt the ice-beds. We poked a hole in the roof and lit up a brazier, fed and watered and mucked out the cows for something to do, and worried ourselves silly imagining that we were starting to show the first symptoms of the fever.

Which was why we weren't there when Thorstein Eirikson died. He hung on a long time, Black Thorstein told us, longer than any of the others in our crew, though one of the farmhands outlasted him by a day. By an odd coincidence, Grimhild died at almost the same time – we could hear her ranting and cursing towards the end, even out there in the cattleshed. Anyhow, when there was just Black Thorstein and Gudrid left, they came out and told us what'd happened. Both of them seemed well out of it, like they were way past caring. Black Thorstein asked if we'd mind helping him with the burials once the thaw came, since it'd be a big job for a man on his own. We said that'd be fine, no problem. Then he said, did we think he could come with us back to Eiriksfjord, since he didn't really fancy staying on at Lysufjord, given what'd happened there. Well, we weren't in any position to speak for Leif Eirikson, but the plain fact was that the three of us on our own couldn't handle the ship, but with a fourth pair of hands we'd probably make it; so we said, sure, why not? After that, nobody said anything much, until the spring came.

You know, when I think back on my life, I'm struck by how much of it I've spent sitting still and quiet and miserable; either frozen or soaked to the skin, in fog, or cooped up over winter in some place I really didn't want to be. I dare say it's mostly my own fault, for drifting through my life instead of making up my mind to do something useful and sensible with it, like other people seem to. Maybe that's why I've fetched up here, where most of the year it's so hot you can scarcely breathe, and you don't seem to get the long summer days and long winter nights, and when you first come here from the North you think it's all so much better, until you've been here a while and you find out it's just different. But there you go. For a while, I sort of persuaded myself that places matter; that who you are depends a lot on where you are, and if only you can find the right place to be, that'll solve all your problems and everything'll be fine. But the plain fact is, places make hardly any difference at all. Any place you go to changes soon as you get there, and most of us are like snails, we carry one place around with us on our backs wherever we go.

Well: when the thaw came, after we'd buried the dead, we fixed up the ship as best we could and sailed back to the Eastern Settlement. It only took us a night and two days, would you believe; all that time we'd been so close, but we might as well have been back in Meadowland for all the good it did us.

I think I can honestly say that Leif was pleased to see us; mostly, I think, because we'd brought back Gudrid, and the ship. Probably on balance he was sad about Thorstein, and losing sixteen of his men like that definitely came as a blow. But it's like my old mother used to say: you can't blame a man for looking on the bright side. At a stroke, he'd cleared out both his brothers from under his feet, and surely Gudrid would have to marry him now.

She didn't, of course. Nor did she marry Black Thorstein,

who'd come to Brattahlid with pretty much the same idea in mind. He at any rate took it quite well. He borrowed a horse, rode back to the Western Settlement and sold up the farm, live and dead stock, the lot; then he came back to Eiriksfjord, bought a place as close to Brattahlid as he could find, and carried on with his life. I heard at some point that he married again, though I don't know if it's true, or any details. Any rate, he went back to being a miserable bastard, and kept himself to himself.

Leif did one thing that surprised me. Not long after we got back, he took the ship up to Lysufjord, got permission from the new owner to dig up the bodies of all the people who'd died over the winter, fetched them back to Eiriksfjord and had them buried there near the little church that Eirik had built for his wife. That's stuck in my mind because it wasn't the sort of thing he tended to do, but I guess he had his reasons. But he never raised the subject of bringing Thorvald's body back from Meadowland – which, you'll remember, was the big idea behind Thorstein's trip. Nothing more was ever said about that. In fact, I believe the whole Meadowland business would've been quietly forgotten about, if Leif'd had his way. But it wasn't, of course; because later that summer, that bastard Bits arrived from Norway, and fell in love with Gudrid, and everything started all over again.

CHAPTER
NINE

A little later, Eyvind came over and sat by me. He had a big axe in one hand and a whetstone in the other. The sun was high, so he was wearing a broad-brimmed hat to keep the bright light out of his eyes.

'It's all right,' he said, as he noticed me looking doubtfully at the axe. 'I was planning to wander up to those trees up there on the skyline, cut out some dry wood for the fire. Kari and young Harald have been a bit free with the charcoal, and I think it may get cold tonight.' He grinned. 'Listen to that,' he said, 'you can tell I've been in these parts too long. Back home, Greek cold'd have everybody sweating.'

'You two start every other sentence with *back home*,' I said, maybe a little irritably 'I take it you don't really like it here.'

He laughed. 'Are you kidding?' he said. 'Soft beds, all the food you can stuff down your face; no work, unless you count prancing around with a spear in your hand trying to look fierce. And we – Kari and me – we hardly even have to do that any more. No, we live on the charity of the regiment, on account of our long and distinguished service.' He snorted. 'And that's all bullshit,' he added, 'though don't go telling young Harald I said so. He thinks we're heroic veterans: we drove the Bulgars out of the north and held back the Saracen hordes in Sicily. Me, I've never even seen a Saracen, not a live one, at any rate. We were the reserves, see. Got off a ship, marched up some mountains, hung around for a few days in camp, marched down the mountain, came home. I guess the mere rumour that we'd come was enough to make the Saracens give up and run away. Or something.' He drew the stone along the axe blade a few times, and the coarse, grating hum set my teeth on edge. 'Kari finally left you in peace, then.'

I nodded. 'He was telling me about how Thorstein Eirikson died of the fever,' I said. 'But then he mentioned someone called Bits, and suddenly he didn't want to talk any more. He got up and went off over there. Last time I saw him, he was telling Harald what was wrong with the way he makes porridge.'

Eyvind frowned, as though puzzled. 'Bits,' he repeated. 'That's odd. The only man he could've meant was Bits Thorfinn, and I can't see why that'd make him go all moody.'

Resignation makes me curl my toes. 'Who's Bits Thorfinn?' I said.

Bits (Eyvind said) is actually short for Bits-and-pieces-that-make-up-a-man – assuming that Kari was talking about who I'm assuming he meant, and that'd have been the right point in the story. In our language, it's not nearly such a mouthful: *karlsefni*. It's just a pain saying it in full in Greek. So we'll call him Bits.

First time I met Bits was in the yard at Brattahlid, maybe a month after we got back from the Western Settlement. I'd been mucking out the milking ewes, and I was staggering across the yard under a huge forkload of sheep-shitty bracken. Couldn't see very well where I was going, and suddenly I crashed into something hard. Needless to say I let go of the pitchfork, and for a split second it was raining bedding and sheep dung. Then I heard someone apologising.

'Sorry,' said the voice. 'My fault.'

Well, he was a liar, whoever he was, but I didn't mind that. Most people, women and kids included, would've punched first and then yelled at me for not minding where I was going. Anyhow, I wiped the crap out of my eyes, and I saw this man standing in front of me, all covered in the stuff.

He was a short bloke; that was the first thing you noticed about him. Unfair, really, because he had broad shoulders, arms like legs, strong chin, piercing eyes; if he'd only been nine inches further off the ground you'd have called him distinguished-looking, or if you happened to be female, probably handsome. But when a man only comes up to your chin, that's the first and abiding impression you get of him. A short bloke.

'That's all right,' I said. 'Should've been looking where I was going.'

'Never mind.' He smeared a handful of shit off his face. 'Tell me where the stream is, and we'll call it quits.'

'I'll show you,' I said.

Well, I took him to the stream and we washed ourselves off, as best we could. Then he stuck out his hand and said, 'My name's Thorfinn Thordsson. Pleased to meet you.'

'Likewise,' I mumbled. I could tell from his accent he was an Easterner: Norwegian. 'You're off that ship,' I said. 'The one that put in last night.'

'That's right,' he said, smiling nicely. 'Actually, that's my ship. We're trading timber for furs and smoked cheese. Leif Eirikson kindly agreed to put us up over winter.'

Just my rotten luck, I thought; because as soon as I'd heard that a Norwegian ship had put in, I'd made a decision. When it sailed back to Norway in the spring, I was going to be on it. Not that I was yearning for the seafaring life after a whole month on warm, dry land; I just wanted to get away – from Brattahlid, from Leif Eirikson, and from my boyhood pal Kari.

I can't really explain what the matter was; but ever since we'd got back from Thorstein's disastrous trip, I hadn't been able to settle. Not all that surprising, I suppose: being one of three survivors out of a crew of twenty, and burying the ones who hadn't made it in a mass grave scooped out of the gravel, tends to set you thinking about a whole range of things. Anyhow, I'd come to the conclusion that I was through with pissing my life away into the mud. Didn't matter where I went, so long as I got away from these people; because as long as I was with them, I wasn't ever going to make anything of myself, I'd just be someone who sat in a corner, wet through, scared and bored. Fair enough, taking passage with a trading ship wasn't a very good way of changing all that, but I wasn't planning on staying with the ship once it'd reached the East. What I figured on doing was stuffing a big bag full of furs, selling them in Norway for what I could get, and having a go at trading. I didn't know spit about it; in fact, I probably wouldn't ever have considered it, only I'd had the good luck to find a dead bear up on the high pastures. You only see them once in a blue moon, but Greenland bears have white coats, and they're worth a fortune in the East. I had that skin off and into a bucket full of beaten eggs so fast you wouldn't credit it. My plan – sounds daft, but what did I know about anything? – my plan was to go to Norway, or maybe Sweden, walk up to the King, and give him my white bearskin. According to all the stories, His Majesty would then give me twice the skin's value in gold, invite me to stay at court and probably let me join his personal guard, just to show how wonderfully generous he was. So, you can tell, I'd thought it all through really carefully. And, just when I needed one, here was a Norwegian ship; and what'd I just done? I'd nearly flattened its captain in the yard, and covered him in sheep shit.

Anyway; there I was, wet from the stream and all my dreams shattered around me, shaking this small bloke by the hand. I told him my name, explained I wasn't anybody, just a hired hand, but he didn't seem to mind that. Usually you can see a very slight change in someone's face when you tell them you're just the help, but the short bloke just carried on smiling, like it didn't matter.

'Well,' I said, once he'd let go of my hand, 'I'd better go and rake up the yard before I get yelled at. Sorry about—'

He shrugged. 'Please,' he said, 'forget it.' Then he smiled again, nodded, and walked away. And that was the first time I met Bits.

So what are you supposed to think about a man like that? I guess you'd say he was weak: some clown charges into you in the yard and covers you in shit, obviously you bash his head in. If you don't, it's because you're afraid, you've got no balls. Or maybe he's sly, he's after something. But the thing about Bits was, he didn't seem to care. He looked at you, decided whether he liked you or not, and carried on from there. They called him Bits-and-pieces because nobody could ever figure what to make of him; but I never had that problem. He was the most straightforward man I ever met.

I didn't actually see much of him after that, not for a while. He was moving around a lot that summer, using

Brattahlid as his base while he went round the Eastern
Settlement, selling his timber, buying furs and cheese. He'd
come back most evenings, of course, but he'd be sit up at the
top table with Leif and Freydis – and Gudrid, of course. I
tried to find out a bit more about him from his crew, but for
some reason they weren't very forthcoming; as though they
didn't like me asking. Protective, almost. All I got out of
them was that he was quite rich, well thought of in Norway,
shrewd in business, had a knack for staying out of trouble,
liked everything quiet and sensible. Most of his men had
been with him for ages, just peacefully trotting back and
forth along the same routes each year, carrying the same
lines, dealing with the same people. In fact, they told me,
they hadn't got a clue why he'd suddenly decided to branch
out into the Greenland trade. But if the skipper reckoned it
was worth doing, that was just fine by them. Apart from that,
they told me, there wasn't anything to know.

Autumn came on, and then the season for slaughtering
the stock, so we were all kept busy, and I'd more or less put
Bits and his ship out of my mind; when you've got plenty of
work to occupy you, you don't tend to brood so much.
Then one day, quite out of the blue, Bits came to find me.

I was outside the long barn, doing one of my least
favourite jobs in the whole world. We'd slaughtered the old
bull a few days earlier, and Leif wanted his hide for boot
soles. It took four of us to get the thing off; then we dunked
it in a bucket full of lye to soak the hair off, and stretched it
and scraped all the bits of meat and skin off the inside, rinsed
it and wrung it out; and the next step, as I'm sure an edu-
cated man like you won't need to be told, is to cure it; and
the best thing to cure a hide with, goes without saying, is
brains. Now it's a sign of our Heavenly Father's blessed providence that a bull's head holds exactly the right amount of

brains for curing his hide, not a scrap more nor less; and what you do is, you scoop up a big handful of brains and you start kneading with your fingers—

'Would it be all right,' I said, 'if we skipped all this?'

Anyhow (Eyvind went on) there I was, bits of white crud oozing out between my fingers, and Bits Thorfinn comes strolling up to me and asks if I could spare him a moment or so.

'Sure,' I said. 'What can I do for you?'

He looked away for a heartbeat or so, like he was utterly fascinated by the sight of a bowl of lukewarm water. 'I'd like to ask you if you feel like joining my crew,' he said.

Well, you could have blown me over with a sneeze. All that time I'd been trying to think of some way of broaching the subject, and here he was – *him* asking *me* – straight out. 'Yes,' I said, because why the hell mess about? 'I'd like that,' I added, just in case I wasn't making myself clear.

'That's good,' he said, with a little smear of a smile, like gravy in your beard after you've eaten. 'But you haven't asked me where I'm going.'

It hit me like a boot in the nuts, and I didn't need to ask, I knew. He wanted me along because – for some reason I couldn't possibly begin to fathom – he was planning on going to Meadowland.

'That's a good point,' I said.

The little smile broadened. 'You're ahead of me, I can tell. And you're right. I'm planning on sailing to the Wine Country. Does that change things?'

That puzzled me for a bit. Not long, though; but long enough to make it look like I was in two minds, because he went on: 'If you don't want to go, that's fine, I quite understand. But if you'll hear me out, I'll tell you why I believe it'll be different this time. Well?'

'I'm listening,' I said.

He nodded, then leaned his back against the stretching frame. He was always leaning on things, Bits, like an old cat. 'For a start,' he said, 'we're going there with a definite plan in mind. Seems to me that it all went badly before, with the Eiriksons, because neither of them really knew what they wanted to do. Just going there was as far ahead as they'd thought. That's not my style. Before I start something, I like to have the whole thing sketched out in my head, like a boat-builder's plan, and everything's got to be measured and sorted so it all fits together.'

He looked at me, but I didn't say anything, so he went on: 'My idea is to start up a proper settlement there; basically, do what Red Eirik did here. Build a farm, get settled in; then, when we're properly established and we know where our next meal's coming from, we share out the land between ourselves and turn it into a real settlement, a community. There's enough people here in the Eastern Settlement who're starting to feel a bit cramped, wouldn't mind moving on; and once we're up and running, we'll have people join-ing us from Iceland, maybe even from the East. Once we've got eighty families or so, we'll be big enough to look after ourselves and keep going. I've given it a lot of thought since I came here and heard all about it, and I believe we'd have a very good chance of making it work. It's splendid grazing country by all accounts, plus there's all that timber, fish, game – even iron ore, which is more than you can say for this place. The key to it, I reckon, is doing the thing prop-erly: enough people, enough livestock, enough provisions to see us through the first winter, including an allowance for stuff lost or spoiled on the trip over. So, what d'you reckon?'

I thought for a while before I answered. 'For a start,' I said, 'you got the name wrong. It's not Wineland, it's Meadowland.'

Easy mistake to make, of course, specially for an Easterner, with an accent. See, in our language, it's almost the same word: *vinland*. Only, if it means 'wine' it's pronounced *vin*, but if it's 'meadow' it's more like *veen*.

'Oh,' he said.

'That's right,' I went on. 'So if you'd got an idea in your head of running cargoes of grapes back to Norway and making a fortune, forget it. And if anybody's been telling you there's wild vines growing all over the place, that's bullshit. We came across some, on Leif's expedition, but we never could find them again, no matter how we tried.'

The way Bits was quiet for a while after I said that, it was plain that he'd been counting on finding grapes under every bush; but he just shrugged and said, 'Well, no big deal. But there *is* timber there, isn't there?'

I nodded. 'Oh yes,' I said. 'Bloody great forests, far as the eye can see.'

'Good.' You could almost see him booting everything to do with grapes out of his mind, then slamming the door. 'That's all right, then. But you haven't answered my question.'

I allowed myself a bit more time; then I said: 'I'm really grateful to you for asking, but I've got to say no. Plain fact is, I've had it with that place. Don't ask me why, I couldn't tell you. Now I'm not trying to tell you your scheme's a washout. I think it could succeed, I certainly hope so. But I won't be joining you, I'm afraid.'

'Oh,' he said again. 'That's a pity.'

Bits looked so sad that I wished there was something I could do. And then it hit me; genius. One stone, two dead birds. 'Tell you what, though,' I said. 'You want to ask Kari. He's been there on all three trips. He knows the place just as well as me, maybe even better. And I know he's not settled here, any more than I am. You take my tip and ask him, he's a good man.'

Bits frowned, like he was being made to do something he'd rather not. 'I'll be straight with you,' he said. 'I know Kari's a friend of yours, but he's not the sort of man I was looking for. He does his work but no more, if you see what I mean. What I'm after isn't farmhands, it's men who'll go off and build their own farms, once we've sunk our roots in, if you follow me. That's why I'd rather have you than him. But if you've made your mind up, I won't try and nag you into anything. The project won't work unless the people I take with me all want the same thing: they've got to believe that they aren't working for me, they're working for themselves. But anyhow,' he added, 'that's beside the point. Thank you for listening to me, anyway.'

And he straightened up, turned round and walked away, leaving me standing there with squished-up bull's brains all over my hands, and a feeling like I'd been kicked in the nuts by a large, strong horse.

If it'd been anywhere else— If he'd wanted to sail up the Greenland coast, or north-east to Permia, where the sea-ice is six feet thick at midsummer, or anywhere in the world, I'd have said yes and thank you without a moment's thought. But no, it had to be bloody Meadowland; because if it'd been anywhere else, I wouldn't have been asked or wanted. I was bound to that miserable place, as though my feet were planted there. Simple choice: stay at Brattahlid the rest of my life, carting shit and turning hay and dragging myself up the mountain to the shieling in the freezing cold to move on another man's flocks; or go back to that warm, lush, hospitable place on the edge of the world, which I never wanted to see again as long as I lived.

It comes back to that old question, doesn't it? Are you always the same person wherever you are, or do you change as you move about? For instance: at Brattahlid I was just a pair of hands; there wasn't anything I could do that couldn't be done better by someone else. I hadn't chosen to go and live there, and they hadn't chosen me; I'd been sort of inherited from Bjarni Herjolfson, like old junk found left behind in the barn when someone sells up and moves on. In Meadowland, though, I was practically the founding father – me and that worthless bastard Kari, who I'd somehow got myself chained to as well. In Meadowland, I was the man who knew where the sweet-water streams were, the best places to build fish traps, which direction the wind came from in winter, where the best grazing was, where Thorvald Eirikson was buried. In Meadowland, I could have my own farm; there'd come a time when I could walk out my door and climb the mountain and look down over Eyvindsfell and Eyvindsmark and Eyvindsvatn, all mine as far as the eye could see. Just by a simple bit of ordinary journeyman magic – get on a boat, sit still and quiet for a few days in the wet and the mist, get off the boat and go ashore – I could get rid of who I was born to be and turn myself into somebody else, like the shape-changers in the old stories, the men who can turn themselves into wolves and bears and eagles. As I stood there in the yard, I could hear that other man's voice muttering in the back of my head – *this Thorfinn Bits isn't like the Eiriksons – he's a serious man, he knows what he's about. It'd be quite different going there with him. There's nothing at all wrong with Meadowland: compared with here or the Old Country it's bloody paradise; what's been wrong each time so far is the bunch of losers you've been with. Like Kari, for instance; and you've had it from the horse's mouth, this time Kari isn't going to be there. You know perfectly well, all your life he's been holding you back, screwing everything up for you; well, now's your chance to be rid of him. Look, all you need to do is go to this Thorfinn Bits and say you've changed your mind; and then you'll be free and clear, finally you can be who you were meant to be.* But, I said to myself, he would say that, wouldn't he? He wanted to go back there, because Meadowland was the only place he'd ever get to exist. Meanwhile there was this other voice; and all it was saying, over and over again, was: *don't go, don't go.* It wasn't giving any reasons, that voice. It didn't have to. It had my full attention.

Well, Bits went off again the next morning, didn't come back for three days; and when he did come back, didn't he ever cause trouble.

I wasn't there at the time; I was piling up cordwood in the woodshed, so it'd be handy for the house once the snow came. So I missed the big scene indoors, when Bits marched up to Leif Eirikson and told him that he and Gudrid, Thorstein's widow, were planning on getting married.

I always miss the good shows – like the classic horse-fights and wrestling matches that people talk about for years afterwards, or the really spectacular fights and shouting matches. By all accounts, that was one of the best. It's no use trying to describe it to you, they all told me, you had to have been there.

Well, I wasn't; so all I can tell you is the outline. Leif wasn't happy, not at all. Ever since Gudrid came back after Thorstein's death, Leif had been convinced it was only a matter of time. It was destiny, he reckoned. He'd rescued Gudrid from death on the rocks, and she belonged to him. Stupid Thorstein had tried to steal her, and look what happened to him. Leif hadn't pressed the issue since she got back, because he wasn't an idiot, he wasn't going to dance over her feelings in nailed boots. Give her time, don't rush anything, and just like apples grow on trees, when the time was right she'd come round and see it was the right thing. And now this bastard, his winter guest, this *short* bastard, had nipped in at the last moment and robbed him right under his nose.

Leif couldn't say that, of course; so he lashed out in the only direction open to him. Fine, he said, if you're hell-bent on getting yourself killed, you crack on and do it, and well rid of you. But if you think I'm going to let you take my sister-in-law out there to be shot dead by the leather-boat people, or die of fever, or starve or get eaten by bears or God only knows what, then you must be even more stupid than you look. She's under my roof, my responsibility, and I say she's not going.

It'd probably have been all right if Bits'd flown into a temper; if he'd bashed Leif round the head, even, or pulled a knife, anything like that. Where I come from we're used to people flaring up, and there's nothing like a few painful blows or a stab wound to make you ask yourself: is this really such a big deal, like something I'd be prepared to die for, or is it really not that important? But no. The more Leif shouted and raved at him, the calmer Bits became. Leif was yelling; Bits didn't yell back, in fact his voice got softer and softer, so Leif had to quieten down just to hear what he was saying. And Bits said: I appreciate your concern, but it's her choice. I've thought it through, and I wouldn't be taking the woman I love with me if I thought there was any serious risk she'd come to harm. On the contrary; I'm taking her there because that's where I can give her a better life, the sort she deserves. You do see that, don't you?

Well; it was as though our Heavenly Father'd stuck His

thumb into the cone of a volcano, just when it'd started to bust open. All that heat and fire, and nowhere for it to go. After a while, Leif stopped shouting; it was like he was drunk and having a desperate row with someone who wasn't actually there. Instead, he just turned on his heel and stomped out, leaving Bits standing there with a sad look on his face, like he was saying, why can't people just be reasonable about things?

I knew as soon as I heard about it that we were in for another long, tense winter; and I wasn't far wrong. Bits carried on like nothing'd happened. He sold the rest of his timber, laid off various deals and loans based on his property back East, and started laying in supplies and buying stuff for the journey; also, he saw to all the arrangements for the wedding. In the end it was a quiet business – at least Leif had the sense and the grace to stay well away for a day or so – and it all went off with the minimum of fuss and aggravation. Bits seemed very happy that day; I'm assuming Gudrid felt the same way, but she wasn't the sort to show what she was thinking, not if she could help it. Of course, a lot of the Brattahlid and Eiriksfjord people reckoned she was only marrying Bits so she could get away from Leif; and if that really was the reason, I can't say I blame her for it.

At the wedding dinner Bits announced that he and his people'd be sailing for Meadowland just as soon as the thaw came. We'd all guessed that for ourselves already, but hearing him announce it was something else.

He'd be sailing, he said, with three ships: his own, plus Leif's ship, which he'd bought off him (before the falling-out, presumably) and another *knoerr* he'd picked up from a man from the Western Settlement who'd just moved down. Ninety men and fifteen women would be going along with him, which meant there'd be plenty of room on the ships for livestock, including a ram, a boar and a bull. Everyone knew what that meant, of course. This time, he was planning on staying out there and doing it all properly; not like the Eiriksons.

Getting through that winter was like walking uphill in thick mud; every step heavier than the last, and getting more difficult rather than less as time went on. It was so bad indoors that I volunteered to help shift the stores Bits had brought from the long barn down to the boatsheds, just for the chance to be outside, in the freezing cold. It set me thinking: Bits had obviously planned everything down to the last detail, and being a trader he thought mostly in terms of objects. So there was a barrel of boot-nails, and seven big wooden reels of heavy linen thread; a box of the very best whetstones, from Gotland in Sweden; a box of flints, from the east of England; three large jars of beeswax; a wooden pot of blacksmith's flux; a bag of lumps of yellow sulphur, from the Old Country; five big coils of wire; crates of tools I'd never seen before, let alone knew what they were for; all the things that sooner or later you'll desperately need but never think about until it's too late. Bits had thought of them, though; and it struck me that someone with that much about him might just be enough to make the difference between success and failure, even in Meadowland.

By the time we got around to unloading the last cartload it was just past sundown. Everything had been loaded in a particular order, so that the things likely to be needed first had to go in last, so they'd be on top of the stack, and handy. Practically the last items were five long wooden crates, and four big apple-barrels – except that what was in them wasn't apples, you could tell that by the weight. Took three of us just to roll the bloody things along the ground; and I got to wondering, as we manhandled them down the plank and into the shed, what sort of item was small enough to go in a barrel but really heavy, and also didn't rattle or shift about as the barrel rolled. Well, I had my own ideas about that, which set me thinking about the crates that seemed to go with them. Not quite so heavy, those crates, but they weren't packed with feathers, either.

'Careful with those,' Bits called up to us as we handed them down off the cart. There's always some clown who thinks he knows best, though; in this case, a man called Hrapp something-or-other, I can't remember now. Anyway, he thought he could take the whole weight of one of these crates, and it turned out he couldn't; the crate slipped off the cart sideways, landed on a corner and smashed open. Turned out I'd been absolutely right in my guesses. It was full of weapons. Spears – short-headed Norway pattern and long-headed French type; Danish beard-axes, the sort that's not much good for cutting or cleaving wood, but works a charm on arms and legs; even a bundle of five swords, packed up in straw and tied into their scabbards.

We all stood there, looking. Quiet? You could've heard a mouse fart.

Bits came bustling up; he wasn't pleased. 'What's the matter?' he said, sounding a bit guilty. 'You lot never seen a spear before?'

Nobody said anything, but I wouldn't have been surprised if at least one of us had said *yes*. Don't get me wrong; where I come from, we don't mind a bit of a scrap now and then. But there's a difference between settling a long-standing argument with a hand-axe or a big knife, and actual weapons. See, we like to think we're practical people; and if a thing's not going to get used, we don't bother with it. So maybe, somewhere about the farm, you may find an old spearhead or a cracked old bow with wormholes in the riser; tucked up in the rafters, maybe, or hung on the wall so long you don't even notice it any more. But when you see a crate full of weapons, obviously newly made, with the oil still glistening on the wood, you stop and ask yourself what's going on.

I'd guessed, of course; I was also prepared to bet, though I don't suppose I'd have found any takers, that in these heavy barrels were mail shirts – apart from a ship, the most expensive thing a man can own where I come from, because it'll take a blacksmith all winter just to draw down the wire, coil it and cut it off into rings, and then another winter patiently linking them together, hammering the ends of each ring flat, punching a hole, cutting a rivet, sliding it into the hole and peening it shut, eighty thousand times. For a start, I don't think any of us had guessed that Bits was quite so incredibly rich. Kings can afford mail shirts by the barrel, and some of the bigger earls out East; and the King of the Greeks, of course, he's got factories where a thousand men do nothing else all day, all year. I'd never seen one in my life, and I'd never expected to, either.

Now when I was a kid back in the Old Country, there was this old man who had a small farm at the other end of the fell; and everybody knew who he was because he was dirt poor, only had three cows and half a dozen sheep; but if you went in his house you'd see swords and helmets and shields, all greased up against the damp and wrapped in wool; put together, they'd have been worth enough to buy the whole valley, assuming you could find anyone who wanted to buy them, but the old man'd rather have sold his fingers. Years ago, they told me, he'd been a real blood-red viking, sailing up and down the fjords every season robbing the ships, or going out to Finland or Permia and making a nuisance of himself round all the coast villages. All the time he was away, of course, his farm went downhill; his brother was supposed to look after it, but he caught a fever and died, and when the viking finally learned some sense and came home, there was next to nothing left. So yes, there's people who have weapons just for the sake of it; but Bits wasn't anything like that. If he'd spent an earl's ransom on the things, it was because he figured they'd be needed.

I guess we were all thinking the same thing, just then: the leather-boat people, who'd killed Thorvald Eirikson. It was a stroke of bad luck for Bits that the crate had smashed open, but it must've been at the back of other people's minds beside mine. The big difference between Meadowland and Greenland – or Iceland, come to that – was that there were people already living in Meadowland, and maybe they wouldn't want to share.

Nobody had anything much to say after that. We got the weapons back in the crate, tied down the lid with ropes of twisted hay, and put it with the others, at the back of the barn. Then we went back to the house, where it was quiet as the grave and there were other things to think about.

But next day three of the men who'd been the first to join up went to Bits and said they'd changed their minds. They didn't say why and he didn't ask, because there was no need. That was just the start. Next day, ten out of the fifteen women cried off, and that meant ten less men, too. Before long, the party was down from a hundred and five to sixty-four, with another twenty wavering.

Bits took it quite well, or that was the impression he gave. It was just as well, I overheard him saying, that they'd changed their minds now rather than later; and there was still time before they were due to leave for recruiting others to fill the empty places. The general view, though, was that he was kidding himself. The most striking thing was that four of his own crew, Easterners who'd been with him for years, announced that they'd be staying over when the thaw came. Needless to say, Leif was delighted; told them they could stay as long as they liked, he'd be glad to have them on the farm, or he'd ask around the neighbours to see if anybody was looking to take on more hands, if they didn't want to stay at Brattahlid. He was rubbing it in, of course, trying to encourage more of Bits's men to leave him, hoping to scupper the whole project and so keep Gudrid within arm's reach. He could've been a bit less obvious about it, maybe, but that wasn't his way. Bits pretended nothing was going on, and that just made Leif angry.

So; while everybody else was changing their minds about the project, why should I be the only one left out?

The point is: I'd had those leather-boat people in mind all along. It was a shock, yes, actually seeing the weapons. But unlike the others, who'd heard the story of how Thorvald died but hadn't really thought it through, I'd already taken it on board; and I'd realised that that wasn't why I had this bad feeling about Meadowland in general. So for me it was the other way about; the fact that Bits was taking weapons with him made me feel better about the idea, not the opposite. Far as I was concerned, the spears and mail shirts were just like the boot-nails and the wire, or the bull: they told me that Bits was taking it all far more seriously than the Eiriksons had ever done, and that could only be good. Looked at from the other direction, the worse things got around Brattahlid, the more I wanted to get away from there; and if the only ship out of Eiriksfjord was headed for Meadowland, then so be it. It came down to a simple choice, really: who would I prefer to take my chances with, the leather-boat people – or the household at

Brattahlid? Put like that, it didn't need a whole lot of thinking about.

Well; if you make up your mind to do something, might as well do it in the best possible way. I could've waited till I had a chance to talk to Bits nice and quiet; but instead I went up to him when he was talking to Leif – rare thing, at that stage – and a bunch of other people, and I pushed my shoulder in between Bits and Leif, and said in a loud voice, 'I changed my mind. If you still want me along, I'll come.'

Bits looked blank for a moment, then grinned all over his face. I couldn't see Leif, of course, I had my back to him, but I wouldn't have minded the loan of one of those mail shirts, to keep Leif's scowl from coming out through my chest. I knew, see, that what Bits wanted, and Leif didn't, was a big vote of confidence, from someone who mattered. Normally, that wouldn't have been me; in this case, though, because I'd been with Bjarni Herjolfson and then Leif and Thorvald and Thorstein, and everybody knew I'd refused to go this time, of course it mattered that I'd changed my mind. It was just the sort of thing, my deciding to join up, that could save the whole project from falling apart.

Ah well. Sometimes I get these good ideas; and then I have to live with them afterwards.

There wasn't any going back after that. Leif Eirikson hated me now, which meant I couldn't stay at Brattahlid; and I had nowhere else to go. You ever wondered what it must be like to be a fish with a hook through your lip? Just ask me – I can tell you.

Much later that day, just as we were all turning in to go to sleep, I went up to Bits and asked him straight out what was in the barrels. I didn't say which barrels I was talking about; I didn't need to.

'I think you know,' was all he said.

'Mail shirts,' I said. He nodded. 'Well,' I said, 'that's all right, then.'

He looked at me for a bit, then grinned. 'You know,' he said, 'you've really screwed things up for yourself here; with Leif, I mean. Not that I'm not grateful.'

'Doesn't matter,' I said, trying to sound like I meant it. 'I mean, it's not like I'll be coming back here, is it?'

Bits nodded slowly. 'You've got the picture,' he said. 'And you're all right with that, then?'

'If I wanted to be here, I wouldn't be going away,' I said. It sounded really profound when I said it, too.

'That's fine, then,' said Bits.

But there was still something bothering me, though really it was none of my business. 'Just one question,' I said. 'If it hadn't been for Gudrid, would you be reckoning on staying there for keeps?'

He took a moment before he answered. 'Yes,' he said. 'That was the idea all along.'

Usually, I know when I'm being lied to; this time, I wasn't sure. I'm still not sure, to tell you the truth. I never heard Bits tell a lie, before or since, so I've got no way of knowing what he looked or sounded like when he was lying. Or it could've been true, at that. Not that it matters all that much, I suppose.

'Well, obviously it matters,' I interrupted. 'It goes to the root of his motivation, surely. And that's important, if anything is.'

Eyvind shook his head. 'Don't see why,' he said. 'Good people do bad things for good reasons; bad people do good things for bad reasons. A hundred years from now, nobody'll know or care why any of us did what we did. All that matters is actions, and what comes of them.'

I frowned at him. 'Do you really believe that?' I asked.

He scratched his head. 'Not sure,' he replied. 'I guess it depends on the action, doesn't it?'

Anyhow (Eyvind continued) that stopped the rot, as far as people quitting the project went. But none of the men who'd already cried off changed their minds; nor any of the women, either. We were stuck at fifty-nine men and five women. Bits said it'd be enough; no bad thing, in a way, because less people meant less supplies needed for the journey, so there'd be space left over for more of the stuff we'd be likely to need once we actually got there. Bits was a great one for seeing the bright side; if you chopped off his leg, he'd say, 'But think how much I'll save on shoes.'

We brought forward leaving-day by a week, because it was getting painful to be at Brattahlid. Bits wanted an early start, so those of us who were going made a point of getting up while it was still dark and creeping out so as not to wake anyone else. We'd finished the loading the previous evening, right down to our personal kit, so all we had to do was stagger down to the boat shed and draw the ships down into the water. With Bits in charge, the operation was completely successful, which meant there wasn't anybody to see us off as we ran the ships out into the sea and clambered aboard. You couldn't have asked for a better departure: the sea was calm and flat, the wind was moderate but in just the right direction, and it wasn't raining. I guess you could say that a big crowd waving us goodbye'd only have slowed us up, maybe even made us risk missing the tide. And anyway, why would I be worried? Since I didn't have any family there, there'd have been nobody to wish me goodbye. Except Kari, of course; and the whole point in going was to get away from him. Even so.

Even so.

But he wasn't there, because I looked, even while we were drawing down the ships. Good riddance, I thought. Finally, after all those years, I was rid of him. Probably I only looked just to make sure he didn't come sneaking up at the last moment. I'm sure that was the reason.

And then we were under way, and there was plenty else to think about. Needless to say, I was on board our old ship, the one that'd originally belonged to Bjarni Herjolfson. Bits wasn't on board, of course, he was on his own ship. He'd put his forecastle-man in charge of ours, a man called Ohtar Kolbeinson; an Easterner, but a good man in his way. We were carrying a lot of cargo: mostly livestock, also some tools, clothes, bundles of cloth, and our own rations for the journey.

Once the sails were set and we were riding a nice fresh south-westerly wind, I found myself a place to sit, and sat on it. I'd learned to do that early during my previous jaunts. If you leave it too long, all the best places get taken, and you end up huddled in the middle of the deck, when where you want to be is at the side, snuggled under the rail for choice. That way, you get some shelter from waves in hard weather; the spray breaks against the rail and sloshes down on the poor buggers sitting in the middle. Once you're a day into the journey, you'll be bloody lucky to change your sitting-place, unless you find someone who's willing to swap with you. Your sitting-place is your only bit of personal space, you see; so it's simple human nature to want to keep it to yourself and to get all stroppy if someone else tries to muscle in on it. Blood's been spilt for less on a long voyage.

Anyway. There was a big, tall barrel at the aft end of the cargo stash; I made a beeline for it and spread my stuff around, like I was building walls and marking out boundaries with hurdles. I reckoned the barrel'd shelter me in front,

same as the rail sheltered me on my left side. Really pleased
with myself, I was; and I was grinning like an idiot and con-
gratulating myself on getting possibly the best berth on the
ship when the lid of the barrel started to move.

I was so taken aback, all I could do was crouch there and
watch. Gradually the lid lifted up, and I was on the point of
yelling to the others when I saw a pair of beady little eyes
twinkling at me from under the barrel lid. Familiar? Oh yes.
I'd have known those eyes anywhere.

'Eyvind,' he hissed. 'That you?'

It was Kari, of course. Stupid bugger'd stowed away till it
was too late to turn back.

I couldn't manage to get any words out, I was so – well,
if you've been paying any sort of attention, you can guess
how I was feeling without me having to tell you.

'Don't just sit there, Eyvind, you stupid bastard,' he hissed
at me. 'Help me get out of here, before I suffocate.'

I couldn't have moved if I'd tried, and I didn't. It was like
there was this ridiculous idea in my head of making him stay
in the stupid barrel all the way to Meadowland; or maybe
he'd die in there and I could fish him out with a boat-hook
and throw his shrivelled corpse into the sea for the sharks
and the whales to bust their teeth on.

By now, most everybody at our end of the ship had
noticed that there was a strange head poking up out of a
barrel. There was pointing and yelling, and Captain Ohtar
came scrambling across the hold, walking on the backs of the
cows, to see what the hell was going on.

'Stowaway,' was all I could say, and I pointed. Ohtar
looked where I'd shown him, and did this great big comical
double take.

'Kari?' he called out. 'What the hell are you doing in that
barrel?'

He knew Kari from Brattahlid, of course; in fact, they'd spent quite a bit of time together over the winter, playing chess. Kari cheats, but Ohtar didn't seem to have noticed.

A couple of men grabbed Kari under the shoulders and out he came like a snail from its shell; all filthy dirty, of course, because the barrel he'd been lurking in also contained charcoal. They dumped him down on the deck, right up close to me for some reason, and Ohtar came and stood over him.

'Just a moment,' Ohtar said. 'Bits told me quite clearly; he said you weren't coming with us.'

Kari grinned at him, stupid great oaf. 'Change of plan,' he said.

'Does Bits know?' Ohtar asked.

''Course not,' I broke in. 'Bits doesn't want him, so he's crept on board and hidden.'

Ohtar looked puzzled half to death. 'Why'd you want to do a thing like that?' he said.

Huge grin from Kari. 'To be with my old mate Eyvind, mostly,' he said; and everybody stopped staring at him and started staring at me instead. 'Also, you need me on this jaunt. Remember, I was the first ever to set foot on Meadowland. Probably, if we took it to law or whatever, it'd turn out that the whole island belongs to me by right of being there first. So you see, it's not up to Bits to say if I can come or not.'

'I don't know,' Ohtar said slowly. But he'd figured it out the same as the rest of us by then. We couldn't go back, so either we'd have to take Kari with us or bash him on the head and chuck him in the sea. I know which choice I'd have gone for, but nobody asked me.

CHAPTER
TEN

'What's he been telling you?' said Kari. 'Whatever it was, don't believe a word of it.'

I smiled at him. 'He was telling me how you both came to join the third – is it third, or fourth? Anyway, the expedition led by the man with the funny name.'

Kari sighed, all the way up from the soles of his ancient boots. They were rather too large for him but had been, at one time, extremely magnificent; and I had my suspicions about them. At the very least, I guessed, their previous owner hadn't parted with them willingly. 'You mean Thorfinn Thordsson,' he said.

'I think so,' I replied. 'Eyvind just called him Bits.'

Kari let out a rather forced laugh. 'Wonderful language, Greek,' he said. 'Me, I'd translate it a bit different: Scraps is more like it. Like, a pile of offcuts left over from other jobs, and your workman's looking to make a bit on the side putting them all together and passing them off as the genuine article. That'd be more like it.'

I scratched my chin. 'So you didn't like him much?'

'You could say that,' Kari said.

I glanced over my shoulder. Eyvind had gone off to the

stream for his daily wash. The Northerners are obsessive about washing, and I believe that's why so many of them look older than they actually are. As I see it, the human skin is just soft, thin leather; if you're continually getting it wet, sooner or later it'll start shrinking and shrivelling. If they used oil and a scraper, like we do, their skins would stay supple and they wouldn't end up looking like dried figs by the time they turn thirty. But there you are.

'He'd just got to the bit where they found you hiding in the charcoal barrel,' I said.

Kari looked blank. 'What charcoal barrel?'

Don't ask me why he told you that (Kari said). The truth is, Thorfinn kept on and on at me to join up, because he needed one of the old hands from the earlier trip, but nobody wanted anything to do with it. I told him to get lost, but he was one of those aggravating little men who won't take no for an answer. Then he told me he'd kidded Eyvind into going, so I gave in. I knew Eyvind'd expect me to go along if he was going. We've been around each other so long, he'd be lost without me.

Now I think about it, I can see where he's got that charcoal barrel thing from. See, I wanted it to be a surprise for him, me joining up after I'd sworn blind I wasn't going to. So I snuck aboard the ship before everybody else and hid behind a big cask in the hold — *behind* it, mind you, not *in* it, there's a difference — and once we were under way I hopped out and said, 'Look, it's me!' or something of the sort, I don't remember what. Anyhow, he pulled a long face like he wasn't glad to see me, but that's just Eyvind mucking around. He always acts miserable when he's happy.

Thinking about it, that was probably the easiest trip we had; at least, I can't remember very much about it, so it can't have been too bad. More luck than judgement, mind you, because Thorfinn was a pretty bloody awful navigator – God only knows how he'd managed to flit backwards and forwards from the East all those years without coming to harm. Hardly knew which way up to hold a bearing-dial. Luckily for us, we weren't on his ship. We were on Bjarni Herjolfson's old tub, yet again, and we had Thorfinn's forecastle-man, Ohtar, as our skipper. He wasn't the sharpest arrow in the sheaf, but he got us there, and that's about all that needs to be said.

You want to know why I didn't like Thorfinn Scraps? I'll tell you. He was weak. Weak and ignorant, and they don't go together very well. Now Thorvald Eirikson was easygoing, but that's not the same as weak. Thorvald didn't stomp up and down the deck yelling all the time, but you wouldn't have answered him back, or not twice. Thorfinn Scraps was the sort of man who wouldn't make up his mind till he'd asked two or three people, and then he'd do something that was a bit of each idea but also a bit of his own, in other words a right mess, and it'd usually go wrong, as you'd expect. Scraps of ideas, you see, all bunged together like a poor man's stew. He deserved his name, all right. Maybe you can get away with that sort of thing when you're plodding the same old trade-routes year after year with the same crew, and so everybody knows what they've got to do without having to be told. Now Thorfinn's crew were a good bunch, far better than he deserved. Search me why they put up with him. He owned the boat, I guess.

Anyhow, we made the Meadowland coast about a day's sail north of Leif's Booths, and turned south. It was funny seeing the place again. A lot of the men were on edge, looking out for the leather boats. Can't blame them for that, but it made me nervous. The way I saw it, we'd spent a hell of a lot of time at Leif's Booths, on and off, without ever seeing another living soul; it was only when we went poking about north that we ran into the leather-boat people, so really there wasn't anything to be afraid of. But when you're not worried about something, and everybody else around you's pissing down their legs, it tends to make you really jumpy. Great start.

Well, we reached the Booths next day, and there they still were, which was good. Stood to reason, if the leather-boat people had really got it in for us they'd have wrecked the place, pulled the houses down and burned the timbers. Instead, apart from the grass getting long on the roofs, you'd never know we'd been away.

We landed, and the first thing that clown Thorfinn does is go charging off up the beach, leaving the rest of us to pull the ships up, take out the tackle, all that. We've just about finished when Thorfinn comes back, looking dead worried.

'Are you sure this is the right place?' he says.

Eyvind says yes, he's pretty sure. Thorfinn scowls, like he doesn't really believe him. 'So where's all the fields of self-sown wheat?' he says. 'It should be just starting to green up at this time of year. I've got two dozen brand new scythe blades and ten flails in the hold.' Typical of the man.

He'd bungled the supplies, too; he'd fetched along every kind of useless tool you could think of, but bugger-all for us to eat, short of slaughtering the cattle we'd brought as breeding stock. But there's definitely such a thing as fool's luck, because the very next morning we woke up, and there on the beach was a beautiful stranded whale.

Rorqual, we call them; I don't know what the Greek word would be, assuming you get them down here in the warm waters. Anyhow, it was the biggest specimen I've ever seen. Seventy feet if it was an inch, and blubber two fingers thick—

★

'Excuse me,' I said. 'Do you mean to say you people actually eat those things?'

Kari stared at me as though I'd just spat in his wine. 'Of course we do,' he said. 'There's not much better eating than a fat whale steak; and it keeps practically for ever, if you can bring yourself to leave any.'

'Amazing,' I said.

'You bet,' he replied. 'Fantastic stroke of luck, when you get one just dumped on your doorstep, so to speak. Back home, though, it can be a problem; because as soon as word gets about that there's a whale, everybody from miles around comes running with their axes and buckets to get a slice, no matter whose land it's washed up on. And then you can bet there'll be a fight or two; regular pitched battles, sometimes. Then you get all the bad feeling, which leads to feuds, which leads to lawsuits and killings and God knows what else.'

'Over whale meat,' I said.

He nodded. 'Give folks something worth fighting over, what d'you expect?'

But this time (Kari went on) there was none of that; because there was just us, no neighbours wanting a share. Talk about luck. But to hear everybody talk, you'd think Thorfinn'd planned it all, maybe sent a message ahead to have it ready and waiting for him when he arrived, like a Greek gentleman's picnic. Truth is, if it hadn't been for the whale, we'd have been back in the old routine, spending all day fishing or grubbing around for the wild corn, and no time to spare for building sheds or putting up fences for all that livestock we'd brought with us.

But anyway; I wasn't complaining, because instead of mouldy porridge I was stuffing my face with prime whale, and who cares where it came from or how it got there? So that was all right; but precious little else was.

I'll tell you a funny thing, though. After we'd finished up the whale, and we were rolling up the last of the blubber in the skin, guess what we found underneath, squashed into the sand: Thorvald Eirikson's canopy stuts. You remember I told you, Thorvald had slung them overboard when we'd made landfall and they'd sunk like stones. Well, there they were, a bit rotten and wormy, but I knew they were his because he'd had THORVALD cut into them in masons' letters up one side. I was going to tell Thorfinn about it – he'd been moaning on the way over because he'd forgotten to bring any canopy struts of his own – but it slipped my mind, what with one thing and another, and by the time I remembered some fool had split them up and used them for guy-rope pegs.

Soon as the fencing was done, Thorfinn orders us to turn the stock out. Me, I could see straight off, the grass was very green and lush, and the animals'd been on hay and barley all the way from Greenland. Now any boy'll tell you, don't let a young calf stuff itself full of fat new grass or first thing you know, it'll scour and die. But Thorfinn was lucky yet again, he got away with it. The calves turned a bit funny for a while, kicking and bucking and prancing about – it'd have been a right laugh if we hadn't been expecting them to keel over and die at any moment – but they calmed down eventually and then they were fine, except they'd gone a bit wild and we had a hell of a job handling them sometimes.

But while they were still doing all that frisking about, Thorfinn was watching them with a huge grin on his face, saying it was obvious they liked it here and were going to be happy. Bloody merchant, see, hadn't got a clue about livestock. I wanted to tell him, they're skipping around like that because they've got really bad guts-ache; but I didn't say anything. He wouldn't have listened.

First job on the list, once we'd unloaded the ship and got everything into store and under cover, was building sheds for the animals. No problem about that, with all the timber you could ever possibly want just a few hundred yards up the slope. So we got axes — Thorfinn had brought three dozen, twelve per ship; brand spanking new, with iron heads and twisted-steel edges, must've cost him a fortune — and we spent three days just felling and trimming, splitting the logs down into rails, and dragging them down the hill. It's hard work cutting lumber, but after being cooped up on the ships, even though we'd had a reasonable crossing, we didn't mind; it was good to be able to stretch our backs and loosen up. Evenings, we sat in the longhouse, with a bloody good fire of birch logs, beer we'd fetched from home and all the whale you could eat. Instead of arranging the seating the usual way, with a high table for the bosses and a long table for the rest, Thorfinn just had one table — planks on trestles, really — and he and Gudrid sat in the middle with the rest of us sitting wherever we liked, ever so informal and relaxed. That was his style, and a lot of the men thought it was a good thing. Not me. Far as I was concerned, it was weakness — he knew he didn't have the strength of mind to be respected, so he wanted to be liked, to be our friend. That's fine, but you don't take orders from your friends. A leader's a man who says, Do this, because I say so, or else; so you do it, even if you think it's stupid or downright dangerous, and that's your side of the bargain kept. If the leader gets his side wrong, then it's between him and Odin, or our Heavenly Father or whoever it is who decides who wins the victory and who gets slaughtered. If you're in charge and you're basically saying, It's not my decision, I'm just going by what everybody else wants, then it stands to reason, our Heavenly Father won't know what to think, because let's say half the men in the group deserve the victory and the other half don't. Screws everything up, and puts the blame on the little people who should only be asked to carry out their side. No good ever comes of it, either up North or down here.

Anyway. We got the pens built, and after that we raised sheds and byres and a barn. The women were busy with the first brew of beer. Thorfinn had a couple of the men who were good with tools make him a plough, because he reckoned both wheat and barley would grow there, no problem at all. We were getting a decent yield of milk from the cows, the fowls were laying, the ice was slow coming so we carried on taking the boats out fishing much longer than we'd expected. In other words, we all just got on with ordinary everyday things, the sort of stuff you don't think twice about, like when you want to walk you don't issue separate orders to each joint and each toe for each stage of the operation, you just get on with it. That was fine, it was a good time, and autumn melted away into winter before we realised how the time was getting on. But that was all right, too. What with cheese and dried fish and the remains of the whale, not to mention the beer, which came out pretty good, we'd got enough in hand to see us through pretty well: fuel wasn't an issue; the house was warm and weathertight and big enough that we could go to sleep without someone's toes in our ears. It wasn't a whole lot different from being in Greenland, except in some respects it was better. Everyone was getting along just fine; no feuds, no personality clashes or fallings-out or any of that stuff. Really, you couldn't complain. Best of all, of course, we hadn't seen or heard anything of the leather-boat people, which'd been the one thing nobody ever mentioned and everybody kept thinking about.

Really, though, you had to laugh. That clown Thorfinn'd fetched along a whole load of mail shirts. I heard the story about them from one of his men; they'd come in the first place out of a big burial mound somewhere on the Danish-Swedish border, there'd been some horrible battle and at the end of it they'd slung all the dead in a ditch and covered them in earth and stones. Some time later, a bunch of the local lads went out there with mattocks and shovels, broke the mound open and salvaged all the gear. These mail shirts – well, some of them were in a bit of a state, else their owners wouldn't have wanted burying; but the Danish lads got some wire and patched them up, and soaked off the rust in salt and vinegar, so they looked pretty good. Then they sold them cheap, as salvage, to some trader or other. He sails to Norway, tries to offload these mail shirts, but the buyers take one look at them and they can see they've been in the ground a bit too long, because the rings've got a bit thin where the Danish lads soaked off all the rust. Then Thorfinn comes along, and the trader figures him out for what he is, an idiot. So, one night at the earl's house, where all the foreigner traders are sitting round drinking with the earl's men, he challenges our Thorfinn to a game of chess. Thorfinn doesn't mind that, he fancies himself as a chess player; they play the game, the trader loses on purpose. Right, he says to Thorfinn, for the next game let's make it interesting: your two hundred ells of Icelandic striped cloth against my three dozen mail shirts.

Well, if the shirts'd been any good, that'd have been a bloody stupid bet; as it was, it was rather more than they were worth, and a sight more than he'd given the Danes. Anybody with half a brain would've seen there was something wrong, but Thorfinn rubs his podgy little hands together and says, Right, let's do that. The trader plays, and once again he loses on purpose.

Of course, everybody's really impressed; here's a man who backs himself at these apparently crazy odds, then loses, then gets up from the table and yawns like he really doesn't care, thanks the other man for an interesting game and says he'll have his men bring the shirts over to Thorfinn's ship in the morning. Just the sort of showing-off that goes down a treat with your landed gentry out East, where they all like to play the big, brave viking; and this earl's no exception. He calls the trader over; the way you handled losing that game, he says, was really classy; most men'd be in tears gambling away a fortune like that, but you just shrugged it off like it doesn't matter. I'd like to give you a present, the earl says, worthy of your honour and breeding. So what does the earl do but pull this huge gold bracelet off his arm and hand it to the trader, plus a fine brooch with jewels in it, and a big load of flour, and a sword, and God only knows what else. So the trader goes away with all this lovely loot, the earl's made himself look good in the eyes of all his chums for his princely munificence, while our Thorfinn wets himself with joy because he's got three dozen mail shirts for nothing.

Anyhow; Thorfinn's got these things, and for the first week or so he puts one on every morning, just in case the leather-boat people attack, and he waddles round the place in it, joining in all the work to show what a good man he is, felling trees and hauling lumber and all the rest of it. But even a rusted-out mail shirt is heavy, especially round the shoulders and neck, and you've got to wear a thick wool shirt under it, else it chafes your skin raw, so it gets pretty warm in there; so he's sweating like a pig and staggering around the place, and because he's short the stupid thing comes right down below his knees anyway. Naturally people start sniggering, but that means he daren't just take the shirt off, else he'll lose face; so he's stuck in it. What with the damp and the sea air and the sweat, the shirt's getting all red with rust and stinky, so every night he's got to dump it in a barrel of sand and roll it up and down the barn to polish it up— Well, eventually he's had enough, and one morning he comes out to go to work with the rest of us, and the mail shirt's not there; everybody stops and stares, and a few of the men grin and maybe start whispering, but of course Thorfinn's suddenly blind and deaf; and that was the end of that. But you can see what I mean when I said Thorfinn was a fool, with fool's luck. He always had this knack of getting things wrong – not so wrong that the ship sank or everybody died, but just wrong enough to spoil his good fortune and take the shine off everything.

Even so, that was a good winter: far and away the best winter I'd spent in Meadowland, though that's not saying a lot. When spring came and we were able to go out and about again, there was something, I don't know, different about everything. Let's see; it'd be completely wrong to say we were starting to think of Leif's Booths as home, it wasn't like that at all. Home – well, I guess you could say that none of us were the home sort. Thorfinn, for example. Presumably he was from some place originally, in Norway; but I never heard him talk about it, and from what his men said, he'd been moving around for years and years, trading and so forth – didn't even spend winter in the same place twice if he could help it. His crew'd stuck with him because they were that way too, they had nowhere to go back to, so as far as they were concerned home was people rather than places. As for Eyvind and me; we'd been raised in Iceland, couldn't wait to leave Drepstokk to go with Bjarni

Herjolfson; we'd ended up at Brattahlid because we'd joined up with Leif Eirikson, and then he decided his wandering days were over, so we were stranded, like that poor sod of a whale. So what did we all do, our funny collection of drifters? We sailed off the edge of the world to Meadowland, with our ships full of useful and practical things, to make new lives for ourselves in the wide-open country. Dreams, dreams – to my mind, Meadowland wasn't my shining future beckoning to me across the sunset, it was more like a bit of bramble caught in my trouser leg, pulling at me and digging in tighter the more I tried to pull away. So no, we weren't starting to see Meadowland as where we belonged. It was more like we'd been washed up there after a horrible storm, and now it was daybreak and the wind and rain'd died off, and sure we were stuck there but at least it was turning out fine.

Spring's when Meadowland's at its best; it's actually not so bad then, particularly if you like flowers and stuff, though they don't do a lot for me personally. It helps, of course, if there's plenty to do. Work's a bugger, but it does take your mind off other things. Lambing came on, and turned out pretty well. The spring pasture suited our Greenland cows; poor bloody animals, they were used to grass like short green wire, so the lush, fat stuff was a real treat for them, and pretty soon we had as much milk as we could drink and loads left over for butter and cheese. It's a sad reflection on people, but how they feel depends an awful lot on what they're getting to eat. Dried fish and a few leeks pulled out of the roof-turf will keep you alive when the snow's deep, but it makes you miserable. Cheese and eggs and a spit-roast duck now and again, and you don't mind waking up in the morning so much. It's as simple as that, really.

Thorfinn was happy as a lamb because the wheat he'd

sown was starting to come through. Gudrid and the other women grumbled now and again, because they were so busy making cheese and churning butter that they were way behind on darning and mending. We had a man working practically full time in the little smithy, bashing out nails by the bucketful, and we all took it in turns to sit by the charcoal heap as it burned through – nice job, that, particularly if you've got a big jug of beer handy. Thorfinn spoilt things a bit because he was so full of bright ideas, things he wanted done; you couldn't settle into a pattern, because one day he'd want a dozen men to drop what they were doing to go off into the woods to cut ash coppice for arrow-shafts; next day he'd tell you, Leave that and see if you can find any decent withy-beds for making baskets, and the day after that it'd be clay for pots, or putting up a row of frames for stretching hides on. So we had a dozen clever projects started at any given time, then put aside and not finished because he was off on some other new craze. But it was all right, he'd say, there'll be plenty of time to finish off later; and in the meantime, he wanted six men to cut turf, or dredge gravel.

Spring just sort of melted away, and then it was summer, the busy time of year. That wasn't too bad, either: long, warm days, the first cut of hay, folding the stock on the home meadows. It still wasn't home, but we were beginning to feel that the place quite liked us, and that's important even if it does sound dumb. Thorfinn started talking about when the best time would be for a bit of surveying, because at the rate we were going on maybe this time next year we'd be well enough established to think about splitting up, going out and staking our claims, deciding where we'd build our farms. The key to all that, he said, was the hay. If we could get a good enough cut, we could feed the stock over winter without having to slaughter. That way, there'd be the makings of a herd big enough to supply each of us with, say, a house-cow and two heifers, in a year or so. Either that, he went on, or fill two of the ships with timber, send them back to the Eastern Settlement and load up with livestock on the return trip; only there, of course, the problem'd be timing, being sure that the ships could get there and back before the start of the cold weather – and if we had half our manpower sailing the ships, would that leave enough of us for the second cut of hay, which was what we'd be relying on to feed the stock?

That's the way Thorfinn thought about things, like a puppy chasing its tail: full of energy, round and round in circles. The more he thought about things, the more complicated they got, until you started to wonder how in hell you'd ever managed to do difficult stuff like breathing or walking without falling over. Instead of telling him to shut up gabbling and get on with it, though, everybody listened carefully and nodded and said, Yes, that's true, good point, until everything outside of routine'd pretty much ground to a halt. Well, it was a change of pace after the spring, when we'd started jobs first and thought about them after, but I can't say it was an improvement.

It was a warm morning in the middle of all this, and either we were thinking long thoughts about haymaking timetables or not thinking of anything at all. I can remember quite clearly, all I had on my mind that morning was a pulled muscle in my back and what we were having for dinner. It all began so quietly, I can't actually tell you what happened to start with. The first thing I noticed was the bull, roaring its head off in the long pen.

Even that didn't register with me to begin with, because that bull was a noisy bastard at the best of times. Thorfinn'd been letting the stupid creature gorge itself on the new grass since the start of spring, so it had colic pretty much all of the time, and when its guts ached it made sure we all knew about it. Well, when a noise goes on all the time you quickly stop hearing it; only that morning, the sound of its roaring suddenly changed, just a little bit.

I was on charcoal duty that day; I was down by the lumber stacks with a saw, cutting cordwood into short logs to go in the middle of the heap. With the saw snicking away I didn't notice the change in the bull's hollering until someone drew my attention to it; he'd stopped work and straightened up, listening.

'What's the matter?' I asked him.

He made a be-quiet gesture at me. 'There,' he said. 'Hear it?'

'Hear what?' I said.

'The bull,' he replied; and then, yes, I heard it. 'What's got into him?' he went on.

Just then I looked round, and I could see about a dozen other blokes laying off what they were doing to listen, so I wasn't imagining things. 'Let's go and have a look,' I said to the other man – can't recall to save my life who it was, sorry. He nodded, so both of us downed tools and strolled over towards the pen.

About fifty yards away, we stopped dead. There were about half a dozen strangers on the other side of the pen, close in by the rails, standing absolutely still.

Sounds bloody silly, of course; but we didn't immediately figure out who they were, because we all thought of them as the leather-boat people, and these ones didn't happen to have their boat with them. They didn't look all that different from us, see; they had buckskins on, and quite a few of our people had made themselves buckskin shirts or trousers, so as to save the wool for best. At that distance, you could see they all had black hair, but we were just too far away to notice that their skins were a bit browner than ours and they didn't have beards.

But eventually the little bells rang in our heads, and we realised: it was them, the same lot that'd chased Thorvald Eirikson's men and killed Thorvald himself. That was when we started panicking.

Well, we panicked a bit; but then someone pointed out that there were only six of them, and they weren't actually attacking. What they were doing, of course, was standing dead still and most likely pissing down their legs in terror. Pity we didn't know it at the time, of course; but the reason why they were scared stiff was that none of them had ever even seen a cow before, let alone a great big noisy bull.

Sometimes I think about that moment, when I've got nothing better to do with my mind. We were scared of them, they were scared of the bull; but a bull's just a farm animal, and they were just men, so where did the fear come from? Simple: never seen one before. It's natural, it's *sensible* to be scared of things you don't know about or understand. That's what we learn when we're kids, the first time we reach out and grab at the pretty red and yellow fluttery thing and find out the hard way that it's fire. And then I get to thinking; Meadowland didn't scare me particularly the first time I saw it, or even the second, or the third. It was only when I got to know it — maybe I'm kidding myself if I say I ever understood it, but I guess that's my privilege, as an explorer — that it started to throw shadows in my mind. Now, you're a Greek, you know about a lot of clever stuff; shouldn't that have been the other way around? Or should the leather-boat people have gone prancing up to the bull assuming it'd be friendly, and only got the jitters once it'd gored a few of them?

Anyhow. They were standing there, still as trees, and we didn't know it was because they were frightened. Now a stranger walking towards you and then standing still and staring in your direction's always an unsettling thing, and really all you can do is stare back until something happens. So that's what we did.

What struck me wasn't how different they were from us, but how alike. I'd say they were a bit shorter than us, though maybe I'm thinking more about the other ones we came across later on. They had straight black hair pulled tight into a knot at the back of the neck. Like us, they were wearing coats that came down a hand's span below the knee; like ours, theirs had the fur on the inside, except round the neck. Under their coats they had buckskin shirts, and trousers down to the ankle, with tanned-hide boots on their feet. I couldn't see any weapons, except that one of them had a bow in his hand and a quiver on his back; but you'd expect that, of course. Four of them had some sort of leather packs or satchels on their backs, and one of the other two was carrying a kind of basket made out of strips of birch bark.

So really it goes to prove the old saying about who you are depending on where you are. Back in Iceland or the Eastern Settlement, if you looked up from your work and saw six men looking like that headed towards you, maybe you'd be curious, if they were strangers, but no way would you be scared; just as you wouldn't be frightened at the sight of a penned bull. What the hell: first time I came to the City, there was this funny-looking brass statue on a short pillar, in a small park near the river. I strolled up to look at it, and bugger me if there wasn't a horrible shrill whistling noise, and then the statue began spinning slowly round and round, and moving its arms up and down. Scared? When I finally stopped running, I realised I'd wet myself. But nobody else in the park even took any notice of it. They were too busy gawping at the crazy foreigner.

Which is what we were both doing, the leather-boaters and us, as though there was a mirror with an invisible frame set up in the middle between us. I don't know, maybe I've thought it all right out of proportion over the years. Maybe it was no big deal. I can't say.

So we stood there, and for a short while nothing much happened. Then, right out of the blue, that useless bloody bull started snorting and bellowing, scratching at the ground with its front hooves, carrying on the way they do when they've been overfed and kept penned too long. That was too much for the leather-boat people; they turned round and ran like hell, their bundles bouncing against their backs.

Well, soon as we saw they were frightened, we all brightened up no end. Couple of our men started laughing; the leather-boat people must've heard them, because they stopped running and looked round, just in case they were being ambushed or followed. But the bull carried on bellowing, and now it was running up the pen towards them, so again they turned and bolted, stopped and looked back at us, like a herd of bullocks when you clap your hands and yell.

'Don't think we need worry too much about them,' said Thorfinn. 'Pretty timid bunch, they strike me as.'

That cheered up most of us – not me, because a few minutes ago we'd been just as timid, or more so – and a couple of the men started jeering and calling out names and whatever. But I was thinking: they've come here to see us, and they've brought bundles and a basket. If they were planning on attacking us, how were they going to go about it – smother us to death? Seemed to me it wasn't too smart to go acting all aggressive till we knew what was in those bundles.

Or maybe I thought that a bit later on, with hindsight. It's been so long now that I can't be absolutely sure.

'I know,' someone called out. 'Let's turn the bull loose. That ought to be a bit of fun.'

Most of us turned to look at Thorfinn; but either he hadn't heard or his mind was somewhere else. Anyhow, he didn't say anything, and next thing, a couple of the blokes – Illugi was one of them, I think, and Thorkel Snot – dashed off, vaulted the pen rails, nipped across and threw open the pen gate.

Off goes the bull. Now by and large, he wasn't a bad-natured old boy; not naturally vicious, like some are. But he was frisky, and now and then he liked to run. I think it was just his way of letting off steam; and if you stood still till he was right up close and then suddenly spread your arms out wide and shouted, he'd stop dead still like he'd just run into a tree, look at you for a bit and then wander off and graze. But you had to know that, of course; and the leather-boat people didn't. Far as they were concerned, we had a tame monster and we'd just set it on them. They didn't hang about, just took to their heels. Good runners, all of them, very impressive turn of speed and they could keep it up over distance.

Well, even I was laughing now, because there's something about the sight of other people being chased by a bull that'd make a corpse grin. We carried on laughing for a bit; but then the bull, who was enjoying himself no end, started to gain on them, and instead of just running straight, they veered off, heading straight for the houses.

That wasn't quite so funny. 'The bastards,' someone said; and Thorfinn started shouting out names; you, you and you, get to the houses and bar the doors quick. He needn't have bothered, we were way ahead of him. The leather-boat people were making such good time, they almost beat us to it, at that; but about half of us got indoors and put up the bars, while the rest of us, including me, scuttled into the yard to keep them out of the barns and buildings.

Luckily, the bull had had enough by then. He stopped running, gave us all a dirty look, and ambled off for a feed. But the leather-boat people were in the yard, with a crowd of us all round them; they were shouting at us – not fierce or angry shouting, more a case of trying to make us understand them by sheer force of noise – and we were yelling back. They couldn't understand us any more than we could understand them, but I should think they got the general idea that we weren't friendly and they'd done something wrong.

Well, for quite some time Thorfinn just stood there, catching his breath. Eventually, though, he held up his hands and yelled, 'Quiet!' – which did the trick. We stopped shouting, and so did they. Then it was all dead quiet for a bit; they stared at us and we stared at them and nobody moved a muscle. You know how it is when you go to a farm where you're not known, and the dogs come bounding out right up at you, barking their heads off. You stop dead still, and when you aren't moving it's like they can't quite see you; they're puzzled and wary, and they growl a bit with their ears back, as if to say, where did he vanish to? And then the farmer or someone comes out and calls them off, and they wander away wagging their tails, and everything's fine. I think on this occasion we were the dogs and they were the stranger, though the edges were a bit blurred, if you see what I mean.

We could have gone on standing there for a very long time, I think; but then one of the leather-boat people, stocky sort of middle-aged bloke, took a couple of steps forward, very slow and careful, knelt down and started untying his bundle. When he unrolled it, we could see what was inside: all sorts of different kinds of fur, squirrel and marten and fox and rabbit and wolf. Poor bastards had only come to trade with us, and we'd treated them like a bunch of vikings.

I think most of us had the good grace to feel really, really stupid. I know I did; and so, fair play to him, did Thorfinn. At any rate, he looked round and waved towards the houses to unbar the doors. Meanwhile the other five leather-boat people had rolled out their bundles, all more of the same, so obviously they were prepared to give it another go. Pretty good of them, I think, in the circumstances.

Mind you, we didn't actually want to buy furs; we'd got plenty of our own, after half a year's hunting and trapping. But that didn't really matter. We obviously needed to make it up to them for being so nasty. Question was, what did we have that they might want in exchange? It wasn't like we had anything much, certainly nothing to spare – if we hadn't needed it, we wouldn't have brought it with us.

I suppose that was what was going through Thorfinn's mind, as he stood there with a sort of dozy grin on his face, his idea of a warm smile of welcome. That was about as far as he went, where diplomacy was concerned; and if that's how he went about trading back in the East, God only knows how he managed to stay in business.

Then we had a stroke of luck; mostly, I think, because Gudrid and the other women remembered their manners, which was a sight more than could be said about the rest of us. Out they came, with jugs of milk and a big dish of bread, butter and cheese. Trust women to know what to do, when the men're doing their best to screw everything up.

Anyhow, Gudrid marched up to the leather-boat people – she was about six months pregnant at the time – smiled nicely and sort of waved the milk and the food at them.

They hesitated for a moment or so; then the man who'd been the first to unroll his bundle took a step forward. He was looking at the food on the tray like he had no idea what it was. I think he may have taken a deep breath, summoning up courage or whatever; then he grabbed a pat of butter and took a big mouthful.

You never saw such a look on a man's face. It was like he'd wandered into Heaven in the middle of dinner. He chewed, then stopped, then chewed a bit more; then he chewed very fast, and bit off another big faceful; then he swung round and held out the rest of the pat to his mates, jabbering away at them with his mouth full. They all tried some, and a heart-beat or so later it was like we all didn't exist, and all that stuff with the bull hadn't happened. They swooped down on the dish like a flock of rooks; one of them tried a hunk of the cheese, and that went down pretty good as well. Gudrid was a bit taken aback, like you'd expect, but she coped well; she looked round at the woman behind her and told her to get some more butter and cheese, quick. By then, the leather-boat people's leader or whatever he was had started drinking the milk, straight from the jug because nobody'd thought to pour any into a cup for him; and we all just stood and watched, and a bloody good show they were put-ting on, at that.

After they'd cleared the dish of everything except the bread – they didn't seem the slightest bit interested in it – the boss put his hands on the shoulders of two of his mates, as if to say, Steady on; then they talked together for a bit, very fast and earnest. By then, fresh supplies of butter and cheese had shown up; but instead of pouncing on it, they hesitated, like they were thinking, or doing sums in their heads. Then the boss looked Gudrid in the eye, to get her attention; he pointed at the empty dish with one hand, and his bundle of

furs with the other; then he sort of waggled his eyebrows, as
if to say, Well, what about it?

'Fuck me,' someone just behind me said. 'He wants to pay
for his dinner.'

Gudrid scowled at whoever'd just spoken, typical woman's
what-will-our-guests-think-of-us scowl; no need, of course,
since the leather-boaters didn't have a clue what'd just been
said. Meanwhile, their boss did the pointing and eyebrow-
waggling thing again, and it was pretty clear that that was
exactly what he meant: his bundle of furs in exchange for
the cheese and butter that they'd just gobbled.

First off, Gudrid stared at him like he was mental; then
she nodded very fast. I don't think the leather-boaters nod
like we do, because their boss didn't seem to have a clue
what she meant by it. He backed off a bit, so she smiled,
knelt down and pulled the furs toward her. He waggled his
eyebrows a bit more, and his mate scooped up his bundle
and came and stood next to him. The woman with the fresh
supplies put her dish down on the deck, and they scrambled
to help themselves. After that, it was pretty plain sailing: six
dishes of butter and cheese for six bundles of fur. When
they'd done scoffing the sixth helping, they stood there
waving their hands in a friendly sort of way for a bit, then
turned round and walked off. We opened up our circle to let
them pass and away they went – giving the bull a wide
berth, understandably, but otherwise all nice and happy and
friendly. We watched them till they were out of sight.

'What the hell,' someone said, 'was all that about?'

Actually, now I come to think of it, that was me.

CHAPTER
ELEVEN

'Your friend Kari,' I said, maliciously, 'was just telling me about your first run-in with the locals.'

Eyvind put down the water jug he'd just filled and looked sideways at me. 'Was he, now,' he said.

I nodded. 'He'd just got to the bit where they'd eaten the cheese, then left,' I said. 'Then Kari got a bad pain in his stomach and went off somewhere. Is he all right?'

'Him? Oh yes, fine. It gets him sometimes. Had it for years. I keep telling him, it's because he bolts his food. What did he tell you about Bits and the leather-boat people?'

A rose or a fruit tree is always improved by judicious pruning. There are many occasions on which the same can be said of the truth. 'He told me,' I said, 'that all they wanted in return for their bundles of furs was a few platefuls of butter and cheese. Is that right?'

Eyvind laughed, and poured water into two cups. 'Bits had it all figured out, right from the start, soon as he set eyes on them,' he said, handing me a cup. 'See, the leather-boat people don't go much on growing stuff, apart from a bit of that funny sort of corn they have out there; and they don't keep any tame animals to speak of. Mostly they live off the big deer in the forests; and the thing about wild meat is, it's all lean. No fat. That's all right in a hot place like this, but where it's cold most of the year, you need a healthy dose of fat in your diet to keep you going. So, far as they were concerned, butter was the most amazingly wonderful stuff they'd ever eaten.' He sighed, as though recalling a good memory. 'So,' he went on, 'soon as Bits realised they were there to trade, he sent in to the house for butter and cheese, which we'd got plenty of, and in return we got, what, a hundred silver marks' worth of furs. Just what we needed for the cold season. Like I told you before, they don't come much shrewder than old Bits.'

I decided to be a little bit of bramble snagging on his sleeve. 'You say Thorfinn deduced all that the moment he saw those people?' I said. 'How come?'

'Ah,' said Eyvind. 'He explained it to me later. He said, none of the other expeditions'd come across these people, not till Thorvald got killed, and we'd been there ourselves a whole summer and winter and spring and not seen anything of them; so, he reckoned, they couldn't be farmers, living all the time in the same place, or we'd have seen their fields and houses. No, he figured they must be wanderers, following the deer as they move around in the big woods. He'd already guessed that before we got to Meadowland, actually; but when he saw them, he noticed that they didn't have what we'd call cloth, that's like wool or linen or cotton. All their clothes and shoes and everything were buckskin and hide and fur. It wasn't the first time he'd been among people like that, see; there's a whole load of them right up north, in Finnmark and Permia, wandering around after the big herds of reindeer they have there. Very much the same sort of people, Bits said, except bigger and taller. And he knew the Permians go nuts over butter and cheese, so it stood to reason that this lot'd be just the same.'

'I see,' I said. 'You're right, he was shrewd.'

'Got to be, if you want to get on as a trader,' Eyvind replied. 'It's a basic skill of the job, being able to size people up at first sight.'

'A useful talent,' I agreed. 'So,' I went on, 'you were on good terms with the locals after that.'

A frown flitted across Eyvind's face. 'For a while,' he said.

But Bits wasn't absolutely happy with the way things'd gone (Eyvind went on). He didn't like the way those people had been able to walk right in on us like that, without us noticing. Fine so long as they were friendly; but what about if they turned nasty for any reason? Like, maybe the ones who came to trade were from a different clan or whatever from the ones who killed Thorvald? Bloody good point, that; they'd most likely still be sore over Thorvald killing the people he had found sleeping under the boats. What if they came creeping up on us out of the wood? And besides, even if that was all forgotten about, a smart man like Bits knew all too well how quickly things can go wrong when you're among strangers, and you don't even know the language. You can give mortal offence without even knowing you've done it.

So the day after the traders came to visit he sent us off into the woods to cut a big load of twelve-foot stakes, and we built a good strong palisade right round the house and the buildings. First we dug a ditch, four feet down, and threw the spoil up behind us so that it made a nice, solid bank about three foot high; and we drove the stakes into that, each one down four feet, to leave two-thirds of its length above ground. Once we'd got all the stakes in, close enough so a rat couldn't squeeze between them, we sharpened the tops of the posts to make them awkward to climb over; and we put in a proper gate and everything. Everyone felt a damn sight safer after we'd done that, I can tell you.

Not long after we'd finished that job, Gudrid had her baby. We were all outside, just putting the last few touches to the palisade, and suddenly we could hear this kid squalling. Bits dropped the sledgehammer he was holding and dashed in through the gate. Then the penny dropped for the rest of us, and we all dashed in after him. Turned out it was a boy; the first Northerner to be born in Meadowland. They called him Snorri, and you can bet your life he got spoiled rotten by all of us. Sort of a symbol to the rest of us, I suppose you could say; like it meant we weren't just passing through, we were there to stay.

'Talking of which,' I interrupted. 'I've been wondering. There were four other women along on this expedition besides Gudrid, right?'

Eyvind frowned. 'Yes,' he said. 'But they aren't important.'

I smiled at him. 'You'll excuse me saying this,' I said, 'because for obvious reasons I can't claim any real understanding of this subject; but there were, what, sixty men and five women, and one of those five was the boss's wife. How could the other four not be important? I'd have thought you'd have been fighting to the death over them.'

Eyvind's frown deepened. Northerners can be a bit scary when they're tense, even an old codger like Eyvind, and if he'd told me to drop the subject, I'd have done so. But he said: 'It wasn't like that. They weren't—' He hesitated. 'Let's say, they weren't things of beauty.'

'Even so,' I said. 'Sixty men, out there for the best part of a year—'

He looked away. 'And let's just say,' he went on, 'they weren't there exactly out of choice. Not theirs, anyway.'

'You're embarrassed about something,' I said.

He was getting annoyed. 'Well, maybe it wasn't the best decision Bits ever made. But he needed to make up the numbers, and there's men's work and there's women's work, and none of the Eastern Settlement women were particularly keen to go. So he had to do the best he could.'

I could feel that I was onto something; not, perhaps, something I'd actually want to know, but I've got this confounded itch of curiosity. 'Well?' I said.

'It wasn't his fault, really,' Eyvind snapped. 'Mostly, he was just doing someone a favour. Like I said, he needed women for the expedition, and they were all he could get. And then, just before we were due to leave, he got word from one of the other farms that a viking'd just put in, and he'd been to Ireland and he'd got slaves for sale. Females.'

'Ah,' I said.

'Well.' Eyvind pulled a strange sort of face. 'The story the viking told him was, they'd been raiding on the west coast of Ireland — used to be a good place years ago, but it'd become too much like hard work. Anyhow, the viking attacked this abbey, out in the middle of nowhere, soft target; and those Irish abbeys always used to have loads of gold and silver plate, stuff like that. Not this one, though; the viking said he'd seen richer cowsheds. But he'd gone all that way, spent a small fortune fitting out the ship and all, he had to do something. So he grabbed a bunch of the nuns, for ransom. Seemed like a good idea, he said. But it turned out that this abbey'd fallen on hard times. Some sort of religious thing; it wasn't, you know, in the mainstream. Point is, they'd fallen out with the local church bosses years ago, which meant that they weren't getting any money, and nobody'd joined up for a very long time, so all that was left was a bunch of old crones; and when the viking sent a message to the bishop demanding a ransom, the bugger practically laughed in his face.'

'I see,' I said. 'Not very good, then.'

'Not really. For two pins, the viking would've turned them loose and told them to get lost, but that'd have been really bad for business – set a precedent, if you follow me. So he was stuck with them: six leathery old nuns that nobody wanted. All he could think of was, take them to Greenland because not many slave traders bother going up that far, someone might give him something for them. Two of them died on the way, which really didn't help. By the time he got there he was willing to give them away to anybody who'd take them. Which was a shame, really, because they were tough old things, hard workers so long as you let them do their praying and stuff. And Bits knew Gudrid'd be pleased, because she was really into religion, like women so often are.'

'And was she?' I asked. 'Pleased, I mean.'

He shrugged. 'Once she'd got used to them, I think,' he said. 'Of course, they only spoke Irish and a bit of Latin; and Gudrid only spoke Norse and a *tiny* bit of Latin that she'd learned off priests, so it was a bit fraught for a while until they figured out how to talk in sign language. But anyhow, that's the answer to your question. Having them along really wasn't a problem in the way that you meant.'

'I see,' I said. 'Thank you for explaining.'

Anyway (Eyvind continued), life went on nice and pleasant over the summer. Nothing much happened after Gudrid had the baby, and we didn't see anything more of the leather-boat people. Not till autumn was beginning to set in.

I can remember where I was, the second time they showed up, because of what happened just before.

There was this man called Ohtar; he'd been the captain of

our ship on the way over, and a pretty good job he'd made of it. He'd been with Bits for years and years, practically his right-hand man. After we'd been in Meadowland for a bit, though, he turned a bit strange. Moody; sometimes, instead of getting on with what he was supposed to be doing, he'd sit up against the wall of the house and stare out at the sea; or else he'd go off into the woods for a whole day, and only come back when it was getting dark. I think Bits tried to find out what was bugging him, but either he didn't answer or he said he'd got the guts-ache or something. Eventually Bits decided that the best thing to do would be to leave him to work out whatever it was for himself.

Anyhow, I always got on reasonably well with Ohtar, though for some reason I'd always given him a wide berth when he was in one of his funny moods. You get a feeling about people sometimes, as though there's a thick thorn hedge all round them that you can't actually see, but you know it's there all right whenever you blunder into it.

Well, this time I'm telling you about, Ohtar was sitting on a barrel in the doorway of the long house; not doing anything, just sitting with his hands on his knees, looking up at the forest. Just inside the door, the baby was yelling its head off; but Ohtar didn't seem to notice. I'd have carried on by and left him to get on with it, but I'd just been sent back from the home meadow – we were turning the second cut of hay – to fetch Bits's hat, which was hanging up on its usual hook in the back room, so I had to go past Ohtar to get into the house. Maybe he heard me, or I brushed against him on the way through; he jumped up and grabbed my shoulder so hard that I felt something give way under his fingers.

'Watch it,' I said. 'That hurt.'

He looked down at me – he was a tall bastard – and for a

THOMAS HOLT

moment it was as though he was having a problem remembering who I was, or what business someone like me could possibly have around a well-ordered household.

'Sorry,' he said quietly. 'I thought you were someone else. That friend of yours.'

I hate it when people say that. For some reason that I've never been able to get my head around, people quite often get Kari and me mixed up. Which is bloody ridiculous; all right, we look a bit alike, and maybe we sound a bit similar, which is only to be expected when you think we were brought up together, we've been everywhere together, done the same things, shared the same experiences. But anybody with enough brains to fill a walnut shell can tell he's nothing like me.

'Thorfinn sent me back to get his hat,' I said.

Either that didn't register with Ohtar or he wasn't interested. 'Your friend,' he said, 'is a menace.'

I nodded. 'Tell me about it,' I said.

'It's all his fault,' Ohtar went on. 'Everything that's happened here, and everything that's going to happen, too. That's why I'm waiting here, see.'

I agreed with a lot of what he was saying, but even so there was something about him that was worrying me. 'Is that right?' I said.

'Yes,' Ohtar said. 'I'm going to kill him.'

That wasn't what I was expecting to hear. 'What's he done to you?' I asked. 'Been borrowing your boots without asking?'

'He's bad news,' Ohtar replied, looking at me thoughtfully. 'He was the one that found this place, wasn't he? Bjarni Herjolfson told you all to stay on board the ship, but he sneaked off and swam ashore.'

'That's right,' I said. 'Just the sort of stupid thing he does.

Like, suppose he'd got lost or swept down the coast in the current. We could've been stuck there a whole day looking for him.'

'Wilful,' said Ohtar. 'That's going to be the death of me, wilfulness. Oh, it's not such a bad thing, knowing what you want and making sure you get it. But thanks to him, I won't be going home with the rest of you. I'm upset about that.'

He was still gripping my shoulder like a forester's vice. 'What makes you say that?' I asked.

'Oh, I saw my fetch today,' he said. 'No mistaking it.' He made it sound like a tiresome thing, an unpopular relative announcing he's come to stay the winter. 'I was stacking cordwood behind the house and a shadow fell over me. I looked up to see who it was, and there was your friend Kari. He looked at me for a moment, and I knew it wasn't really him.'

There's not a lot you can say to someone who's in that sort of mood. 'You sure about that?' I said. 'I mean, people are always thinking they've just seen the fetch, and then nothing happens to them and they realise it was just their imagination. Then, one time in five hundred, they think they've seen the fetch and next day they're dead, and everybody says, "You see?"'

'Excuse me,' I interrupted. 'What's a—?'

'When you're about to die,' Eyvind said patiently, as though he was teaching the alphabet to a backward child, 'you see the fetch. It's a sign, to let you know.'

'Oh,' I said. 'What does it look like?'

He shrugged. 'Could be almost anything,' he said. 'Or anybody. Quite often it's someone who looks just like you, as though you'd looked in a pool of water. Or it could be someone who's already died, or a friend you haven't seen for years and who was miles away at the time you thought you saw him. Sometimes it's a person you met once, years and years ago, and suddenly bump into again, for no reason. Or just a stranger; or someone you see every day. Point is, when you see the fetch, you *know*.'

'That's silly,' I pointed out. 'If it can be anyone at all—'

'Mphm.' Eyvind moved his head slightly. 'That's what I used to think.'

Ohtar looked at me (Eyvind said), and he frowned a bit, and then he said, 'So anyway, that's why I'm waiting here for your friend Kari. I suppose you're going to go and warn him now.'

I shrugged. 'But hang on,' I said. 'If it really wasn't him you saw but the fetch pretending to be him, what's the good of killing Kari? Won't solve anything.'

'It was all his fault,' Ohtar said. 'Least I can do is take him with me.'

It wasn't the moment for it, but I laughed. 'I know the feeling,' I said. 'Strikes me I've been taking him with me all my bloody life, like those little round hairy seeds that snag on your sleeve as you go by. Has it occurred to you that if you're about to die soon and you kill him first, maybe you'll be stuck with him in the next world for ever and ever?'

Ohtar sighed. 'I can't help that,' he said, 'I don't make the rules. You know, it's a funny thing. When you're a little kid, your dad tells you about Valhalla; and when you're older, the priest tells you about Hell, and the strange part is, both of them sound pretty much alike, except that your dad says that's where you'll go if you're good, and the priest says that's where you'll be headed if you're bad. You know what I've figured out? It's only just occurred to me, but it makes good sense. Both of them, they're actually one and the same place; but if you're a viking you want to go there, and if you're the quiet, peaceful sort you'd hate it there, and Heaven's the place for you, sitting still and quiet·indoors on the right hand of God for ever and ever, like it's a winter that never ends. And of course, a viking'd hate that.' He shrugged his shoulders. 'The fact is,' he said, 'where you are depends on who you are, and that's all there is to it. Like us being here,' he added. 'Once you look at it in that light, of course, it all starts to make sense.'

I'm an old man now, and one of the rules I've lived by is that as soon as someone starts telling you the world makes sense, you can bet anything you like that his brain's come undone. Mind you, I'd come to that conclusion already.

'I see what you mean,' I said. 'But maybe you should hold off on killing Kari, just for now. I think it'd be better that way.'

Ohtar looked down at me. 'You're saying that because he's your friend,' he said.

'Yes.'

'Fine.' He yawned. 'That's as good a reason as any, I suppose. You'd better take Thorfinn his hat, before he starts wondering where you've got to.'

I got the hat and started off back to the meadows, thinking how awkward it was going to be having a nutcase around the place, and wondering what Bits could do about it. I hadn't got very far, though, when I heard a woman screaming.

I knew it wasn't Gudrid, because she was in the house with the kid, and the screams were coming from out front, in the yard. Had to be one of the Irish women, not that it mattered particularly who was doing it. I dropped the hat and raced off round the side of the house, just in time to see a big furry bundle sail over the top of the palisade and land in the dirt, just shy of the midden.

There was another bundle lying close to it, and one of the Irish women standing by yelling her head off; hardly surprising, of course, but I wasn't fussed about it because I knew the bundle for what it was. The leather-boat people had come back for more trading, and since we'd built the palisade and they couldn't get in the yard, they were slinging their wares inside to show us what their intentions were.

'It's all right,' I called out, but of course the stupid old cow hadn't got a clue what I was saying. Then a third bundle flopped on the ground right by her feet; she screeched like a chicken with the fox on her tail, and scuttled towards the house.

Nothing to worry about, I thought, but I'd better go and fetch Bits; so I ran off through the back gate and down to the meadow, and found him and the rest of the gang coming back up. They'd seen the leather-boaters coming down out of the woods, they said, and this time there were quite a few of them, perhaps two dozen.

'But that's all right,' Bits added. 'We've got plenty of cheese.'

When we got back to the yard there were loads of bundles lying there. Bits knelt down and opened one up; beautiful furs they were, and cured better than we could've done it. Bits grinned.

'This is a stroke of luck,' he said. 'If they'll trade us stuff like this, we could fill a ship and send it back to the Old Country.' (He meant Norway, of course, not Iceland.) 'With what these'd fetch over there, we could buy everything we'll ever need for the settlement; and we'd get traders coming out here to buy before long, once the word gets about.' He stood up. 'Better open the gate and let

them in,' he said. 'It's bad business, keeping customers waiting at the door.'

So a couple of the men went to open the gate, while
someone else ran inside to tell them to fetch out all the
cheese and butter we could possibly spare. When the house
door opened, I saw Ohtar peering out round the door
frame; and he had his axe in his hand. I didn't like the look
of that, because I wasn't absolutely sure that I'd talked him
out of killing Kari; he'd given in a bit too easily for my
liking.

They didn't look much different from the first lot, those
leather-boaters. Shorter than us, for the most part, and thin;
but well-built and wide across the shoulders, lean like dogs
rather than scrawny. They seemed nervous but anxious to be
friends; and bearing in mind what Bits'd just said, we were
keen to be friendly back. Out came the butter dishes and
wooden plates full of cheese, and jugs of milk with the cream
on top. To start with, the leather-boat people were happy
just to stuff their faces, like the last time; but while they were
eating and drinking, I noticed that they were looking round,
taking an interest. Mostly, I saw, they were looking at all the
things we had that were made of metal; when the sun flashed
on a brooch or a buckle or an axe-head, they'd look up and
stare for a bit, as if they'd never seen the like before.

Then I studied them for a while, and thought maybe they
hadn't.

For instance, there was one tall man with grey hair. Instead
of a belt round his middle he had a strap of twisted hide, and
it was tied in a knot rather than fastened with a buckle. In it
was tucked an axe, but the head wasn't steel, it was chipped
stone – some kind of flint or agate. That made me look at the
rest of them, and sure enough, there wasn't a single bit of
metal to be seen. Our lot, on the other hand, were positively

sparkling, because the sun was out; we Northerners like showing off, you see, and anything made of metal's valuable, so you like to wear it where people can see. We like shiny brass cloak-pins and finger-rings, or silver or gold if we can afford it; and of course you don't go anywhere without your knife and your axe, they're your basic everyday tools you use for most everything you do. Also, the men who'd come back from the meadow had their pitchforks, and some of them had billhooks for splitting withies into ties. All the sort of thing you'd never usually notice; unless, of course, you'd never seen bright, shiny things like that before.

I looked over at Bits, and I could see that he'd reached the same conclusion; but he was worried. 'Listen, all of you,' he said – he could say what he liked, because of course the leather-boats couldn't understand a word – 'I want it under-stood, nobody's to trade anything made of iron or steel with these people unless they check with me first. Butter's one thing, but weapons are a different matter entirely.'

Common sense, really; still, it had to be said, in case there was anybody who hadn't figured it out for himself. And sure enough, it wasn't long before a couple of the leather-boats started pointing at things like axes and knives and making unmistakable how-much-for-that gestures with their eye-brows and their hands. But Bits just looked stern and shook his head, and they seemed to be getting the message. So they went back to wedging cheese into their faces, while we cut the bindings on the bundles and had a look at what we were getting.

I was knelt down over a thick wad of squirrel pelts when a man called Ketil Mordsson came over to me. He looked worried, and I asked him what the matter was.

'Don't suppose you counted them on their way in,' he said.

That seemed a funny thing to ask. 'No,' I replied. 'Why?'

'I did,' he replied. 'Eighteen, I made it. And there's only sixteen now.'

I thought: that's an odd thing to be worrying about, and an odd thing in itself. 'Maybe two of them ate so much butter they've gone outside to throw up,' I suggested. 'If I was stuffing myself like that, it'd only be a matter of time.'

Ketil shook his head. 'You seen the way they've been eyeing up our knives and axes?' he said. 'You heard what Thorfinn said just now. I don't like that there's two of them missing all of a sudden.'

Now I could see what he was getting at; and I thought about Ohtar, inside the house with his axe and in a funny mood. 'Where's Gudrid,' I asked, 'and the kid? I can't see them, they must be indoors still.'

He frowned. 'That's a point,' he said. 'Come on, we'd better have a look.'

I really wish we'd thought of that earlier, but we hadn't. As it was, we were ten yards or something like that away from the door when a leather-boater came flying out, running so fast that his feet hardly seemed to be touching the ground. A moment later, out came Ohtar. He had his axe in his hand, and the blade was all smeared. Then, inside the house, Gudrid started screaming her head off.

Everybody froze and spun round; except Bits. He grabbed the man standing next to him — just so happened it was Kari. 'Get that gate shut,' he yelled in his ear, 'and someone get that bastard.' He meant the leather-boater who'd just come out of the house, and he didn't need to explain — we were way ahead of him. A couple of men made grabs for the runner but he swerved round them; and then Thorhall Eyes stuck out a foot and tripped him, and he went sprawling on the ground, all flying arms and legs.

I'd stopped to watch; but Ketil Mordsson was in the house already, pushing past Ohtar, who'd stopped dead and was standing there, his axe hanging from his hand, like he'd just been woken up while sleepwalking. Gudrid stopped yelling; and Ketil came back out, just as Thorfinn shoved past him, going in.

'It's all right,' Ketil told him. 'She's all right, so's the kid. There's one of them in there dead, though.'

So then we were all looking at Ohtar. 'That's right,' he said, rather awkwardly. 'I killed him.' He paused, then went on: 'They came in snooping around.' He hesitated again, then added: 'One of them was creeping up behind Gudrid, where she wasn't looking. He was going to snatch the kid, so I chopped him.'

The rest of the leather-boaters had realised that something wasn't right; they were edging back together into a circle, looking at each other, one or two of them talking softly. I could see them feeling for their axes in their belts without looking down, and I had a really bad feeling about what was going to happen next. It was like when you've cut three parts of the way through a tree on a windy day, and as it sways you look up and you can see it's almost ready to go but not quite. Do you step back clear, in case it comes down, or do you nip back in under it for the couple of good cuts it'll take to finish it off? That's what it felt like: one more misunderstanding, or a movement getting taken the wrong way, and we'd have a battle on our hands; we'd kill all of them, and they'd kill two, maybe three of us while we were at it. It was all very ugly, so it was just as well we had Bits in charge. He came out of the house, saw where we'd got to and clapped his hands together hard to get our attention.

'Open the gate,' he said, loud and firm but not shouting,

'and let them go, all of them. Just let them go,' he repeated. 'There's been no harm done, far as we're concerned.'

As the gate swung open, the leather-boaters edged towards it, not taking their stares off us for a moment. 'They were trying to steal an axe,' I heard Ohtar call out. Bits must've heard him but he didn't react.

'What about the dead man?' Ketil asked.

'Soon as they've gone, take him outside about a hundred yards and dump him. If they want the body, they can come back and take it without having to come in too close.'

One of the leather-boaters wasn't budging. He was standing his ground and saying something loudly, asking a question. Then the man who'd run out of the house said something back, and it struck me that quite likely the rest of them, the ones who'd already gone outside, didn't know yet about their man getting killed. My guess is that that was why Bits was in such a hurry to get them outside the palisade, before they realised what'd happened.

Anyway, the last few of the leather-boaters left; two of his mates had to come back and drag off the man who'd been shouting. We got the gate shut, and then Ketil and a man called Mord Fish brought the dead man outside. Ohtar must've given him one hell of a scat, because the top and back of his head were split right open, like a knotty log where you have to drive in wedges to free up the axe. I'm no expert, but I don't see how you could've done that except from behind.

'What a bloody fuck-up,' Bits said when he saw the body. I have to say, I turned my head away. It was only the second time I'd seen a man killed with an axe, and it's not something you get used to easily.

We waited a bit; then Bits had them open the gates and drag out the body. The men who did it said they hadn't seen any sign of the leather-boat people; I guessed they'd run for it, and only found out later that they were one short.

After that we all stood round for a while, and nobody said much. Ohtar sat down on a pile of logs and put his face in his hands. I think Bits went indoors to see how Gudrid and the baby were getting on. A couple of the women started collecting up the plates and jugs; I saw one of them brushing mud off a big hunk of cheese that'd been dropped. It was a strange atmosphere, like we were all kids who'd been caught doing something naughty and we were waiting to be yelled at.

Bits came out, and straight away he said, 'Right, things are going to get difficult from now on. You can bet what you like that they'll be back, and next time there's going to be a lot of them, and they won't be coming to trade. Now we should be all right behind the palisade, but what I'm worried about is the cattle.' He paused, like he was waiting for someone to argue; then he went on: 'I want a dozen of you to go up in the woods and make a clearing, where we can hide the cows. Mord, you and Helgi take the bull and let him loose in the small pen – that'll stop them coming up the track to the gate. We want to make sure we fight them where we want to, and the best place for that's going to be out back of the barns, between the lake and the woods. If they want to come at the gate without coming past the bull, that's where they'll have to go. Any questions?'

Nobody else had anything to say, so Bits had us pick up all the bundles and take them inside; no point in all those valuable furs getting trampled underfoot, he said. Meanwhile, he had Ohtar and Ketil and me fetch out the weapons that he'd brought in the ship: the spears and swords, and the bows. The lids had warped up tight on the crates, so we had to bash them in with the backs of our axes. We also pulled out the barrels full of mail shirts; but when we'd stove in the lids and tried to turn them out, they wouldn't budge. See, nobody'd given them any thought since we got there, and I think the sea water had got into them during the voyage; anyhow, they were all rusted up together into a huge brown lump. Soaking them for a week in salt and vinegar might've done something for them, but we didn't have time for that, so we let them bide where they were. I think Bits'd forgotten all about them, because he didn't mention them at all.

Everybody was a bit quiet and thoughtful while we were handing out the weapons, and nobody really wanted to be given one, like they weren't too happy about touching them. Bits called out who was to have what; I didn't get anything, not that I minded. We'd both got our hand-axes, of course, and when things get nasty it's always best to keep it simple and stick with what you know. Bits had one of the swords, and he folded his cloak over his left arm like a shield, very professional; that was Bits for you – everything he did, he made it look like he knew what he was about.

Bits told me to give a spear to Ohtar; and while I was over there I said to him, quiet so people wouldn't hear: 'So that was your fetch, then.'

He looked up at me. 'It's not over yet,' he said.

I shook my head. 'Was he really going to grab the kid?' I asked him, but he didn't answer, and I didn't want to make a big thing about it. For what it's worth, though, I don't believe in fetches, apart from the ones you carry round with you all the time. I still can't make up my mind whether Ohtar was under the tree when it fell or whether he was the tree himself. There comes a point, I guess, where the difference is too slight to be worth bothering with. Anyhow, Ohtar took the spear from me and pricked his thumb on the point to see if it was sharp. That surprised me; it'd been lying in the crate all that time and it'd got all fogged up with rust. It was always damp in that corner of the long barn, where we'd stored them.

Since then, of course, I've been a proper soldier, here down south where you're always fighting some war somewhere; and I've learned that battles are one part sheer muscle-snapping effort and ninety-nine parts standing or sitting around waiting for something to happen, and the one part is probably the best of it, even though that's when people get themselves killed. Maybe that's why we Northerners make such good soldiers: we can handle the useless waiting better than you people. After all, we sit around all winter waiting for the spring; we sit in our ships while the sea-spray smacks us around; we know how to bide quiet and save our energy, the way dogs and other animals do. But I for one don't like it – I can feel the time pressing on me, like toothache. I have to make an effort to find something to think about, and even that doesn't always work. When we fought the Bulgars and the Saracens, back in the old emperor's time, the officers always said I was a terror for fidgeting. Seems to me that every place I've been and everything I've done has been more waiting than doing; and I've wasted all that time by chafing against it, instead of finding a use for it. Not that it matters a lot. These days, of course, the emperor pays me for my time, whether I do anything useful or not. I tell you, if I'd come down here when I was young Harald's age, I'd be running the empire by now.

Anyhow, we didn't have long to wait. Two days later – it seemed longer, because we couldn't do anything while we were waiting, couldn't go out to see to the stock, couldn't even walk round the yard collecting the eggs – two days later they came back.

It was early morning, about the time you'd be looking to drive the cows back to the sheds for milking. There was a thin grey mist hanging low, the sort that starts about four feet off the ground and collects round trees and buildings like wisps of wool snagged in the thorns. By mid-morning it'd all have burned away; but it was good cover for the leather-boat people, coming up through the woods. We had the bull in the pen directly facing the point where the woods were nearest to the palisade, on purpose to force them to come between it and the lake. It was a good strategy, based on what we knew about the way they liked to fight, which wasn't much. They'd killed Thorvald Eirikson with a volley of arrows, and that was about the limit of what we knew; so Bits's idea was to cramp them up so that only the ones on the outsides could shoot at us. We'd meet them head on at the narrowest place, hold them there if we could, while a couple of us would sneak round, open the pen and drive the bull into their rear.

Good strategy. After all, we had nothing to gain from killing them: what we wanted to do was persuade them that they didn't want to fight us, now or in the future; and up till then at least they'd been mortal afraid of the bull. If it suddenly turned up out of nowhere, right up their arses while their attention was on the fighting in front, there was a fair chance they'd panic and run for it, maybe even be scared enough to leave us alone for ever. For good measure, Bits decided, we'd drive up the young bullocks as well. You and I know that a dozen young bullocks may act tough, but the worst they'd ever do to you is try and lick you to death; the leather-boat people didn't know that, though. Anyhow, we reckoned that it might work, and we couldn't think of anything better in the time available.

Bits had put Sigurd Eyes up in the top hayloft, with two

others to relay what he said back to the rest of us inside the house. Sigurd had been up there the best part of two days, so you'd have had to forgive him if he'd let his attention wander. But he saw the leather-boaters as they started walking out of the woods, and he called down how many of them he could see as they came: first five, then a round dozen, then a gap and then another fifteen. We were all sitting on the benches in the hall as the relay called out the numbers, all of us frantically adding up the total in our heads. All told, it came to eighty-one; so we were outnumbered, but not badly. Actually, Bits had assumed that there'd be more of them than there were of us, which was why he'd picked a tight place for the battlefield: a small area turns a large force of men into a hindrance rather than an advantage.

They had bows and arrows, the relay told us; also spears and axes with stone heads, and small round shields made of leather stretched on a birchwood frame. None of them had what we'd call armour, needless to say since they didn't use iron or steel, but quite a few of them were wearing three or four layers of fur coats, which would quite likely cushion a half-hearted cut or turn a long-range arrow. All in all, it sounded like they knew what they were doing, which was more than could be said for most of us. Oh, we weren't complete virgins when it came to fighting; half a dozen of the older men in Bits's crew had fought vikings once, in the Norway fjords, and nearly all of us had played at sparring with sticks against our fathers and brothers, back when we were kids. Where I come from, you don't really tend to learn fighting; it's assumed that you know how, by light of nature. Earls and rich farmers' sons may spend an hour or so with an old farmhand who was a viking in his youth, learning a few guards and passes and maybe a bit of footwork, but most of us have better things to do with our time.

Still, we were ready for them, or as ready as we'd ever be; and we listened as the relay told us that they'd seen the bull and didn't like the look of it – they were following the path up beside the lake, exactly as we wanted them to. When Bits heard that, he nodded to Mord and Hrut and Grim; they were in charge of the archery detail, a dozen or so men who had some idea of which end of the arrow you're supposed to pull on. The archers got up and filed out; they were to get up onto the roof of the cowshed, which was hard up by the palisade on the lake side, and shoot arrows into the leather-boaters as they passed. With luck they'd drop one or two, and then skip out of the way before the enemy could shoot back; that was supposed to stop them in their tracks and give the rest of us time to assemble at the side gate, ready for our glorious charge.

So the archers went out; the rest of us sat very still, giving them time to get in position. Kari was next to me; for some reason I couldn't fathom, Bits had entrusted him with a long-handled Danish axe, though Kari's never been able to split a cord of logs without missing his mark and knocking the axe-head off. I had my hand-axe, of course, and my knife; and I was trying to make up my mind what I was going to do. Sensible thing, of course, would be to find some big, tall, broad bugger and stay close in behind him for as long as possible; but a part of me was saying that the right thing to do was to get up front and engage the enemy. And then there was Kari to consider; someone was going to have to look out for him, since he wasn't to be trusted to take care of himself, and it seemed unlikely that anybody else'd be inclined to bother. Mostly I was thinking, how much will it hurt, to have a chunk of sharp stone forced through my skin and inside me? What if I'm not killed dead, but they cut off my arm or my hand or my leg? Or I could get bashed over the head, and you can go blind from that. Back home, you see men who've been in battles and had bits of themselves chopped off, and some of them learn to cope pretty well with just one hand or one leg, and some of them would've been far better off dead, for all the good being alive does them. Which would be worst, crippled or blinded? Or what if we lost, and all of us were killed except me, and I was left lying in a messy heap of dead bodies with both legs busted? Before a battle, it's really, really hard to think about anything except pain. If you've never been in one before, you think back to all the horrible accidents you've seen – men who've fallen off roofs or been crushed by falling trees or gored by bulls. You think of the terrible damage that can happen to a body, the splintered bones and the raw flesh, fouled with mud or dust and small bits of stone and twig. You think of needles of smashed rib poking up through skin, and how much it hurts when you bash your head on a branch or a rock, hard enough to break the scalp. I suppose there's men in this world brave enough or vicious enough to think of other things before a battle, but there's not many of them. You don't actually dwell much on the possibility of dying, or what that'd actually mean. Most everybody just thinks about how much it's going to hurt.

When Bits told us it was time, I stayed close to a man called Bjarni Grimolfson, who was one of the men who'd fought the vikings; he was with his best mate, Thorbrand Snorrason, and Ohtar joined us just as we were leaving the house. I looked round for Kari, but he'd lagged behind and I couldn't get back to him through the crowd in the door-way. I worried about that all the way across the yard to the side gate.

We were about two-thirds of the way across the yard when I heard yelling from outside the palisade; the archers had let loose too early, before we were where we were meant to be. Some of the men started to run, and for a while we were bumping into each other, shoving and stumbling and getting in a tangle, not a good idea when you're all pressed up together and every one of you is carrying something sharp in his hands. I was sort of swept out of the gate along with the rest; I was holding my axe down by my right knee, so nobody'd cut himself on it, and I couldn't draw my knife for fear of injuring somebody, so it had to stay on my belt. Bjarni'd got behind me somehow and he was trying to get past me but he couldn't; his shoulder was wedged in behind mine and he was shoving me along, so fast that I couldn't find my feet or my balance. Then for some reason we stopped short, and I was pushed forward. I ran into the back of Thorbrand Snorrason and trod on the calf of his left leg; he tried to turn round but he was wedged in too tight, so he swore at me instead, and I was more scared of him smashing my face in for being clumsy than I was of the enemy, just for a moment or so. Then we were moving again; and an arrow dropped down out of absolutely nowhere. It came down almost vertical, grazed the side of Ohtar's head, skidded off his collar and fell feathers-down right in front of me. I heard it snap under my foot. I could feel Ohtar's blood on my nose and cheeks and I told myself, it's all right, even tiny scratches on the scalp bleed like shit; Ohtar didn't seem to have noticed he'd been cut. Then something else came down out of the sky, whirred over my head and landed with a very solid, chunky sort of noise, and I heard someone behind me yell. Again I was thinking, it's not when people yell that you ought to worry, it's when they're hurt and they're quiet; that's when it's serious. Someone told me that once, I can't remember who; I'm not sure whether it's true or not, but it's the sort of thing that goes through your mind at times like that.

Then I heard a voice up ahead shouting, 'Fuck it, they're slinging rocks!' Of course, I couldn't see anything much, apart from the back of Thorbrand's head, but we all came to another sudden sharp halt, like when you walk into something solid in the dark. You can tell when the men in front of you are scared; it's a lot of little things, like the silence when they all go very quiet, the way they stand dead still for a moment, the smell when some poor bugger in the line shits himself in terror. It's bad enough when you can see what's going on, or you know what the sudden new danger's likely to be. When you haven't got a clue, other than someone up ahead yelling about flying rocks, it's bloody terrifying. You don't know if it's an ambush, or enemy reinforcements have turned up, or a sudden attack on the flank, or there's some brilliant tactical ploy your commander hadn't been expecting; or it could be cavalry or catapults or Greek fire, or even bloody elephants for all you know. What filters back to you is, it's very bad and it's happening far too close, and you're jammed in the middle and can't get out. That's when men start trying to turn round and push their way to the rear, and pretty soon everything's fucked up and a hundred times worse than it need be.

I wasn't the first man to lose it and start shoving, and I wasn't the last either. Not that it made much odds; these things happen so quick, it doesn't really matter. I got myself turned round; at one point I was nose to nose with Bjarni Grimolfson who was staring at me from a few inches away like he couldn't figure out what in hell was going on. Then I managed to slip past him, and Thorbrand shoved past me; I slipped and went down on one knee, landed hard, felt my kneecap go crunch on a stone or something. Just what I needed, I thought, to be caught up in this mess and be hobbling along, not able to run. So many people were pushing and shoving past that it took me a while to get up and back on my feet again, and even then I couldn't keep up, they just slipped and squirmed past me and I was still struggling for my balance. I got both feet planted and found out, to my great joy, that I could actually put some weight on my bashed knee, when I noticed that the man pushing past on my left-hand side wasn't anybody I recognised. He was one of the enemy.

That was a very bad moment. I remember thinking, I could just reach over, right now, and run the edge of my axe across the back of his knee, and that'd be him sorted; but if I did that, and somebody noticed, the rest of them'd tear me to pieces. Screw that. So I stopped looking round, fixed my stare dead ahead, saw that the man in front of me was Thorbrand, and kept going, fast as I could. Someone or something clouted me a horrible great scat in the small of the back but I pretended it hadn't happened, and my guess is it was just an accident. If it was one of the leather-boat people trying to harm me, he was pretty half-hearted about it and didn't try again.

So there we were, in full retreat, with the enemy at our heels; not so good, really. I hadn't got a clue what'd gone wrong, or how I was supposed to get out of it; but then we stopped dead again. I crashed into Thorbrand's back and my knee crumpled; I went down hard on my face, and I felt someone's feet on my back, then on my neck – the bastard was walking over me to get to wherever he wanted to go. I lifted my head just a bit, and all I could see was a heel, in a cured-hide shoe sewn up with sinew thread, standing still about six inches from my nose. What happened in the next few moments after that, I'm rather foggy about. There was a yell, a bit of foot-shuffling, and then something big and heavy fell across my shoulders and didn't move at all. My head was pressed sideways, and I saw a hand reach down and pick up an axe off the ground. Then I think someone's foot must've bashed into the back of my head, and I was completely out of it.

CHAPTER
TWELVE

'Did he tell you,' Kari asked, 'how I saved his life?' I paused before answering. 'Maybe he was going to,' I replied, 'but then Harald called him away to take his turn on watch. So you saved him, then?'

Kari nodded. 'Well,' he amended, 'as good as. It was me pulled him out from under the pile of dead bodies, and realised he was still alive. That counts, wouldn't you say?'

'I should think so,' I replied. 'Was he grateful?'

'Oh, you know how it is,' said Kari, with a shrug. 'You wake up after taking an almighty scat on the head, you don't really know who you are or where, or what's been going on; and people say all sorts of dumb things without really knowing it.'

'So I gather,' I said. 'So what did Eyvind say?'

Kari frowned. 'He was lying there on the ground,' he said, 'eyes shut, head all sticky with blood; and he opens his eyes and looks at me for a bit like he'd really been expecting to see someone else, and he says, "Oh fuck, don't say you're here too."'

'Strange,' I said.

'I thought so. But apparently, he was pretty well

convinced that he'd been killed in the fighting, which meant he was either in Heaven or Valhalla; and seeing me, I guess he assumed I'd been killed as well, which obviously upset him. I mean, we've been friends a long time. It was sort of touching.'

'That explains it,' I said. 'Obviously. But he was all right, was he, apart from the bang on the head?'

'More or less. He was a bit giddy for a while, threw up a couple of times. I reckon he was lucky to get off so lightly, being right in the thick of it like that when it all started to go so badly wrong. All thanks to that fuckwit Thorfinn, of course.'

Kari yawned, and wriggled a bit so that his back was resting against the tomb gatepost. The afternoon sun was pleasantly warm, and I could smell the dust. 'Were there many killed in the fighting?' I asked. 'You said something about a pile of bodies.'

Actually (Kari said), bearing in mind what a screw-up Thorfinn made of it, we were bloody lucky. Two dead, one broken leg and a dozen or so with cuts and bruises. The worst of it happened where Eyvind was. The man next to him, Thorbrand, was killed by an arrow; we found him lying on his back with half a flint arrowhead sticking out from right between his eyes, and he had a weird sort of stunned look on his face, like he hadn't believed a bit of stone tied to a stick could be so dangerous.

When he went down, the leather-boaters thought they'd won; they started crowding forward, shoving us back, and that was when Bjarni Grimolfson got killed. Stabbed in the guts with a flint spear; and the man who'd killed him grabbed his axe out of his hands and swung it round his head with a horrible yell and lashed out at the nearest target –

Ohtar, I think it was; he was off-balance and looking the other way, but luckily for him the leather-boater missed him completely and drove the axe into the ground. It hit a stone and the back horn of the blade snapped off like an icicle and nearly put his eye out. Bloody fool dropped it like it was on fire – I suppose he thought it was bewitched or accursed or something – and turned and ran like a hare.

That put a bit of a check on their advance, and maybe they'd have buggered off and left us in peace if it hadn't been for Thorfinn's brilliant plan of turning the bull loose in their rear. Stunning piece of thinking, that; because, of course, what happened was that they were far more scared of the bull than they were of us, and the men at the back of the mob just wanted to get as far away from it as they could. Last thing they wanted to do was go *towards* the bull, so their only way out was through us, or over us, whatever it took. So there was the bull driving them along, and they were pushing us back just as fast, and we had nowhere to go because our backs were to the palisade. We'd have been really screwed.

'Just a moment,' I interrupted. 'It sounds to me like you had a much better view of what was happening than Eyvind did.'

'That's right,' Kari replied. 'I was up on the cowshed roof, with the archery detail.'

'I didn't know you were an archer.'

He grinned. 'I'm not. But it was a damn sight safer up there; and when they started chucking those rocks at us out of their catapult—'

'Catapult?' I queried.

'Didn't Eyvind tell you? Oh yes, they had a sort of siege-engine thing – a bit rough and ready compared to your wonderful Greek machines, but it did the job. Basically it was like a giant spoon with a very long handle, powered by ropes of twisted hide. It threw a rock as big as your head, very scary. Could've done a lot of harm if they'd been able to aim it any sense.'

'Good heavens,' I said.

'I know what you mean; them not having any kind of metal, but being smart enough to make a siege engine. That was the thing about them, see: they weren't dumber or smarter than us, just a bit different, and there were more things we had in common with them than there were differences. I mean, we were wearing the same sort of clothes, ate a lot of the same sorts of food, which is a way of saying we were living off the same land. Main difference was, we stayed put in houses and they wandered around living in tents. But that's beside the point. Yes, I was up on the roof there; I doubled back as soon as our boys started to give way – I didn't fancy getting caught up in a crush where I couldn't move my arms and legs, and the roof seemed a good place to go. I was still doing my bit in the battle, mind, because I sat up on the roof and threw down several of the rocks their siege engine'd slung up there. I hit one of the bastards, I think I may've smashed his arm, or his collarbone. Anyhow, it looked like it hurt, and served him right. Can't blame me for getting out of harm's way, can you?'

'I guess it's what I'd have done,' I said. 'Of course, I'm only a clerk.'

Like I was saying (Kari went on), it was looking pretty bad for our side: two dead, and we hadn't killed any of them by that stage. They were pushing us right back, and our lot were trapped up against the palisade, nowhere to go.

Remember, we hadn't got any armour, no helmets or shields. I was really worried, I can tell you.

But you'll never guess how it ended, or who saved us. Of all people, it was Gudrid, Thorfinn's wife. To this day I don't know what prompted her to do it. My guess is, she got so pissed off watching from the house while her idiot husband was trying his best to get us all killed that she finally couldn't stand it any longer. She came running out of the side gate, up the side of the battle; hair all down on her shoulders, waving her arms and yelling bloody murder. Then she sees where Thorbrand Snorrason was lying dead, and that seemed to be the last straw. She grabs the sword out of his hand and waves it in the air, shrieking at the leather-boat people, really ferocious. They don't know what to make of it: are they supposed to fight her, or what? One of them comes up to her, all wary, like when you see two cats fighting; he's got a spear, and he makes a couple of feeble pokes in her direction, like he's trying to shoo a contrary old sow back into the pighouse. Gudrid yells all sorts of stuff at him — he can't understand a word, but he gets the general idea — and he takes a step back, waggles his spear-point at her like he's getting ready to feint. What does she do? She rips open her bodice, pulls out her right tit and slaps it with the flat of the sword. I could hear the smacking noise right up where I was; it was like hands clapping.

That was enough for the leather-boat man; he drops his spear, swings round on his heels and runs for his life. Gudrid lets out a whoop they could probably have heard back in the Eastern Settlement; she's jiggling the sword with one hand and her tit with the other, and the rear end of the enemy column starts backing away; meanwhile the bull's roaring like hell behind them, kicking and prancing about, and between Gudrid and the bull it's all too much for them. They start to break and run. The front end, who can't see what's going on behind them but know that their mates have just turned and run away – they stop pushing forward against our men, and we push back at them. Ohtar sticks his spear into one of them as he's trying to look back over his shoulder – goes in one ear, comes out the other, you never saw the like – and then it's more or less over. They're all running like mad for the wood. Someone up on the roof manages to drop one of them with an arrow; the shot doesn't kill him, it's being trampled on by his mates that does that. I clock one of them with my lump of rock as they go by, but not enough to stop him; our boys catch another two of them who trip over as they run, and pretty well tear them to bits. And that's the end of the battle.

I can picture Gudrid in my mind, standing there like she's just woken up out of a really strange dream. She drops the sword on the ground, does her bodice up really quick, scampers back in the house and slams the door. Some of our men – the ones at the back, mostly – are jumping up and down and yelling, because we've won. The ones up front are more stunned-like, can't figure out what the hell just happened. Thorfinn – he's at the back, been there all the time – he's shouting orders but nobody's paying him a blind bit of notice. I hop down off the roof; I'm worried sick because I lost sight of Eyvind when our lot started giving ground and falling back, and I reckon he must've been killed. There's a ring of men round Thorbrand's body, but nobody seems to want to do anything, they're standing there gawping like they'd never seen a dead man before. I pull Eyvind out from under him, and that's when he says, 'Oh fuck, don't say you're here too.' And that was our great and glorious war against the leather-boat people; nearly lost by a moron and a bull, but saved by the same bull and by Gudrid's knockers. I

tell you, when your officer cadets read up on their great battles of the past when they're learning how to be generals,
they ought to study the Battle of Leif's Booths. It'd make
war a lot more interesting if they did.

As victories go, it was pretty sour. It'd been far too close;
and two of us had been killed. Made no odds that we'd
killed twice that number of the enemy; it wasn't as though
we could eat them or cure their hides for shoe-uppers or
anything, so it wasn't like when you stand around after a
hunt looking at the bag, thinking about how well you've
done. About the best that could be said for it was, we were
still alive, and we weren't going to have to waste too much
time getting rid of bodies. Actually, that's a real issue sometimes, after a battle. Sometimes you can just let 'em lie, once
you've buried your own; but if you're in your own territory,
you've got to tidy up. Last thing you want to do after fighting a battle is spend a day digging ditches.

But we made the effort; we buried Thorbrand and Bjarni
where they fell and heaped up mounds over them, and we
dug a trench out back for the leather-boat people. Just
pitched them in; one of you grabs an ankle, someone else
grabs a wrist, a little swing and a heave, and down they go.
Anything else is a waste of energy.

Eyvind was still pretty banged up, so we took him and a
couple of others who'd been hurt into the back room,
Thorfinn and Gudrid's bedroom, and laid them on the bed
where they'd be nice and comfortable: wounded heroes, see.
The rest of us flopped out on the benches. I don't think most
of us slept that night – I got the feeling of lying there in the
dark surrounded by sixty-odd people all awake and thinking.
Weird, that is.

Next morning, we tried to go to work same as usual, like
nothing had happened. Felt all wrong. For one thing, all of

us kept glancing up from what we were doing towards the woods, just in case a bunch of enemies had appeared out of it since we last looked. Normal work around the place didn't seem important any more. Milking or scraping down the yard or splitting logs or mending fence rails; there didn't seem any immediate need to get it done, because where was the point? We all knew we'd be leaving, sooner or later.

All of us realised that, I think, pretty much as soon as the fighting stopped; but it was two or three days before anybody actually said anything, and even then it was just a hint here and there. I remember I was out in the marsh with a man called Sigurd Eyes; we were picking up chunks of bog-iron for the forge. Nasty job, that: you had to stand or plod about, over your ankles in greasy grey mud, bent over all the time, looking down for the right size and shade of black. Each of us had a big fat oak bucket, and we knew better than to go back till both buckets were full.

We'd been at it quite a while before either of us said anything; then Sigurd came straight out with it, which surprised me; I knew him quite well by then, of course, because all of us knew everybody else inside out, after being cooped up tight there for so long. But I'd always figured him for the type that gets on with it without thinking: gets up in the morning, does his work, eats and goes to sleep with never a thought beyond the job in hand. He was a Greenlander, Eastern Settlement; I'd known him slightly from Brattahlid, though he was from one of the outer farms.

'How long do you think it'll be?' he said to me.

'What?' I replied.

He frowned, like I was being dumb on purpose. 'How long before we pack it in and go home,' he said.

'You think it'll come to that?' I asked him.

'Bound to,' he replied, all matter-of-fact. 'We can't stay here, not now.'

I guess I knew exactly what was in his mind, but just for my own sake, for devilment, I played dumb; suppose it was easier arguing with him than with myself, inside my own head. 'Because of the battle, you mean?'

'Of course.' He stooped, and a bit more iron clinked in the bucket. 'We couldn't ever settle. It'd always be at the back of our minds – will it be today, when they come back.'

'I don't know,' I said. 'We beat them once, didn't we?'

Sigurd laughed. 'More by luck than judgement. You know that. If it hadn't been for Gudrid—'

'Yes, well,' I said. 'Maybe she spooked them so badly they won't ever set foot round here again. Her and the bull,' I added.

He shrugged, like it was a non-issue. 'Even if they never come back, we'll spend the rest of our lives waiting for them,' he said. 'It's, I don't know, trust. We can't trust this place any more. Any day it could suddenly turn on us again and attack us. It's like a marriage, living somewhere: got to have trust, or it's nothing but trouble. It'd be like living on the lip of a volcano, like the poor people do back in the old country.'

'But it's good here,' I said. 'At least, it's starting to get good. It's warmer and the grass is better, and there's timber; and the way things are going, the rate we're building the herd up, it won't be that many years before we can start branching off and setting up our own farms. You tell me, where else do you know of where you can still do that? And it's the only way the likes of you and me are ever going to have our own places.'

He sighed. 'True,' he said. 'But it won't happen. Nobody's going to wander off two days' walk from here, out in the wilds on his own. All packed in tight together we might just be safe. Singly, out there, no chance. Fact is, we should never've listened to Thorfinn Thordsson. We knew about the locals, because of what happened to Thorvald Eirikson. That ought to have been enough to warn us.'

'All right,' I said, straightening up for a moment. 'But the plan's always been that we're just, you know, the pioneers. Soon as we're up and running here, Thorfinn'll send the ships back and bring in a new batch of settlers, till there's enough of us here that the locals won't dare mess with us. That'd solve that, wouldn't it?'

'If he could get anybody to come.' Sigurd shook his head. 'Listen, you're talking about bringing out women – and kids, even; otherwise the settlement doesn't stand a chance. You might find a few men daft or desperate enough to come out here, even with the threat hanging over us; women'd have more sense.'

'I don't know,' I said to him. 'I think now we've come so far, put so much work in—' I tailed off, and he didn't say anything, and we finished the job off in silence. The rest of the day I couldn't keep my mind on what I was meant to be doing; I scat my thumb with the hammer, knocking pegs in fence rails, and tore a hole in a hide I was scraping down. It was like an itch or a stone in your shoe: sometimes you could put it out of your mind and then it came back, and everything I did seemed to be soiled with it, like the hems of your clothes when you walk in the mud.

Eyvind was up and about again after three days' good rest. There was nothing visibly wrong with him, but he was sour and quiet, didn't want to talk. I guess we were all wait-ing for Thorfinn to say something, but the days went by and he carried on giving out the day's orders each morning, telling each of us what we'd be doing, same as normal. But there was a sort of forced ordinariness about him, if you get my meaning; he was having to try and act natural, which of course is very hard to do if you're trying to do it. Meanwhile summer was getting on; if we were going to leave, we'd have to make the decision before the autumn started, so we could put by the stores for the journey.

Then one day – it was evening, we'd come in from outside, and Gudrid and the women were getting the place tidied up for dinner – it so happened that they'd had the bundles of fur out, the ones we'd had off the leather-boaters in trade. It was Thorfinn's idea: pull 'em down out of the rafters and check them every now and again to see the damp or the moth hadn't been at them. Anyhow, when we came in from work the furs were all laid out on the tables, and the women were about to pack them away again. Gudrid looks over at Thorfinn, and asks him, 'Where should we put these?'

He looks at her like he doesn't get the point of the question. 'Back up where they live,' he says.

She shrugs. 'All right,' she says. 'I just thought, we might as well get them bundled up and pack them in some hay in a barrel.'

Thorfinn frowns. 'Why?' he says.

'For the journey home,' Gudrid answers.

And all of us listening, of course; standing there, waiting for him to answer. You could've cut the silence like cheese. He took a long time, like he was thinking about it; and he didn't look round at us or anything, but he really didn't need to.

Eventually, 'That's a good idea,' he says; and Gudrid nods to the women, who fetch out the old rags and the wool waste, and she asks a couple of the men to go out back and fetch in one of the empty barrels. And that was it; that was the moment we knew the settlement had failed, and we were going home.

Thorfinn never made what you might call a formal announcement or anything; but in each morning's daily orders, there'd be two or three jobs that were to do with preparing for the journey – like sending men up into the woods to gather beech-bark and moss for caulking the ships, or drying or curing some bits of meat instead of cooking them for the evening meal. Simple as that, and at least there wasn't any fuss. But we had Gudrid to thank, because none of us could ever've raised the question straight out with Thorfinn. He wasn't that kind of man.

Now the only question was, could we be ready in time before the cold set in, or were we going to be stuck there another winter, waiting for the spring weather? There again, Thorfinn made it difficult for us all by not saying anything straight out about our plans; it was like he'd told us all about it, but none of us'd been paying attention, and we didn't dare admit we'd not been listening. We kept waiting for him to tell us to start overhauling the ships; he had us out drawing pitch off the pine trees and twisting ropes and putting up supplies, ready to start the overhaul, but before long everything, all the materials were up together but still no word from Thorfinn.

Meanwhile, as we were waiting, we had another death: Ohtar this time. It started off as a septic finger and then it got really bad. His whole hand swelled up, fever set in, and in the end he couldn't talk or hardly move at all. Sad way for him to go; he was the quiet, solid type, the sort you need on a long-haul job. Talking to him was like digging gravel out of a stream; bloody hard work, and just when you think you've got a good spadeful, it slides off the blade back into the water. He was hard going in winter, when there was nothing to do; but if you were doing a job of work together, you could turn your back on him and know that his part was as good as done. Got to admit, I'm the opposite; I'd always rather talk than graft, and I'd be useless on my own, because the thought that unless I do it, it won't get done would put me off even starting.

When Ohtar'd been on his back for three days and it was pretty clear that he wasn't ever getting up again, some of us took it in turns sitting by him, just to keep him company. Not sure he appreciated it, but we did it anyway. When it was my turn, and we were alone in the house, everyone else out at work, he beckoned me over and grabbed my wrist. It was plain enough that he was off his head by then, but if he wanted to talk that was what I was there for. Also, I don't think I could've got my hand free without cutting off his fingers.

'That mate of yours,' he said, in a raspy, painful sort of voice. 'He about anywhere?'

I shook my head. 'He's off up the woods,' I said. 'Won't be back now till it's dark, I don't suppose.'

That seemed to bother Ohtar. 'Give him a message from me,' he said.

'Wait and tell him yourself,' I replied; because he was sounding urgent, like he didn't expect to be still alive come nightfall.

'Just in case,' he said. 'Tell him I was right after all, about the fetch.'

Well; crazy stuff, like you'd expect from a man dying of the fever. 'I'll tell him,' I lied.

'Tell him,' Ohtar went on. 'Tell him that that wasn't all I saw. I didn't say anything before, because I was waiting to see if the fetch was a true fetch. If it was, I'd know the rest was true too. You see that, don't you?'

'Makes sense to me,' I said.

'Tell him,' Ohtar went on, 'that I was out back of the house one night, and the moon was full. I wasn't doing anything, just getting logs, and I ran into a man I'd never seen before. He looked like he was someone I knew, but I couldn't remember him, and he definitely wasn't one of us. I was going to ask him who he was and how he'd got there, but I couldn't get the words out, somehow. Anyway, he nodded to me like we were old friends passing on the road, and went on; but then he stopped and turned back, like he'd just remembered something he'd been meaning to tell me.

'"It'd all have been different," he said to me, "if only you'd landed a mile or so further south. But no, you had to know best."

'I didn't like the sound of that,' Ohtar went on. 'What I mean is, it didn't make sense, but it felt like I understood what he was getting at. So I asked him, "Who are you?"

'He grinned at me – scary sight, that was – and he said, "Who you are depends on where you are, and I'm here. Come on," he added, "you've been here all this time, you should know me by now." Again, I sort of felt I understood, though I couldn't have explained it to you then, and I can't now.

'"What do you want?" I asked him, and he shrugged his shoulders.

'"What do *you* want?" he asked me back, and I didn't know what to say. "There you are, then," he went on. "That answers your question for you, surely. If you don't know, how can I know? And if you don't know why you're here, how can you know who you are? Of course, you and me'll have plenty of time to get acquainted, but the others are just passing through, so it doesn't matter. But I always liked you; you've always been the job in hand, no matter where; on a ship, forecastle-man, I reckon that means you're everywhere, and you make it into just the one place. I guess if you've got to settle down, there's worse places than this."

'He was starting to get me down, but then he raised his hand and waved; I blinked, or I got something in my eye, and when I next looked he'd gone. I went after him, but I couldn't see him anywhere. Any rate,' Ohtar went on, 'not till now. But here he is again.' He was looking past me, over my shoulder. 'You should've told me you knew him, Kari,' he said, 'though I suppose I should've guessed.' Then he breathed out, long and slow, and sort of folded up back onto the bed; he was still breathing, but he'd gone all limp and boneless. He hung on for another day but he didn't wake up again; and then we buried him under a mound at the edge of the meadow, close by the woods.

Ohtar dying like that seemed to help Thorfinn pull himself together; because the day after we buried Ohtar, he told us to make a start on overhauling the ship. That was good news, because we reckoned we still had time to sail home before the cold weather, if we got a move on. But it didn't work out that way. Two of the ships were fine, didn't need anything doing to them except caulking and pitching and a bit of ropework. The third, though – Bjarni Herjolfson's old ship, the one Eyvind and me'd always sailed on – was in a terrible state. Don't ask me how it got like that when the other two stayed sound; but the strakes were so rotten that in places you could break off a handful and crumble it up with your fingers, and you could poke a hole through the boards with your thumb. It was so bad that it might almost've been better to tear out the sound bits and build them into a whole new frame, but we didn't want to admit to that, if you see what I mean – it'd have been too depressing. So Thorfinn decided we'd patch it up, cut out the rot and splice in new timbers; he tried to make it sound like it was just a few weeks' work, but he wasn't fooling anybody. Luckily, we had more than enough good, seasoned wood for the job, which meant we stood a chance of getting the work done before the *next* winter set in. That was the most we could hope for; so, like it or not, we were there for another four months, at Leif's Booths.

I've known some slow winters, but none quite as bad as that one. Gudrid wasn't talking to Thorfinn, not really, since the battle; if they needed to talk about something to do with the running of the house, they'd do it in the hall, in front of everybody, and they were so polite to each other, you could tell how brittle things'd got between them. We carried on working on the ship far too long into the cold season; result, five men went down with cold fevers, and it's a wonder none of them died. Worse than that, we were so busy with the ship we didn't have time for curing fish or smoking meat – we'd finally come to terms with it and slaughtered all the livestock, but somehow a lot of the meat didn't get preserved, so it went bad and had to be thrown away. Upshot of that was, there wasn't enough food – but by the time we'd noticed, it was far too cold out to go hunting or fishing. So we had to go on strict rations, which didn't improve matters. A couple of men took it badly, panicked the rest of us; they were talking about killing the four old Irish women, since we didn't need them any more and the rest of us could share their rations. Gudrid put a stop to that kind of talk, but sometimes it's worse, shutting people up when they're in that sort of mood, there's the risk they'll just go ahead and do it anyway, in the middle of the night when everybody else is asleep. So the rest of us were on edge about that. Thorfinn said he didn't trust the men who'd been suggesting it, wanted to take their axes and knives off them; they said they'd kill him if he tried it, and he backed down. Gudrid moved the old women into the inner room, with her and Thorfinn, and that solved the problem, but now we were practically at each others' throats all the time, so nobody dared say anything, all day long; we just sat, or lay on the floor, and time passes very slow indeed when you reach that stage. It was like hanging by your fingertips off a ledge, with a bloody great drop if you let go. You've got to hang on, you daren't move, but you know it's only a matter of time before your fingers start to slip. As if that wasn't bad enough, it was a harder winter than usual. We couldn't face being hungry *and* cold, so we piled the fire up high and tried not to figure out how long the wood was going to last at the rate we were getting through it. I think we were down to three days' supply by the time the thaw started and we were able to get up into the forest to cut some more. It was just as though Meadowland was getting spiteful with us for wanting to leave, though she'd made it pretty clear that she didn't want us around any more. Sounds strange, but I've known people like that, so why should places be any different?

Well, we got through. Nobody starved, or froze, nobody killed anybody else; we hung on, and then the snow turned to rain, and we were through into spring. You'd have thought that once we were out of the house, outside in the fresh air, with food to eat and the prospect of going home to look forward to, things'd have lightened up and the tension would've melted away. It wasn't like that – I think we'd all come too far over that winter. You never saw men work so hard as we did, fixing up the ship; but that almost made things worse, if possible. We'd got past the unskilled stage of the job, and most of what had to be done was up to the carpenters to do. They were going slow, because the last thing they wanted was to fuck something up and have to start all over. The rest of us thought they were crazy, or doing it on purpose; there were a couple of fights and a lot of shouting and temper, and that slowed things down even more. I think all that saved us was that we were too tired – what's that clever Greek word – too *demoralised* to smash each others' faces in. It'd have needed too much effort, and we didn't care quite enough to do anything that energetic.

Middle of spring, we were finally all done. We dragged the ship down to the sea and floated her; she was letting a bit of water in, but we pretended we hadn't noticed. Loading the cargo cheered us up a little bit, because we were absolutely determined to hold Thorfinn to his promise about share and share alike. He hadn't meant it to apply to trade, of course, only to what we got from farming at the settlement; but we weren't having any arguments about it. We had the furs we'd traded with the leather-boat people, and two good loads of timber. If you took a few steps back and thought about it clear-headed, a share of just over one-sixtieth of that lot would still amount to a decent wage for the time we'd spent. Not enough to buy a farm in Iceland, maybe, but better than nothing. There were a few cracks about who we could dump over the side on the way home, so as to bump up our shares, but that was just kidding around; a month or so earlier, you'd have been worried if your name had come up.

I remember, the night before we were due to sail, I went outside to take a leak. After I'd run dry, I noticed Eyvind standing in the open and looking up at the stars. Now, we'd got on better than most over the winter; I guess we'd been friends so long we couldn't fall out if we tried really hard, there wasn't that much difference left between us, after we'd been through everything together. But for a couple of days before that evening we hadn't had a chance to have a chat together; and I wasn't cold or in a hurry to get back indoors, so I went over and said: 'What're you looking at?'

He looked round; he hadn't noticed I was there. 'Nothing,' he said. 'Just thinking how glad I'll be never to see this bloody place again.'

I couldn't argue with that. 'Dumb, isn't it, that we've spent so much time here, when we both hate it so much,' I said. 'Beats me how we kept letting ourselves get dragged back here.'

For some reason he looked at me all crooked, like I was trying to be funny. 'Well,' he said, 'this is definitely the last time I'll stand here. I've given this place a good slice of my life and I've got bugger-all to show for it. If we get blown out and drown on the way home, at least I won't be buried here.' He laughed. 'It's like feeding a dog begging at table: you do it once and it'll never leave you alone. Well, it had Thorvald, and then we had to give it Ohtar and Thorbrand and Bjarni Grimolfson. I'm glad it won't get me as well.'

Eyvind gets like that sometimes. I'm used to it. You are too, probably, after listening to him. If you take no notice, he gets a grip and goes back to normal. 'Fine night,' I said. 'Any luck, we'll get clear of the coast and the current before the wind gets up.'

'Hope you're right,' he said. 'You know, there's times when I have this horrible feeling that I've put my foot in a snare, and the more I try and pull away from the things that hurt me most, the tighter they grab me. This place,' he said, looking away. 'Some people. But it seems to me that that's only to be expected – I mean, ever since we left the Old Country, I've lived a good share of my life on ships; and what's a ship but a way of going from place to place, yet always taking the same place with you?'

A lot of people were starting to sound like that, so I wasn't too worried. Let 'em finish, and usually they get better. 'Right,' I said.

'A ship's a place,' he went on. 'It's a wooden platform with sides, you can sit on it or stand or sleep, you can live all your life in that small space. But it can take you anywhere – here, or Norway, or right down the bottom end of the world, to the Big City or Saracen country, or the hot place where the blue men live. You can go there, as far from where you were born and meant to be as it's possible to go, but always you take that wooden cage with you.' He laughed, don't ask me why. 'Like the Eiriksons,' he went on. 'Leif, Thorvald, Thorstein – they all came here to get out of Eiriksfjord, but instead they brought Eiriksfjord out here, along with the stores and the supplies and the tools and the other necessities from home. And see what happened? Killed two of them, screwed up Leif so he can't ever give it away – his life's a shambles, because he wanted Gudrid so much, he thought this place had given her to him but instead it keeps taking her away. It's dragged her out here, and Thorfinn Bits along with her; it's trashed him, and look what it's done to you and me. Look what it's done to *me*,' he said, and he sounded like he was getting a bit overwrought; he got like that when he was a kid and he knew he wasn't going to get his own way; but he was always a strong-willed man who never got what he wanted. 'I could go anywhere, I could go to Constantinople, and I'd still be stuck on the ship that took me there. With you,' he added, and I really don't know what he meant by that.

I wasn't quite sure what to say, but I had to say something. 'When we get home,' I said, 'I say we quit seafaring for good. Get away from Brattahlid; maybe head over to the Western Settlement. Sure, it's a bit bloody sparse over there, and the winters are no fun, but that means they need good hired men, we'd be treated right. Maybe even, if we knuck-led down and got on with it, maybe one day we could get a place of our own. No, seriously,' I went on, when he pulled a face. 'Let's face it, you and me, on our own we'll never raise the money, not for land and stock and gear. Together, though— Well, anyway,' I said, 'it's a thought, it's some-thing to aim for. Better than being here.'

Eyvind looked at me for a bit, and I couldn't see what he was thinking, which is unusual. 'Whatever you say, Kari,' he said. 'Whatever you say. Only—'

'What?' I asked.

'Only,' he went on, and it was like he wasn't actually talk-ing to me, 'I think that'd be pretty much like being on a ship, specially in winter. And I keep coming back to one thing, though it sounds pretty stupid if I say it.'

'Go on,' I said.

'I keep thinking of when we first came here,' he said, 'with Bjarni Herjolfson; and he said, that night when we were at anchor, he said for none of us to go ashore; but you did. He told us not to, but you didn't listen. You left the ship – and here we still are, all these years later.' He shrugged. 'Forget it,' he said. 'Forget I said it. It doesn't mean anything.'

'All right,' I replied. 'I haven't got a clue what you're talk-ing about, anyhow. But think about what I said, the Western Settlement and maybe trying to get a place of our own.' I made an all-around-me gesture with my arms. 'This lot here, this was always too far away, out of our league, not to men-tion the leather-boat people being here already. But I think the Western Settlement might be just the place. The right place, for you and me.'

'You know, perhaps you're right,' he said, but he didn't seem very happy about it. 'Or we could save our money and buy a ship. There, that'd do just as well, wouldn't it?'

I wasn't so sure about that. 'Not the same, though, is it?' I said. But he changed the subject.

'You know what?' he said. 'I've been getting those dreams again.'

'Oh,' I said, because that wasn't too clever. I knew what he was talking about; but dreams are always weird, and they don't mean spit, no matter what people tell you.

In Eyvind's dream, he's married, got his own farm, got two grown sons working with him; and then one morning he wakes up, and there's his wife in the bed next to him, stone dead; and when he looks closer, she's actually been dead for years and years. All the skin's shrunk back to the bone, her hair's grown out, her nails are long and crooked and her skin's like parchment. He jumps up and runs into the hall, yelling; and there's his sons and the hired men, lying on the benches, and they've all been dead for years too. He runs outside, and the grass is all long and choked with weeds, everything's overgrown and falling to bits, the roof-turf has grown down and joined in with the grass on the ground; it's like they all went to bed one night and didn't wake up, everybody died in their sleep twenty years ago, except him. So he runs down to the fjord, and there's the ship, Bjarni Herjolfson's, drawn down onto the beach and ready to sail; and everybody on board's dead too, Bjarni and Red Eirik and the Eiriksons, just like up at the house. And the crazy thing about it is, he told me once, he knows that he's the only man still left alive in the whole of Greenland; and when he dies, the settlement'll end and the grass will grow back over it all, and pretty soon people will have forgotten it was ever there.

Well (Kari went on), not long after that we finally got away. I'd been expecting that we'd have a really shitty run back to Greenland, to match the luck we'd had while we were at

Leif's Booths, but actually it wasn't too bad. The winds were lively but didn't smack us around too much; we went a bit off course and ended up crossing from Slabland to north Greenland, then down the coast to the Western Settlement. It'd changed a lot since I was last there – you'll remember, they'd had the bad plague that killed Thorstein Eirikson – and we passed a lot of empty farms, or places where they'd had to let a lot of the pasture go. I said to Eyvind, if we just helped ourselves to one of those abandoned places, nobody'd give a damn; but I guess he'd thought it over and decided that he was against the idea, because he didn't show any enthusiasm.

We put in at Lysufjord for water, then followed the coast down. Thorfinn said he was making for Brattahlid and a squall pushed him further on; me, I don't think he ever intended landing there, because he wanted to keep Gudrid away from Leif, now that she'd gone all cold towards him. So we ended up at the southern end of the Eastern Settlement, back at Herjolfsness, where we'd first arrived, round about the third week of summer. Herjolf was long dead by then, of course, and Bjarni was the farmer.

We stayed there a week, all of us together; but then Thorfinn said he was going back north to Eiriksfjord, because he wanted to spend winter at Brattahlid. Truth was, Gudrid made him; Brattahlid was the nearest thing she'd ever had to a proper home, and she wanted to go back.

But Eyvind and me, we stayed. We'd had enough of Brattahlid, and seeing Bjarni again, and a few of Herjolf's people who were still alive and who'd come over from Iceland with him, we thought we might as well stay there, if Bjarni'd have us. I'm not saying he was keen, but he felt obliged. After all, he'd been the one who'd brought us out there to start with.

So there we were, almost home again; and it wasn't much, in fact it'd got a bit run-down since Herjolf's day and it wasn't a patch on the old place back at Snaefells in Iceland, but it was the best we were likely to get, after being out of things so long. Eyvind and me both agreed, compared to Meadowland it'd do us just fine, and we made a solemn vow by the Holy Cross and Thor's hammer and all that stuff that we weren't ever going anywhere again, alive or dead. We had the rest of summer and the whole of autumn to settle back in; and winter at Herjolfsness was like being in heaven, after that bloody terrible four months at Leif's Booths. The work was lighter, too, or else we'd hardened up a lot; Bjarni was pleased with us and the newcomers there, the ones who'd joined the household since we left, were a good bunch, decent people. When spring came, I decided there really wasn't any need to go off up to the Western Settlement, like I'd planned. We were a damn sight better off as hired men at Herjolfsness than we'd ever be as our own masters up there. Pity, I thought, that we hadn't known that earlier, before we left in the first place. And whenever I felt like I was getting itchy or pissed off with being the hired man, I just looked out west over the sea, to where Meadowland was, and said to myself, yes, but at least I don't ever have to go back.

'So that was the end of it,' I said. 'You and Meadowland, I mean.'

Kari looked at me and smiled, all sad. 'Oh no,' he said. 'We went back, one more time.'

CHAPTER
THIRTEEN

Of all the stupid, inconvenient moments to be rescued—

Harald was shouting, waving his arms at us; and when I looked in his direction, I could see a cart, with our escort in front and behind. They'd found a blacksmith, and finally they'd come back to fix our busted axle.

Kari looked, and laughed. 'Doesn't time fly,' he said. 'See, if only I'd had me to talk to, all through those long winters and boat trips, think how much less miserable my life would've been.'

I sighed. I was nominally in charge of the expedition; so it was up to me to go and brief the blacksmith (though I knew absolutely nothing about mending axles), arrange payment, useful sort of clerkly things, my job. I thought to myself: Lucky Leif Eirikson would've known about technical ironworking stuff, so would Thorvald or Thorfinn Bits. And they'd been *bad* leaders.

The blacksmith was a Greek, of course, so he wanted to talk. As we covered the few yards from his cart to ours, he told me that it was really inconvenient being called away at a time like this, he had a stack of work on, lamp-stands and reaper-blades and pot-hooks to make, if it hadn't been the Imperial service he'd have stayed at home and screw the bonus payment. (What bonus payment? I wondered.) Also, he didn't have his proper portable anvil, he'd lent it to his brother-in-law who had a whole lot of chains to overhaul, so he was going to have to do the best he could with an old helmet-stake stuck in a log-end, so I wasn't to expect bloody miracles, even assuming he could get a welding heat with just two sets of small bellows and two flat stones for a forge, though that'd depend on the men working the bellows, who'd have to be a couple of my men, since he was on his own, well, there was the boy, of course, but he needed the boy as his striker and he couldn't do the two jobs at once, and with the best will in the world it wouldn't be his fault if the weld didn't take if it was my two men slacking on the bellows that was to blame.

'Fine,' I said, when at last he paused for breath. 'Understood. Just do the best you can.'

He stared at me as if I was mad, or being deliberately awkward, or both. 'If you could've got the cart back to my shop,' he said, 'there wouldn't be a problem, I got a four-hide double-action bellows there, you can pump the bugger with just your little finger and it'll breathe fire like a dragon.'

I pointed out that if the cart had been in a fit state to get to his workshop I wouldn't have needed him at all. He didn't deign to reply to that, and I thanked Heaven for small mercies.

Harald Sigurdson unloaded the gear from the blacksmith's cart and set it up; he did a splendid job, I think – except that at the last moment he contrived to drop a big, heavy metal thing (the blacksmith told me the technical name, but I wasn't listening) on his foot, doing himself an enormous amount of damage in the process.

Back in the City they'll tell you that the Varangians are a stoical lot. Varangian prisoners captured by the enemy will endure days, even weeks of torture and never say a word. Maybe; but only because the Saracens and the Bulgars never thought to drop heavy blacksmithing tools on their feet. Try that, and your problem will be to get them to shut up. Clearly, his injuries ruled Harald out for bellows-working duty; and the escorts made it plain that they were far too tired after their long trek to undertake the work; so that only left Kari and Eyvind. To their credit, they agreed and set to work quite cheerfully; even I could see that they were blowing up a good, hot blaze in the improvised forge, and the blacksmith stopped moaning about the fire and turned his attention to something else.

Which left me sitting on a rock, watching a procedure that meant nothing to me at all, waiting, when I really needed to know what on Earth could've induced Kari to go back to Meadowland one more time. After I'd been on the rock three hours or so I considered going over and asking him to tell me as he worked the bellows; but then the smith started bashing something with his hammer, sparks flew in all directions from the white-hot axle, and I stayed where I was.

Blacksmiths are strange people to watch when they're working. Most of the time they stand perfectly still, staring mournfully into the fire like an old man remembering his youth, while the bellows creak and wheeze. Just when you're sure that they've fallen asleep on their feet, like horses do, they suddenly lunge forward, grab their hammer, sweep all the other tools off the anvil with a majestic surge of the forearm, and set about their chunk of dazzling iron with the savagery of a Turk slaughtering civilians. Just when you think you're seeing some actual work getting done at last, they stick their bit of metal back into the fire, and go back to silent standing. For the first half-hour it's a fascinating sight. After that, you tend to lose interest.

After what seemed like a very long time, the blacksmith said something to Kari and Eyvind, and they stopped working the bellows; then he upended a pot of charcoal over the fire and came over to talk to me. It wasn't going well, he said; the axle was horrible, a piece of shit, whoever made it ought to be ashamed; it was impure, filthy, stuffed full of sand and clinker and rubbish that meant it wouldn't weld, get it up to a heat and it just burned away like tallow. There was nothing for it, he concluded, with a shake of the head so tragic that Aristotle would've written a book about it, but to go back to his workshop and forge a brand new one, from good, clean, honest, *Greek* iron. It would take time, it would screw up his whole schedule for years to come and it most definitely wouldn't be cheap, but there was absolutely nothing else that could be done.

'Right,' I said. 'Well, thanks. How long—?'

He cut me off with a sharp sigh. Obviously that was one of those questions you simply don't ask. 'I'll be quick as I can,' he said. 'Probably, best thing'd be if I called in my sister's boy and my cousin, assuming they can be spared; and I'll need a load more charcoal, the clean stuff, that's if they've even got any. Anyhow, I'll do what I can. After all, it's for the government.'

He rolled sadly away, and for reasons I couldn't quite follow, the escort went with him; so, after a day of almost exaggerated bustle and action, I was back where I'd been before: me, Kari, Eyvind and Harald, waiting.

'So tell me,' I asked Eyvind – Kari was on watch – 'whatever was it that induced Kari to go back to Meadowland?'

Eyvind scowled past my shoulder. 'You want to ask him that,' he said.

'Well, I can't,' I said irritably. 'He isn't here. So I'm asking you.'

He sighed. 'It's not as simple as that,' he said.

When we got back (Eyvind said), Gudrid and Bits and the rest of the party went back to Brattahlid; but Kari and I stayed on at Herjolfsness. That is, I thought I'd be clever and stay on there, after Kari'd said he was going with Bits and the others; but as soon as Kari heard, he told Bits he'd changed his mind, and then he went to Bjarni Herjolfson and asked if he could stay too. I actually pleaded with him not to stay; I reminded him about his plans for moving out to the Western Settlement, where he could take over one of the abandoned farms and be his own master. I'd never be able to forgive myself, I told him, if he let the opportunity slip past him just for my sake.

Didn't bloody work; so Kari stayed, and we dug in at Herjolfsness and got on with our lives. It was funny, being back with that crowd. Most of them were people we'd known from Iceland; but when we'd left with Bjarni to go trading they'd been kids, and suddenly they'd come over middle-aged or old. And then I stopped and thought about it, did the figuring on my fingers; and you could've stolen my legs and replaced them with rake-handles when I worked out that it had been twenty-five years – twenty-five years – since we left Drepstokk and sailed away with Bjarni.

I couldn't believe it. All that time, a lifetime, wasted; I hadn't actually noticed it before, but now I realised I'd grown old too, rather more than the kids at Herjolfsness who were now grown men and the men who were now too old to work. Twenty-five years – that meant I was forty-two, which makes you an old man in the North. The best years of my life had melted away in a dream, a recurring nightmare of fog at sea and long winters at Leif's Booths – and where had it got me? Nowhere: I was right back where I'd started, only rather worse. I was in Greenland rather than the Old Country, and I was forty-two years old.

But at least, I promised myself, at least I'd finally woken up; and it'd been bad and I had nothing to show for it apart from my share of the fur money – did Kari tell you that on the way home the ship carrying the furs got swamped by a real lumpy bastard of a wave, and half the furs got spoiled? – but at least I was still alive, still in one piece, on my feet, able to do a day's work and earn my keep. It was time, I reckoned, to close the door on all that and make the best of what I had left. There wouldn't be a farm for me now, I'd be a hired hand until I got too old, and then I'd be a nuisance sitting by the fire, a grace-and-favour man, pleased to be given some stupid little chore that the kids couldn't be made to do. I'd get stiff and deaf and blind, and I'd die when the house was empty, when the men were all out at work, and soon after that they'd forget I was ever there. Like it mattered to me; at least I wasn't in Meadowland any more, and I'd never have to go back there again.

Once I'd got all that sorted out in my mind, I discovered that actually things weren't quite so bad. Perspective; there's a wonderful Greek word. It's all perspective. Once I'd told myself I wasn't much more than a walking corpse playing out my last few sad years, I found that life at Herjolfsness wasn't so bad after all. We cut the hay, turned it, got it stacked and thatched; and Bjarni came up to me when we'd done thatching the last rick and asked if I was planning on staying for good, because if I was, it'd be all right with him. That made me feel better straight away. I was doing something right – in Meadowland you just got on with it, and nobody said good or bad, because it didn't matter, there wasn't anybody else to do your work so you couldn't be fired or sent away. I told Bjarni that as far as I was concerned I was there for good, and he shrugged and said, Fair enough – and that was that. I'd come home.

And then there was the girl. Well, that's how I thought of her, because when we left Drepstokk she was eight, little Bergthora, and her mother used to yell at her because she'd be out back of the barns playing with the dogs instead of helping churn the butter. Next time I saw her she was thirty-three, and her second husband had died of the fever the previous winter, and her face was thin and full of lines. She had a son who was fourteen and a daughter who was ten – crazy, I thought, how can little Bergthora have kids who are both older than she is? – and they were both getting a bit wild, they needed a father. I'm not quite sure why I married her, but it turned out to be a good move. We didn't see all that much of each other – you don't, when you're hired hands on a big farm, where all the men work outside all day, all the women work in the house or the outbuildings, and then everyone eats and sleeps together in the main hall – but sometimes at night, when she was asleep on the bench next to me and I was lying awake – I often had trouble sleeping after Bits's expedition – I used to pretend that we'd been married for twenty years, I'd been there all that time, and the boy and the girl were my son and daughter, not the offspring of two men I'd never even met; and I'd convince myself that it was true, this fantasy, because if it had been true, if I'd never been away, then here was where I'd have ended up, in that place; like when two of you go for a walk, and one of you takes a short cut that goes badly wrong, through the bog, up and down the fell, and then you meet up again on the road that you should've taken in the first place. I won't say I was happy at Herjolfsness; but it was the best time of my life, absolutely no question about that.

'So you didn't go back to Meadowland with Kari,' I interrupted.

'I'm coming to that,' Eyvind replied.

Red Eirik had three sons and a daughter; Lucky Leif, Thorvald who was killed by the leather-boat people, Thorstein who died of the fever, and Freydis, who stayed home. Let me tell you a bit about Freydis.

She was, what, a year or so older than me, and she was married to a man called Thorvard, who lived at Gardar, on the far eastern side of the Eastern Settlement. I can save a lot of words by telling you that Thorvard was generally known as Space, because that's all he was: a space where a man could've stood. You could be in the same house with him for a week and never know he was there. Each morning he'd put on his coat and go out, get on with his work on the farm, and you'd forget he existed. As far as everybody was concerned, the farmer at Gardar was Freydis Eiriksdaughter, and anybody with any sense didn't go there.

There were plenty of stories about Freydis, and some of them were even true. Like when her stockman challenged the Einarsfjord people to a horse-fight—

'Excuse me?' I said.

'Horse-fight,' Eyvind repeated. 'It's a bit of fun for the long summer evenings. You get the nastiest, most vicious horse in your herd, the one you gave up trying to break years ago, and your neighbour brings along his; you haul them into a small cattle-pen, and you prod them with goads till they're good and mad; then you get out of the pen quick. The horse still standing at the end wins.'

'I see,' I replied.

'It's meant to be just a way of letting off steam,' Eyvind went on. 'But people do like to gamble, and once money comes into it, there's always the temptation to cheat. Pity, because that leads to bad blood, which leads to feuds, killings, law cases and God knows what. Still, it's a pretty sight, two bloody great horses kicking and biting shit out of each other.'

There was this horse-fight (Eyvind went on); and the Gardar boys reckoned it was in the bag, because they had this really mean, savage bastard of a stallion. Biggest horse you ever saw, so they say, black with a white teardrop on its forehead; nearly killed a shepherd once, and a terror for kicking down the rails and running off. Only reason they didn't knock the bugger on the head was, they were saving it for fighting. The Einarsfjord men had a chestnut stallion, not so tall at the shoulder but solid, just a mass of muscle. They'd fought it three times already, and it'd pulped the opposition, so they were pretty sure of themselves.

The day of the fight came round; all the Einarsfjord people trooped down to Gardar to watch, they brought a picnic supper and a big barrel of beer, and Freydis sent out two more barrels so as not to be outdone. She'd let it be known she wasn't happy about the whole business; reckoned the stockman hadn't asked her first (which wasn't true, but that's what she told people) and she couldn't see the good that'd come of her prize stallion getting all busted up in a fight; so she stayed in the house and watched through the doorway. If she thought it'd spoil everyone's fun, her not being there, she was a bit off the mark. They were all having

a great time, the visitors as well as the locals – particularly the
Gardar people, because they didn't get much company.

After they'd all had a drink or two and a bit of socialising,
the Gardar stockman brought out his horse, and the
Einarsfjorders brought out theirs, and the fight was on. Now
the Gardar stockman, name of Hrapp, was almost as much of
a bastard as the horse. He was from the Hebrides, and they're
all a bit rough round the edges out there; but Hrapp got
slung off the islands for being a nuisance, which says a lot
about him. The long and the short was, he was a bit happy
with his goad, planted as many scats on the Einarsfjord man
as he did on the horse, and there was nearly a free-for-all
before the horse-fight even started. So feelings were running
a bit high when the horses eventually got around to doing
the business. The thing was, that nasty old black stallion of
Hrapp's took one belt too many off the Einarsfjord horse,
and decided it didn't like rough games after all. It picked up
its heels and ran, and the chestnut chased it round the pen a
couple of times and then ignored it.

Well, the Einarsfjord lot were pleased about that, you can
imagine. They reckoned they'd won a few pennies off the
Gardar people, plus they'd taken Freydis down a peg or two.
So they were all cheering and chanting and throwing stuff at
the black horse, which stood there trembling up the far end
of the pen. Hrapp was stomping up and down looking very
unhappy, while the Einarsfjord man was making a few
choice remarks about him in particular and Hebrideans in
general.

Out of the blue, Freydis comes storming out of the house.
She was a short woman, with a little round face and a
pointed-up nose, and to look at her you'd have thought she
rolled across the ground rather than walking; but she goes
right up to Hrapp, snatches the goad out of his hand and

gives him a scat round the back of the head with it that sends him staggering; then she hops up over the rail into the pen, marches up to the black stallion and lays into it with that goad so hard that it's a wonder it didn't snap.

First off, the horse rears up and tries to smash her head in with its front legs; then it has a go at sideswiping her onto the rails and crushing her ribs. But she's quick on her feet, is Freydis: she sidesteps and darts in and out, all the time whacking at the horse on its shins and ribs, or stabbing it in the neck and belly. So the horse turns round so as to get a kick at her with its back legs, which is what she's been after. Soon as she's got a clear shot, she punches the goad into the horse's arse, and off it goes like a shooting star, prancing and lashing out, hurting like buggery and scared out of its wits. The Einarsfjord horse sees it coming, reckons it's come back for some more fun, and leaps out at it; gets its teeth round the black horse's ear and shreds it. Doesn't realise its mistake till it's on the ground, front leg busted, ribs stove in, the Gardar horse dancing round trying to stomp on its head; and that's the end of the fight. Freydis stands there with her arms folded while Hrapp and the men get their horse under control; Hrapp gets a broken collarbone in the process, and one of the farmhands gets kicked in the head, dies two days later.

Of course, the Einarsfjorders aren't happy at all. They all reckon the fight was over when the Gardar horse bolted the first time, and there was no call for Freydis to go setting it on a second time. They're yelling all sorts and shaking their fists, but Freydis looks past them like they aren't there and she can't hear anything; and eventually they cut their horse's throat and go home. Freydis has the dead horse flayed and the hide tanned and made into winter boots for the shepherds. For weeks afterwards, they say, she was going around with a big smile on her face, nice as pie to everybody, they'd never known her be so pleasant. She made her peace with Hrapp straight away, said there were faults on both sides and he was still the best stockman in Greenland so why not just forget all about it; and when his body was found out on the fells, beginning of autumn, not a single bone unbroken, everybody reckoned it must've been the Einarsfjorders being sore losers.

Anyhow, that's Freydis, and you can see why life at Gardar tended to be a bit exciting at times. One thing you had to say for her, she wasn't afraid of anything on land or sea; and she was always close to her family, particularly her father and her brother Thorstein. She even managed to be civil to Gudrid while Thorstein was alive, but after he died and Gudrid married Thorfinn Bits, it was as much as Freydis could do to say a couple of words to her without spitting. For some reason Freydis was always down on her brother Leif, at least to his face, though by all accounts you didn't dare say a word against him when she was around if you valued your skin. But every time she went to Brattahlid she'd find some excuse for giving him a hard time. If it was autumn and the cows were still out, she'd bollock him for overgrazing; if he'd brought them in, she'd call him a fool for wasting good hay while there was still grass above snow. If he bought stock, he'd always paid over the odds; if he sold an animal, he'd practically given it away. That sort of thing, all the time, relentless, like water dripping; and Leif never cussed her back or anything like that. He'd just sit still and listen, and I've seen him myself gradually freezing up till he was so tense that if he'd toppled out of his chair onto the floor he'd have shattered in pieces. And once she'd gone home again, if anybody said anything against her, even hinted, he'd fly into a rage, knock a man's teeth down his throat; I don't think anything ever got him so worked up as someone bad-mouthing his sister.

Well, not long after Bits came back to Greenland, Freydis made up her mind it'd been far too long since she'd been to visit her brother, so she and Thorvard Space and a few of her men set off for Brattahlid. Just so happened that, a day or so before they arrived, a ship put in from Norway. It belonged to a couple of brothers called Helgi and Finnbogi; they were Icelanders originally, from the Eastfjords. Helgi was the elder brother, about forty-seven or forty-eight years old, and Finnbogi was maybe four years younger: traders, quiet men. They'd hit it off with Leif straight away, and of course Leif'd told them all about how he'd discovered Meadowland; and then Gudrid and Bits had joined in and said how it was a nice enough place, but you wouldn't want to live there; but if you had a good ship and wanted to turn a profit, there was all that timber just waiting to be felled, not to mention furs and all that. They were just trying to impress their guests, they didn't mean anything by it. But when Freydis showed up – she hadn't thought to send ahead to say she was coming, that wasn't her style – everybody was still talking about Meadowland, of course.

A friend of mine from Leif's expedition, man by the name of Thord Horsehead, was sitting close by the top of the table, the first night Freydis was there. She had Leif on one side and Bits on the other; the two Icelanders were sitting opposite. That was Freydis all over: had to be in the centre, so everyone was in reach.

Thord told me Leif had put him up on the top table that night so he could tell Helgi and Finnbogi some details of his expedition that'd slipped his memory, something about the currents in the bay; he reckoned they went one way, Bits insisted they went the other, and Leif wanted Thord to back up his version. Well, Thord did as he was told, and Bits thought about it for a moment and explained how they were both right – the currents changed with the phases of the moon, or some such shit. Leif got grumpy and sulked because he hadn't been completely right. The brothers asked Thord a few questions, sensible and to the point. Gudrid broke in with some detail that all of them had missed, which supported what Bits had said. All very pleasant and civilised, if you turned a blind eye to Leif being snotty.

Freydis had always had the gift of being able to drink like a man. When she'd had just about enough, her face glowed red and her voice got louder, and she tended to lean across the table and talk right into your face. 'Sounds to me,' she said to Helgi and Finnbogi, 'like you're thinking of going out there yourself.'

The Icelanders looked at each other; it was like they had the knack of being able to talk to each other without saying a word. 'The thought had crossed my mind,' Helgi said. 'But it sounds risky to me.'

Freydis laughed. She had a nice voice. 'The savages, you mean? They aren't anything to worry about.'

Awkward silence. Leif still sulking; Gudrid looking down at her empty plate and frowning, Bits stroking his beard, my friend Thord trying to pretend he wasn't there. 'Really,' Freydis went on. 'No problem. I mean, if Gudrid could make them all run away just by waggling her tits at them . . .'

Bits started to say something, but thought better of it; Gudrid caught her breath and scowled at Freydis. Probably, Thord told me, Freydis didn't even notice. 'No disrespect to Gudrid and Thorfinn,' she went on, and everybody must've noticed the order she said their names in, 'but they didn't handle them right, that's all. Got to be firm. Give 'em a good smack on the nose, they won't bother you. Besides,' she went on, 'you probably won't see hide nor hair of them. I think they wander around, like the Lapps do, following the deer herds.'

The Icelanders were quiet for a moment. Then Finnbogi said: 'Actually, it wasn't the locals we were concerned about. It's just – well, it's a long way away, and a lot of open sea to cross, and it sounds to us like the weather's very unreliable. We're traders, we like to stick to well-tried routes. We need to know exactly where we're going to be and when. I mean, it's no good showing up in Norway with a cargo of stuff when you've missed the fairs and the King's court has moved on up-country.'

Freydis waved all of that away with her solid little hand. 'If you fill your ships with timber,' she said, 'you'll find a buyer any time, here or back in the Old Country. No question about that.'

'It's not that simple, though, is it?' Bits interrupted. He was quite red in the face now, though he was talking rather softly. 'You can't just turn up, load up and go on. It takes time to fell enough timber to fill a ship.'

''Course it does,' Freydis said, all sweet and patient, like Bits was a backward child. 'Which is why you need to be a bit organised. You have a permanent settlement. Soon as the ships are loaded they sail home; and while they're away, you fell and trim out the next load, so it's ready and waiting for when the ships come back. You could get it down so nice, you could fit in four, even five round trips in a summer. Keep that up for five years or so, you'd be nicely set up. You see,' she went on, 'where all the others screwed up, my brothers and Thorfinn here, no offence, they never really figured out what they wanted to do, or else they had a whole load of cock-eyed ideas. You—' (She was looking at Leif.) 'You couldn't make up your mind whether you were founding a new settlement or you were just there to cut lumber;

result, you fiddled around for a season or two, gave it up and came home. Thorvald was the same. Thorstein was so hopeless he couldn't even find the place.' Leif fiddled with his cup, turning it round with his fingertips; Gudrid, Thord told me, just looked sick. 'And you—' (Bits this time.) 'You wanted to go and play at farming, but look at you, you're a trader, same as these two; you'll never make a farmer in a hundred years. You couldn't build a settlement because you couldn't believe in yourself being a farmer; you were in the wrong place, you couldn't be yourself. What I say is, there's this bloody wonderful opportunity out there, it just needs someone with a bit of sense to work out how to make the most of it.'

Thorvard Space – he was there too, of course, but down the table a bit – suddenly pipes up and says, 'That's right, that's absolutely right. Marvellous opportunity going to waste, all it wants is a good leader.'

'I agree,' said Helgi unexpectedly. 'We were thinking that ourselves. But as you said just now: Thorfinn here's a trader, and that's what we are. If things didn't work out for him, who's to say they'll work out for us? I mean, I don't know anything about how you go about founding a permanent settlement.'

Then Gudrid turned her head and treated Freydis to a bit of a stare. 'It seems to me,' she said quietly, 'that the three of you should go into partnership – I'm sorry, the four of you, I was forgetting Thorvard. It sounds like you've got it all planned out in your head, Freydis. I suppose that's only to be expected from Red Eirik's daughter.'

Leif opened his face to say something, but Freydis got in first. 'Actually,' she said, 'that's not a bad idea at all. To tell you the truth, I'm getting sick and tired of Gardar. No room to expand, that's the problem. There's only the little strip of grazing, no bigger than a rug, between the sea and the fells.

I think I could get to like the idea of a smart little venture like this one.'

Helgi and Finnbogi went all quiet again, thinking about it. 'We've only got the one ship, of course,' Helgi said. 'Don't suppose we could get enough lumber on one ship to make it worthwhile – not if we're going to have a permanent base as well as the ship's crew.'

'Oh, that's no problem,' Freydis said quickly. 'Leif'll lend me his ship, won't you? I mean, he's not going anywhere, he's a farmer now, and that ship's been there and back so often that it knows the way.'

Finnbogi frowned. 'I thought you sold the ship to Thorfinn?'

She laughed. 'Oh, he did. And when he came home, he bought it back off him, God only knows why. I mean, what on earth is he going to want it for? Waste of good money. But there it is, so it might as well be used.'

Leif kept his mouth grimly shut; so Gudrid said: 'And there's the houses too, of course. If you use them, it'll save you all the time and effort of building. Isn't that right, Leif?'

Thord told me that Leif went very still for a moment or so, like he didn't trust himself to move. Then, very slowly, he said, 'You're welcome to borrow them.'

Freydis laughed. 'You always say that,' she said. 'But face it, you aren't ever going to use them again, they're no good to you. Or are you going to charge me rent, your own sister?'

'I said,' Leif repeated, 'you can borrow them. That's as far as I'll go. Same with the ship.'

Freydis shrugged. 'Fine,' she said. 'Doesn't make any odds, in practice. Anyhow, I think we're nearly there. We've got ships, we've got a base ready-made, we know the way, and getting a crew won't be a problem around here, it never is.'

Finnbogi shook his head. 'Our crew won't all want to go,

I can guarantee that. Some of them have been with us a long time, they'll say they're getting too old to go dashing off having adventures.'

'Well.' Freydis shrugged. 'You'll be able to find some people here in Greenland. Or what about the Old Country? Bet you there's any number of men – hired hands and the like – who'd jump at the chance of a bit of land, house of their own. Iceland's getting very small these days. And you're headed back that way, aren't you? And there's loads of time for you to recruit and be back here well before the end of the season.'

Thord looked at the Icelanders, expecting that they'd be all reserved and doubtful. But not a bit of it, they were beginning to warm to the idea. 'It's true, Helgi said, 'there's plenty of manpower in the Eastfjords. We wouldn't have to pay them anything, just give them their shares in the proceeds, along with the rest. And if there's houses there already built, all we'd have to find up front would be the cost of stores and gear.'

'And a settlement,' Freydis interrupted, 'once it gets going, they'll need their flour and their malt, same as anybody else, and livestock too, of course. Which means the ships won't be coming back empty, and we get to turn a profit both ends.'

Thord said it was like when you light a lamp in a dark room; suddenly he understood what Freydis had in mind. She'd be in charge of the permanent settlement. It wouldn't be a partnership, not really; once she was there, she'd turn into her father, the way Leif and all her brothers had wanted to do, and failed. (And that was why Leif was squirming in his seat and swelling up like a bullfrog; he'd tried to become Red Eirik and failed, and now he was there in Brattahlid, running the farm Red Eirik had built, his father's hand-me-down, when what he'd always wanted was to start completely fresh, like the old man had done.) That was why Freydis was putting into the brothers' minds the idea that they could make more money if the settlement and the ships were run separately, and the settlers had to buy their flour and malt and stuff from the brothers. The surprising thing, Thord told me, was that as far as he could tell he was the only one there who'd tumbled to what she was up to.

'We'll have to think about it,' Finnbogi said. 'There's a lot of details—'

'Of course,' Freydis said. 'I wouldn't want you to agree unless you'd both thought it through very carefully. I wouldn't want to go into business with anybody who'd make a decision like this on the spur of the moment.'

If you ask me, though, she knew she'd won. Finnbogi and Helgi were detail-solvers by nature: give them a list of small, practical problems to sort out, and already they were involved, in their minds, committed. Like, the best way to get someone to help you with a real bugger of a difficult job is usually to ask their advice; they think about it and say, well, you could do it like this; and then you say, yes, but I'm a lousy carpenter (or smith, or mason, or whatever); and then your friend says, that's all right, you leave that side of it to me – and you've caught him. That, I reckon, was how Freydis snared the brothers; it was just the sort of thing she was good at. Everybody thought of her as a loud woman, which was probably why they never expected her to be sly, and weren't on their guard.

Next thing I heard, back at Herjolfsness, was that the brothers had gone back to the Old Country; and so I put them out of my mind. It was only later, when I happened to meet Thord on the road and he told me about what had happened that evening, that I began to feel a prickle down the back of my neck, warning me of danger. Wasn't hard to persuade myself I wasn't at risk; so what if Freydis and these Westfjord men did go into partnership and set off for Meadowland again? Nothing would ever make me join them, and since I wasn't even at Brattahlid any more, I was well out of the danger area. In fact, I told myself, it'd be no bad thing if Freydis left Greenland. I'd always thought of her as the sort of woman who starts blood-feuds, which are something I can do without, thanks all the same. They were all very well in Iceland – kept the population down, no bad thing in a small country – but we couldn't spare the man-power here in Greenland for that kind of indulgence.

I guess my wife must've been thinking along the same lines, because not long after the news came that Finnbogi and Helgi were back at Brattahlid, she made a point of asking me if I was thinking of going to Meadowland again.

'Not bloody likely,' I said.

'You sure?' She looked at me. 'You told me you didn't want to go the last time. Or the time before that.'

'Different then,' I replied. 'For a start, I didn't have you. I was at Brattahlid, where I never really wanted to be. Now I'm here, and probably as near settled as I'm ever going to get. Besides, even if I was twenty years younger I wouldn't go there again.'

She studied me for a bit, then nodded firmly. 'Good,' she said. 'Because I'll tell you this now, if you were going, I wouldn't be coming with you. And while I think of it, there's a baby on the way.'

While I think of it . . . 'You sure?' I said, soon as I'd caught my breath.

'Positive,' she replied. 'You don't look pleased.'

'Balls,' I said. 'I'm bloody overjoyed.' Meant it, too; though why it came out as a growl, I can't say. Mind you, when we talked, Bergthora and me, it was usually more shouting than talking. She was a strong-willed woman, in her way. So maybe it was just force of habit.

'Well,' she said, 'that's good. I'd like for our kid to grow up knowing his father. Most of the girls reckon it's something of a mixed blessing, but I think it's more of a help than a hindrance.'

I can't remember what else we said, and anyhow it's none of your business. But that bit of news just made me all the more determined that I wasn't going to go back. I'd rather die first.

'Sorry to interrupt,' I said. 'But I'm not sure I understand. Yes, I can see why you didn't like the place much. Bad experiences, and so on. But to say you'd rather be dead than go back there; it's a bit strong, isn't it?'

Eyvind scratched his head. 'My feelings *were* strong,' he said. 'I had a very bad feeling about the place. It's like an old story we tell up North, about the man who goes to visit the trolls. You know it?'

I shook my head. 'What's a troll?' I asked.

'This young man,' Eyvind said, 'goes to spy on the trolls, who live behind a great door in the side of the mountain. All his life he's heard about how rich they are, great piles of gold and silver, swords and armour, more than all the carls in Norway put together. So he creeps up among the rocks to where he can spy on the door and watch the trolls go in and out; and one day, a party of trolls go in and they don't shut the door properly behind them. The young man grabs his chance; he dashes over to the door and drags it open. Takes all his strength, but he makes a gap just big enough to squeeze through. And as soon as he's through to the other side, the door slams shut and he can't open it again.

'So off he goes to find the trolls. He's so scared he pisses himself, because everybody knows trolls'll kill you soon as look at you, if the fancy takes them. But he's got no option, he needs a troll to open the door. So on he goes; and he hasn't gone far when he meets two people. But they don't look like trolls. They're tall and handsome and noble, a man and a woman, and they smile at him and say welcome to Troll Hall. It takes him a while, and then he figures it out. Trolls are only ugly and savage on the outside, on the other side of the door. Inside the door, they're beautiful and kind and gentle, and they take him to see the king, and the king invites him to dinner – which is wonderful, all the food he can eat, all served off gold plates in a hall that makes the King of Norway's house look like a woodshed. In fact, he gets on famously with the trolls; they really like him, though he can't see why, and they want him to stay as long as he likes, and the long and short of it is, a week later he finds himself marrying the king's daughter and being made an earl.'

'Good heavens,' I said. 'Is this a true story?'

'I guess so,' Eyvind said. 'Wouldn't be much point passing it on down the generations if it's just a load of lies. Anyhow, he's really pleased he came, because the troll princess is beautiful and he loves her like crazy, and he's rich and powerful and all the trolls treat him like he's really important. And then one day, the trolls are roasting lamb for dinner, and he thinks, lamb's nice, but what it really needs to bring out the flavour is a bit of rosemary. But there isn't any in Troll Hall, they've never even heard of it; so he says, that's fine, I know where I can get some, I won't be long; and he hurries to the gate in the mountainside, and to his amazement he can pull it open with one hand, just like the trolls do; and he goes back out into the sunlight, and the door slams shut behind him and vanishes.

'Of course he panics, he wants to go back, because his life there is so good. But he can't find any trace of the door. He scrabbles about among the rocks, digs up the turf with his nails, no trace of any door. What's more, he's knackered, so tired that he can hardly stand up, and deadly thirsty too.

'Close by there's a spring, so he goes to have a drink; and in the water he sees his reflection, and guess what? In just over a week he's gone from being a young man to a shrivelled old bag of bones, eighty if he's a day. He's really scared at this and desperate to get back to Troll Hall; he sees a farmhouse in the distance, which he can't remember having seen before, so he staggers off to see if he can borrow a mattock and a spade to dig for the gate with.

'The farmer lends him the tools; and just on the spur of the moment, he asks the farmer how long he's been living there. Forty years, the farmer says. Our bloke thinks about that; then he asks who's the king of Norway these days; and the farmer says, we don't have a king right now, Earl Hakon threw him out and he's in charge. Our man's never heard of Earl Hakon; he says, are you sure? King Halfdan's been thrown out? The farmer looks at him all sideways and says, you mean Black Halfdan? That's right, the man says; and the farmer tells him, Black Halfdan died well over a hunded years ago.'

Eyvind stopped. I waited to see if there was any more, then I said: 'That's a nice story. But I don't see the connection. I mean,' I went on, as he pulled a face, 'the man in the story liked being in Troll Hall, though you still haven't explained what a troll is; and he wanted to go back. So Troll Hall can't be Meadowland.'

'The man in the story was an idiot,' Eyvind said. 'And it was all his fault. He should never have gone anywhere near the trolls to begin with.'

I frowned. 'That's not right,' I said. 'He was doing really well, once he was there. His only mistake was leaving, to get the rosemary. If he hadn't done that—'

'I know.' Suddenly, Eyvind grinned. 'And the way some people tell the story, it wasn't a door in the mountain but a ship; and the captain told him plainly, don't go ashore; and his friend said the same: don't go ashore, stay here. But he didn't listen and swam ashore in the middle of the night; and while he was looking for the rosemary, the ship sailed away and left him stranded; and he's been there ever since.'

CHAPTER
FOURTEEN

'Whatever he tells you,' Kari interrupted, his hand on my shoulder, 'don't believe a word of it. So, what's he been telling you?'

Eyvind looked past me, at Kari. 'You're on watch,' he said.

'Harald's turn,' Kari replied cheerfully, sitting down next to me and ripping a huge bite out of an apple. I was amazed his remaining teeth could handle that much force without snapping.

'Where'd you get that?' Eyvind demanded.

'Off the blacksmith,' Kari said with his mouth full. 'He had plenty, he won't miss this one.' Eyvind sucked in a deep breath, like a disapproving viper. 'Or this one either,' Kari added, flicking another apple at him with an unexpected twirl of the wrist. Eyvind had to use both hands to catch it before it hit him in the eye.

'Thanks,' Eyvind grunted; but he took the apple.

'Welcome.' Kari crunched. 'Not that they're up to much, compared to what we used to have back home. Too small and dry, sort of a dusty taste.'

Eyvind nodded. 'Same with the pears,' he said. 'But you can't fault them on grapes.'

Kari looked up and grinned. 'Grapes aren't everything.'

'That's no lie,' Eyvind said, with feeling. 'Remember that crazy German, Tyrkir? We never did find any more vines.'

'We didn't really look,' Kari answered. 'Not after that autumn, with Thorvald, when there wasn't any booze.'

'Well, of course not,' Eyvind grumbled. 'No point looking for what isn't there.'

It was a bit like watching a fencing match, an exhibition bout between two former champions, now old and retired. As they bickered, they deliberately left an opening for the counter-attack, and from time to time they rested, under the guise of momentary agreement. I tried to imagine what it'd be like, this kind of measured, bloodless sparring, day after day for more than fifty years. Was it the itch you never can quite reach with your fingernails, or did there come a time when there was nothing else left? 'Eyvind was telling me,' I broke in, 'about how Freydis the daughter of Red Eirik tried to persuade the Iceland merchants, Helgi and—' I frowned. 'Helgi and what?'

'Finnbogi,' Eyvind muttered.

'That's right. Anyway, how she tried to talk them into a partnership, to go back to Meadowland and start a logging operation.'

Kari clucked, like an annoyed chicken. 'That woman,' he said. 'You know, I reckon she was the worst of the lot. Has he got to the bit where—?'

'No,' Eyvind said sharply. 'Don't say anything, you'll ruin the story.'

Kari smiled. 'I'll leave that job to you, then,' he said. 'Don't mind if I just sit here and finish my apple?'

Eyvind sighed. 'Go ahead,' he said.

★

When they announced their plan (Eyvind said), nobody was all that surprised. Word had got around, so we were all prepared for it.

The brothers came back from Iceland with a full crew, thirty men – about ten of their original crew and twenty Icelanders, half a dozen of them fetching their wives along with them. When Freydis saw the six women she was livid; the Brattahlid people were sure she was going to call the whole thing off, but she calmed down quite quickly and let the matter drop without saying a word. A term of their deal, we learned, was that Freydis would take thirty men on her ship, and the brothers would have the same number on theirs. Finnbogi said that since he and his brother had allowed some of their crew to bring their wives, it'd only be fair to let Freydis's crew do the same, so that it'd be the same for both parties. Freydis went along with that, and there the matter rested. Finnbogi said he was sorry for breaking the agreement, though he couldn't help mentioning that the agreement said thirty *men* each, and didn't mention women at all, so there hadn't actually been a breach. Then he thanked her for being so reasonable.

Freydis had been going to announce who was in her group as soon as the brothers got back to Greenland; but she put it off, saying she'd wait till everything was settled. I think the main reason was that she couldn't find enough men willing to go. All of us who'd been there before said no, we weren't going, no matter what we were offered – money, land, anything. That put a lot of people off joining, as you'd expect. There's always some, though, who won't listen; and you can bet that they'll be the ones that no sensible captain'd choose. Time went on; the brothers and their thirty-six Icelanders were sitting around at Brattahlid, waiting for Freydis, and she was getting desperate. She'd managed to

scrape together twenty men out of the two Greenland settlements, but that was all.

The day she came to Herjolfsness, Kari and I were in the
barn. I was up in the hayloft, Kari was down below—

'It was the other way around,' Kari interrupted. '*I* was in the
loft, pitching hay down to *you*. That's how come she spoke
to you first.'

Eyvind frowned. 'You know what, he's right. I'd been up
top in the morning, but at midday we changed places.'

'Told you,' Kari said with a smirk. 'His memory's not
what it was, see.'

'My memory's fine,' Eyvind snapped, as though Kari had
touched a nerve. 'But it's just a detail, it's not like it matters,
and it was a long time ago. All right?'

Kari shrugged. 'I was just pointing out, you got it wrong.'

'Fine. I got it wrong. Can I get on now, please?'

Like he just said (Eyvind continued), I was down below; he
was chucking the hay down, I was picking it up and pitching it into the back of the small cart, so we could take it up
to the stock on the middle pasture. We'd been at it all day
and I had a headache, so when I saw a shadow in the doorway, I was glad of the interruption. I wasn't expecting
Freydis Eiriksdaughter to come through the door.

'You Kari?' she asked.

Well, she caught me off guard. 'No,' I said.

'Right, so you must be the other one, Bare-arse Eyvind.'
I nodded. 'I'm Freydis, Red Eirik's daughter. But you know
that.'

'Yes,' I said.

'Fine.' Freydis sat down on the tailgate of the cart and
spread her skirts out; she was wearing blue, and the hem was

muddy. 'In that case, you know I'm sailing for Meadowland any day now. I need you two with me.'

Really, I didn't want to hear her say that, not when my head was already hurting. 'It's nice of you to say that,' I said. 'But it's not possible. Sorry.'

'Balls,' said Freydis. 'I just saw Bjarni Herjolfson, he said he could spare you. So there's no problem.'

That set my head off worse than ever. 'It's not as simple as that,' I said. 'For one thing, I've got a wife. Baby on the way.'

She shrugged, like I'd said something irrelevant. 'So? They can come too.'

'Yes, but—' It's difficult, when you're talking to a farmer, and you're just a hired man. You don't know what you can say and what you can't. Sure, Freydis wasn't *my* farmer; but you can't tell someone who owns a whole fjord to fuck off and die. She'd complain to Bjarni and get me thrown out; or if she felt really insulted she'd send one of her men up to put his axe in my head, and then sort out compensation with Bjarni afterwards. (Twelve ounces of silver was the going rate for a hired man back in the Old Country, but that was if the killing was unprovoked; if I insulted Freydis, in law that'd be assault, so she could claim a discount. I'd heard stories that back at Gardar she had a big wooden chest full of leather bags of silver, all weighed out and ready – twelve ounces for a hired man, a hundred for a farmer's son, and so on, to save mucking about. It'd belonged to Red Eirik, apparently, and she'd helped herself to it when he died.)

'Yes, but what?' she said. 'Look, I need a couple of men who know the country. I'm offering good terms: share in the profits and five ounces of silver each on top. That's more than either of you two deadbeats'll ever see.'

'You're right,' I said, 'it's a lot. But I'll be honest with you, I really don't want to go there again. That's all there is to it.'

Freydis pulled a face. 'Scared.'

'Yes,' I replied. 'And not just the leather-boat people. I have a bad feeling about the place. In fact, if you want my advice, forget about the whole idea. No good'll come of it if you go.'

'Shut your mouth,' she said, like she was scolding a dog. 'I don't give a fuck what you want, I need somebody who knows Meadowland, and you two've been there more times than anybody else. I've arranged it with Bjarni. You'll be well paid. That's the end of the discussion.'

'Sorry,' I said. 'No.'

'I don't take no from the likes of you,' she said. 'Call that friend of yours down here.'

Well, I could do that. I shouted 'Kari!' a couple of times, but he stayed up there, and who could blame him? So after a bit she pushed past me and scrambled up the ladder. 'You,' I heard her yell.

A bit later she came down again, alone. 'Well,' she said, brushing hay off her skirts, 'that's settled, then.'

I looked at her. 'Kari's agreed to go?'

'He's coming,' she said, 'same as you, whether you like it or not. I'll send a cart for you when we're ready to leave.' Then she stomped out.

'Has she gone?' Kari hissed down from the loft. I looked up, and saw his face peering at me round the edge of the hay.

'What did you say to her?' I asked.

'Same as you,' he replied, 'but she wouldn't listen.'

'Are you going?'

'To Meadowland? Fuck that. No, I'm staying.'

'She doesn't seem to think so,' I said.

'Fuck her,' Kari said. 'Look, she can't make us go. What do you think she told Bjarni?'

I shrugged. 'God knows,' I said. 'We'd better have a word with him.'

So we did, that evening. When we told him we'd been talking to Freydis, he pulled a sour face. 'Her,' he said. 'Bloody woman. Look, you sure you want to go to Meadowland with her? She's nothing but trouble.'

Kari opened his mouth to say something, but I got in first. 'Is that what she told you?' I said. 'That we want to go?'

He raised an eyebrow. 'Don't you?'

'Of course not,' I said. 'Told her so, as well.'

'Oh.' He shrugged. 'She came busting in while I was in the smithy, told me you two'd sent a message to Gardar asking if you could join up. She'd come to ask me, as a matter of courtesy, if I minded. I said it'd be a pain in the arse, since it'd leave us short-handed, but if you two were dead set on going, I reckoned I owed it to you.' He frowned. 'That's not how it is, then?'

'Too bloody right it's not,' Kari broke in. 'We wouldn't go back there for the otter's ransom, not after last time. We like it here,' he added. 'Don't we?'

I nodded like crazy, and Bjarni shook his head. 'Well,' he said, 'I'm glad to hear it. Quite apart from not wanting to lose two hands at this time of year, I wouldn't want you two to come to harm. And any trip she's organising—' He sighed. 'You two'd better watch your step,' he said. 'It's a bad idea, getting on the wrong side of Red Eirik's lot, any of them. But she's worse than Leif, if you ask me. Tell you what,' he went on, 'I'll put you on inside work and yard work till after she's sailed. I have an idea it wouldn't be safe for you out in the fields while she's still in the country.'

We thanked him and went into the hall. Very thoughtful and considerate of him, but not exactly calculated to cheer us up. The best thing, we decided as we talked it over that night, would be if she found the extra men she was looking for pretty quick; then she wouldn't need us, and maybe she'd leave us alone. It wasn't looking hopeful, though, if she was prepared to come all the way from Gardar on the off chance of bullying us into joining.

The next few days were a bit tense, but then we heard some good news: Freydis had found ten more men, which meant that she now had the full thirty she was allowed by the deal she'd struck with the Icelanders, and Kari and me were off the hook.

The story of how she came by her new recruits made me all the more glad I wasn't going. By all accounts, they were the survivors of the crew of a ship that had belonged to a couple of berserkers, from somewhere in the Hebrides. Now you don't know what a berserker is, and you can count yourself lucky; they're a real pain in the bum, and it's a good thing that you don't hear of them nearly as much as we used to when I was a kid.

Berserkers are men who like to fight; in fact, it's what they like best, more than good food or land or money or sex or anything. They aren't necessarily the best fighters around, but they always win, because they really aren't bothered one way or another whether they survive the fight or not – what they care about is killing you. You can't beat that. Doesn't matter how fast you are on your feet or how good your reflexes are or how hard you can hit or how long you practise sparring; deep down, you and me, what we want most out of a fight is to still be alive at the end of it. That's why the berserker wins the fight before it starts. They make the most of this, of course. They don't bother with mail shirts or helmets, because armour only weighs you down; but they'll have beautiful old swords, gifts from earls or dug up out of graves. Once they've got a reputation, they go around taking

anything they want, doing what they like, anything to pro-
voke a fight. Mostly, of course, sensible people clear out till
they've gone away, but from time to time you get some fool
who wants to make a name for himself, or who thinks that's
what he wants until it's too late. Very occasionally, you'll hear
of some farmer's son who's taken on one or two berserkers
and sorted them out; and there's no better start in life for an
ambitious young man, always provided he lives to tell the
tale.

These two berserkers – brothers, they were – started off in
Denmark, till they got chased out by the king's men, so they
got hold of a ship and thirty-odd men who were past caring
what they did, and went raiding along the southern coast of
Norway. The king got fed up with this and sent five ships to
deal with them, but they cleared out in time and headed for
Iceland, where there aren't any kings to spoil things. They
had a rare old time in the Eastfjords; and then for some
reason they took it into their heads to try their luck in
Greenland. But a storm caught them on the second day out,
blew them way off south; one of the berserkers went over
the side, and his brother jumped in to save him and got
drowned too. By the time they made it to Gardar, only
twelve of them were left, what with one thing and another;
and two of them didn't fancy any more long sea voyages.
Freydis gave the other ten a choice: join up with her, or get
back in what was left of their ship and take a chance on getting back to Iceland.

Well, that more or less put the lid on it, as far as we were
concerned at Herjolfsness. If Freydis had men like that staying at Gardar, the sooner she set off on her expedition, the
happier we'd all be. As it happened, the two men who didn't
want to join up got slung out of Gardar and turned up on
our doorstep. Bjarni Herjolfson was a hospitable sort as a

rule, but even he was in two minds about having them under his roof. They told us their sorry tale, and promised faithfully that they were through with all the raiding and stealing and the viking stuff. Also, they said, they'd been wanting to quit for some time, but the berserkers were vicious bastards who didn't like anybody leaving the crew, so they hadn't dared. There might have been some truth in that.

'It was terrible,' one of them said, a short, wide man called Bersi. 'They'd pace up and down the ship, grabbing people and bashing their faces and saying they'd chuck them overboard. One man tried to leave; he swam ashore during the night, and the brothers made us turn back and go look-ing for the poor bugger, and when we caught him they killed him right there, on the spot. They just didn't care what they did when they were in one of their moods.'

Bjarni, who was obviously in two minds, asked them why the whole crew hadn't got together and stuck a knife in them while they were asleep, or rolled them over the side.

'You wouldn't dare,' the other one said – Starkad, his name was. 'We talked about it, when they weren't there sometimes, but nobody had the guts for it. You'd make your mind up, but then you'd think, what if I'm stood over one of the bastards with a knife in my hand, and just as I'm about to do the business the bugger wakes up and sees what I'm about? No, we kept our faces shut and tried to get on with it. But we're really glad we're here now and not on that ship any more.'

As far as that went, I could see what he meant: he was glad to be out of a bad place, and so was I. Even so, I didn't want to have anything to do with either of them, just in case they changed their minds about giving up on the old ways. They gave the impression that they weren't in any hurry to leave, but they didn't seem inclined to work either, and that was unusual. When you go to someone's house and you're not anybody important, you can't just sit round in the hall all day with the women, when all the men are outside working; you feel an idiot, for one thing, and it's boring. Also, your host may be patient or laid-back, or he may not. I mean, everybody works, don't they? Even rich farmers and earls get outside and work, if they're not crippled or anything like that.

'Not here,' I pointed out. 'Or hadn't you noticed?'

Eyvind shrugged. 'Never could understand that,' he said. 'But then, you're Greeks. And it's so fucking hot here most of the time, I can see why you'd rather stay indoors and keep still, if you've got the choice.'

I shook my head. 'That's not the point,' I said. 'Our nobles and rich men don't work – not what you mean by the word, anyhow – because it'd be demeaning. The fact that you don't have to shows you're one of the better sort.'

'Well.' Kari made a gesture with his hands that was intended to signify universal tolerance. 'Like he said, you're Greeks, you've got a funny way of looking at the world. Mostly I guess it's because you value everything in terms of things – money, gold and silver, furniture, clothes, whatever. The man with the most stuff is on top. Back home, everything's about people. So, if you want everyone to think you're better than they are, you prove it by what you do, not what you have. Which is probably,' he added with a grin, 'the reason why the Eiriksons went to Meadowland. They had to outdo their father, or else they'd just be the Eiriksons for ever and ever; the only thing anybody'd have known about them was who their dad was. That's failure, far as we're concerned. Here, though, it means status and glory

and power, which—' He sighed. 'I'm glad I don't understand you people,' he said. 'You could hurt your head
bending it round that kind of notion.'

Anyway (Eyvind went on), Freydis made her mind up about
when she was setting off. Now she had her thirty men, she
was in a hurry to get moving, so there'd be time to fell a load
of timber and load the ships up before the end of the sailing
season. She'd be cutting it pretty fine as it was, but the dangers didn't seem to bother her. She didn't come round
Herjolfsness again, or send messages or anything, so we reckoned we'd been let off the hook.

The night before she was due to set sail, me and Kari were
up on the roof, patching a few places where the turf was getting thin, when the two berserkers' men, Bersi and Starkad—

'Maybe I should tell this bit,' Kari interrupted.

Eyvind glared at him. 'Why?'

'Because you're getting it all wrong,' Kari said. 'First, we
weren't on the roof, that was the day before. You've forgotten. When it all happened, we were in the yard, scraping
down. And it wasn't the two of them, it was just Starkad.'

Eyvind was silent for a moment or so. Then he frowned.
'You're right,' he said. 'Which is bloody odd, because I have
nightmares about that, but in my dream we're up on the
roof, and it's both of them, not just Starkad. But yes, what
you said is how it actually happened.'

'Right,' Kari said. 'So—'

So we were in the yard (said Kari) and we'd done about two-
thirds, and stopped for a rest. Starkad comes running in; he
sees us, collapses against a wall and says, 'Thank God for that.
I thought I wasn't going to find anyone.'

'What's up, Starkad?' I asked. 'You look like you've been running.'

He nodded. 'From the long meadow,' he said. 'It's Bersi. He was tethering the bull, and it lashed out and kicked him in the head. He needs fetching back here, so someone can take a look at him.'

Naturally we hurried after him, fast as we could go. It's a fair step from the yard at Herjolfsness to the long meadow; it's up a steep slope, down into a combe and up the other side. Starkad was plunging ahead, like a dog that's been kept in for two days in bad weather; he'd stop and look back at us, then race on. Bersi was lying at the foot of a big stone outcrop. He was flat on his face and not moving.

'Kari,' Eyvind called to me, 'you're nearest. Go and see if he's still breathing.'

I took a few steps toward him, and then there was this bloody awful noise, like all the trolls under the mountains were drunk and having a party. I swung round to see what was up, and there behind me, in a half-circle blocking all my lines of retreat, were a dozen men.

I knew straight away who they were: they were the berserkers' men, and they were meant to be several hours away out to sea, not hiding behind piles of rock and jumping out on people going by. I had a bad feeling about what they were up to.

I yelled at Eyvind to run for it, but he was way too slow off the mark; they grabbed hold of him and chucked him down in the dirt, and one of them pulled out a knife and pricked him with it, just under his chin. You didn't need to be brilliantly clever to figure out what that meant: hold still, or we kill your mate here. So I stayed where I was, and Bersi got up off the ground and tied my hands behind my back with a bit of old rope.

'Welcome to the party,' he said. 'Glad you could join us after all.'

Well, there wasn't a lot I could do, was there? Should've seen it coming, I suppose. Should've figured that Bersi and Starkad wouldn't have been allowed to leave the berserkers' crew just like that; not by their mates, not by Freydis. Should've thought to ask what Bersi was doing tethering the bull up on the slopes, rather than bringing it back to the farm. But I only thought about that later, lying awake in the middle of the night and beating myself up for lack of anybody else to take it out on. At the time, I was mostly thinking, no, you bastards, you can't do this; which was a waste of time, of course, because they just had. I suppose the real mistake I made was believing we'd got rid of Freydis just by saying no. She wasn't that sort of woman.

They had a little two-wheel cart hidden among the rocks. They dragged us onto it, and a couple of the berserkers' men came along to keep us company, knives drawn. I thought we'd be going to Gardar, but instead we went straight down to the coast; to a little fjord that didn't even merit a name of its own, where a ship was riding at anchor. I knew that ship. I knew it very well.

They didn't untie the ropes till we were on board and the ship was too far out for us to risk jumping overboard and swimming ashore; till then, we lay on top of the cargo in the hold, along with the other useful stuff. I was thinking, they may have got me but I'm buggered if I'm going to do any work; I'll just lie here all the way to Meadowland.

That didn't last long. When they untied us, Freydis came stomping down off the foredeck to look at us. She stood there for a bit, hands on hips, frowning; she was wearing a man's coat several sizes too big for her, and big heavy shoes with nailed soles.

'Now then,' she said. 'We've got off to a bad start, but I don't want that to be a problem. I've been to a lot of trouble to get you here, because I know you can be useful; but if you turn out to be more trouble than you're worth, I'll have you slung over the side. Understood?'

I'll say this for Freydis: you never had any trouble understanding her – or believing her, either. 'Understood,' Eyvind said, and I nodded.

'Fine,' she said. 'In that case, here's the deal. Same as for the rest of the men: everything we make out of this project, I take half off the top, and everything else is equal shares for everybody. That includes you, provided you pull your weight. Got that?'

We both nodded this time; and I have to admit, I caught myself thinking, well, that's not so bad. Now we're here and we've got no choice, we might as well be paid. 'What do you want us to do?' I asked.

'Your part starts when we get there,' Freydis answered. 'Till then, just stand your watches and make yourselves useful. You know the drill, you've both done this before.'

'Who's navigating?' Eyvind asked. It was a valid question, but he had a nerve asking.

'Me,' Freydis said. 'And no, I've never done it before, but I know what to do. If Leif could do it, stands to reason it can't be difficult.'

Neither of us said anything, because there wasn't any point. Nothing we could do about it; neither of us knew about navigation, that's the captain's job. I knew you used a bearing-dial if you had one, and you got your bearings from the stars, if you had to go out of sight of land. Any kid knows that, and presumably Freydis knew it too. She'd have made it her business to find out how many days we had to follow the north-west Greenland coast before heading due

west, how long to hold that course. If we got blown off –
well, if that happens, usually it's anyone's guess, you keep
going and hope that sooner or later you reach land, and that
it's somewhere you recognise. It's a horribly dangerous way
to carry on, and it always strikes me as a small miracle that
anybody ever gets anywhere without being drowned; but
people do it, I've done it more times than I can remember,
and I'm still alive, aren't I?

Three days out, still following the coast, and the fog came
down. Wind died away to nothing, sails flopped, we sat
there on the decks, couldn't see more than a yard or so in
any direction. I knew that when that happens, you just sit
still and wait. Freydis, though: first time at sea, she was
bloody terrified. She went up and down the ship, asking
everybody what to do. We all told her, there's nothing you
can do, just sit it out, but that just rattled her even more.
'There must be something,' she kept on saying. 'They should
have oars on this bloody ship, like they've got on warships.'
Well, she wasn't inspiring confidence; but mostly we ignored
her. She wasn't so free with her threats, which made a nice
change. That wouldn't last, though, once we were moving
again.

Three days we sat there. It gets so boring you can't stand
it any more. It's like when you've rubbed your heel raw in a
new pair of boots, and every step's torture, but you've got to
keep walking. Each stride forward makes the sore worse,
but the alternative is to sit down in the wilderness and starve.
Eyvind and I scratched the lines of a Tables board on the
deck with a brooch pin, and made pieces out of bread-crust.
Wasn't long before some of the others wanted to join in, and
we couldn't very well say no to them; but neither of us are
anything special at the game, so pretty soon we were out of
the game and watching – and there's few things in life as

boring as watching someone else play Tables. I did my bit; I tried to cheer up Miseryguts here by chatting about old times, but that just made him gloomier.

Mid-morning on the fourth day, the wind started to blow. Fuck me, did it blow; it scooped us up and practically threw us away from the shore. There were those waves that rear up way over the top of the mast and hang there for a second, like you wouldn't believe water could. When they come down you say to yourself; well, it wasn't the best life, but it was better than nothing. Then, just when you think it's all over, the wave coming down sort of slides under the ship; you're up in the air, hull right out of the water, and it's any-body's bet whether you'll flop back down and get a soaking, or whether the ship's frame will finally spring its joints and fall to bits around you. The cargo tries to bust its way free of the ropes; something gets loose and someone yells your name; you don't want to move, it's the last thing you want to do, but you do it anyway, because you can't disobey orders on a ship just becase you're scared stiff or nothing'd ever get done. You try and stand up, and then the deck slams into your heels; you're flying, then you land on the palms of your hands and your kneecaps, and you yelp because it bloody hurts, but a moment or so later the same thing happens again. You slide across the deck and your shoulder slams into a barrel or the mast or something just as hard. You can't feel anything from your shoulder to your wrist, and you're grabbing like crazy with your other hand for something to hold on to; and still you're dead set on doing the job you were told to do, and somehow or other you do it. By then, of course, someone else is yelling to you, do this or do that. You've long since forgotten the wet, the cold, the pain; in fact, it's good you've got this scary, impossible job to do, because it keeps you from noticing stuff that'd make you give up completely otherwise. Mostly you focus on the job, because that helps you shut out the rest of the shit, the danger and the state the ship's in and the wave hovering overhead like a giant hawk. Time doesn't seem to pass the usual way; you know it's been longer than a heartbeat and less than a day, but in between you can't judge, you're lost, like a ship in fog.

Then it stops; wind dies down, waves behave themselves, people stop moving about and flop down on their knees or their backs where they are. Some of them drop off to sleep just as they are. If you're me, you can't do that; you've got to drag yourself up on deck and take the best look you can at the damage that's been done. A spar's been torn down, and a whole load of your precious rope is mashed up into felt, there's leaks sprung in half a dozen places, timbers ripped off the side. You look at all of that and in a cold, closed part of your mind you're calmly saying, well, we can splice that, we can weave those ripped-up ends into a rope, we can lash that down so it won't come apart any further; that'll take a whole day, that'll only take a watch and a half, there's nothing at all we can do about that till we make landfall. The rest of you just blanks out; there may be another squall on its way, but you can't be bothered. Like the fat man said when the bull'd chased him halfway round the pen: the bugger'll just have to gore me, then.

When the wind dropped, of course, we hadn't got a clue where the hell we were. We'd lost two out of three water-casks, and the sail was just rags, beyond patching. We had a spare sail, of course, so that was all right; but the spare sail's what you use to catch rain when you're short of water. Starkad the berserkers' man was hanging off the rail, trying to look at the sternpost; there were dowels snapped and nails pulled out, and some poor fool was going to have to hang out over the stern by his feet to make that lot good. Wasn't going to be me, I was absolutely sure about that; but then Starkad called out, 'Here, Bare-arse, you get over here and give me a hand'; Bare-arse is Eyvind, of course, and I took one look at him, head sagged against the rail, dead to the world, and I hopped up and said, 'That's fine, I'll do it.' And I did—

'I don't remember that,' Eyvind said.

'Don't suppose you do,' Kari replied. 'You were shattered. I think your eyes were open, but you weren't hearing anything. That's why I went in your place.'

Eyvind frowned, as though he was a devout monk who'd just heard irrefutable proof that God doesn't exist. 'You never mentioned anything about it before,' he said.

'Subject never came up,' Kari replied, perfectly reasonably. 'And it was just one of those things. I'm sure you've done stuff like that for me before now, when it really mattered; when I've been asleep or I've had a bash on the head, whatever.'

Anyhow (Kari went on), we sat there two full days trying to fix up the ship as best we could, though it was a losing battle, we knew. It was an old ship; wasn't exactly new when Bjarni first had it, and since then it'd been back and forward across that same bit of sea, taken one beating after another. Comes a time when a ship just gives up; everything starts to go at once. Planks pull off nails, tear out great chunks of rotten wood so you can't just draw the nails and knock 'em back in. Cracks get to the point where there's no strength left, and nothing firm enough to anchor a bit of twine to. Basically, there was nothing holding the ship together beyond cussedness and force of habit; and we were lost in the middle of a very big sea, with a woman who'd never governed a ship before as our captain.

The thing is, you don't just give up, even when it's bloody obvious you've come to the end of the rope. You think, this is completely ridiculous, might as well not waste your energy; but someone calls out to you, do this, do that, and you do it, and you don't think, you stop thinking. You look at a piece of wood and you know it's going to break sooner or later; but somehow or other sooner and later never come. The wood hangs on, like the man dangling off a cliff by his fingernails. Call it strength of will, call it bloody-mindedness. Time drips by, and you're not dead yet. Doesn't make any sense, but you ask anybody who's been to sea, they'll tell you that's how it is.

When the wind came back, it was mild and gentle, which is another way of saying too slow. It was good because anything stronger would've been enough to shred the ship; but it was bad because we were running out of water fast, and though it pissed down with rain for two full watches we had nothing except pots and cups to catch the water in. Rain tipped down and flooded the bottom of the ship, but we couldn't drink that because it got mixed up with the salt water coming in through the leaks; so there we were, bailing out water fast as we could with our three remaining buckets, while our throats were dry as rawhide. Did you know you can get half a drink of water just by wringing out your clothes over a cup? That's assuming you're sodden wet enough, but pretty soon we were, so that was all right.

The wind died away again just as the water ran out and it came on to rain again. Freydis had us take down the sail and spread it out to catch enough to fill our one remaining cask. That gave us a few more days, but that didn't do us much good while we were still both lost and becalmed. The thing

is, when you're sitting like that in the middle of an endless
sea, you know that really there's no reason the wind should
blow today rather than tomorrow or the next day; makes no
difference to the wind, one way ot the other. But it makes a
difference to you; if it blows today and in the right direction,
most likely we'll make it. If it blows tomorrow, then it's
about fifty-fifty. If it's the next day, our chances are one in six
or one in seven.

It blew on the third day. By that time, we'd all gone dead
quiet. No one called your name, because there wasn't anything to do. When the wind started to come up we didn't
even notice it to begin with; we were actually moving when
I realised what was happening. Even then, all I thought was,
it's too late, a whole day too late; the wind'll blow, the ship'll
make it to Meadowland and be run aground, but we won't
be there to do anything about it because we'll all be dead.

But this time it was a good, running wind. It was smooth
enough not to shake us apart, but it carried us along much
faster than we'd have guessed, all the way to land.

Not, of course, the land we were trying to get to. It was
first light, I remember, and Eyvind happened to be looking
that way. I was facing back, out over the ship, and I saw men
sitting up and staring back over my shoulder. Then one of
them called out, 'Well, is this it or isn't it?', so I looked
round, and I recognised it. Forestland.

'Fuck that,' Freydis said when we told her; she'd been
lying on the cargo wrapped up in three blankets. 'Fuck
where we are – is there any water?'

So Bersi and one of the Gardar men launched the boat,
and they were gone a very long time. After a bit, Freydis and
a couple of her people started arguing – if the boat didn't
come back, should we try and bring the ship itself close in to
land so we could swim ashore, or should we cut our losses

and try somewhere further down the coast? At some point someone yelled for me – my local knowledge, presumably – but I pretended that I hadn't heard. If the boat didn't come back, we were through. Taking the ship in would wreck it, and we'd all drown; if we kept going till we reached somewhere we could beach it, thirst would get us. The boat or nothing; and right then, I didn't care.

'Like a berserker,' I interrupted.

Kari looked at me. 'What?'

'Like a berserker,' I repeated. 'Those people you just told me about. You said they don't care if they survive or not, and that's what gives them their strength. Same with you.'

Eyvind laughed. 'Not really,' he said. 'A berserker's always got something he wants, usually something of yours, or just fame and glory. We didn't *want* anything. We just didn't give a damn.'

I thought about that for a moment. 'I disagree,' I said. 'I think this berserker business answers a question that's been puzzling me all through this story—'

'Don't you want to hear what happened?' Kari interrupted.

'What? Oh, I guessed. The boat came back with water, or else you wouldn't be here talking to me.'

Kari scowled. Eyvind laughed. 'So,' he said. 'What's the question?'

'Simple,' I said. 'Why'd you do it? Not you two personally,' I added. 'You two never really had any choice in the matter; you got caught up in the action, like bits of thorn in a sheep's coat. No, I was thinking about the Eiriksons, why they kept going back there; and why Leif would never give away the houses, only lend them.'

'Fine,' Kari said after an awkward moment. 'You've

thought about it. You Greeks are supposed to be good at thinking. What did you come up with?'

I smiled. 'It's the berserker thing,' I said. 'You do these crazy things because you don't care. I mean, listen to yourselves. You come from a country that's piss-poor; over here, your earls would be peasants. You've got nothing. You live in houses with grass roofs, and everybody's got to go outside in the cold and the wet and work. Also, by the sound of it, there's far too many of you to fit in those funny little countries of yours. I don't know much about them, but the impression I get is that they're mountains with little fringes of grass round the edges. Iceland won't even grow corn, you said. So, because there's too many of you to stay home, you wander off adventuring. You go all over the place. You get in a ship and sail away, not even knowing if there's a country out where you're headed, or just open sea and ice. You'd have to be absolutely crazy to do that; either that or you don't care. Berserkers.'

There was a long silnce. Then Eyvind said: 'Have you finished?'

'No,' I answered. 'Because, surprising as it may seem, you aren't the only ones. I can think of another race that acted the way you do, many years ago. They lived in a poxy little country, mountains with a few pockets of dirt at the bottom of the folds, and there were way too many of them to fit. So they got on ships and sailed all over the world; they took amazingly stupid risks, and they fought big, powerful enemies and they won. All these years there hasn't been a word for them, but now I've found one: berserkers. Pity that most Greeks couldn't even pronounce it, because that's what they were.'

Eyvind sighed through his teeth. 'Now have you finished?'

'Yes.'

'Good. You're wrong. You've sat there all this time, we thought you were paying attention, but you've completely missed the point. And, I'm sorry to say, you don't understand us worth pigshit.'

I'd offended him; which was odd, because I thought I was paying him an enormous compliment, comparing him and his tribes of barbarians to us, the Greeks, rulers of the world, the greatest and wisest people ever. But either he'd missed the point or he had a different view of the world.

'All right,' I said. 'What's the real answer?'

He shook his head. 'Just asking the question shows you don't really understand. Maybe you don't want to, I don't know. Look, do you want to hear about what happened, or don't you?'

The boat came back (Eyvind said) and they'd found water. It'd taken them a long time because the water was a little spring deep in the woods; they'd had to lug the empty barrel out there, fill it with nothing more than their cupped hands and their hats, and finally fetch the barrel back and get it into the boat without spilling it all. It must've been an exciting story, how they managed all that, but nobody was in the mood to listen. They were thirsty, and they wanted a drink.

We sailed on; and nothing much happened till we reached Meadowland, and Leif's Booths. It was mid-afternoon when we rounded the point and I saw the place again. Mixed feelings. Yes, I was delighted I was still alive, after I'd quite definitely given up hope, and yes it'd be bloody marvellous to get off the ship and onto dry land. But I had to tell myself to be happy, it didn't come of its own accord. That place, again: I kept asking myself, why here, why does everything

I do wind up with me here, of all the bloody awful places? Just for once, couldn't it be somewhere else?

I was whining happily to myself in this vein, when I noticed something different, or something odd; something that wasn't as it should have been, anyhow. Took me a moment to figure out what it was, and I realised it wasn't because it was anything out of the ordinary. Quite the opposite, in fact. It looked so very familiar, which was why I overlooked it for a long time.

There was smoke coming from the chimney-hole of the main house. Somebody was at home.

CHAPTER
FIFTEEN

When Freydis saw it, of course, she did her block. She jumped up, staggered her way to the rail (there was a bit of a surge blowing up) and stared for a while. Then she started yelling, 'Bring us in, quickly, now!'

By the time we were all the way round the point, so that we could see the whole of the bay, we had an answer to the mystery. There was a ship dragged up on the beach, and Freydis recognised it. Nothing to panic about; Helgi and Finnbogi had beaten us to it and got there first.

Well, you'd have thought Freydis'd have been pleased; they'd arrived before us and laid a fire in, so at the very least we could go ashore, warm and dry ourselves, and quite likely they'd have some dinner cooking; all chores we wouldn't have to deal with ourselves. Good.

But Freydis was absolutely livid. You know how, when they're really upset about something, some people stop yelling and go dead quiet. I'd never seen Freydis go like that before, and I guessed it was because this was the first time I'd ever seen her get properly angry. For the life of me, I couldn't figure what it could be that'd got to her so badly.

But her face was white, with little red spots in the middle of her cheeks, and she wasn't saying a word.

Freydis went ashore – couldn't wait for the boat to get in tight. She hopped over the side and waded, with her skirts floating up round her waist. Soon as she was on the beach she tripped on something and when she got up she was grinning, because what she'd fallen over was a canopy strut. Trouble was, it wasn't one of hers, though she'd done the usual business as soon as we were in sight of land. But hers were all carved and fancy, imported, and the one she'd gone arse over tip on was just plain oiled wood with a few twiddly bits top and bottom. That really hacked her off; no need to ask whose struts they were.

Anyhow, she set off marching up to the main hall, wet skirts flopping round her knees like the flap of a netted fish drowning in air. Starkad and another of the berserkers' men went after her, but they couldn't catch her up except by running. Kari and I followed on at a safe distance, just to be nosy.

She stormed up to the house door and shoved it open, and went right on in. You know, she reminded me a lot of Bjarni Herjolfson, that time he came back from Norway and found his dad had buggered off to Greenland. Anyhow, in she went, and there were some women there, fixing dinner.

'What the fuck are you doing in my house?' Freydis yelled.

Naturally, they looked at her like she was a frost-troll or something. Most of them didn't even know who she was. I don't remember any of them screaming, but probably that was just shock.

'Where's Finnbogi?' she snapped. 'I want a word with him. And you can leave that and get packing. I want all this shit out of here now.'

You could've heard a mouse cough. Then one of the women – I think she must've known Freydis from Brattahlid or somewhere – mumbled, 'They're all up the woods, I think they're marking trees for felling. If you like, I can take you up there.'

Freydis didn't bother answering. She was chalk-white now, like a dead body. She turned on her heel and marched out, saw me, grabbed me by the arm and said, 'In the woods. Where are they likely to be?'

Actually, I could answer that. There was a ride; Leif had started it, and Thorvald and Bits had carried on with it, quite some way into the forest, for hauling out felled lumber. Chances were that Helgi and Finnbogi would've seen it and gone there, if they were choosing what to fell to start making up a cargo. I tried to tell her where it was, point to it, but either she wasn't taking it in or I wasn't explaining clearly. 'Shut up and take me there,' she said.

So I led the way; Freydis followed, and Kari tagged along behind like the pedlar's dog. Freydis walked quick when she was in a mood; I was supposed to be leading her, but I could only just keep up. Days of sitting around on a boat, see; your legs get stiff. Anyhow, we toiled up the hill into the wood, following the ride. Someone had been using it; there were footmarks everywhere, and ruts where logs had been dragged out.

We came on them quite suddenly; the track curved a bit, and there they were. I saw the brothers, Helgi and Finnbogi, and four or so other men; Finnbogi was cutting a cross in the bark of a tree, marking it for felling. Soon as Freydis saw him, she shot past me, nearly knocked me over, and bounded up to Helgi so fast that she was on him before he looked round. He opened his mouth to say something but never got the chance.

'What the fuck do you think you're playing at?' she yelled. 'Stealing my houses.'

It was like Helgi'd walked into a wall in the dark; he never saw it coming till it hit him. 'I'm sorry,' he mumbled, 'I don't know what you're—'

'My houses,' Freydis repeated. 'And now you're up here felling my trees. You thought I'd drowned, you arsehole, and now you're robbing me.'

Helgi stepped back a bit, because she really did look like she was going to go for him. Then Finnbogi came over and stood between them. 'They aren't *your* houses,' he said. 'Leif only lent them to you. And besides, you weren't here, we were cold and wet and the houses were empty. What were we supposed to do?'

A moment later, he'd shrunk back as well; Freydis spun round and shoved right up close to him, so he'd either have to push her back or get out of her way. 'What you were supposed to do,' Freydis said, 'was keep the hell out of my houses. And instead, they're stuffed full of your junk.'

Finnbogi pulled a puzzled face. 'I don't see the problem,' he said. 'I mean, the house is big enough for all of us, and we're partners, aren't we? But since you feel so strongly about it,' he added quickly, 'we'll clear out, you can have them back. Give us a couple of days—'

'Not a couple of days,' Freydis growled at him. 'Tonight. Come morning, anything I find in there belongs to me. You understand?'

'Well, yes,' Helgi said. 'But what's your problem? And what you said about the trees. I really can't follow that. The whole point is, we fell timber and ship it back home. But now you're saying—'

Freydis lunged at him. I never saw a man skip so fast; he jumped backwards and dodged behind the tree that his brother had just marked. I think that ended the debate, because the Icelanders sort of faded away among the trees, like elves in a story. A few heartbeats later, we were on our own, just the three of us.

'Bastards,' Freydis said. 'I never ought to have trusted them. We're going to have to watch them very close, very close indeed.'

You get moments like that sometimes. It's when you've sort of resigned yourself to things going badly, but deep down inside you still believe it'll all come out right in the end; and then something happens, and that little light in your heart goes out, and you know you were right all along. It's a cold, lonely feeling, and I'm sick to death of it.

Well, neither of us said anything; there wasn't anything to say, and Freydis didn't really seem to know we were there, she was more talking to herself, preoccupied. Kari and me, we followed her back to the houses at a distance, just in case she started off again. We didn't talk; I was thinking, surely she knows Leif only lent her the houses; but that didn't seem to matter. Some people see the world the way they want it to be, and anything different is someone else's mistake. I felt sorry for the Icelanders, and even sorrier for me.

When we got back to the houses, we found the Icelanders had got there before us; they were fetching all their stuff outside, and Helgi had got two horses in the shafts of a cart and was leading it round into the yard. I was surprised to see two horses and a cart; they must've taken up a lot of the cargo space on his ship, but I guess he reckoned he'd need them for logging. Maybe because of that they didn't seem to have brought much gear – a few chests and presses of clothes, not much flour and bacon, a load of axes and saws but not much else in the way of tools. It'd be rough on them, having to build a new house for themselves without the right equipment, and if I'd been them I'd have kicked up a fuss. I'm glad they didn't, mind.

They were obviously in a hurry to get away as fast as they could; but Freydis was in among them, getting under their feet, looking at every damn thing before she'd let them load it up, in case it belonged to the house rather than them. She didn't find anything like that, though she argued the toss about a three-legged stool and a pair of bellows, till Finnbogi dragged up three or four witnesses to swear they'd seen them aboard the ship on the way over. I don't think Freydis believed them; she called them all liars and said the things had been left there by her brother – though how she could've known when she'd never set foot there before she didn't explain, and nobody asked. After they'd gone, though, she pounced on Kari and me and asked us over and over again, wasn't that Leif's stool and the bellows Thorvald had brought from Brattahlid? We said no the first five times, and maybe the last two. She wasn't pleased with us, but she let us go in the end.

Meanwhile, they were fetching in our stuff. Truth is, I hadn't seen much of it, because it'd all been covered up with hides on the way over – we'd begged her to let us strip the hides off and use them to catch rainwater, but she'd flat-out refused, she wouldn't let us risk the stuff underneath getting spoiled by sea water. We'd all assumed it must be flour and malt and smoked meat. When the hides came off, though, we saw what her precious cargo really was: furniture, and tapestries, and the famous bench-boards that had belonged to Red Eirik, the ones he lent to someone and got into a blood feud over. Bersi the berserkers' man got into a right state about that, because it meant there wasn't much room left for useful stores. 'What the hell do we need all this shit for?' he said. 'You planning to eat this stuff over winter? Because there'll be fuck-all else.'

Freydis acted like she hadn't heard him, so he came up closer and repeated what he'd said, right in her ear. 'And we could've died of thirst,' he went on, 'because you wouldn't let us take the hides to catch water, and it was just to keep the salt off all this junk.'

Like I just said, Freydis was carrying on like he wasn't there; and then quite suddenly, she spun round, grabbed a farrier's hammer off a pile of tools, and cracked Bersi on the side of the head with it. I won't forget the noise it made in a hurry: a thick, chunky sound, like slamming an axe-poll against a stump. His legs seemed to melt under him and he flopped down in a heap, like a wet coat you shrug off when you come in from the rain. Then she put the hammer back where she'd got it from and carried on unpacking cups and plates from a barrel.

Nobody gave her any trouble after that, not about the furniture or the hides. But we were none of us happy about the situation. Because the journey had taken longer than we'd planned, and we'd lost stuff over the side in the storms, we didn't have more than a month's food in hand. No cows or sheep or other animals on our ship; somehow, when we saw there weren't any, we'd got it into our minds that the Icelanders were bringing them, but they'd brought horses instead and besides, we weren't on speaking terms with them. So: no milk, cheese, butter. Four hens and a cock-bird between thirty-five of us. Another nasty shock, specially for Kari and me who understood the implications: just two small barrels of malt, enough for two weeks' beer at the very outside. But we had very nice tapestries: one old one of warriors arriving in Valhalla, and a very pretty thing with women in blue dresses picking flowers, which Freydis told Starkad was French.

After we'd been there three days, and nothing much had

got done apart from unloading the ship and repairing the palisade – top priority, Freydis said, though I got the impression it wasn't the leather-boat people she wanted to keep out, it was the Icelanders – we had a bit of a meeting. Freydis had gone off on her own, to see what Helgi and Finnbogi were up to. They were building a house on the other side of the lake, and Freydis went at least twice a day to the edge of the wood, where she could look down at them without them seeing her. When she went off on the third morning, Bersi and Starkad came round and called us all into the long barn. We sat on the floor or leaned up against the wall, while those two and another of the berserkers' men, Grimolf, stood up at the far end, looking nervous.

'Right,' Starkad said, when everybody had settled down, 'we'd better keep this short. Looks to me like we've got a problem.'

He wasn't getting any arguments about that.

'Question is,' he went on, 'what're we going to do about it? The way I see it,' he went on, ignoring a few suggestions from the rest of us, 'we've got two choices. We can either carry on like we are, and probably starve to death or get caught out by the locals and killed, or else we can have a change in who calls the shots round here, and sort out something sensible among ourselves.'

There was a bit of muttering, and I noticed it was mostly coming from the Gardar men. There were about twenty of them, people Freydis had brought with her from her farm. One of them – we'd clean forgotten about him up till then, which gives you an idea of what he was like – was Freydis's husband, Thorvard Space.

Now don't get me wrong about Thorvard. He was a funny man; in fact, he was two men. When Freydis was around, he was so pale and thin you practically couldn't see him, and if you could he was just this shapeless drip of a man, like a skin without any bones or meat inside. But when she wasn't there, you noticed he was actually a big bloke, tall and broad across the shoulders, great big hands like rake-heads. Anyhow, when Starkad said all that about getting rid of Freydis, up bobs Thorvard Space, and his face is as red as a sunset.

'Just this once,' he said, very slow and gentle. 'Just this once, I'll forget I heard you say that, Starkad; and I'll assume you were just talking for yourself, and not the rest of you arsewipe vikings. But if I hear another word against my wife in this place, I'll kill the man who says it, and you've got my word on that.' Then he sat down; and I looked out the corner of my eye at the Gardar bunch, and they were all sit-ting there grim and stern-looking, giving the berserkers' men the long, cold stare. Just goes to show, you should never speak first and then think after.

Well, that was the end of the meeting; and Starkad and Bersi and Grimolf had a bit of trouble getting out of the barn, because wherever they tried to go there were Gardar men standing in the way, like they were just waiting to be shoved aside. Very ugly indeed, the whole feel of it; and I can't remember ever feeling more scared. Cold sort of feel-ing, right to the bone. See, Kari and me didn't really belong to either side, the berserkers' men or the Gardar mob; fig-ures, really, since we'd been dragged along kicking and screaming, so to speak. But it meant we were nobody's friends, so if it did blow up into a right old mess, we'd be fair game for either party.

If I'd ever kidded myself it'd blow over and we'd all settle down, it wasn't for long. Things just got worse. I'm guessing someone told Freydis about what Starkad had said; she got all uptight and quiet, which was worse than when she was roaring around the place yelling. Then there was Starkad, who wasn't going to forgive her for bashing in his mate's head with the hammer, and the rest of his lot, who were furious with Thorvard for calling them vikings. Everywhere you went, you saw men walking quickly across the yard or outside with their axes in their belts, not talking to men from the other faction. At night, in the house, with precious little to eat and nothing to drink, it was bloody awful. Not much better during the day, because there wasn't anything to do. Freydis wouldn't send us out to hunt or gather food, even though we were nearly at the end of the flour and stores; she didn't want the berserkers' men going off somewhere plotting against her, and she wanted her own people close, for protection against Starkad and his lot and also against the Icelanders, who she was convinced were going to sneak across when she wasn't looking and rob her, or worse. She was still going out twice a day to watch them, and often she'd take one or two of her men with her; when they came back they all had that grim look, so I guess it was starting to rub off on them. Once or twice I heard Thorvard whispering with some of the Gardar blokes, something about waiting till they were ready or biding their time till the enemy were off their guard; then, as soon as they saw me, they'd go quiet and stare at me, which I really didn't like at all. Obviously they were planning something, but there was no way of knowing who they were figuring on dealing with, Starkad's people or the Icelanders.

Came the day when the food ran out. When Freydis heard there was nothing left, she got into a right old state, though I can't see how it could've come as a surprise to her. First she had two of her men drag Bersi in from the yard; they held him up against the wall, and she accused him of stealing the flour for the vikings (which was what she called the berserkers' men, to their faces as well as behind their backs). First Bersi just said no, he'd done no such thing; but it was plain she didn't believe him, or didn't want to believe him, and he was getting very scared, you could see that.

'It wasn't me,' he repeated; and then I guess he had a flash of inspiration, because he added: 'It must've been them. Finnbogi's lot, the Icelanders. They must've snuck in here while our backs were turned and stolen that flour.'

I happened to be looking at Freydis when he said that, and I swear that her face sort of lit up, like a lamp glowing bright when you blow on the wick. She didn't say anything, but you could see that, as far as she was concerned, that had to be the right explanation.

Well, Bersi could see from the look on her face that he was part-way off the hook, but not free and clear; you could almost hear the grindstones in his mind slowly turning. 'Stands to reason,' he said, in a very wobbly sort of voice. 'They filled their ship up with that cart and the logging gear, and those horses. Probably fed all their grain to the horses, so no wonder they've run out.'

I guess Bersi realised that wasn't a clever thing to say at roughly the same time the rest of us did. Freydis gave him a look that would've flayed the skin off most people, and then said: 'It's my fault, I'm too trusting. Leif should've told me they were no good, but I expect he wanted me to fail. Probably suit him if I never came back. I know for a fact that he had more than his fair share of Father's things when he died, but it was no use trying to say anything.' She scowled; she had a way of scowling like she was rinsing all the anger off her face, and then she'd smile. 'Well, we'll see about that, when the time's right. Meanwhile,' she went on, all brisk and businesslike, 'we need food, before winter sets in. No point doing their work for them. Right, I want foraging parties, first thing in the morning. You—' For a horrible moment I thought she meant me, but she was looking over my shoulder at a Gardar man called Styr Otter. 'Fishing. Take the ship's boat, I want cod for drying and salmon for the smokehouse. Bersi, you can make yourself useful for a change; take two of your men and pan for salt, we'll need plenty. I want you' – now she was looking at Thorvard Space – 'to lead a hunting party in the woods, there's deer everywhere, you can see their slots all over the place. And you two' – this time it really was our turn – 'Leif was always talking about the wild corn that grows here. You'll know where to find it. I want enough for flour for the winter, and brewing.'

No point telling her you couldn't brew with the stuff; we'd tried, God knows. Kari nodded brightly, I think he'd have agreed to anything just to get out of her way. 'And while you're at it,' she added, 'you can bring in, say, fifteen bushels of grapes. Take four men, we need to move quickly.'

There was a lot more of that sort of thing before she was done; and in each case it was, *Take five men* and *Choose half a dozen men to go with you*; Kari told me later that he'd added it all up, and she'd given orders for at least a hundred men, even allowing for double shifts. But we were all right; since we knew there weren't any vines, we wouldn't need four men to help us find them.

Gathering wild corn was just fine by us, because it got us well away from the house for most of the day. It was hard work, mind; stooping down all the time, lugging heavy sacks, two hours' walk at least in the morning before you even started picking, and all as far back again at night. I've worked as hard in my time, but never harder; and nothing nice to look forward to, like you've got at home, a good meal and a drink, friendly company in the hall and a good feeling about your life. I guess I kept myself going by telling myself, this can't go on, sooner or later it'll get sorted out and we'll all be going home, back to Herjolfsness where I belong. Funny, actually, that it took all that time away, all those journeys to the very edge of the world, to make me understand that the place I ought to be was pretty much the place I started out from.

We were out one time, mid-morning, and we'd been working since first light. It was getting harder and harder to find any stuff worth picking, but we'd been lucky and come across a patch big enough to fill our sacks. We carried on till noon, then we sat under the trees for a breather while the sun was high. You'd laugh if I said it was hot; a Greek'd freeze to death. But picking that wild corn was enough to work you up into a muck sweat even on a cold day, which was part of the pain of it; you'd be frozen going out, sweating while you were there, chilled to the bone going home. But anyway.

We were sitting under the trees, not talking or anything; I may even have closed my eyes for a moment or so. But then I felt someone's shadow on my face. Now, obviously my first thought was the leather-boat people; so I sat up before I even opened my eyes, and tried to tug my axe out of my belt, only it was stuck. But then I heard a voice saying, 'Steady on,' and I knew it wasn't them, so I looked up.

I didn't recognise any of them, but it wasn't genius to figure out that they were Icelanders, Helgi and Finnbogi's lot. There were six of them, standing looking at us. They didn't seem tense or anything like that. I noticed they had long axes, and one of them had a long cross-cut saw over his shoulder.

Of course, I wasn't sure whether we were on speaking terms or not; but they seemed fairly relaxed about us, which was just as well. One of them sat down next to me, and the others followed suit. 'Mind if we join you?' the first one said; I nodded, and Kari said, 'Help yourself.'

'Sorry,' the stranger said, 'I don't know either of you; but my name's Einar, this here's Skeggi, and this is Svein' – and so on, I can't remember the rest of their names. I said who we were, and Einar nodded. 'You're the two who came here with Lucky Leif,' he said.

'That's right,' Kari replied. 'And Thorvald, and Thorfinn Bits. Actually, we were with Bjarni Herjolfson, the very first time.'

Einar seemed impressed. 'You must like this place a lot,' he said.

Well, it'd have taken far too long to explain. 'It's all right,' I said. 'But a lot depends on the company, if you follow me.'

Einar looked at me, all thoughtful. 'It's all right back at our place,' he said.

'I don't doubt it,' I replied. 'How's the house coming along, by the way?'

'The house? Oh, we finished it a while back. We're all settled in now. It's a bit rough and ready, but it keeps the rain off and the cold out.'

'That's good,' Kari said. 'So, where are you boys from? In the Old Country, I mean.'

'Eastfjords,' Einar replied, and before long we were chatting away nice and pleasant, about people we knew, distant relations we shared, because in Iceland everybody's somebody's cousin. They say in Norway that you can shut up a load of Icelanders in a house in October, and let them out again in spring when the snow thaws and they'll still be having the same conversation, about whose great-aunt married whose third cousin back in Laxriverdale, and whether their second child was a boy or a girl. I know it's one of the big jokes with foreigners against us Icelanders, that we're all inbred as buggery, but I think it's a good thing we all know who we are; and hearing that kind of talk out there, in bloody Meadowland – I'll admit it, I was pretty close to tears.

The fact is, you see, home isn't a straightforward thing. Partly it's a place, but partly it's people. I mean, you can be with the same bunch, like a ship's crew, for years and years, going all over the place, trading or whatever, but that's never home; not when you wake up every morning and there's a hill or a mountain on the skyline you don't know the name of. So you pack in the seafaring and go back to the farm, but everybody you ever knew is dead or moved away, and that's not home either. Or you can be in a place like Meadowland so often and so long you know it by heart, you can walk around with your eyes shut and not bark your shins, and you know the people you're with, because you've been through winter with them; and it still isn't home, because you know perfectly well the place doesn't want you there, any more than you want to be there. Home's such a bloody delicate thing, one slight change or one thing missing and it's screwed up for ever; and a man's better off blind or missing a hand or a leg than being away from his home. Greeks I've talked to since I've been here, they think we Icelanders are soft because the most a court of law can do to you back home is make you an outlaw, so you've got to leave your house and move away to another part of the country, or overseas. Soft; I don't think so. I think it's the cruellest thing you can do. I mean, everybody dies sooner or later, but having to live in the wrong place, in a place that's not meant for you to be in – that's cruel. And I never even did anything wrong.

Anyhow, we talked away with the Icelanders for a long time, till they realised it was getting late and they were supposed to be meeting up with another party to do a job. See you around, they said, and they went on, while we just sat there.

A bit later, we got up and carried on gathering the wild corn; and Kari said, 'This is stupid. I mean, look at us, men our age, and all we've got to eat is wild stuff off the ground. Pigs live better than this.'

My mind had been working along much the same lines, I'll admit. So I said to him, 'Are you thinking the same as me?'

'Could be,' he said.

'I was thinking,' I said. 'We could go over to the Icelanders' house, see if they've got bench-space for two more. I mean, they're felling lumber, which means they're planning on going home come the spring.'

'Earlier, maybe,' Kari said.

'Possibly even that,' I said. 'And what's more, they'll be heading back to the Old Country.' I thought about it for a moment or so, then I added, 'Don't know about you, but I'm sick of Greenland.'

Kari nodded. 'Whole place smells of Red Eirik,' he said. 'Like here. Everywhere you go, you can smell him.'

Well, I wouldn't have put it quite like that, but I could see what he was getting at. We didn't say much more about it all the rest of that day, but next day and the day after we kept coming back to it; and pretty soon we reached the hard place, which was how Freydis'd take it if two of her crew went over and joined up with Finnbogi's people.

There wasn't any need to talk about Freydis much, we both knew what we'd seen. The only way either of us could see it working was if we timed it just right and went over to the Icelanders just when they were getting ready to sail. Of course, we'd tell them to forget about any claim we had on shares in the timber proceeds, we just wanted to get away from there and back to Iceland. The question was, would they give us a ride out of the kindness of their hearts, and my guess was that they probably would. After all, I didn't imagine they'd be coming back again, deal or no deal, and if helping us pissed off Freydis, that'd more likely make them want to help us rather than the other way about.

'But we want to be sure,' Kari said, one time when we were going over it yet again. 'No point showing up on the off chance the day before they sail. They'd be more likely to tell us to get lost, and if Freydis found out that we'd tried to go with them, she wouldn't be happy. No, we need to have a talk with them first, see how they take it. For one thing, how are we going to know when they're going to leave, unless they tell us first?'

Seemed to me that what Kari was suggesting was a bit risky. All it would take would be for one of the Gardar lot to see us talking with the Icelanders, and we'd be in trouble. On the other hand, I could see he had a point. Anyhow, we couldn't agree, so we let it slide, and the year was slipping away. I never knew a place like Meadowland for time just melting away, like beer in a leaky barrel. You'd think time'd crawl along, like it usually does when you're suffering, but it wasn't quite like that. The days could seem very long sometimes, but they soon went by, without you really noticing. You know, I've thought about this stuff for a good many years now, and I think where you are makes all the difference. Who you are is all about where you are, and it bends other things too, like how quickly time passes, and what's right and wrong. Strikes me there's nothing more important than place; everything else falls in with it.

Anyway, we'd been on gathering wild corn for maybe a month, and we'd got pretty well all there was. Suddenly one morning, Freydis calls us all together. There's now enough food for the winter, she says, so there's going to be a change of plan. We're all off food-gathering and on felling timber.

'We've got to be quick about it, too,' she said, 'before the Icelanders get all the good stuff. They've got a head start on us, but we can get ahead if we work hard.'

I took that as meaning that the deal they'd struck back in Greenland, that we'd be the permanent outpost and they'd do all the hauling and shipping of the lumber, was now dead and buried. Fair enough; like I said just now, I didn't see Finnbogi and his people coming back here again once they'd taken their cargo home. But this business of making it into a race struck me as plain stupid. After all, the forest was so vast we'd never even bothered trying to explore it: the little bit that Finnbogi's lot could fit onto one medium-sized *knoerr* was neither here nor there. Also, it increased the chances of our lot running into theirs; if the Gardar people met up with the Icelanders, there would probably be a whole lot of trouble, and there was no need for anything like that.

But never mind. Next day we were all up bright and early, off to the woods with axes and hooks and saws and rope. Freydis drove us at it like a plough-team. There was none of the careful surveying and marking we'd seen the Icelanders doing; no, if it was tall and had leaves on, she had us cut it down and trim the brash, and then leave it where it lay. In a couple of days we'd felled more than enough timber to make up a cargo for our ship, and we were all expecting to be put on to hauling what we'd cut. Not a bit of it. Next day we cut another big load, trimmed it, left it where it'd fallen. Even the Gardar men thought it was all a bit odd. For one thing, we weren't just felling oaks, like the Icelanders were; a lot of what we'd felled was birch, which isn't a lot of use for a lot of things, and rots into pulp if you leave it in the cord too long. In fact, what Freydis put me in mind of was when a fox gets into the hen-coop and runs round and round after the hens, picking off any that're a different colour or breed and then killing the rest too. Fox'll only take one or two birds to eat, the rest he kills just because they're there. Same with Freydis. She was acting like she was planning on cutting down every last tree in Meadowland, not because she wanted to sell the trees as timber but because she wanted them all dead and out of the way – well, yes, that's right, so that the Icelanders couldn't have them.

Still, it was something to do, and it's easier to forget about the big picture when you're busy. I can't say as felling timber is my favourite job; too dangerous, for one thing. A hundred-foot tree is a treacherous bastard when you've cut three parts of the way through and it's starting to creak. You can stand there and look at it, figure out which way it's going to fall. You can rope it up to the trees next to it, or you can have your mates pull on the rope so it'll drop neatly where you want it to go. But one time in five it'll have the last word, twisting or splitting, getting hung up in the neighbouring branches so it's dangling there ready to go at any moment; and when you finally get round to those last few strokes of the axe, watch out for the butt-end of the log. It dearly loves to kick back as the tree goes down. One of our men, Geir Something-or-other, got careless that way, and the kickback smashed three of his ribs.

Mostly, I'm glad to say, Kari and me were on trimming duty, cutting off the branches, clearing and burning the brash. It's hard work, but you're less likely to get squashed flat, unless someone drops a tree in the wrong place and you're under it. Mostly it was hand-axe work, which jars your elbows and strains your hands and wrists. At least we were doing something useful, because the branchwood wasn't fit to ship and was only good for burning. So we made cords and faggots, more than enough to keep us going through yet another Meadowland winter.

By the time the wind started to turn cold, we'd been logging practically non-stop for over a month, and we'd had enough. We wanted a rest, possibly even a bit of fun before we had to barricade ourselves indoors till the thaw. Someone suggested getting up a few sports and games; races and wrestling and the ball-game, or even a swimming match if anybody felt brave enough to get in the freezing-cold water. The idea went down well. Slogging away cutting timber, the Gardar men and the berserkers' men had put most of their differences behind them. There were a few hard cases, obviously; one or two men who held grudges because of accidents or near-misses at the logging, and a couple of long-running feuds between men who just didn't like each other very much. But that sort of thing's normal, and if you can't cope with it you'd best find a remote bit of land nobody else wants and stay there.

Starkad the berserkers' man and Freydis's husband, Thorvard Space, saw to most of the arrangements for the sports; they were good at that sort of thing, details and such like. They sorted out who was going to take part in which events, the order they'd go in, making sure that two deadly enemies weren't put together in the wrestling, that kind of thing. It took them a day or so, while the rest of us cleared a bit of space and marked out the courses and rings. We were all ready to go, in fact, when Freydis calmly announced that while we'd been busy with all of that, she'd gone over to the Icelanders' house and invited them to join in.

Stunned, was what we were; and I guess Finnbogi's men must've been the same, or more so. Anyhow, while we were all standing there wondering if we'd heard her right, she said how it was a real shame and a stupid waste of time and effort, us and the Icelanders not talking to each other. It didn't matter whose fault it was, she said; far as she was concerned, she was happy to forgive and forget, with winter coming on and everything. This'd be the perfect opportunity to clear the air and sort things out, so that come the spring we could get on with the job we were all out here to do.

I think Thorvard Space might've said wonderful, what a good idea; but the rest of us just stared at her, until she got annoyed and stomped away. We couldn't make it out; not after all the work we'd put in felling lumber, and not having anything to do with the Icelanders since practically the day we arrived. The general view was that Freydis was up to something; Bersi went around saying it was an ambush, and suddenly at some point when they weren't expecting it we'd round them all up and cut their throats, like slaughtering the cattle at Yule. Actually, that thought had crossed my mind, but not for long. Oddly enough, I wasn't nearly as surprised as the rest of them. I figured that for some reason Freydis had simply changed her mind. I think there's some people who have very strong minds, just like others have very strong arms or backs; all the Eiriksons were like that, I reckon, they'd get an idea into their heads and then they'd bend the rest of the world till it fitted the way they saw it. That was my guess, but you never knew anything for sure with Freydis. She was like one of those trees I was talking about just now: you never really knew which way she'd fall.

Naturally, sports day had to be put back a bit to give the Icelanders a chance to sort themselves out; which had the effect of building up the excitement at our place. You'd have thought that with all the bad feeling and attitude we'd had since we'd arrived in Meadowland, we'd have been way past getting excited, like a bunch of kids. Not a bit of it. Grown

men, grim-faced old bastards like the Gardar lot, or evil
buggers like the berserkers' crew, with nothing on their
minds except whether they were going to get picked for the
ball-game team. Crazy. But like I keep saying, nobody was
his usual self in that place. Maybe it was because we were
there on our own, so far away from anywhere and anyone
that we might as well have been the only people in the
whole world; whatever the reason was, those stupid games
mattered. Men who wouldn't have bothered to walk from the
barn to the yard to watch a horse-fight back at Brattahlid or
Herjolfsness were up in the morning dark running ten laps
of the palisade or down on the beach chucking great big
rocks around. Kari here was dead set on going in for the
swimming, but I managed to talk him out of it—

'Talk me out of it, you arsehole,' Kari interrupted. 'You said
that if I put in for the swimming match you'd cut my hamstrings while I was asleep.'

Eyvind sighed. 'You knew I was just kidding.'

'Did I? Well, maybe I knew you wouldn't go that far, but
you made no bones about it — if I went in for the sports
you'd be really snotty about it, moaning and groaning at
me. Didn't leave me much choice.'

'It was for your own good,' Eyvind snapped. 'And you
can't say I was wrong.'

Silence for a moment or so. 'Still don't see where the
world would've come to an end if you'd let me go in for the
swimming race,' Kari said doggedly. 'Not that I cared all
that much. It was just bloody typical, you telling me what I
could and couldn't do.'

'Really.' Eyvind was scowling ferociously. 'Well, if you'd
listened to me the first time I told you not to go swimming—' He stopped; and the looks on both men's faces told

me that Eyvind had gone too far. 'All I said was, don't go getting involved, it's all going to turn nasty. That's all I said. Apart from the joke about your hamstrings.'

'That's not quite how I remember it,' Kari said quietly. 'But what the hell, it's a long time ago. And you're telling the story.'

That made Eyvind flare up a bit. 'You don't like how I'm telling it, you carry on,' he said. 'My throat's getting sore anyhow. No, you go on, I'll just sit here quiet and listen.'

Like he was just saying (said Kari, as Eyvind lay on his back with his hands folded on his chest), everybody was in a high old state over these games. Me, I think it was just because we'd been living on our nerves so long, it was good to have a chance to let off steam; plus, the Gardar men and the berserkers' men had been wanting to have a go at each other for some time, but obviously they'd reined back from actually sorting things out with axes and knives, because we were all stuck there together. It was good to have a chance of settling scores without half of us ending up dead.

Well, the Icelanders came over early. They fetched their women along; more to the point, they brought a barrel of beer. It was leftover provisions from the journey, they said, and they'd been saving it for a special occasion. Now, one barrel between sixty-odd men is a piss-poor ration, but we hadn't tasted beer practically since we left Greenland; far as we could gather, the same went for them, and yet here they were sharing their last barrel with us. I think a lot of us changed our minds about the Icelanders on the strength of that, at least as long as the beer held out.

So we had a drink or two to clear the air and relax our muscles, and then it was time for the foot-race. Five laps of the palisade, and Finnbogi put up a fur-lined coat and a new pair of boots for the winner. That annoyed Freydis, who'd been wondering if she should have prizes; she'd asked around, we all said yes but she'd decided against it. So she had a word with our runners – there was a Gardar man called Kolskegg, I remember, and Starkad's kid brother Flosi, and a couple of others – and told them they'd better win, or else. Now sometimes Freydis did make jokes and kid around, but she always looked so grim and ferocious when she was doing it that it was just as well if you assumed that she was being serious.

Helgi and three men I didn't know were running for the Icelanders. Finnbogi asked Freydis to start the race, but she told Thorvard Space to do it for her. He stood up on a log and yelled out, two, one, go, and they set off at a hell of a lick.

I don't know about you, but the sight of a bunch of men running in a big circle doesn't really get my blood up. Sprinting and hundred-yard dashes I can just see the point of, but pounding round and round the same circuit doesn't grab me. I was looking in the other direction when the race ended, watching some rooks mobbing a hawk; apparently, Flosi won, with one of the Icelanders second. Freydis was grinning all over her face, and Finnbogi handed over the coat and the boots very graciously, I thought. Anyway, that was the race safely out of the way, and everybody happy, even Freydis.

Next was the throwing match, where you've got to chuck a big rock further than anybody else. Now I was so sure that one of the Gardar men, can't remember his name offhand, was going to win, I even had a small wager with an Icelander over it, my knife against his hat. I'd watched our man practising, see, and I couldn't imagine anybody doing any better. Pity, it was a good knife, and I'd had it a long time. Serves me right for gambling.

For the swimming, we'd tarred over a barrel and anchored it with a rope tied to a big stone: first man to touch it was the winner. I still reckon that should've been me; I could have taken the Icelander who won it, easy. The water was freezing cold, mind; even though the swimmers covered themselves all over with lard, they came out blue and shivering. There was a fur blanket for a prize, courtesy of Helgi and Finnbogi; very suitable.

Anyhow, our side was two-one down at this point, with wrestling the next event, and Freydis was getting upset; so she pulled out one of the berserkers' men and made Thorvard Space go instead. He wasn't happy, but he had to do it, because she said so. Don't know what else she said, but whatever it was it put the fear of God in old Thorvard. Never seen anything like it, he fought like a mean old bear, and the Icelanders didn't stand a chance. Freydis had insisted on giving the prize for that one – Helgi had brought along a fancy whetstone, but Freydis told him to keep it, she'd got a better prize. But when Thorvard came out the winner, I guess she must've changed her mind, because she made Helgi give him the whetstone after all.

All square, then, as we came to the ball-game. Now the most you can say about the ball-game is that it doesn't usually lead to as much bad feeling as horse-fights do. True, more people get killed or crippled actually playing it, but there aren't so many blood-feuds as a result. The rules are a bit complicated; the gist of it is, there's two teams, and they take it in turns to face off against someone from the opposing side. Each team has a base-line, and the object of the game is to knock or carry the ball over the other side's line: that's called scoring. Each of you has a bat, but strictly speaking you're only supposed to use it for hitting the ball, and then only at the start of the game; soon as one or other of the players has smacked the ball, you drop your bats and try to grab or kick the ball over the line. Apart from the offside rules, which are so complicated nobody really understands them, that's about it; everything else is fair. When everybody's had a go, the game's over and the team that's scored the most lines wins. It's not for the faint-hearted, obviously, but most people manage to keep their tempers, and it's bad form to send out your team's giant against the other side's dwarf. It's a good way for two men who don't get on to work out their differences without using weapons, and it can be good fun to watch, if you like that sort of thing.

It was pretty obvious that the first pair were holding back; there was a lot of running about, but they hardly laid a finger on each other, and the crowd got impatient after a bit, so they called it a draw and came off. Next up were Helgi, for the Icelanders, and Thorvard Space for the home side. They were under a bit of pressure from the crowd to put on a better show, but you could see that neither of them wanted to start anything that could spoil the party. Helgi was the better runner, he was light and quick on his feet and had a good eye for the ball; but Thorvard had the brute strength, which meant he won the off – that's where you see who can hit the ball with the bat, right at the start – and sent the ball a long way down the field towards the Icelanders' base-line. Helgi went scampering after it, got to it way ahead of Thorvard, picked it up and started to run.

Thorvard runs in for a tackle and launches himself at Helgi, who dodges; Thorvard ends up crashing on the ground, but he gets his hand to Helgi's ankle and pulls him down. The ball skips out of Helgi's hand and goes rolling over the sideline, which means it's out of play. Now, here's where the offside rule gets complicated, because the player who puts the ball out of play forfeits the put-in to the enemy – in other words, if Helgi put it out, Thorvard gets the put-in, and the other way about if it was Thorvard's fault. What came out afterwards was that Thorvard reckoned it was his put-in, because Helgi was in possession when the ball was sent out of play. Helgi reckoned the opposite, because it was Thorvard's tackle that made him drop it. Anyhow, Helgi tries to get up to grab the ball, but Thorvard won't let go of his ankle. Helgi thrashes about with his leg to get it free and, by accident or on purpose, kicks Thorvard on the nose. Blood everywhere, naturally. Thorvard jumps up and swings at Helgi, who ducks out of the way, stands on the ball and goes down with a hell of a bump. The ball scoots straight over to Thorvard; he picks it up, just as Helgi stands up again. Thorvard throws the ball, hard as he can, and it hits Helgi smack in the face. True, Helgi's standing with his back to his own base-line, and our side reckons it was all in the game, Thorvard was just putting the ball in, chucking it towards the line, like you do. The Icelanders, needless to say, start yelling that it was deliberate. In other words, we're a heartbeat or so away from an all-out pitched battle when Freydis runs out onto the field, gets between Helgi and her husband so as to stop them going for each other, and gives Thorvard a smack round the face that sets him staggering. Of course, the Icelanders all cheer, and even our lot can't help laughing at the sight, because Thorvard's a huge bloke and Freydis had to stand on her toes to reach; and by the time Thorvard's head's stopped spinning, the mood's changed and everybody's happy again, except possibly Thorvard, who doesn't count.

Well, Finnbogi had the sense to agree when Freydis asked him to call off the rest of the match; it was only fair, he said, because that way, the whole of the sports day was a draw, too, and what could be better than that? At which, Freydis puts her arm through his and leads him back to the house for dinner, and we end up all mixed in together, instead of the Icelanders on one table and us on another, as was originally planned. There's no beer left, and the food's a bit sparse, but we're all such good friends by now and anxious to be nice that nobody seems to notice. Freydis cleans up Helgi's cuts and bruises herself, and she sits between the brothers on the top table.

I don't know where Thorvard got to after the ball-game, but he wasn't at the dinner, and my guess is that Freydis told him to make himself scarce so that there'd be no awkwardness between the brothers and him. The Icelander I sat next to at dinner reckoned Freydis had saved the day and done a fine job; he'd obviously got her all wrong, he said, and he was glad about that. It was stupid that we'd been there all that time and not said a word to each other. There were faults on both sides, he figured, and now we could put it all behind us and get on with loading a cargo and making some money.

When he'd finished saying all that, all I could do was nod and say, yes, right, you bet. For all I knew, he might even have been right – I didn't know what they'd been saying or doing over their side of the lake, after all, maybe they'd been as twitchy and suspicious about us as we'd been about them. Naturally, I hoped the air had been cleared once and for all, and it was going to be apples and honey all the way from now on. But I wasn't convinced, and neither was Eyvind. Mind you, he's a gloomy bugger at the best of times, so that was nothing to go by.

We finished dinner, and the Icelanders didn't seem to want to hang around very long afterwards; I guess they wanted to leave while we were all still friends, before anything happened to screw up the peace. There was the usual formal exchange of presents between Freydis and the brothers. She gave them each one of Thorvard's wool shirts, and they gave her a dinky little hand-axe, which they said they'd had their smith make specially, out of the local bog-iron. Freydis seemed very taken with it, particularly because it was Meadowland-made. That was a nice touch, she said.

Well, that was the end of that. The Icelanders went home, and we sat around for a bit in the hall, talking things over quietly. It was all a bit subdued, after all the excitement, but I happened to overhear Freydis talking very fast and enthusiastically to Starkad and one of her men from Gardar, about how we could all get a move on with loading the felled timber, now that things had been patched up with Finnbogi, and maybe we might even get a ship out before the cold weather closed in. That sounded good to me, particularly since I'd made myself a promise that if a ship did leave for the Old Country, I was bloody well going to be on it. I got off to sleep straight away, which was unusual.

Next morning, I woke up before the rest of the household. I needed to go to the outhouse for a piss, so I made my way outside careful and quiet, so as not to wake anybody. I was halfway across the yard when I heard a *tink-tink* sound. I looked round and there was Freydis, kneeling down at the barn corner. She had the little axe that Finnbogi had given her, and she was bashing away with it at a bloody great big stone. She was hitting so hard that sparks were coming off, and she kept at it till she missed and gave the handle a hell of a scat on the edge of the stone. The handle snapped and the head flew off, at which point I made a dash for the bog before she saw me standing there watching. Later on that day, I heard her telling someone to reset the edge and put a new handle on it.

CHAPTER
SIXTEEN

One morning (Kari went on), Freydis got up early. It was dark, of course, and she woke me as she bumped into the partition on her way out. She'd put on Thorvard's cloak – presumably she grabbed the first thing she could find – and she wasn't wearing any shoes. I assumed she was going out for a pee, so I turned over and went back to sleep.

Later on, when we went out to work, I saw that there was a heavy dew, and I could see footprints in the grass going up out of the home meadow towards the lake. I remember thinking, that must've been Freydis, where was she off to so bright and early?

I was working that day with Eyvind and a Gardar man called Thorketil; he was all right, for one of Freydis's people – you could talk to him without getting scowled at or knowing that what you'd said would be reported straight back. We were cutting coppice for charcoal-making, and there was a good stand of middling-high birch on our side of the lake; I suggested we might as well try there. Maybe it was wondering about those footmarks that put it into my mind, I don't know.

We'd been working for a bit and had stopped to put an edge on our hooks when a couple of the Icelanders came up through the ride. Since peace had been made and we were allowed to talk to each other, they came over to say hello. I knew one of them from the sports day, a man called Mord Squint, who'd been one of their swimmers. We chatted for a bit about the sports, the ball-game mostly, but I could tell that Mord wanted to talk about something else.

'We had a visitor over our place this morning,' he said.

That made me feel a bit pleased with myself. 'Let me guess,' I said. 'Freydis Eiriksdaughter.'

Mord looked a bit disappointed. 'You know about it, then,' he said.

'No, we don't,' Thorketil interrupted. 'Don't pay him any mind, we don't. So what did she want?'

Mord sat down on a tree-stump. 'It was all a bit strange, really,' he said. 'Me and Snorri here were just about to set off for work – we'd been talking to Helgi, being told what to do today. Finnbogi was still in bed, he can be a bit slow getting started in the mornings. Anyhow, I happened to look up, and there's your Freydis stood in the doorway. Don't know how long she'd been there, and she was looking straight past us like we weren't there, at Finnbogi. I guess he noticed we'd stopped talking, because he propped himself up on his elbow and yawned, and saw her.

'"Hello, Freydis," he said, all nice and polite. "What're you doing here?"

'She didn't stir from the doorway, like she was afraid to come in – no, it was more like she was superstitious; you know, like the people who won't walk over burial mounds, or under ladders. "You'd better get up and come outside," she said. "I need to talk to you."

'All this as though Helgi didn't exist, mind; not to

mention Snorri and me. "All right," Finnbogi says; he grabs a coat, stuffs his feet into his boots and stomps out.

'They go a little way off, to where there's an old fallen tree lying on the ground. Of course, Helgi and Snorri and me, we pretend to take no notice, but we stop talking, and we're earwigging like mad. I'm pretty sure that Freydis didn't realise we were listening. We were out of sight behind the door frame, but we could hear every word, and I could just see them through the crack between the door and the frame.

'Freydis sits down on the old tree, and after a moment Finnbogi sits down beside her. Neither of them says anything for a bit – it was like when you first go courting, and you and the girl are both too shy to speak. Then Freydis says, all pleasant: "So how are you lot getting on?"

'"Not bad," Finnbogi replies. "Like you said back in Greenland, this is a good place. I've never seen grass like it, and you certainly weren't exaggerating about the timber. There's definitely money to be made here, and it wouldn't be a bad place to have a permanent settlement, assuming we don't get any more bother from the locals. But we haven't seen anything of them – don't know if you have? – so maybe after the last time they've decided to leave us alone."

'He waited for Freydis to say something but she didn't. So he went on: "The fact is, the only thing that's been putting me off this project is this problem we seem to have been having with each other. Bugger me if I know what it's all been about, but if we've got it under control at last, don't see why we can't make a go of it after all, along the lines we agreed back in the East. As far as I'm concerned, it was all a lot of unfortunate misunderstandings, and if you haven't got any problems with us, we haven't got any with you. And that's about it, I reckon."'

Well, Eyvind and I looked at each other, but we didn't say

anything, and neither did Thorketil, though you could see he didn't know what to make of it. My guess is, Freydis had been saying a lot more to her own people, from Gardar, than she ever said to the berserkers' men, or to us; and it's a fair bet that she'd been going on to them about what a bunch of thieving, cheating bastards the Icelanders were. So he was puzzled, but pleased as well, just as we were.

'So then what?' Eyvind asked.

'Well,' Mord went on, 'Freydis didn't seem to react to what Finnbogi'd just said, one way or the other. She just sort of let it lie for a moment or so. Then she said, "Actually, what I wanted to talk to you about was the ships."'

'That must've taken Finnbogi a bit by surprise, because none of us had given the ships much thought since we got here. I don't know,' he added, 'what about your lot?'

'I don't think anybody's mentioned the ship for a long time,' Thorketil said. 'Why, what did she say?'

Mord frowned, then he said: 'What she wants to do, apparently, is swap: you get our ship and we get yours.'

I couldn't make head nor tail of that. 'What did Finnbogi say?' I asked.

'He was as taken aback as you are,' he replied. 'I mean, for one thing – no disrespect – your ship isn't a patch on ours. It's old and it's small, and besides, we know our ship, how it handles, what its funny little ways are. But that wasn't what got me. Put me straight if I've got this wrong, but wasn't it the plan that your lot was going to stay here, while we shuttle back and forth with the timber?'

'That's how I understood it,' I said.

'Me too,' Mord said. 'In which case, surely, we'll be using both ships; so what does she want ours for? In any case, even if she's dead set on keeping one of them here while we're away, surely it makes better sense to use the larger one for carrying cargo. We can get half as much again on ours as we could on that old *knoerr* of yours.'

All I could do was shrug my shoulders. 'What did Finnbogi say?' I asked again.

Mord laughed. 'I think he was so stunned at it all, he didn't know what to make of it. But you should know her by now. If she makes a suggestion, it's not generally open to negotiation. If she wants our ship for something, I don't see as we've got much choice in the matter. I mean, if Finnbogi'd said no, you can't have it, do you really think she'd leave it at that? Anyway, Finnbogi said yes, that'll be fine, we'll do that, then. I was standing next to Helgi in the doorway, remember, and he nearly choked, which shows you what he thought about it all. Usually, the brothers talk things over ever so carefully before they decide anything; but Freydis had clearly made up her mind, and Helgi wasn't about to rush out there and ask his brother, in front of her, what the hell he thought he was playing at. Anyhow,' Mord said, 'that's the news from over our way. Something to think about, if you ask me.'

That was no lie; and after the Icelanders had gone, the three of us talked all round it, trying to figure out what the scam was, what she was up to, but we couldn't think of anything that'd fit the facts. It was pretty clear that Freydis had something in mind, and that something was the reason she'd decided to make peace with the Icelanders, after treating them like shit ever since we'd got there. But before we could understand what she was planning, we'd have to figure out why she'd taken against Finnbogi's people in the first place, and none of us really knew what was behind that, except that it was something to do with Leif's Booths, and finding them making themselves at home there when we'd arrived. That was the core of it; but that was as far as we could go.

Truth is, trying to explore Freydis's mind was like Bjarni Herjolfson pointing his ship at the unexplored north-western sea and setting sail.

We worked for a bit, and then it was time to go back for breakfast; the sun was up and the dew had gone, and all three of us were curious to find out if anything had been happening back at the house. So we hurried back, and we found the whole crew standing about in the yard. The house door was shut, and people were glancing at it from time to time, like they were waiting for some announcement to be made. It was all very odd, and it made the palms of my hands sweat.

I saw Starkad and Grimolf, two of the berserkers' men, standing by the barn wall, and I headed over to see if they knew anything about what was going on. I knew Starkad couldn't keep anything to himself for very long, and Grimolf wasn't much better; they were nattering away in low voices, so obviously there was something to talk about. When I asked them straight out what was happening, they tried to look blank, like there was nothing unusual; but they couldn't keep that up for very long.

'It's Freydis,' Starkad said. 'She's had a row with Thorvard Space.'

Well, that was nothing special. 'So?' I said.

Grimolf shook his head. 'I was in the house,' he said, 'around going-to-work time. I'd stayed behind to put new laces in my boots, and I was waiting for Starkad here to get himself moving – we were supposed to be mending fence-rails together. Anyhow, I was just about to go outside when I heard them talking in the inner room; so naturally, I stopped where I was and listened.'

I could believe that. Grimolf had thief's ears, nothing was safe from them. 'Well?' I said.

'It was comical, really,' Grimolf said. 'Thorvard was still in bed, I guess, and Freydis must've been climbing back in with him, because he moaned about her feet being cold and wet; and then he sort of paused, and asked where she'd been, so bright and early. Don't suppose he meant anything by it, just ordinary husband-and-wife grumbling; but Freydis took it the wrong way or something. "If you really must know," she said, "I've been over Finnbogi's."

'That took Thorvard by surprise. "What the hell did you go over there for?" he asked.

'"To ask if I could buy their ship," she says, like it's the most natural thing in the world. So Thorvard, who's still three parts asleep, remember, asks what she wanted to do that for. "Because I want something bigger and better than that old wreck of my brother's," she says. "Why do you think?"

'"Fine," Thorvard grunts. "So what did they say?"

'Then Freydis makes this sort of pig noise. "It wasn't what they said," she tells him. "More like what they did."

'"Well?" Thorvard says. "What did they do?"

'Now Freydis starts yelling at him. "They said no," she says. "And when I tried to reason with them, they got nasty. Really nasty. Helgi hit me, right across the face; and then he grabbed my arms from behind, and Finnbogi tried to – to touch me." She stopped for a moment. You could've heard a mouse cough. "I managed to slip away; they came after me but I hid in the wood. They had six or seven of their men out searching for me."

'Another pause, then Thorvard says, very quiet so I could hardly hear, even with my ear right up against the partition: "Is that true, Freydis? Did they really—?"

'She screams at him, is he calling her a liar? He doesn't say anything, and she starts sobbing, and going on at him: he's pathetic, she's twice the man he is, if a bunch of thieves like Finnbogi's men can do that to his own wife and he won't do anything about it; he doesn't say anything, not that I could hear. This wouldn't have happened if she was back home in Greenland, she says, where she's got a brother who'd look after her, instead of a useless gelding of a husband who can't get it up any more; and loads more stuff like that. Still no answer from Thorvard, and now she's screaming at him that unless he does something she'll divorce him right then and there.

'Then I heard him moving,' Grimolf went on, 'and it struck me that if he was coming out, it wouldn't be very smart if he caught me eavesdropping on such an intimate conversation. So I got out of the house pretty quick.'

'He told me what he'd heard,' Starkad interrupted, 'and then we went and told Bersi, because I didn't like the sound of that at all, all that stuff about Thorvard doing something; I thought we'd better get the rest of our lads together, in case there's trouble. You know how things have been between the Gardar boys and us, after all.'

'So then what?' I asked.

'So then,' Grimolf went on, 'Thorvard comes rushing out of the house, all red in the face and shaking. He grabs hold of the first men he finds, tells them to get everybody together here in the yard, because there's a job needs doing that'll take all of us to do it. Then he goes back in the house and slams the door, and I heard the bar go up. And we've been waiting here ever since.'

I left them, and went to find Eyvind. Thorketil had gone to talk to his mates, and the Gardar men were all huddled up together round the side of the house. It was one of those times when you can feel trouble's on the way, but you can't quite figure out where it's coming from or what it's all about. There wasn't any reason not to believe what Grimolf had told me, but it didn't make any sense, not after what we'd heard from the Icelanders. I couldn't make it out. Naturally, I told Eyvind what I'd heard, and he was as gob-smacked as me; in fact, he was all for slipping away quietly before anything started that we might not want to get caught up in—

'That's right,' Eyvind interrupted. 'And I bloody well wish you'd listened to me.'

Kari scowled at him. 'Yes, right,' he said. 'And then what do you think would've happened to us?'

Eyvind didn't answer that; Kari shrugged, and went on, 'Credit where it's due, it wasn't because he was scared or anything, I'm not suggesting anything like that.'

'Thank you so bloody much,' Eyvind grunted. 'But of course I was scared, and so were you. You'd have to have been simple not to be scared in a situation like that. Truth is, we'd both been scared ever since we found ourselves on the ship with Freydis, headed back there. You learn to live with it, like with toothache, but sooner or later there comes a point where you can't blank it out any more. Which was why I told Kari we ought to get out of there, go and hide in the forest or something.' He paused, and they looked at each other. 'Luckily,' he went on, 'Kari told me not to be so bloody stupid.'

Kari shrugged. 'I was thinking the same thing,' he said. 'I wanted to run away, same as you. But there was a voice in the back of my head telling me that whatever happened, it couldn't be worse than being stuck out in the forest on our own, in Meadowland. I guess I was thinking, if something's going to happen to me, I'd rather it was an axe in the head than dying out there in the woods. I was more afraid of

Meadowland than just plain ordinary death, if that makes any sense.'

Neither of them said anything for a long time; then Kari carried on with the story.

We stood around in the yard for most of that day (Kari went on). To start with, everybody was talking, but after a bit it got very quiet. There didn't seem to be anything worth breaking the silence for. All we could do was wait and see what happened.

Sometime around nightfall, the door opened, and Thorvard called us in. We sat round on the benches, in our usual places. Freydis wasn't there, and the door of the inner room was shut; Thorvard was up at the top table, and there was a chess set in front of him; the way the pieces were set, it looked like he'd stopped in the middle of a game. Time wore on; we ate dinner and got ready for sleep. Thorvard got up a few times to put wood on the fire, but he didn't say anything to anybody, and nobody had the nerve to go near him.

I can't imagine that anybody slept much. I lay awake all night, staring up towards a roof I couldn't see in the dark, until gradually light blurred in through the smoke-hole. I was in a sort of daze, I guess: awake, but not thinking anything in particular; my mind skimmed over a whole lot of things, like someone skating on ice. At times, it was almost as if I was remembering things that hadn't happened yet; I could remember Freydis leading us down to the beach, where we stowed provisions on board the Icelanders' ship, then cast off, leaving them behind; or else I was back in the skirmish with the leather-boat people, when Ohtar got killed. Other times I thought about being on the ship with Bjarni Herjolfson, catching sight of this place from a long way out – I was back where we'd only just arrived, nobody had set foot on Meadowland yet. My memories were all stirred up together; like when they're making cheese from the fat milk, and they stir in the cream that's risen on the top overnight, breaking up the crust and mixing it in till there's just the smooth, even texture of the milk. All the separate journeys – Bjarni, Leif, Thorvald, Thorfinn Scraps and Freydis – blended together; it was like they'd all happened simultaneously, like I'd only come to this place one time, and each set of events was happening in a different part of the settlement, and I was standing out on the porch, watching each one in turn. I saw a picture once: a painted book, like they make in monasteries. It was supposed to be the different seasons of the year, all jumbled together on the same page. In one corner, they were ploughing; in another, they were scaring birds off the sprouting corn; in another, they were cutting and binding, and so on, as if time was flat, and if you got up high enough you could see everything happening together. It was that sort of feeling, lying there in the dark; crazy, I know, but it felt really vivid and lifelike, it made much more sense than the idea that I was lying on a bench in Leif's Booths on my fifth visit to the same place. I argued to myself, which is more likely: that I've come to this same godforsaken place five times, or just the once? I felt like it was that night I swam ashore from the ship, after Bjarni Herjolfson had told us that we weren't to go ashore, but I had to know better; and then I thought I'd hit on the real explanation – that I'd gone ashore that night and stayed there, never swum back to the ship at all; that, all these years later, I was still here, I'd never left and gone to Greenland, gone back to Greenland, Brattahlid and Herjolfsness. After all, how probable was it that a man'd spend his whole life going round and round in circles, like a tethered goat on the end of its chain, with the stake driven in right here, at Leif's

Booths? I was trying to make some kind of sense of all the stuff I thought I knew; and in the end I realised there was only one thing I knew for certain – that nobody owned Leif's Booths, because the owner refused to give the place away, he'd only ever lend it, and that was why nobody could ever stay here, and nobody could ever really leave.

So I was thinking all this crazy stuff, and daylight kind of crept up on me while I wasn't looking. The door of Freydis's room opened, and she came out. It was still very early, and she was barefoot, wearing one of her husband's cloaks because it was the first thing that came to hand in the dark.

'Get up,' she said, to all of us.

So we got up off the benches, reached for our boots and coats and hoods, and our axes. Men were pinching at their eyes to rub the sleep out, yawning, clearing the fog. I heard the milk-can clink on its hook, and the leg of a table dragging on the floor as it was pulled out. I heard someone coughing, an axe-head bumping on the wooden partition, ashes shifting in the hearth as someone poked life into the fire. The start of every day sounded like that in Leif's Booths, like every day was the same day over and over again; so maybe this day would be just like all the others, where we all wake up, go out to do the early morning chores, and when they're done we come back in for breakfast. I remember, I prayed, to our Heavenly Father, and Thor too, to be on the safe side: please let today be like all the other days, and if that means having to stay here for ever and ever, well, there are worse places to be and worse ways to spend a life. Only, please don't let the circle be broken *today*; if only we can get this day safely over and done with and out of the way, maybe everything'll work out and be just fine.

I was on my feet now, and I looked at Freydis. She was drinking water out of a wooden bowl, and it was dribbling down her chin onto her chest. Thorvard was coming out of the inner room; he had something wrapped in a cloth, and he was peeling the wrapping off. Starkad was watching him too (he was much closer to him than I was) and I heard him say, 'Thorvard, what've you got there?' Thorvard didn't answer, but he wound away a turn of cloth, and I saw a sparkle, gold and red, and I recognised that the thing he was was holding was a sword.

So I thought: thank you, Thor and our Heavenly Father – thanks for nothing. But it'd been a long shot anyhow, because when did the likes of them ever listen to the likes of me? I noticed that something was missing; something hadn't happened that should have. Took me a moment to figure out what it was, and then I knew. Nobody'd asked what this morning's jobs were: nobody'd asked, because we all knew.

Freydis put down her bowl and wiped her mouth on the back of her hand. She looked slowly round at us; maybe she was counting us, I don't know. Then she nodded, very slightly, at Thorvard, and he walked to the door. He had the sword in his hand, no scabbard; maybe it didn't have one. I'd just put my axe in my belt, it's second nature first thing in the morning, you aren't dressed without it; but today it didn't seem like all the other times; it was like I'd somehow done it on purpose, rather than out of habit. I remembered I'd sharpened it the day before yesterday and hadn't used it much since, so it probably still had a good edge on it.

We were all on our feet now, except for Eyvind—

Kari paused, and looked at his friend for a moment. 'You want to tell the next bit?' he asked.

But Eyvind shook his head. 'You carry on,' he said, and looked away.

★

Well (Kari went on), Freydis noticed him still sitting on the bench. 'Get up,' she said.

But he didn't stir. 'I'm not feeling too bright,' he said. 'It's my head. I think I'll stay in this morning, if that's all right.'

Nobody moved or made a sound; the two of them just looked at each other for a bit. Then Freydis said, 'Get up. I need all of you for this.'

'You don't need me,' Eyvind said.

'No, all of you,' Freydis replied. 'Thorvard.'

Thorvard came back down the hall towards Eyvind, and everyone stepped back to let him through. I remember the look on his face; it was blank, like he wasn't in there. Before Thorvard reached him, Eyvind stood up. 'It's all right,' he said, 'I'm coming.'

'That's fine, then,' Freydis said. 'Come on, we're wasting time.'

I saw Starkad and Bersi look at each other, then look away like they were both embarrassed at something they'd done, or not done. Their lot, the berserkers' men, were all up the front end of the hall, with the Gardar men bringing up the rear. I tried to remember if that was how they usually slept in the hall, but now I came to think of it I wasn't sure, one way or the other. Everything seemed different somehow, and I wasn't sure that these were the same people I'd come to Meadowland with, this time or any other. Their faces looked the same, but to me they felt like strangers.

When we got outside into the open air, I was surprised by how early it still was. It felt like half a day had passed since Freydis had woken us up; but the dew was still fresh and wet on the grass – the fat, sweet grass of Meadowland that was going to make us all rich, every man a farmer or an earl – and the early sunlight was still straining through the trees, faintly stained with pink and green. Eyvind and me, we tried to stay at the back, as Freydis led the way at a cracking pace, stomping along like a mother who's angry with the kids; Bersi was up front with Thorvard, but Starkad hung back to talk to us. He looked guilty, no idea why. I noticed he had a long knife, what we call a *sax*, dangling off his belt; it was so long that it was bumping his ankle-bone as he walked, and it was getting on his nerves. I hadn't seen him with it before.

'You two,' he said. 'I know you were in that thing with the savages, the leather-boat people, but that wasn't a proper battle. You ever done any real fighting?'

Both of us shook our heads.

'Didn't think so,' Starkad said. 'You don't look like you have. You can always tell, if you know what to look for. It's a sort of flinching, very quick, when anyone moves.'

'You must've done a lot of fighting when you were with the berserkers,' Eyvind said.

'Me?' Starkad shrugged. 'A bit. More than I'd have liked, that's for sure.' He frowned, like he was carrying on another conversation at the same time with someone we couldn't see. 'Look,' he said, 'really it's pretty simple. Always keep your eyes fixed on the other man, right? Got to pay attention, that's the main thing. When someone hits out at you, use your feet, get out of the way; don't try blocking or parrying unless you've got absolutely nowhere to go. When you want to hit, feint high and cut low; go for the kneecap, the shin, the inside of the knee if you can; it's the oldest trick in the world, but it always works. Don't try and hit too hard, you're only wasting strength and slowing yourself down. Basically, that's it, all there is to it. You got all that?'

I nodded. 'You think there'll be a fight?' I said.

'Hope not.' Starkad shook his head. 'Yes, I can't see how it's to be avoided, if we're going to try and steal their ship. I don't think Freydis'll be happy till she's forced them to fight us. You know, I used to think it was bad when I was shipping with the berserkers; but she makes them look like kittens. Just remember,' he went on, 'feint high, cut low and whatever you do, don't just stand there rooted to the spot. Got to keep moving, or you're dead.'

He pulled a tight little smile, like he was letting us know how sorry he was to hear we hadn't made it; then he hurried up and went forward to talk to Bersi. 'So that's that, then,' Eyvind said to me. 'We're going to pick a fight with Finnbogi's lot. That's so stupid.'

Couldn't argue with that, but what was I supposed to do about it? So I nodded, and we carried on walking. Nobody else was talking much, except us.

When we got to the edge of the lake, Freydis stopped and went 'Shhh!', loud enough to be heard back at the Booths. I guess that was her idea of being a military leader. Past her I could see the Icelanders' house in the distance, all blurry and grey in the morning haze. I couldn't see anybody about. Maybe they're all still in bed, I thought; or maybe they saw us coming long since, and they're lurking in ambush, and we'll all be killed. Fact is, I was just starting to feel scared.

Now I'd been scared before, obviously, but this time was different. It's like when it's your turn to get up early and go and feed the calves, and it's so bitter cold out, soon you can't feel your fingers or your toes. Usually I feel fear in my stomach, like a finger twisted in my guts; my knees go, and my bowels and bladder, and it's like there's something stuck in my throat so I can't breathe right; all I want to do is drop to the ground and curl up in a ball, like a hedgehog, with all my spikes facing out. This was different: maybe it was more horror than fear, like I was walking right up to something so nasty that I couldn't bear to be near it. Maybe it wasn't going to kill me, or else I'd have felt the other kind of fear, but that wasn't the issue, really. I was cold, and sweating at the same time, and if I'd had any feeling in my legs I'd have run away, and the hell with what happened to me afterwards.

We went round the lake and came to the door of the Icelanders' house. They'd worked hard on it, like they meant to be there a while. They'd stripped a wide patch of turf to build the walls and the roof – a few wisps of grass were just beginning to show on the bare earth – and the house itself sparkled all over, with drops of dew caught in the grass. I'm used to it, of course, but people from other places always take a while to get accustomed to the fact that we make our houses out of turf, that they're growing things, alive. I met a German once, who'd been to Scotland and seen the turf houses there, and he said they gave him the creeps, because who wanted to live inside a living house? It was like being inside a burial mound, or a grave. I look at it the other way: who wants to live in something brittle and dead, something piled up on top of the ground instead of shaped out of it? But Meadowland was different, as always. We'd come there for the rich, fat grass – grass that dripped with butter, as Leif said once – we walked on it and lived under it, and it grew so well, so fast and rich; but it hated us, and I hated it right back. It couldn't wait to close over us for good. There's all those stories about sailors who land on a small island in the middle of the sea, and when they light a fire the island starts to move, and they realise it's not land, it's the back of a whale or a sea-dragon. I'd laughed at those stories, I thought they were just plain dumb, till I came to Meadowland; because that place was alive, a big, broad-backed monster; and the houses there, Leif's Booths, were its mouth, and if you stayed inside too long it'd digest you.

Freydis was being a great leader again. 'You six, round the back,' she said, without making it clear who she meant, so nobody moved. 'And I want three of you under each sky-light, in case they try and shin out over the roof. Bersi, Starkad, when I tell you, bust the door down.'

Stupid woman; you try busting in a house door, with just your boot and a hand-axe. They looked at each other, hesi-tating; but Thorvard walked straight past them and put his hand to the latch. It was open, and the bar wasn't up.

So he went in; and I guess the Icelanders didn't get up as early as we did, because they were all still asleep. I heard drowsy voices asking, who's that, what're you playing at? But Thorvard started grabbing them, hauling them up by their shirt-fronts or their hair and bundling them out, like unloading cargo from a ship. As they came out, arms twisted behind their backs, eyes blinking, like you do when you're still mostly asleep, Starkad and Bersi caught hold of them and slung them down on the grass, and as each one fell one of our men put his boot on the poor bastard's neck, to keep him still. When Thorvard had hooked out half a dozen or so, Freydis nodded at the Gardar men, and they went in and helped. I was standing well back, but someone caught hold of the collar of my coat and dragged me forward, same with Eyvind, and we were given an Icelander each to look after; and I put my boot on some man's neck, pressing down hard until I knew it'd be hurting; and I could do it because, like I told you, my feet were numb and I couldn't feel them. I can remember his face, though, and how I jammed his jaw to the ground with my toe, so he couldn't turn his head and look at me.

Thorvard went and pulled out Finnbogi, and Helgi came staggering out after him, yelling, 'Now wait a minute,' or something like that. I think he tried to grab Thorvard's arm, and then someone moved behind him. I didn't see, I was looking at the man under my feet, but I heard that very flat, chunky noise of an axe going into something solid. When I looked up, Helgi was toppling forward, and the hair on the back of his head was a sticky mess.

Finnbogi started to wriggle in Thorvard's grip; and then Thorvard looked at Freydis, and she just nodded, once.

I want you to believe me when I tell you that I didn't want to do it; but I knew I had no choice in the matter. There's a point where a thing's balanced and it tips just a hair's breadth too far; or where the man hanging by his fingernails off a ledge just can't quite hold on any longer. It's the moment when a man breathes out and this time he doesn't stop till all the air's gone out of him, and that's when you go from two possibilities to only one. I was telling myself, I don't have to, they can't make me; but I felt the axe-handle slip up through my belt, I felt the smooth weight in my hand, the weight as I lifted it above my head, to the point where I couldn't hold it up any longer and it came down. I screwed it up, of course; I meant to hit him nice and smart just behind the ear, good and crisp and clean; but I let the handle roll in my hand, and the edge gouged out a big chunk of scalp and blood and skidded off, and I had to do it again, and again, until I'd got the top horn jammed in smashed bone. I had to press down hard on the handle to lever it out again, like when you're splitting logs and you miss the line, and the grain clenches on the axe-head and grips it. Then I stood up and straightened my back; I felt sick and very scared, and mostly I felt really, really stupid, because I'd made a fuck-up of doing this one important job, I'd done it so badly, and there wasn't even anybody I could tell I was sorry.

So; we killed them all, thirty-two men, on the wet grass. Apart from Helgi and Finnbogi, none of them struggled or made a fuss; I don't think they had a clue what was going on, to be honest with you. It was all over, and the only sound was one of the Gardar men, swearing and whining because his axe had glanced off and nicked a fat slice out of his own shin.

Then Freydis looked up – she'd been watching very carefully, to make sure we were doing a proper job – and she said, 'And the women.'

Thorvard straightened up and said, 'Freydis, for God's sake,' but she acted like she hadn't heard him. Nobody moved, we all stood quite still and looked at her, and she frowned slightly, like she was annoyed. Her eyebrows tightened and she pursed her lips; and then she said, 'All right, then. Somebody give me an axe.'

Still nobody moved; so she clicked her tongue, and she pulled out from her belt the pretty little axe that Finnbogi had given her, the one whose handle she'd busted. Then she went into the house. She wasn't gone long, and when she came back out there was blood on the cuffs of her sleeves, and a dab on her cheek, where she must've pushed her hair back behind her ear.

'Set fire to it,' she said; and someone told her, 'It's fresh turf, it won't burn'; and she sighed, like it was so annoying. 'Just pull it down, then,' she said. So we lugged the bodies inside, and four of the Gardar men who'd brought long axes went in and cut through the sills and the joists. They got out in good time; the roof just sagged in the middle, like it was tired, and the whole house folded slowly in on itself and kind of sat, then lay down, as though it was curling up to go to sleep. 'We should've looked inside,' Freydis said. 'We'd have found all the things they stole from us. But it's too late

now, and I can't be bothered with it any more.' Then she
sighed again, and turned round, and headed back the way
we'd come.

Kari stopped talking; he folded forward, with his hands
crossed over his chest, and he looked very old. I turned my
head away, and Eyvind was watching me. He nodded. 'Me
too,' he said. 'Right up to the last moment I was going to
refuse, I was going to do something to stop it. But I didn't.'
He shook his head slowly. 'Things like that happened all the
time in the Old Country: men cut down in the fields or on
the road, whole families burnt to death in their houses –
they'd wedge the doors shut from the outside, nail bars over
the skylights, and get a fire going under the eaves till the turf
caught. But there was always a reason; a bad one, mostly, a
blood-feud or a matter of honour, but a reason we could all
understand; and they knew when they did it that it'd be
their turn soon, nobody ever expected to get away with it,
so when they lit the fire it was like they were burning their
own houses too. It wasn't good, sure, but in a way it was fair,
and at least we all knew why it had to be done.' He shrugged
his thin shoulders. 'It all happened just like Kari said. Must
be getting on for twenty years ago now, but I can remember
it like I'd just come from there, like my coat's still wet with
the dew.'

Kari lifted his head. 'When are those idle buggers finally
going to get that wheel fixed?' he said. 'No disrespect, but
you bloody Greeks—'

'So what happened after that?' I said.

When it was all over (Eyvind said; Kari just shook his head
and didn't say anything), Freydis led the way back to Leif's
Booths, and we all followed, like ducklings. She kept well in

front of us, but someone told me that halfway back she
started smiling.

It was still early, of course, the whole job had been very
quick and easy, so it still wasn't even time for breakfast. We
hung about outside the door, until Freydis came out again.
I noticed she'd changed her apron, but she was still wearing
the dress with the bloodstained cuffs. She started giving out
jobs, like it was an ordinary day. When she'd finished,
though, she cleared her throat loudly, and we all stopped and
looked at her.

'One last thing,' she said. 'If any one of you ever says a
word about what just happened, to anyone, ever, I'll have
him killed. When we get back to Greenland, if anybody
asks after Finnbogi and the Icelanders, we just say they stayed
on here. Pretty soon everyone'll have forgotten all about
them. That's all.'

Freydis had her way on that score, but she needn't have
bothered threatening us. I don't think anybody ever mentioned the killing of the Icelanders; there wasn't any point,
we'd all been there, seen it all, been part of it. The whole
business just lay quiet, always in my mind but never brought
out into the open. Fact is, we didn't talk much at all, bar-
ring the usual work stuff, like who had the staffhook last
and the log basket needs filling. The only chat beyond that
was a little bit of growling between the Gardar crew and the
berserkers' men; they tended to stay out of each others'
way, mostly, but there were a few flare-ups, always short and
brittle, and nobody actually pulled a knife or took out an
axe. I could tell the berserkers' men weren't happy, though.
Starkad did tell me he was worried, in case his lot were
going to be next – that was the closest anyone ever came to
mentioning the forbidden subject – but I thought he was
fretting unduly. Freydis mostly acted like the berserkers'

men didn't exist, except first thing in the morning, when she was handing out the day's work. She got very sharp with Thorvard, I noticed; she'd criticise him in front of the men or behind his back, which she never did before. He shrank back inside himself like a snail. I never saw him say more than two words to her, and he was always the first out of the house and the last back. If you came across him during the day, he'd look straight past you. He was always working, hard enough for two men: felling and trimming lumber, dragging logs and building cords. One day I saw him beside the lake; he stood for a long time looking at the mess where the Icelanders' house had been, and then he opened his coat and pulled out that sword of his; it was wrapped in old cloth, but it was plain enough what he'd got there. Soon as he'd got it free of his belt, he slung it out into the lake as far as he could get it to go. When I told Kari, he was all for swimming out there and trying to find it, before it got all rusty and clagged up. I managed to talk him out of it.

For the best part of a month after the killings, Freydis had us clearing ground, digging turf, cutting and driving in fence posts and rails, like she planned on building more barns and sheds. One day I was round the back of the shed that Bits had used as a stable, and I found the Icelanders' cart and their horses, tucking into a big mangerful of hay. A couple of days after that, Freydis told one of the Gardar men to take the cart up to the woods to pick up kindling and stuff, and he seemed like he knew what she was on about, so I guess she'd told a few people it was there.

The cold was coming on, and we'd had the first light dusting of snow, when Freydis called us all together when we came back in for dinner. Time was going on, she said, and if we wanted to get back home to Greenland before winter set in we'd better see to the ship. She'd been to have a look at it, she said, and it was in a hell of a state. There were timbers rotted through, the rigging was shot and the sail was in shreds. Luckily, we could sort it all out by stripping what we needed off the hulk of the other one, Bjarni Herjolfson's old ship; soon as we'd finished the overhaul, we'd be on our way home again.

Nothing like a bit of an incentive to get you moving. We had the Icelanders' ship fixed, caulked and ready to go inside of ten days. Freydis came to inspect it and said it'd do; then she told us to drag Bjarni's old ship well aground and set it on fire; we didn't need a second ship, she said, there weren't enough of us to man two of them, and she didn't want anybody coming along and stealing it.

So we did as we were told; we dragged what was left of the old *knoerr* well inland, piled well-dried brushwood and brash up in the hold and set it alight. Made me feel strange, doing that. It'd never been a wonderful ship; it was old and creaky when Bjarni first bought it, and it had been a long way since then. Just pulling it apart for materials, though, and then burning it: that struck me as a vicious thing to do, as well as wasteful. Kari figured it was because Freydis was worried that she'd got the numbers of the Icelanders wrong, and that some of them had been away from the house and were still alive out there someplace; she didn't want to leave the ship behind in case they sailed back to Greenland after we'd left and told people back home what she'd done. That's the best explanation I can think of, but I don't think it's true. I think Freydis just liked destroying things, if she couldn't have them. When the fire was going well, it put me in mind of stories I'd heard when I was a kid, about how in the olden days, when an earl or a king died, they'd put him on his ship, set light to it and launch it into the fjord, so the dead man could sail to Valhalla or wherever he was going. I don't think Helgi and Finnbogi were on that ship, but there was a funeral feel to it, at the time.

Once the Icelanders' ship was ready and we'd piled on as much timber as was safe to sail with, and a bit more, Freydis told us she was planning on leaving Meadowland in two days' time. Strange; I'd been waiting for her to say that, looking forward to finally getting away from the place, going home, never coming back. When I heard her say the words, though, I can't honestly say I felt anything much. Relief, I suppose; but it was the feeling you get when you're doing a difficult job, making a real bitch of it, and it's getting too dark to see, so you've got to leave it unfinished till the next day. No pleasure, it wasn't like a terrible pain had finally stopped; certainly no joy. We were finally going home: so what? It was too late for being happy now. It was like we'd just lost a big, important battle, and the war with it. No point going home under those circumstances, when you've already lost everything.

We set sail early on a bright, clear morning, with the frost still crisp on the grass. Don't know when I've set out on a long journey worse prepared: only three casks of water, precious little food, no spare sail and the ship riding so low we were close to getting swamped, even though the wind was gentle and even. Usually when you leave a place, you keep turning back and looking at it till at last it slips away out of sight; me, I kept my stare well out to sea until I was absolutely sure it'd gone, like a small child afraid of spiders in the roof.

Anyhow, that was the last I saw of Meadowland, and Leif's Booths. We had an absolutely fucking awful ride home: gales and big waves, fog thick as butter, you name it. In spite of that, though, we held our course, and eventually, with hardly any water left and nothing to eat except the cold pickings off a couple of gulls, we came through a fat slab of fog and saw Herjolfsness; Greenland, home.

'And that,' Eyvind said, 'is really the end of the story. Funny,' he added, yawning a little, 'I've told it a fair few times over the years, but never quite like that. Usually, I put in a bit more courage and nobility and stuff. It's what people want to hear, specially if you want them to buy you drinks.'

He started to get up. I reached out and caught hold of his sleeve. He looked at me.

'But what happened next?' I asked him. 'Once you got home. What became of your wife? And how did you end up here?'

Eyvind grinned at me. 'Oh, that's another story,' he said. 'But it's just about me, and a few other people. I thought you wanted to learn about Meadowland.' He shook me off gently and walked away without looking back.

I turned to Kari, who hadn't moved. 'So what happened?' I asked.

Kari shrugged. 'Not a lot, really,' he said. 'We arrived back at Herjolfsness but nobody seemed particularly glad to see us. They wanted the timber, of course; good straight timber was always in short supply, and you can't build houses without it. But they don't have much money, and what they do have, in the way of trade goods and so on, isn't really worth having. Freydis kept to the agreement, more or less; she took a big slice off the top, but the rest was shared out equally between all of us, and it was worth picking up. Not enough to buy a farm with, though.'

'So you stayed there?'

He nodded. 'For a bit,' he said. 'But Bjarni hadn't expected to see us again – Freydis had told him she'd be

staying there with her people while Finnbogi shuttled backwards and forwards with loads of timber. So, naturally, he'd
taken on men to replace us, and even on a big farm like
Herjolfsness you can't afford to hire men if there's no work
for them to do. He was nice about it, but he made it pretty
clear: we could stay there a while till we sorted ourselves out
and the timber was sold; after that, come spring, we'd be
moving on. While we'd been away, Eyvind's wife had moved
on, gone to keep house for an old farmer in the Western
Settlement whose wife had died. Eyvind thought about
going out there and fetching her back, but I told him, forget
it. She was probably happy there, settled. He had no land,
soon as spring came round he'd have no work, no place to
live. I told him, best thing we could do was move on, and
eventually he had to admit he saw the sense in it. Just before
winter a ship from out East stopped at Herjolfsness; they'd
been blown off course and needed somewhere they could
spend the winter. I had a word with the captain, asked him
if he could use two more men. I told him where we'd been,
what we'd done – except for the stuff about Freydis, naturally – and he said he was going East soon as spring came –
Dublin, then Scotland, then Orkney or some such place.
Didn't matter where, so long as it was away. See, I realised
that I'd gone past the point of going home. There comes a
time where you can't, any more, because it's not there. Like,
suppose Herjolf, Bjarni's dad, hadn't ever moved to
Greenland. Bjarni would've carried on as a merchant,
coming home to spend winter with the old man; but eventually, Herjolf would've died, and that would have been the
end of Bjarni's routine, things would've changed so he
couldn't ever go back again, not *home*, if you see what I
mean. He could go back to a place, but not to the man who
made that place what it was. Same with me; I couldn't go

back to Herjolfsness any more, even though the place was still there, the land and the house and the barns and stuff. Even if Bjarni'd said we could have our old jobs back, our old bits of bench to sleep on, I don't think we could've gone back. We wouldn't have fitted; like a knife that's got bent and won't fit in its sheath any longer. And, well; when you've got no home to go to, any place is as good as any other. Any place, except one.'

Kari paused to scratch his head and shift a little. 'I told Eyvind,' he went on, 'about getting a berth for us both on the Easterners' ship, but he said no, he'd be heading up to Brattahlid, see if there was any work going there. I told him, you don't want to do that, go and live there with Freydis's brother; haven't you had enough of Red Eirik's offspring to last you for good and all? He said no, but he'd had enough of being on ships; anywhere else he went from now on would be somewhere he could walk to, else he wasn't going. I could see his point, but I felt it was sad, that we'd been through so much together, been friends all our lives, and have to split up now and go our separate ways. But I didn't want to go to Brattahlid; my second-least-favourite place in the world, or third if you count Gardar. So I said, this is it, then, here's where we say goodbye. And he said, well, yes, it looks that way; and both of us were feeling too awkward to say anything more by that stage, so we left it there

'But all through winter, I kept thinking about it, and by Yule I'd made up my mind, I couldn't go East like I'd planned, I'd have to go to Brattahlid, if that's where Eyvind was dead set on going. I told him so, and he seemed sort of pleased, though I couldn't quite make out what he was thinking. Anyhow, that's how we left it. But then I found I couldn't sleep nights; I'd drop off, and then I'd have this same dream, over and over again, and it was always Freydis and the killing, except it wasn't in Meadowland, it was Brattahlid, and it wasn't the Icelanders she was killing, it was her brothers, Leif and Thorvald and Thorstein – and Thorfinn Scraps and Gudrid, too. It was almost like she'd turned into the place, she'd turned into Meadowland, Leif's Booths, and she was killing them all over again; anyhow, it spooked me out, and I knew I couldn't go to Brattahlid or even stay in Greenland any more. So I decided I'd have to go East in the ship after all. But I couldn't face telling Eyvind, not after I'd made a big thing about staying just so we'd still be together. I felt really bad about it, but I didn't have the courage.

'So spring came, and the thaw; and the Easterners caulked their ship and got it ready, loaded their cargo and all. They were leaving very early in the morning, to catch the wind, and I snuck out of the house while it was still dark and went with them. We all went nice and quiet down to the beach so as not to wake the household, and we were on board and cast off before the sun was up. When it was light enough to see, I looked about me; and fuck me, who did I see sitting in the stern but Eyvind?

'I nearly fell overboard. All that fretting and feeling guilty, and there he was. Of course, I yelled out his name and rushed over to him, trod on a rope and nearly smashed my head in on the rail. "What're you doing here?" I said. "I thought you were going to Brattahlid." He looked at me, with this really strange look on his face, and said, "Apparently not", or something like that. Later, he told me he'd been watching me, not being able to sleep and so forth, and he'd figured out what I was planning on doing, and so he'd changed his mind and decided to come along after all; and he didn't tell me so it'd be a surprise.' Kari stopped and frowned. 'You know,' he said, 'Eyvind and me, we've spent all our lives together, never been apart more than a few days ever, but still there's times when I can't quite figure him out. He can be a funny bugger; but there, every time we think we're going our separate ways we seem to end up back with each other. I said that to him once, and he said yes, a bit like us two always ending up back at Leif's Booths. He meant it as a joke, I know, but it's always struck me as an odd thing to say.'

CHAPTER
SEVENTEEN

Next day the smith came back with a new axle, fixed the cart, overcharged us and went away. We put the gold back in the cart and carried on with our journey, like nothing out of the ordinary had happened. The abandoned tomb vanished behind a roll of hills, the road opened up in front of us, and we left behind the place where I'd heard the story. But not the story itself.

Stories are a bit like those burrs that catch in the hem of your cloak. When you move on, you take them with you, without realising, and that's how the burr-plant propagates itself, riding unseen on the coat-tails of travellers. The story had come a long way, all the way from one edge of the world to the other, snagged on the sleeves of two old men who passed it on to another, to me. Here it is, and you can have it.

It was Eyvind who filled in the rest of the story. Kari was with us, so he didn't explain how he came to be on the Easterners' ship, when he'd told his friend he was going to Brattahlid. Instead, he told me how they'd drifted, with their share of the timber money in their purses, from Dublin to York, York to Winchester, Winchester to Paris and then a pilgrimage to Rome; which didn't seem to have done any good, since they hadn't noticed any miracles happening, or anyway not any good ones; so they decided Rome couldn't have been enough of a pilgrimage for their case history and circumstances, and they'd better go the whole hog and head off for Jerusalem. They got there, somehow or other: no money left, no food, Kari at death's door with the fever, dragging step by step along the road, but they got there at last, to the Holy Land, to the City of God. They arrived one night and lay down to sleep in the first doorway they could find. And next morning: nothing. No miracle.

Nor the next day, nor the day after that. They went to the Holy Sepulchre, but that didn't help. They went to Calvary, or at least they thought that was where it was, nobody spoke Norse and they were just beginning to pick up Greek and Arabic; they went to Bethlehem, and still nothing. At Bethlehem they finally sat down and came to the conclusion that whatever their problem was, the solution to it wasn't a place. By that time, of course, they were screwed; so they walked back to Jerusalem, hoping to run into some charitable fellow-pilgrim going home somewhere North-West who might take pity on them, and there they heard about the City, and how the Emperor's personal guard was made up of Northerners like themselves.

It was, as Eyvind said, a small and pretty crappy kind of miracle; but by then they were happy to settle for what they could get. They had to hang about waiting for three months before they found a ship that'd let them work their passage to Constantinople, and by the time they arrived they were in such a sorry state that the captain of the Varangians didn't want them and told them to go away. Finally, though, their luck changed. They were sitting outside the barracks gate feeling miserable when someone walking by stopped and said their names; they looked up and saw a very splendid-looking man in Guard uniform, gleaming scale armour and a big shiny sword, who said his name was Thorbjorn Asmundson, and he'd been one of Thorfinn Bits's crew, and had stayed with them at Brattahlid. He hadn't wanted to go to Meadowland, this Thorbjorn said, and he'd struck out East, ended up here and worked his way up to sergeant.

Thorbjorn got them into the Guard by vouching for them to the captain, and that (Eyvind said) really was the end of the story. Oh, they'd had some fun since then; they'd been to Sicily with Georgios Maniakes, they'd fought the Saracens and the Turks and the Bulgars and all sorts of other interesting people, and when they weren't fighting they'd lounged around the City having a fine old time, and ever since they joined the Guard (Eyvind said) they'd never had to do what he considered a full day's work. But that wasn't the story, Eyvind said; because really, it was only about the two of them, and who'd be interested?

And that, more or less, was all I got out of them; and when we arrived at Thessalonica, we found a letter from home waiting for us: because we were so far behind schedule, the plan had changed. I was to carry on west with the money and an escort from the Thessalonica garrison, but (for some complicated administrative reason which now escapes me) the Guard contingent was to head back home straight away.

I meant to say goodbye, I really did. I meant to thank them both, in a suitably graceful manner, making it clear that we were now genuine friends, rather than a Greek government officer and two of his hireling guards. I meant to let them know where they could find me once we were all back in the City again, so that we could drink together in a more civilised setting than an ancient looted tomb, and they could tell me other fine stories from the North, experiences and adventures and what Homer calls the glories of Man. But an accountant's idea of the crack of dawn isn't quite the same as a soldier's. I got up early so as to be sure of catching them before they set off, and found that I'd missed them by an hour. When I got back, I went to the Varangians' barracks and asked after them; the captain asked his clerk, who first told me they were dead, then that they'd been pensioned off five years ago, finally that they were still in Greece somewhere, and he didn't know when they'd be back. He promised faithfully, by St Constantine and the True Cross, that as soon as they returned he'd let me know. And so, of course, I never saw them again.

Many years later, I heard some news of them, from another, later Guard captain I met at a finance meeting. If the two men he was thinking of were the same as my two, he said, they'd been pensioned off as unfit for service, on account of old age, and had bought a small ship with the intention of sailing to India; because, he said, they'd never been there. I have my doubts, though. He said that the two explorers were Kari and Eyvind, but the descriptions he gave me were nothing like them at all.

I hoped to get further and better news a few years later, when I met yet another captain of the Guard at some function or other, and he turned out to be none other than our silent, much-enduring comrade, Harald Sigurdson. Actually, I didn't recognise him; fortunately, though, he knew me, and asked (very diffidently) if I was the Greek clerk who'd taken the payroll to Sicily back in the old emperor's time. When I looked at him more closely, I knew who he was. If anything, though, he was even taller and broader, with a leonine mane of hair flowing round his shoulders and a beard you could have stuffed a mattress with. His voice was still high and squeaky, though; but now he spoke flawless Greek with a cultured City accent.

The first thing I did was ask after Kari and Eyvind. But he didn't know any more than I did; he was pretty sure they'd either died or gone away, since he hadn't seen them hanging around the place for quite some time. But, he went on, it was odd that I should have mentioned them, because he'd been thinking about them – and me – rather a lot lately.

'You see,' he went on, pouring me a cup of rather good wine; we'd gone back to his private lodgings, splendidly furnished in the very latest fashion. 'The political situation back in Norway has changed; for the better, as far as I'm concerned. My nephew Magnus has been throwing his weight about rather, putting people's backs up. Things are going quite well for me; I'm negotiating a marriage alliance with Jaroslav of Novgorod, which ought to give me the leverage I need to persuade King Svein Ulfsson of Denmark to come in with me; one way or another, it won't be long before I get Norway back, and maybe a nice fat slice of Sweden and Denmark too.'

'How splendid,' I said, remembering how he'd allowed the two old rogues to bully him and order him about. 'Soon I'll be able to tell all my friends I knew you before you were famous.'

Irony had about as much effect on him as spitting peas at an elephant. 'By all means,' he said. 'And if ever you're in the North, you'll have to come and stay with me, as long as you like. But it's not Norway I wanted your advice about, or even Sweden and Denmark. It's what I'm going to tackle afterwards that's been bothering me.'

I frowned. 'After Norway and Denmark and Sweden, you mean.'

'That's right,' he said, nodding briskly. 'The thing is, with the Northerners you've got to keep them busy. It's like herding sheep: so long as they're moving, they keep together and one half-decent dog can keep them in order. Once they're grazing quietly in a meadow, however, they split up and wander off, and it's a devil of a job making them do what you want. So, once I've dealt with young Magnus and done my deal with Svein, I'll need something else to occupy my mind; and I've pretty well narrowed it down to a choice of two projects. But that's where I've got a bit bogged down, if you follow me. Can't make up my mind which; and that's where you come in.'

'Heavens,' I said. 'Well, I'm happy to advise, of course, but I don't know what value my opinions on strategy and international politics are likely to be. All I know about is adding up columns of numbers.'

He smiled indulgently. 'Ah,' he said, 'that's not quite accurate. You'll see, as I explain.'

'That's all right, then,' I said. 'Please, go on.'

He stretched his legs out a bit – I'm sure he was cramped, Greek chairs are made for normal-sized people – and sat quiet for a moment, marshalling his thoughts. 'The first choice,' he said, 'and, I have to say, the obvious and logical one, has got to be England.'

'England,' I interrupted him. 'That's the sort of triangular island up and across from France? Sorry, but it's years since I last had any reason to read Ptolemy.'

'That's England,' he confirmed. 'And Scotland's on top of it, and Ireland's next to it, due west. First, I've got a fairly decent claim to it – it's a bit complicated, because the English succession's all tangled up with Denmark and Norway and there's no clearly obvious line, which actually makes it easier for me to step in, if you see what I'm driving at. More to the point, it's a big, fat country, splendid grazing, the people are a bit simple but hard-working and docile, and we sort of speak the same language, more or less. They've had it pretty soft for a long time now, and they're a bit too keen on the quiet life for their own good, to be honest with you. Their idea of repelling an invader is to pay him money till he goes away. I reckon that by the time I've sorted out Magnus and Svein, I'll have an army that'll be able to roll the English over as easily as picking apples. Then Ireland'll be the next logical step, then Scotland, Orkney, the Hebrides; after that, possibly the Faroes and on to Iceland, depending on how things turn out. But that's getting a bit far ahead – don't weigh your wool while the sheep are still wearing it, as my grandfather always used to say.'

'Quite,' I said. 'Very sensible.'

'Anyway,' Harald went on, 'England would be a pretty shrewd move for a whole lot of reasons, and it'd make me a player in the big game. I'd be leaning on the Latin Empire from both the north and the west, and if there's one thing I've learned since I've been here, it's that the Latin Empire is definitely where the future lies. France, Germany, Italy, they're all in a real mess. No direction, you see, nothing to unite them, not since Charles the Great's time. But if some-one strong and dynamic were to burst in on the scene, knock their heads together, sort them out and get them organised – well, there's all the manpower there you could possibly want, hundreds of thousands of potential soldiers; and you know better than I do, it's shortage of manpower that's slowly bleeding this place to death. A concerted push from the west, and the Greek empire'd come tumbling down like a derelict barn – no offence,' he added quickly.

'None taken,' I assured him gravely.

'Which is exactly what Christendom needs,' Harald went on, as though I hadn't said anything. 'Unite the Latin and

Greek empires; drive the Turks out of Asia Minor and North Africa and Spain; get the Church put back together again – I mean, I ask you, what a disaster that's been, the two halves of Christendom at each other's throats for centuries and all over the technicalities of how you calculate the date of Easter, it's pathetic; and once we've done that, well, the sky's the limit, really.'

'Absolutely right,' I said. 'It's such a good idea, in fact, I'm surprised that nobody else ever thought of it.'

Harald shrugged. 'It's all about vision,' he said. 'Anyhow, that's one of my choices; and you can tell, I've thought it all through pretty thoroughly. It's the other one that I wanted to ask you about. You see, you were there when those two old farts, Kari and Eyjolf—'

'Eyvind,' I corrected him

'—When they were telling that story, all about the big island over the sea, out west; in fact, you heard the whole thing, I only got bits of it. Anyhow, what I was thinking is, how about it?'

I looked at him. 'How about what?'

'That island of theirs,' Harald said. 'Meadowland, or Wineland, or whatever it was called. Yes, I know they moaned about it and said what a rotten place it was, but, well, you talked to them long enough, you know as well as I do that they were a pair of losers, so what's their opinion worth? Peel away all their whining and stuff, get back to the facts; you've got a great big island, to all intents and purposes uninhabited, absolutely stuffed with valuable timber, magnificent grazing, good climate – it's crying out for someone to take advantage of it.'

'Yes,' I said slowly, 'but look what happened to everybody who tried to settle there; Lucky Leif and Thorfinn Bits, and that dreadful woman who murdered her business partners—'

He raised an eyebrow. 'Murdered?' he said. 'I think I
must've missed that bit. Doesn't matter; the fact is, those
examples don't matter worth a damn. Look at them criti-
cally, what've you got? A few half-baked attempts by a family
of idiots, with no real resources, no planning, no real struc-
ture to speak of; honestly, it's a miracle they lasted as long as
they did. You can't dismiss a project simply because it's been
tried by idiots and failed. Just think of what I'd be able to
bring to it. Well, first, money; resources. I can fit out a
whole fleet of ships – purpose-built for carrying livestock
out and timber back, on the Greek pattern. Then there's
manpower, which is generally the key to any venture. The
North is seething with spare people, men with nowhere to
go and nothing to do. Leave them where they are, they
make trouble; send them somewhere to start a colony, you
gain a useful new possession and you get rid of a load of
layabouts and hungry mouths: two birds with one stone.
Then there's organisation, administration. Damn it, we don't
even have words for them in our language; but since I've
been here, of course, I've learned all about that sort of
thing – supply lines, matériel support, communications, all
the most up-to-date modern techniques. But the most
important thing that I'd bring to the business would be clar-
ity of purpose. I know what I want out of the project; and it
strikes me that's one thing the Eiriksons never had. It's like
they thought that just going there was enough; they hadn't
properly thought through what they were going to do when
they got there. With me, it'd be quite different, of course.
Planned, phased settlement, self-financing, with the profits
from lumber and furs and so forth. Carefully regulated inter-
dependence – no chance of the colonists deciding to kick
me out and go it alone, when they depend on me for their
malt and their flour, and of course I'm the one who'll be

setting the prices and the rates of exchange. If all goes well, it wouldn't be long before I'm making as much out of selling stuff to the colony as I'm getting from what they send me. Wealth, you see, that's the key to everything. I mean, you must appreciate that better than anybody. What's keeping the City and the Greek empire going these days? Not manpower; the Turks and Arabs and Slavs outnumber you a hundred to one on each front. Superior military force? Hardly; you hire barbarians to fight barbarians. And you can do that because you still have this amazing knack of generating wealth; and if I'm going to make my proper mark on the world, that's how I've got to start thinking. Oh, it's not the Northern way. If you want to conquer your neighbours, you ask yourself, who are my bravest warriors, not where's the money going to come from to pay for all this? But that's small-minded thinking, limited, and it won't get you anywhere. And another thing, about this idea of Meadowland. Everywhere you go in the North, and the South too, sooner or later you're going to run up against the power of the Church. Now don't get me wrong, I'm a God-fearing man, and in its place the Church is a damn good thing; but they own all the land and the property, plus they can send you to Hell for ever and ever if you annoy them, which means you've got to tread very carefully so as not to piss them off. But if I start up what'll basically be a whole new country – a whole new world, even – if the Church wants to do business there, it'll have to play by my rules and do what I say. You can see how that alone makes it a more attractive proposition than England, say, where half your people are going to have their first loyalty to the Pope and their bishops, not to you. Really, when you think about it, you've got to admit that it's an amazing opportunity for the right man. Mind, I don't know how big the island is, nobody knows that – one of the first things I'd need to do would be a proper survey, send ships right round the coast, draw a map, so I'd know what I'm dealing with. But it's not unrealistic to suppose that it's quite big – bigger than Iceland, almost certainly, maybe as big as Ireland, even; and every acre of forest we cut for timber is an acre ready to be ploughed and seeded for pasture. I have an idea that sheep'd do really well there; imagine what you could so if you had a near-monopoly of the wool trade. And then there's the natives; there's a source of cheap labour for you. Do what the ancient Romans did, use the natives as your workforce, and when you've got all the work out of them you can, you reward them by making them citizens, thereby increasing your manpower reserves and your recruiting pool for your armies. You just can't do that in the North any more, apart from a trickle of Irish, they're too well organised and defended. But imagine the benefits. Instead of the old style of government, where I allot land to my earls, and they have their tenants, and both the profits and the loyalties get dissipated all down the line, I can keep the best land for myself as royal estates, worked by native labour under my bailiffs; I keep control directly in my hands, and I get the wealth I need for my aspirations in Europe.'

By this time he wasn't looking at me; he was gazing over my shoulder, at a bright vision only he could see. 'I don't know,' he said, 'I really don't. It's a damn shame I've only got a miserable little country like Norway to start off from. If I was King of France, say, or Emperor of the Greeks, I could do both at the same time, England and Meadowland. As it is, I've got to choose; I'm only human, after all, I simply haven't got time to do one and then the other. And I'd hate to turn my back on either of them, but I've got to; it's really frustrating. So,' he went on, remembering I was there, 'what do you reckon? You're a shrewd man, and by now you know as much about Meadowland as anybody. If you were in my shoes, right now, which one would you go for? I'd be really interested to hear what you think.'

What I think; so I thought. When I'd finished thinking, I steepled my hands and did my best to look intelligent; I've practised it over the years, at committee meetings and assessment panels, and if I try I can be quite convincing.

'If you want my honest opinion,' I said, 'I'd go for England. Now I want you to bear in mind that I know next to nothing about the place; and what little I do know is, what, five hundred years out of date, because we Greeks have had bugger-all to do with it since we pulled the garrisons out, back before the Western Empire fell. But I'm basing my advice on what I know about Meadowland; which isn't a lot, since I haven't been there, and all I do know is what Kari and Eyvind told me.

'That said, though,' I went on, 'I think Meadowland would be a bad idea. Again, I'm very shaky on my geography; but after I heard the story, I had a look in the old maps, and read my Ptolemy and my Strabo; and of course none of the places in the story are even mentioned, unless what Ptolemy called Thule is actually Iceland. And that in itself is significant, I believe. Frankly, it's a very long way to go, from Norway to these places. If you wanted to guarantee a practical and efficient line of communication between your base and this Meadowland, you'd need to have a firm grip on all the stepping stones along the way. As a soldier, you know how important that is. If you're relying on the goodwill of independent states for your lines of supply and your transport routes, you're asking to be held to ransom at some point. So, in order to make sure of your communications, you'd have to conquer first Iceland and then Greenland. Now, you know about these places, I don't; you know about the political set-up, the degree of resistance you'd be likely to meet, the level of sympathy you might expect from disaffected chieftains, that sort of thing. But my point is, even if it's a straightforward job it'll take time – years, probably, before you've got enough control to move on to Meadowland itself. And correct me if I'm wrong, but Iceland and Greenland sound to me like poor places, with no valuable resources to speak of; so all the years you're subduing them, there's no income coming in to finance the project, you'd have to fund it out of your other revenues, which puts a strain on your domestic economy. Once you've done that, you can start colonising, yes; but it'll be years and years before the revenues coming in exceed the costs, maybe not even in your lifetime. To be blunt about it: unless you discover large deposits of gold and silver in Meadowland, that you can just dig out of the dirt and cart away to your ships, forget it. Meanwhile, what have you got? Timber. Fine, it's valuable, but it's bulky, you can't ship enough of it quickly enough and cheaply enough to subsidise all your ambitions.' I paused, for effect. 'It depends on how you see things,' I said. 'I mean, if you're prepared to plough all your available resources into the project for years to come, your son or your grandson could stand to inherit – what did you call it just now, a whole new world. Fine; you'll be remembered as a visionary, a great man in context, like Philip the Macedonian. But you'd only ever be Philip, you'd never be Alexander. It all depends, like I said, on what you want; and if you'll pardon me for saying so, from what you told me I think you want to be the Northern Alexander: you want the world and you want it quick, while you've still got time to enjoy it. Meadowland's too far away, and too much of the distance between you and it is covered in water. To my mind, it's as simple as that.'

Harald was quiet for a long time, thinking; then he nodded decisively. 'You're right, of course,' he said. 'It's too far away, and that's all there is to it. England it is, then. Thanks. You helped me clarify my thinking, I'm obliged to you.'

I grinned. 'My pleasure,' I said. 'And when you're King of the whole North and you need a chief clerk, write me a letter and I'll come up and run your exchequer for you.'

'I might just do that,' he said. And the grisly part of it was, I think he probably meant it.

Three years later, to my amazement and, let's face it, horror, that buffoon Harald Sigurdson was crowned King of Norway. I read about it – a small footnote in the regular diplomatic gazette – but nobody I asked knew anything about the goings-on of the far-northern savages: heretics and pagans, uncouth, unlettered, kin to the unspeakable Normans who have caused so much trouble in Sicily and other places in recent years. So I thought no more about him, or any of the Northerners, for close on twenty years; until, a month or so back, there was another footnote in the gazette about a change of regime in England. According to our sources, who are generally reliable, the English king is dead, killed in battle, and the country is now in the hands of William the Bastard, Duke of Normandy. This came as a surprise to our diplomats, who never thought the Normans had the resources for such an enterprise; but, according to the report, they managed it because the English were weakened after fighting off another invasion, only a few days earlier, led by Harald Sigurdson, King of Norway, generally known as Harald the Tyrant. The English victory was a close-run thing, our man in Paris reported; but once King Harald was killed, fighting bravely in the front rank, the

Norwegians gave up and ran away, leaving the English free to march the whole length of their island to fight the Normans and be slaughtered.

Well, then. It's not every day that an elderly accountant like me changes the course of history. The power of Norway is broken and the relentless spread of the Norman menace continues unchecked, all because I persuaded Harald Sigurdson not to go to Meadowland. The joke of it is, the reasons I gave him were improvised rubbish, made up on the spur of the moment and dressed up in long words so he wouldn't see how thin and scraggy they were; because I didn't want to give him the real reason why he shouldn't go anywhere near Meadowland, because he was an idiot and he'd have ignored me.

I didn't want Harald Sigurdson to go to Meadowland because it's obviously an unlucky place. Simple as that. No good will ever come of it, nobody who goes there will ever have any joy of it. Don't ask me to explain why; if you've got this far, you'll understand without me having to construe it for you. What was it Kari said? The old story, about the island that turned out to be a hungry whale, gobbling up unwary sailors who landed their ships on its back. That's about right, I believe. But it goes deeper than that, I think. There are places that do things to people; and I believe Meadowland is one of them. If you go there, it will change you. It seems to me that it's a place that takes your strengths and turns them into weaknesses, as it did with the strong-willed, venturesome Eiriksons. What-ifs are easy in this wonderful Greek language of ours, where you can turn thoughts into things with a flick of syntax. I wonder: what if Red Eirik had gone there, instead of his son? Would Meadowland have turned his weaknesses into strengths?

Maybe; I think he could have founded a settlement there, just as he did in Greenland. But Greenland and Red Eirik moulded the Eiriksons and made them specially vulnerable to the dangers of Meadowland. When Harald Sigurdson asked my advice, I tried to ask myself, which is he, Eirik or Leif? And I looked at him, and thought of all the men and women he was planning on sending to that place, and I knew it was my duty to God and my brothers and sisters in Christ to talk him out of it – not because I thought he'd fail, but because I was afraid that he'd succeed.

So much, then, for the island of Meadowland, which lies further north and west than any other land we know about. I, John Stethatus the clerk, have written these words in the year of Our Lord 1066, with the express intention of advising my lord Constantine the Tenth, Emperor of the Romans, that he and his successors should never, under any circumstances whatsoever, send any expedition or invest any resources or commit any body of men to this remote and dangerous place, which might rightly be termed, in more senses than one, the end of the world. If anything is certain, this side of Judgement Day, it's that the Roman Empire will last until the end of all things, representing as through a glass, darkly, the Kingdom of God in this world. It will only come to its end on that day when, with the blessed apostle, we see a new Heaven and a new Earth, and all considerations of wordly rule and empire cease to have any meaning. Until that new world comes, we who live on the old Earth, under the old Heaven, all have our place, where we were ordained to be. Leaving our place, as Adam left the garden God made for him, we leave behind who we are, and inevitably become someone, something else; turning our backs on what God has ordained for us, we walk into abomination. This

Meadowland, and all other such places, if any, waiting still to be discovered, are not the new Heaven and the new Earth promised to us by the apostle; we must be patient in our place, and wait for them to come to us.

Which is fine, I suppose, as far as it goes: a proper logical conclusion drawn from the facts as they were presented to me. Perhaps I'm biased; after all, I hate travelling by sea, so anywhere I can't go by land must be a bad thing, and to be avoided. And it's easy to block off the places where you don't want to go anyway by stationing at the gate an angel with a fiery sword; God doesn't want me to go there, so I don't have to.

But a man who sits in the same chair all day, looking out of the same window, can't help being titillated by stories of far-off lands, curious and unknown places where the sun burns the soil to sand, or the sea freezes over. And a man who spends his life huddled on the deck of a bobbing ship dancing on the crests of mountain-high waves can't help wishing that he was on dry land, sitting in a chair, looking sleepily into the fire. Kari said about his people, so poor in material things compared to us, that who they were was all they had; and that seems to have been true enough. What made the difference, in Meadowland, was that *who* we are depends so much on *where* we are, because context governs everything. What I wrote just now, about God ordaining a place to each of us, may not be so far from the truth after all, and that's the disturbing thing. Take a man who has practically nothing, and put him in an empty place – a good place, unspoiled, fruitful even without the plough, almost a Garden of Eden – and you've stripped away everything that stands between us and God's original creation, the very essence of Mankind. Shouldn't you see in him a proper return to grace, as he comes back to the garden he was driven out of? Logically, I believe you should; and then I think about Freydis, and about my friends Kari and Eyvind with their axes in their hands outside the house on the shores of the lake, and somehow I'm not so certain any more.

Author's Note

The written sources make no mention of any further attempts at settlement in Vinland after Freydis's return. By 1121, when Bishop Eirik of Greenland tried to find it again, the route had been forgotten. Greenlanders occasionally ventured across to Forestland (Markland) to cut timber; but the Greenland colony itself eventually failed. Scandinavians were still living there in 1410, when a Norwegian ship landed there after losing its way en route to Iceland, but the Englishmen who rediscovered Greenland around 1500 found it uninhabited. Nobody knows for sure what happened to the colony. It could simply have been climate change, overgrazing, and a decline in the demand for its exports as the Norwegian economy weakened. In 1448, however, rumours of a pirate attack on the Eastern Settlement reached Norway, and Eskimo tradition recorded in the eighteenth century seems to confirm that that was how the colony met its end.

In 1071, six years after Harald Sigurdson died at Stamford Bridge, the Byzantine Empire suffered possibly the greatest catastrophe in its 1,100-year history when its armies were massacred by the Turks at Manzikert. Deprived of most of its territory and manpower, it dwindled away until the city of Constantinople was finally sacked by Sultan Mehmet II in 1453, thirty-nine years before Columbus reached the New World.